SHOPPING FOR A CEO

BY JULIA KENT

* * *

I'm thrilled to be the maid of honor in my friend's wedding, but the best man, Andrew McCormick, is a chauvinistic pig with a God complex.

And I can't stop kissing him in closets.

(Don't ask.)

He's the brother of the groom and the CEO of my biggest mystery shopping account, but suddenly he's refusing to be in the wedding. He won't talk about it. Won't see reason.

He's such a man.

And he still won't stop kissing me in random closets.

(Thank goodness.)

I'm a fixer. That's what I do. I can fix anything if given the chance. But when the game is fixed there's only so much I can do.

The ball's in his court now.

Game on.

* * *

Shopping for a CEO is the 7th book in the New York Times and USA Today bestselling Shopping series. When CEO Andrew McCormick and mystery shopper Amanda Warrick find themselves in the unlikely position as maid of honor and best man in the Boston society wedding of the year, an undeniable attraction and dual stubborn streaks add fuel to the fire in this romantic comedy from Julia Kent.

Copyright © 2015 by Julia Kent

* * *

Sign up for my New Releases and Sales newsletter at http://www.jkentauthor.com

TABLE OF CONTENTS

Praise for Julia Kent

at times! I even cried a little. I absolutely love this series!!! I can't wait to see what's to come next!!! This is a must read!"

"Every chapter made my heart beat faster in anticipation. Julia Kent once again pulls at our emotions and allows us to fall in love with the characters all over again.... Very well worth my heart palpitations."

Reader Emails

"I just can't imagine how you come up with this stuff, but am so glad you do!"

"I finally had to write to you and tell you that you are simply one of the most amazing authors. Your humor is perfect. I really do bust out laughing out loud. My family thinks that I am crazy when I do it but I can count on a good read from you especially when it has been a rough day. There hasn't been a single thing that you have written that I haven't fallen in love with the characters. They become real and some of your lines have become a part of our family language. Thank you for sharing your amazing gift."

"Having another fantastic evening as I just finished your latest book and now the fam can go to sleep since the laughing/screaming out loud has stopped... Stomach muscles are sore. Better than sit-ups! :-)"

ACKNOWLEDGEMENTS

To my beta reader friends, I give you my deepest thanks.

To my awesome husband, I give you my heart and the rest of my life.

To my dear friend Gretchen Galway, I give you credit for Josh's best line in the childbirth class. ;)

And most of all, to my readers, I thank you from the core of my soul. You have no idea how important you are to me.

SHOPPING FOR A CEO

CHAPTER ONE

"And when I took little Maisy to the veterinarian for the first time to have her anal glands expressed, the bill nearly made *my* anal glands explode!" my date says with a chuckle, reaching for his pint of Guinness. He finishes the last inch or so of the glass, lets out an enormous belch, then leans in, elbows on the table, cradling his jaw in his hands like he has a massive secret to share.

I lean *back*. As in, away.

"That," he says, reaching for my hand and ensconcing it between both of his, "is when I turned to good old YouTube and decided to DIY."

"DIY?" This guy has more jargon than a sociology grad student.

"I taught myself how to express her anal glands," he crows proudly. "Just did it this morning."

I look down at our hands.

I can live without one, right?

"It takes more vigor than you'd imagine," he murmurs.

That is the worst come on line *ever*.

"Another beer?" the waitress asks, interrupting. She is my new best friend.

I nod vigorously and tug my hand away from his, praying for divine intervention. Or an electric knife to saw off my hand. A beer will have to do. If I get tipsy enough on this date, maybe I'll forget that my hands just rubbed up against—

Hold on there. Pause.

You heard me right. I'm on a date. Except I'm *not* on a date. I'm technically working right now. On this date. I'm dating him *professionally*.

Wait—don't get the wrong idea. I'm not...well, it's not *that* kind of working date. I'm not making three hundred bucks a night to lick his toes or whip him or be a professional escort or anything like that.

(But that's starting to look better and better....)

All I get is my regular paycheck, my meal, and an eighteen dollar mystery shopper's fee for having Mr. Anal Gland Hands sit across the table from me and talk about Maisy the Wonder Schnauzer like she's his girlfriend and I'll be the third in their little poly human-human-dog threesome.

That's right. I'm getting *paid* to do this.

My boss, Greg, got a new account for online dating service evaluations for his company, Consolidated Evalu-Shop, and I'm currently on the prototype date. I have to create the series of questions that future mystery shoppers will answer when they go through all these customer service shops to determine whether the dating service works as the owners expect, and to help improve customer service, client retention, and overall efficiency.

I'm the sacrificial virgin.

Okay, not technically a virgin, but...you know what I mean.

"DoggieDate: The place where dogs find love" is an online dating service for dog lovers.

Snort. Go ahead. Say it.

The motto needs some work.

I'm mystery shopping DoggieDate's entire customer service and online algorithm matching system. This is my first date. According to their system, Amanda

Warrick, age twenty-seven and *noneofyourbusiness* pounds, with a college degree, an interest in chihuahuas and labradoodles, the owner of Spritzy the teacup chihuahua, and a lover of seafood is an eighty-three percent match with....

Mr. Anal Gland Hands, forty-nine, thrice-divorced, a triathletic vegan, an Internet Marketer, owner of Maisy the schnauzer and...

Unpause.

"You know, Amanda," he says, grabbing my hands again. Ron. His real name is Ron. He has a combover like Donald Trump and arms like cords of steel, tanned deep and hairless. "If you're anything like me, you're sick of this dating game. How about we strip off all the bullshit layers and just get right to the heart of seeing if we're compatible?"

Pause again.

This isn't the first time I've done online dating. It's just the first time I've done it professionally. I'm not invested in the outcome here. I'm just doing my job.

But.

I know what Ron's about to say, so pull up a chair. This'll be a doozy.

Unpause.

"So tell me all your secret sexual fantasies."

I totally called it.

"All of them?" I ask, leaning forward. "Because I'm not sure we have enough time for that."

His eyes light up. They're the color of the bay after a big storm, the kind of brownish grey that only comes from stirring up a lot of crap.

I sniff the air. You smell that? It's the scent of desperation.

Or Maisy's anal glands.

It's hard to tell the difference.

I need to focus on work, though. This isn't a real date. If it were, I'd trigger a rescue text from my best friend Shannon and claim she's in the ER and take my escape. Given how often Shannon really *does* end up in the emergency room, I'd have about a one in ten chance of not lying.

"Tell me all about Maisy!" I say, suddenly chirpy.

Poor Ron recoils. "She has nothing to do with my sexual fantasies!"

I didn't imply as much, but the fact that he's so quick to say that freaks me out.

"No, no, of course not," I say in a soothing voice. The waitress brings my beer and I drink half of it in one long ribbon of alcoholic perfection.

Ron unclenches. He has super-short hair (except for the Trump combover right along the bangs) and is clean shaven. Those grey-brown eyes are framed by nothing but loose eyelid skin.

And then it hits me.

He has no eyelashes. No eyebrows, either. That's why he looks like he's so interested in everything I say.

"I just meant," I continue, "that I love my little Spritzy. That's why I joined DoggieDate. I'm wondering what Maisy's like."

Ron relaxes. "Actually," he says with a conspirator's grin, "she's only half mine."

Half? How do you have half a dog? Is Maisy a made-up dog? Does Ron use a fake dog to troll for women?

Or worse, maybe there really is *half* a dog somewhere. In a freezer. Like Jeffrey Dahmer's victims.

"My ex-wife and I share custody."

"Ohhhhh," I say slowly, tipping back the second half of my beer. The waitress notices and before I've put the bottle down she catches my eye.

The Sisterhood Of The First Date Code is enacted. Third beer on the way. Good thing I'm taking a cab home. On my boss's dime, no less. There is no way I'm going through twenty dates like this without beer and a cab.

That's right. Twenty. I have to date *twenty* dog lovers, male and female, in an effort to create as thorough a survey as possible for the hundreds of mystery shoppers nationwide who will evaluate DoggieDate.

Anal glands be damned.

"How do you share custody of a dog?" I ask, intrigued. My third beer appears and I stifle a belch. Only men can burp on dates.

Women have to slowly leak out their CO_2, like a deflating float at the Macy's Thanksgiving Parade. God forbid you let one rip.

"She gets Maisy every other week. We trade off holidays. We each get her on our birthdays."

He's serious.

"Who pays doggie support?" I joke. "Do you meet in a McDonald's parking lot to hand her off in neutral territory?"

"No. Whole Foods. And I make more, so I give Alicia eighty-two dollars a week to help cover Maisy's Reiki treatments."

Oh, God.

"Okay, great," I mumble, nodding vigorously. *Okay, great* is code for *You're batshit crazy.*

It then occurs to me: this is the entire point of these mystery shops. DoggieDate is designed for dog freaks.

If Ron is the norm, then I am, technically, the freak here.

I'm borrowing my mom's teacup chihuahua, Spritzy, for the dates where the men and women want to have our dogs meet. Ron didn't want that. He said the humans needed to make sure we were compatible before taking the very serious step of letting the dogs meet.

Dog Reiki? The man pays eighty-two dollars a week for dog Reiki but he sticks his hands all over his dog's brown starfish to save money?

And *I'm* the freak.

I guzzle the third beer and the waitress gives me a look. She comes over with the check. Ron ignores it.

Oh, Ron.

"I'd like an orange-flavored seltzer," I ask the waitress. She nods and walks off.

Ron snickers.

"What's funny?" I ask.

"Flavored seltzer. You know what they use to flavor those." One corner of his mouth hooks up as his hand brushes against the check folder. He still doesn't pick it up. I'm on an expense account, so it's no big deal. Plus, technically, this is work, so why do I care that the guy won't get the check?

And yet this is a little too close to a date for my comfort.

It has nothing to do with the fact that I haven't been on a real date—one I'm not getting paid to attend —in months.

Not a thing.

"Amanda?" Ron gently nudges my hand.

"Oh, yes?" I'm in la la land, already distracted.

He smiles. "Beaver anal glands."

"Beaver *huh*?"

The waitress sets my bottle of flavored seltzer water on the table. Ron points to it. "The flavoring. They express beaver anal glands to make most of those flavors."

I pour the bottle into the glass of ice and laugh.
As I take a sip, our eyes meet.
He shrugs. "Look it up. For real."
I drink the entire glass in one long motion.
And then I burp the ABCs.

CHAPTER TWO

To my utter surprise (not), Ron ditches me, his phone buzzing suspiciously about two minutes after my spectacular belch. I'm not being hyperbolic: that burp was so good that some frat boys at a nearby table gave me a standing ovation.

Ron's rescue text is so obvious it might as well have had flashing red and blue lights attached to it.

He leaves me with the bill. I pull out the company card and give the waitress a fifty percent tip. She deserves it.

Three beers pool in my bladder and taunt me as I try, repeatedly, to make quick notes about the date to help me write up my survey.

No luck. Can't write. I need to evacuate the beaver funk.

Wait. That sounds very, very wrong....

As I weave to the bathroom, I run through the date in my mind. Dog lovers have different needs from your average desperate single looking for love. Because I am your average desperate single looking for love, I know what I'm talking about.

And DoggieDate has definitely figured out a distinct niche of the dating pool.

A pool I plan never to swim in.

This restaurant is on the Boston waterfront, right along a string of buildings that face the seaport. The bathroom is marble-lined and covered in fake Tiffany lamp fixtures, with glass beads and lots of prism reflections throughout the little enclosed room. I finish my business, scrubbing my hands extra hard as I wash them, and wonder if Ron was telling the truth.

Beaver glands for fruit flavoring in water? Now I've heard everything.

I waltz out of the restaurant, a little loose from those beers. The frat boy table gives me scattered thumbs up, one of the guys following me with his eyes the entire way out. I know this because the double glass doors show his reflection as I walk toward them.

I still got it.

At least, when it comes to impressing twenty-year-old college boys with my belching techniques.

Early spring on the seaport in Boston is fabulous at night if the snow has all melted and you have a warm breeze, which I do tonight. I walk outside and stare at the rippling water, inky black with gilded tips, the moon shining on them, making the waves look like knife edges popping up to and fro. My thick sweater wrap is just enough to prevent me from freezing.

Not as warm as a date's arm slung around my shoulders, but my sweater hasn't recently wiped any dog butts, so I'll take it.

I sit down on a small bench that runs perpendicular to the water and try to find a ride home with the app on my smartphone. I hate these devices. I want my old flip phone, but Greg insists we use these things now to do our mystery shops.

Greg also insists I pretend to date men like Ron.

One down, nineteen dates to go.

In the search for my phone, I find my lipstick. Plum Passion. Who names these things? For the hell of it, I re-apply the color. Not that it will do me any good. After a (fake) date like that, what I need to attract a dog lover is Biscuit Beige. How about Puppy Pink? Burgundy Beagle?

No. Wait.

Frosted Spay.

I lean back against the bench and close my eyes, enjoying a light breeze that lifts the ends of my hair. I'm back to my natural color—boring brown—after years of doing hairstylist mystery shops that involved coloring it. I want to kick off my high heels and throw on some yoga pants, but instead I wiggle to make my Spanx more comfortable and settle for just taking a full breath.

This fake dating stuff is for the birds.

Er, the *dogs*...

My purse vibrates slightly from a text. I know I should read it, but I'm pretty certain it's my mother, and right now, I just want to enjoy being unencumbered by anyone else's expectations for a few moments. Nights like this require a breather, no matter how fleeting.

A man's laugh floats on the air like a smoke signal, followed by the lilt of a woman's giggle. I open my eyes and trace the source of the sound.

A man in a suit is at the stairs leading to the dock, where a smattering of boats are tethered. He's turned away from me, one arm outstretched toward a woman a step or two below him. The cut of his suit in the moonlight screams expensive. He has a cobra back, wide at the top, with the broad shoulders of a swimmer. His jacket is open and I see a hint of his waist, his torso bisected by a thick alligator-skin belt looped into trousers tailored so well across a strong, well-defined ass that I could turn his butt into a work of art if I were a sculptor.

SHOPPING FOR A CEO

He pulls the woman up and turns. I see him in profile.

It's Andrew McCormick.

Oh, sweet holy hell.

I haven't seen him in months. Haven't kissed him since we were in the emergency room after my best friend, Shannon, swallowed the engagement ring his brother, Declan, gave to her as he proposed.

(A tip: don't bury a three-carat diamond ring in a piece of tiramisu at a fancy restaurant as a way of proposing to a woman. *Any* woman. Why ruin the dessert like that?)

I'm the maid of honor for the wedding. Andrew is the best man. We've managed to avoid each other so far, but the wedding is three months away. I knew this day was coming.

But I didn't expect it to be *today*.

My heart starts skipping beats as I take him in from afar, shielded by the angle of my bench. He has no idea I'm watching him. Thick hair, cut short and with the kind of layered sophistication that only comes from a stylist who charges three figures. Shaded eyes that I know are sharp and smoldering, a blend of brown and honey that makes you melt inside. He's in a full suit, tie still snug against his neck, the moonlight reflecting off a white shirt. His grin is contagious, making my own smile widen as I tilt my head and let myself get lost in wondering.

The woman with him climbs up the final step and moves away from him. Basic body language is easy to read. They're not on a date. If they were, she'd move closer.

He's grinning. So is she. Then I see the sheaf of papers in her hands.

A business meeting.

The relief that floods my body makes me looser than the three beers I just had. My heart continues an off-beat pattern more erratic than Red Sox pitching. I have no right to feel relief. I have no need to feel any of these outrageously inappropriate emotions I'm sporting right here, sitting alone, rejected by Mr. Anal Gland Hands and watching the man who secretly kisses me in closets seal some kind of business deal.

That's right. Closets.

And yes—kisses. Plural. My relationship—or, more accurately, *lack* of a relationship—with Andrew McCormick, an executive at Anterdec Industries, the biggest client that my company services, is one filled with mystery, discomfort, complexity, and—

Closets.

Too many closets.

More than a year ago I stormed into his office and made him, his brothers, and his father see reason. I set up a hotel shop for Shannon that brought everyone together to make Declan and Shannon face each other and clear the air.

Andrew and I ended up making out in his office closet.

Three beers in me and all I can do is reminisce. Get a fourth in me and I'll spill the entire story.

And then there was that tiny on-call room in the emergency room where we kissed while Shannon's tiramisu nearly killed her last year.

I eye one of the boats. Boats don't have closets, do they?

He turns toward me, as if that thought were spoken aloud. The clouds look like cotton candy, streaked across the sky. In the intermittent moonlight he looks like a painting, with shadow and light playing on his skin and cloth as if he were a canvas of delight. A playground.

"I'm sure you'll love the houseboat, Andrew. It seems like a perfect fit for your new life," the woman with him says in dulcet tones. Too bad I have hyperacusis and can hear dog whistles.

And secrets from men who kiss me in closets.

"Thank you, Marcy. I'm looking forward to this," he replies. He sounds so smug. So confident. So panty-throwingly sultry with that damn voice that feels like silk being stroked across my neckline whenever he speaks.

"Having your father step down and make you the official CEO of Anterdec would make anyone look forward to—"

"Shhhhhhh," he says, holding one finger up to his grinning mouth. "That's still embargoed information. You only know because the boat is a business purchase." He rests one palm on her shoulder. Her head tilts to the left and she tosses her hair back over her back.

I narrow my eyes.

She gives him a conspirator's smile. "Of course."

I dart to the left, my head hidden by a bush. I can still turn and see him, though. Andrew shakes hands with Marcy the Secret Broker and she walks off. He jolts a little, reaching into his jacket breast pocket.

Phone call.

As he talks, he pulls at the knot in his tie, loosening it. With two practiced fingers, he undoes the top button of his dress shirt. The wind picks up and sweeps his hair into a mess from behind, sending locks across his forehead. He shivers.

I can't stop staring.

CEO? Andrew's officially the CEO of Anterdec Industries now? Has his father really stepped down? I know from Shannon that Declan's been resentful that James McCormick has been grooming Andrew for the position. The two of them posture and jockey for head alpha wolf of the McCormick clan like drunk eighteenth century Highlanders with something to prove and nothing to lose.

Shannon is going to freak out when she hears this.

And I, unlike Marcy, am not sworn to secrecy. Hah.

Andrew walks, pacing on the dock, taking three long strides, turning, then repeating the motion. Deep in conversation, he's talking with someone in confident tones. This isn't a business negotiation. Whatever the topic, it's not a source of stress. Yet his voice is commanding. Controlled.

Assured.

Thick, muscled thighs carry him to and fro. I've seen those thighs in person, sweaty and tight, covered in Lycra. Bike shorts. Back in his office.

The day he kissed me.

The *first* day he kissed me.

I go loose as I watch him, then force myself to twist and sit with my back to him, molding to the bench. I look up at the sky. My eyes close slowly, lashes creating a venetian-blind effect as the stars poke in between layers of the night.

I breathe in the salty air, the waves lapping against the dock's joists.

I breathe out frustration and regret and a kind of ennui that comes from being stuck in a life without...

Closets.

I shouldn't watch. I know I shouldn't. But my lashes pry themselves open as if called by an unseen force and I give in to impulse.

17

SHOPPING FOR A CEO

His call ends and he stuffs the phone into the inner chest pocket of his suit jacket. His back is to me now, his face tipped up. Is he taking in the stars? Ocean waves miles away lead to tiny ripples that lap against the wooden posts of the docks. A fake Boston Tea Party ship sways in the distance, looking about as drunk as I am, except I'm on firm ground.

My phone rings. I lurch up, frantically digging through my purse for it. The sound makes Andrew startle. He turns around and catches my eye.

I freeze. My phone burbles, buried under all my receipts and notes and lip balms and tampons, jumbled into the disorganized mess of my life that I carry around in a three-pound weight on my shoulder.

He gives me a questioning look but doesn't take a step. Then his eyes narrow and he asks, "How long have you been sitting there?"

Long enough to appreciate the hours you spend with your spin instructor, Mr. Sculpted Ass.

His eyebrows rise. Oh, God. Did I say any of that aloud?

I do what any self-respecting woman who has made out with the man twice in private, and who hasn't said a word to her best friend about the second time, and who is coming off the utter humiliation of being ditched on a first date with a guy named Mr. Anal Gland Hands.

I run.

By the time I whip around the corner of the building, there's a yellow Prius cab at the curb. Without even bothering to flag it down, I crash into the door, fling it open, and throw myself in the back seat.

I give the cabbie Shannon's address, then dial frantically as he pulls away. That missed call was from Shannon, anyway. Might as well visit her now.

I look out the window.

No sign of Andrew.

Two thoughts live simultaneously in my floating brain:

Thank God

and

He didn't follow.

CHAPTER THREE

Shannon isn't answering her phone, or her texts, but I have the cabbie drop me off at her building anyhow. Worst case, she's not home.

Best case, she's home and has a pallet of tiramisu on hand. The non-ring kind.

I buzz her door. A small video screen shows Marie's face, sudden and invasive, like a cat that has discovered a hidden video camera. One covered in tuna sauce.

"Who's there?" she asks pleasantly.

"MOM!" Shannon shouts. Her voice is tinny but a relief to hear. "We've told you not to answer for us at our apartment."

"What? I'm being rude now because I want to help? When you lived with your sister you never cared if I answered the door for you."

"No, Amy and I cared then, too," Shannon says flatly.

"Then why didn't you say something! I can't read minds," Marie retorts.

"We did say—"

"Give it up, honey," says a man's baritone. "Don't engage the crazy."

Marie's voice sounds like a teakettle. "I am not crazy—"

Bzzzz.

The foyer for this apartment building looks like something the Greeks built in Athens millennia ago, except with air conditioning and wireless security. A concierge desk sits to the right, with a flank of similarly-dressed women, all with their hair in updos, speaking in dulcet tones on wireless headsets.

It's a little too close to Grey Enterprises for comfort. I've never snooped around Declan's apartment, but I wouldn't be at all surprised to find a Red Room of Pain in there.

When Shannon and Declan returned from New York engaged and ready for wedding planning, he'd set one simple condition: Shannon had to move in with him. She readily agreed and moved most of her belongings, except for Chuckles.

Amy inherited Chuckles. Amy will never let Shannon forget this, and so in exchange, Shannon had Declan help Amy get a job at some high tech business incubator in Waltham where you not only can bring your pet to work with you, they have an on-staff pet groomer and animal shaman who will help read your pet's past lives for you.

Chuckles turns out to have been Vlad the Impaler in an earlier life.

I know, right? I'm not surprised either.

I ride a bajillion flights up to the penthouse, then pause just before the elevator doors open. I'm loopy and loose, and an ache in me lingers.

An ache for what?

Andrew.

His name floats into my head, an unexpected cloud on a sunny day.

No. I'm being silly. Anyone would look good after Ron the Dogbutt Whisperer. Even an animal shaman would be a better date.

I walk into the living room. It's all sleek, smoky grey and wide open glass lines.

22

"I now know way more about anal glands than any human being ever should," I announce.

"Another sex toy shop?" Marie asks.

"No."

"You're working with anal, uh...glands...for fun?" Declan asks. He's less perplexed than he used to be. I think we're wearing him down. He's dressed in the McCormick version of casual, which means his tie is loose. Does the man not own a pair of sweatpants or some cheesy, shredded concert t-shirt from 2003?

"Proctologist mystery shops?" Marie muses. "Hmmm." She turns to Shannon. "Your father's due for his colonoscopy, and the co-pay is ridiculous. Do you think Greg could let Jason become a certified mystery shopper and give him a proctologist shop?" she asks hopefully.

"*Dog* anal glands," I say with a mouth that over-enunciates.

"You mystery shopped a proctologist who works on *dogs*?" Marie asks.

All three of them stare at me like *I'm* the one who's coming up with this stuff.

"No. I went out on a date with a guy who squeezes his schnauzer's ass for fun."

"Oh," Marie says absentmindedly as she puts a yellow sticky note on a giant calendar. "I went out with one of those between dating James and Jason back in the day."

"You mean there's more than one out there?" I ask.

Declan quirks one eyebrow as the door buzzes. Taking his leave with a look of relief, he goes to the monitor, leaving me and Shannon to stare at Marie with twin expressions of confusion.

"What does that even mean, Mom?" Shannon asks as I go in for a hug. I haven't seen her since she and

Declan returned from a business trip that lasted for two weeks in New Zealand, and the hug goes on longer than it should. I've missed her. As she presses her hands against my back I can feel the cool hardness of her engagement ring band.

The ring that has more intimate knowledge of Shannon's body than even Declan. Shannon's Twitter nemesis, Jessica Coffin, chronicled the, uh...transit of the three-carat diamond engagement ring after Shannon swallowed it during the proposal. The hashtag #poopwatch led to more than a little embarrassment for Shannon, but she weathered it all with grace.

Marie raises her voice as if lecturing. "It means you never want to date a man who's obsessed with his dog. They are worse than the ones who are attached to their mothers at the navel. Dog freaks will always put their pets ahead of their women."

"Dad was a vet tech when you two met," Shannon says as she pulls away from me. Her expression is a mixture of happiness and aggravation, which means Marie's been here for a while.

"Yes, but he wasn't obsessed with, you know..." Obviously distracted, Marie's voice tapers off as she looks at the giant dining table, a cross between a tornado and the president's nuclear bomb briefing room. Have you ever seen those reality television shows about the preppers who buy things like coconut flour in 55-gallon drums, or who dehydrate 9,000 pounds of cherries for the day the zombies take over?

Marie's the prepper version of a mother of the bride. Except substitute chocolate fountains and Haggis for the cherries and you get the basic idea.

"Dog butts?" Shannon offers helpfully.

Andrew walks in just then. Of course he does. The man knows how to make an *exit* from my life. Over and over and over. That one he has down to a T.

And now, apparently, he's perfecting the art of awkward *entrances*.

"Speaking of assholes," I murmur.

There goes my heart, beating triple time at the sight of him. But this time, I have the upper hand. I've got the goods on him.

And he knows it.

"You're safe," he says to me in a weird voice. Tight, as though angry, but relieved, as if he cares.

"Of course I'm safe. What are you talking about?"

"You disappeared at the marina."

Now Declan, Marie and Shannon pay full attention to us, Marie dropping everything. Her eyes light up. Oh, no.

No no no no no.

She's already busy planning *one* wedding.

She doesn't need another one, even just in her head.

"You two had a *date* at the marina?" Marie asks in a voice that goes up at the end like a wedding planning erection. Like all the blood in her body swells to fill Something Blue.

"No date. In fact, I just happened to walk along the water and ran into Andrew talking about his new appointment as the C—"

Andrew's across the room before I can finish, his warm, muscular arms around me, lips on mine. He tips me back, like a stage kiss, as if the way his hands press into my waist and back aren't more than a surface-level gesture.

He tastes like wine and nearly two years of questions.

SHOPPING FOR A CEO

I wonder if I taste like beer and nearly two years of frustration.

My thoughts quiver, then fade, as the kiss melts me. If this is just for show, he's putting his heart and soul into it. And his tongue. *Definitely* his tongue. His hands snake down and one cups my ass, the other pulling me tight. His tongue takes its time, like he's at the beginning of negotiations for the deal of his life.

Maybe he is.

The man is in no rush.

"I don't understand," I hear Marie say as if she's a thousand miles in the air, floating on the wind with a hundred helium balloons clutched in one hand. "Andrew is Mr. Anal Gland Hands?"

The spell is broken.

"Does he even have a schnauzer?" she asks a gape-mouthed Shannon, who is staring at me and Andrew like she's spotted Sasquatch and he's snacking on little tempura versions of the Tooth Fairy and Santa's elves.

Andrew pulls away, his mouth covered in my lipstick. Plum Passion. Our eyes meet and he gives me the same damn jaunty grin he flashed the other two times we kissed.

He comes back in to nuzzle my neck. I can't breathe, yet I'm panting. I'm panting so hard my lipstick should be called Panting Panty.

And then he murmurs, "Don't say a word about my being named CEO."

I freeze.

That's *it*? That's the only reason he chased me down and kissed me? To shut me up?

So I do what any self-respecting woman would do to a guy who has now kissed her twice in closets during crisis points in her best friend's life.

I pull back and slap his face so hard my palm turns purple.

From the lipstick.

Marie gasps. Shannon lets out a little scream.

Declan smirks, the kind of smile that has zero mirth in it, and mutters something that sounds like, "Great. Asshole Boyfriend Summit coming tonight. I'm not getting any."

Marie's eyes narrow. Out of the corner of my field of vision, I see her walk up to the enormous stainless steel refrigerator and open the freezer section.

"Shannon," she stage whispers. "We're going to need more ice cream for this."

"Not sure there's enough for this situation, Mom," Shannon answers in a high, reedy voice.

It feels so good to slap the bastard. No, really. It's as if my arm has been coiling, waiting like a hunter sits for days before slaying the perfect beast.

Andrew is a *beast*. A perfectly gorgeous, one-hundred-percent selfish, modern-day Adonis who thinks he can just kiss me in private and I'll let him. Like I'm on a kissing retainer and he can access me at will.

"I'll thank you to stop kissing me. It's not in the corporate contract between our respective companies," I snap. My heart is pounding so hard it's like it's boxing with itself, my ribs the punching bag, my pulse throbbing in time with some rhythm set by the pure fury of being wronged by a man I can't stop being attracted to.

Damn it.

His jaw is open, his hand pressed to the growing red spot on his face where I hit him. My palm tingles from the scrape of skin against five o'clock shadow, and the humiliation of realizing all that passion I felt was just a game to him. Those deep brown eyes stare at me with an intensity that belies everything I'm feeling.

"It should be," he growls.

And with that, he turns and leaves.

"I'll walk you out," Declan mutters.

Shannon gives him a look. Declan walks to the door Andrew's just exited and sighs.

"Salted caramel this time? Two pints or three?" His fingers curl around the doorframe as he waits for an answer.

She looks at me with the deep intensity of a psychotherapist analyzing a feral child. "One bag of marshmallows. One bag of Cheetos."

Declan's eyebrow goes up.

"Mom!" Shannon calls out. "Do we have any butter?"

"Yes. Two sticks," Marie calls out.

Declan flinches. I can see the calculation in his eyes. Dare I ask about the butter? He's a smart man, though, and chooses the path of least resistance.

Silence.

Andrew uses silence, too, I realize as I will my pulse back to a beat that doesn't involve breaking the sound barrier. He uses his mouth to silence me.

Why?

"Fine. I'm buying marshmallows and, uh...Cheetos." Declan's hand is on the doorknob. He's giving Shannon a look that says, *Please don't make me buy tampons again*.

"Aren't you sending Gerald?" she asks in a surprised tone. Gerald is Declan's primary limo driver. Notice that phrase? *Primary* limo driver. The man has back-ups. I'm sure the back-up limo drivers have back-ups, like understudies for Broadway show stars.

Billionaires live lives of fluid grace, where other people are in charge of smoothing all the wrinkles, preventing any hiccups, and making sure they don't, you know...

Have to buy marshmallows, Cheetos and tampons at a convenience store on a Friday night.

It's a wonder Andrew didn't just send his limo driver to kiss me and shut me up. When you hire someone else to do all your dirty work for you...

The tiniest sliver of panic blooms in Declan's moss-green eyes. He controls it quickly. I have to give him credit.

"I could use some air," he mumbles. "So I'll just go."

"Coward," Shannon says with a chortle.

He clears his throat meaningfully. "I prefer the term *ninja*." A swift peck on the cheek and a flick of the wrist and Declan's out the door before she can argue.

Smart man. All the IQ points must have gone into him and his older brother, Terry. Andrew was left with a hot ass, that sultry grin, and a coal-covered soul that whispers evil sweet nothings to his conscience.

Kiss her in the closet in your office, it says. *Kiss her in the hospital closet*, it murmurs. *Kiss her to shut her up*, it hisses.

Bet it wasn't expecting my little slap.

"I should feel triumphant," I whimper as Marie rushes over, glass of white wine in hand, offering it to my lips like she's a priest giving First Communion. "I stood up for myself. I made it clear in no uncertain terms that I am not a woman to be trifled with."

"And it only took you two years," Marie says, nodding. I guess that's supposed to be comforting. Marie can be kind of hit-or-miss like that.

"And three kisses!" I groan between guzzles of white Zin.

Shannon does a double take. "Three? There was a *third* incident?" She scrunches up her face, making her cute little rabbit nose poke out. "When did you—"

"Was it that time Jason and I saw you at the hospital during Poopwatch?" Marie asks. She's wearing this gorgeous, flowing lilac silk wrap and her eyelashes are so long it looks like she contracted them out to an asphalt company. She leans forward on the counter between the kitchen and the living room, eyes wide and fascinated.

Shannon gives me a deadly stare. "You made out with Andrew while I was in the emergency room *choking to death*?"

Busted.

And then she turns on Marie. "And quit calling it Poopwatch."

"Honey, that's what everyone calls it."

"No, Mom, that's what *Jessica Coffin* called it." Shannon frowns. "Wait. You just used the present tense. Calls. Not *called*. She's still making fun of my...of the...of you know—"

"Poopwatch," Marie and I say in unison.

Her hands go up in the air in a show of exasperation. Either that, or she's turned into a gospel singer. "That's not funny!" Jessica briefly dated Shannon's ex, Steve, and had the hots for Declan. As a trend setter in the Boston social scene, Jessica's tweets can make or break a restaurant, though she has lost some of her power. Humiliating Shannon online seems to be Jessica's favorite hobby.

Marie and I look at each other and burst into giggles. We can't help it, even though we shouldn't. Marie places one perfectly manicured hand on

Shannon's shoulder, her fingernails a deep purple with a lilac tip.

"Poopwatch will never, ever not be funny, honey."

Shannon's eyes narrow like she's at the OK Corral and ready for a showdown. "You have one word that pushes my buttons. I have one for you."

Marie laughs even harder.

"Elope."

Marie stops laughing and blanches.

"You wouldn't!"

"Try me."

"But honey, Poopwatch is—"

"Elope!"

Marie's mouth tightens like a drawstring pouch. Her nostrils flare. Her eyes go small and she looks like one of those apples carved and dried to look like a shrunken head.

Except one with the smooth, shiny forehead of a Botoxed woman.

"Fine," Marie says with a sigh. "No more Poopwatch jokes." She reaches for a To Do list with a mad rush of scribbles and cross-outs, additions and arrows. "Does that include the pre-reception slide show?"

"WHAT? What on earth would you have in a slideshow about my...about the ring getting caught in my...about Poopwatch?" Shannon screeches.

Marie smirks. "Gotcha to say the word."

"Elope."

Marie's face falls.

"And you know Declan will jump at the chance if I even whisper that word once," Shannon adds.

"I don't know what to do with you!" Marie says with a sniff, playing the wounded mom. "You're so selfish that you won't have a bridal shower—"

"Selfish? I asked everyone to donate to charity in lieu of gifts and a shower, Mom!"

"—and now you're joking about elopement. It's as if you don't want a big, fancy society wedding with all the glamour and mystique and thousands of eyes on you."

"I *don't*! That's the point!" I can see Shannon's getting wound up in a way that only Marie can wind that key in her back.

Marie turns to me and, as if it weren't at all a *non sequitur*, asks, "Andrew is stringing you along again?"

I burst into tears.

Marie is a pro. Shannon's so outclassed.

"I slapped the CE—, er, a major client! Greg is going to explode when he learns what I just did to Andrew!" I wail, my tears curling down my jawline as I shove a cookie from a tray that Marie made into my mouth.

That's it. I am done. He has firmly taken every cell of my body, melted it, turned it to dust and shaken it so hard I am now just particles on the wind, clinging wherever I land.

"*Greg?*" Marie and Shannon exchange a look, then burst into laughter. "Your boss?"

"Honey, Greg doesn't explode," Shannon says with a quiet mirth. "He'll just bumble along and say nothing about it. Besides, Andrew kissed you without your permission."

Good point.

"But she let him. I saw that. They were evenly matched, tongue for tongue," Marie counters.

"Ewww, Mom!"

"What? Like you and Declan couldn't see it? You don't get close up views like that watching *The Bachelor* on an iPhone while maximizing the screen."

I stop crying and stare at her.

"Not that I do that," she mutters, shoving a rescue cookie in her own mouth.

"That was so unprofessional," I say, chiding myself. "He's a major client. I need to keep my tongue in my mouth."

"And your hands off his ass," Marie adds.

"And my—what? I did not touch his....oh., no." A vague, yet remarkably visceral, memory of my hands scraping against the fine fabric of his trousers, the cashmere turning into butter as my fevered palms met his hot marble thighs and ass makes me pant.

Shannon's frown is like a nonverbal *tsk tsk tsk*.

I guess I did take the opportunity to explore the, uh, terrain.

His spin trainer should be given a Nobel Prize for Sculpture.

My phone buzzes, jolting me. I look at my text messages.

"My mom," I groan. As if the night couldn't get any worse.

"Has Pam learned to say the words 'toilet paper' out loud yet?" Marie asks with a snort.

I sigh. "She can't even say 'menopause.'"

Marie goes quiet and eats another cookie, then mutters, "Can't say I blame her."

It's 11:06 p.m. You said you would be home by eleven, the text reads.

You know where this is going, right? So do I.

I'm at Shannon's place. I am fine. I am running late, I text back. But the text just says Sending, and doesn't go through.

"Has she microchipped you yet?" Marie jokes. I look at her, all blonde and coiffed and smiling. Marie is the opposite of my mother in every way, from energy level to assertiveness, and while I know I should answer my mother's worried missives, and I know she's struggling tonight, I can't. I just can't. Andrew has tasted me, again, and that takes precedence.

Speaking of tastes, I reach for a rescue cookie. At this point, I need a rescue *buffet*. Where the hell is Declan with my Cheetos and marshmallows?

And...pause. Because I know, right? Cheetos and...marshmallows? Here's the trick: you make rice cereal marshmallow treats. The kind with a box of rice cereal, a bag of marshmallows and a stick of butter, all mixed together and pressed in a greased pan.

Except instead of the rice cereal, insert crunchy Cheetos.

Unpause so you can marvel at the amazement that is this delicacy. I know! It's like you've been living a culinary lie all these years.

You're welcome.

Marie waves another cookie at me. "Earth to Amanda!" She points to the dining table. "Declan was just telling me that he loves the idea of a wedding cake in the shape of bagpipes." On the table I see schematics of wedding cakes so complex they look like an architecture firm has designed blueprints for them, complete with pulleys and fire sprinkler systems.

Shannon gives me a look that says anything but. "No, Mom, he was saying the opposite."

Marie inhales, the air whistling past her back teeth. "No, he didn't! He said he'd love a cake made in the shape of bagpipes as much as he loves me." She gives Shannon a doe-eyed look. "There's only one way to interpret that comment."

Shannon and I exchange a look and say, in unison, "Right."

My phone buzzes again. I look.

Mom.

Please respond before I call 911, she texts.

Declan walks in just as I'm texting back the words, *I am fine. Will be home late*. This time, the text goes through. Whew.

He plunks the marshmallows and Cheetos on the counter. Shannon opens the refrigerator door, bends down, and searches for the butter.

Declan "bumps into" her from behind and bends over her, whispering something I imagine is quite dirty in her ear, given the Lauren Bacall laugh that emerges from her.

I watch them, my earlier beers fading, the taste of Andrew McCormick lingering on my tongue, the burn of his cheek etched into my palm.

Shannon gets it all. The awesome, charismatic mother. The billionaire fiancé.

A father.

I don't even have that. Mine left when I was five.

The green cloud of jealousy that fills me feels like a smoke bomb, as if emotional terrorists appeared out of nowhere in a flash mob and pulled the pins, tossing the bombs like hail in a sudden storm cell.

I'm jealous. I can admit it. It's not as if there's something wrong with that. I can hold two opposite emotions in my heart at the same time. I am capable of feeling joy for Shannon and her new life and sorrow for my own trainwreck. Life doesn't have to be either/or. It can be both/and.

As Declan nuzzles Shannon's neck and touches her ass in ways that make me feel like I'm watching the opening to a Showtime after-hours special, I text my mom back with a single line:

In twenty minutes. On my way.

"I have to go," I announce.

Marie's face falls. Shannon and Declan are butting up against each other like horny goats in springtime. I'm seriously worried about how they're both eyeing the stick of butter in her hand.

"But we were just about to look at the plaid gel nails for the bridesmaids!" Marie whines, holding up a full-color brochure from a local spa with—yep—plaid gel nail fills.

"You seriously want the bridesmaids to have fingernails that look like kilts?" I ask, knowing the answer.

"Everything will look like kilts!" Marie gushes. "I've even found plaid matching bra and thong sets for the bridesmaids. And a garter for Shannon."

I swear I hear Declan mutter the word *elope*. Then he distinctly says, "Garters?" in a gruff voice.

"Will we throw plaid rice?" I joke.

"Is there such a thing?" Marie gasps.

"Check out Etsy," I say as I walk toward the door, trying to ignore the lustfest going on in the kitchen. My phone buzzes over and over. Probably Mom, whipped into a panic. "You can find anything on Etsy."

Even if you *shouldn't* be able to.

"Hey! What about the Cheetos and marshmallows?" I hear Declan call out as the elevator doors close.

I close my eyes and slump against the elevator wall, wondering how my night opened with dog butts and ended with plaid fingernails.

CHAPTER FOUR

Living with Pamela Warrick is a physical, and emotional, landmine. She's always been high strung. Neurotic. Tightly wound. A Museum Mom. So anal retentive you could put coal up her butt and get a diamond.

But only in private.

Mom's OCD is like tree pollen in Massachusetts in May. It is just there, a fine layer that coats every surface, appearing with a spectral green hue when it is at its worst. It makes your eyes water and your throat itch, a malady you can't escape. No amount of drugs can stop it. Trust me. I tried, back in high school. And not the kind you buy at a drugstore.

I have heard—and told—all the jokes about her *uptightedness*.

But when you add the fibromyalgia that hit her my senior year of high school, it's like taking obsessive compulsive disorder and living with that on double speed.

With pain.

When she's so picky I can't do anything right, including breathing, I remind myself it's not her fault. And it's not. Getting rear-ended in a compact car by a guy driving the biggest SUV on the market and who didn't even apply the brakes isn't something anyone causes.

Except for the asshole driver who was—that's right —texting.

Sexting, we learned, in the trial. You really do not want to watch those exhibits being paraded around a courtroom.

Neither did his wife.

Because the sexy pictures he received while texting weren't from *her*.

Mom's settlement covered her medical bills, some of her ongoing massage and physical therapy, and about half my college tuition.

But there's never enough money to cover the change in her.

I extracted myself from Shannon's place with promises to return tomorrow. They're not empty assurances, though Declan's look of appraisal made it clear he didn't care so much about the fool's errand of buying weird grocery items at the buttcrack of the day, but did find my flimsy excuse for leaving to be about as sturdy as Donald Trump's sense of feminist principles.

I get out of the cab and walk up the front steps of our house, a rented duplex in Newton, the journey as familiar and comforting in a damning sort of way, as if my life is on infinite repeat and all I can do is march along the deep grooves that my own feet created long before this moment.

"Amanda? Is that you?" Mom's voice is a mixture of concern and anxiety.

"Who else would it be?" I say, realizing my mistake as the words come out.

"Who else? You could be a robber," she answers, outraged at my insouciance. "A rapist. Someone trying to steal that nice computer your boss gave you."

"Right." The less said, the better. Did I mention what my mother does for a living?

She's an actuary. Working right now on terrorist insurance for large corporations. It's like having Josh Duggar work in costume design for Hooters.

Nothing like picking a line of work that feeds into your greatest source of weakness.

"It could be Tommy Lee Jones," she says.

"Right—wait, what?"

Mirth fills her voice. "Hah. Gotcha."

One joke. One little, not-funny joke is all it takes for me to understand her mood. I've cultivated a series of coping strategies for understanding where she is emotionally at any given time.

"You got me," I say, walking over to her old vinyl record player and putting on some Thelonius Monk, the neat, orderly steps for starting the machine done by rote memory, a soothing ritual that cuts through today's craziness.

Mom's passion of vinyl carried over to me. The scratches and bumps make the music gritty and real, and jazz helps her to mellow out.

"What were you doing?" she asks as the music provides a backdrop for our talk.

"Kissing a billionaire," I blurt out.

"Really? There certainly are plenty of billionaires going around now. Shannon got one. Are they handing them out like free samples at Costco now?"

"Hah," I pivot. "Gotcha."

She believes the lie. Wouldn't you?

"Oh, Amanda," she says, moving with great effort. Where I'm taller and rounder, Mom is a pixie. Tiny and high-strung, she says the fibro turns her into blocks of concrete shoved inside a flesh set of tights. Her pain level must be manageable today.

Some days, she can't even joke.

"You'll find your billionaire some day, honey," she says, yawning.

I already have, I want to say. I pinch my own forearm, willing the thought to go away.

Spritzy runs into the room, collar clanging.

Mom winces. "We need to do something about that collar. The metal against the metal makes my silver fillings hurt."

Sound sensitivity comes with her fibro, too.

I pick up the little teacup chihuahua, giving him some love. Spritzy shakes in my arms with an unremitting joy that makes me wonder why on earth I keep spending so much time obsessed with worrying about whether I'll ever find true love.

I'm holding it in my arms right now, all 2.7 pounds of it.

Too bad you can't really date your dog. At least, your dog's personality.

"I can order the plastic tags, Mom. He doesn't need the metal ones." As if he agrees with me, Spritzy nods his head. Then I realize he's licking my hand over and over, his head bobbing. He must taste rescue cookies.

Verbal Mistake Number 2 with my mother. We've been through this before, and....

"It's a waste of money to swap them out. I just need to learn to live with the sound."

And 3...2...1...

Cue a big sigh.

Am I callous for thinking about her fibromyalgia in terms of a rubric? It's like when I create and implement a new mystery shopper's questionnaire for a new marketing campaign. Study the objective. Determine the best way to meet the goal. Meet customer expectations. Exceed customer expectations.

And always, always, manage expectations.

But the true measure of success comes in predicting what happens next.

"I can see you're having a tough time, Mom," I say. My compassion is real. I remember the mom she was before the car accident. I know she doesn't want to be like this. I know pain can change a person.

"I am," she says. Her voice is filled with a thousand regrets and a million feelings she wants to convey but can't. I get it. I understand. I'm a fixer. I can detect nearly any problem in a person's voice, in the way they bounce their legs, in the nervous twitch of an eyelid.

In the taste of a man's kiss when he's trying to silence me from detecting exactly what I'm trained to do.

Spritzy's licking my face now. It's cute, but he's no substitute for Andrew.

"Can I help? Heat up a rice sock for you? Run you a bath?" I ask Mom.

Her voice starts to tremble, the ripples of sound an apology for something she feels sorry for, though it was never her fault. "Thank you. The rice sock sounds lovely."

I plunk Spritzy down on his impossibly-tiny dog bed and make my way to the kitchen. It is spotless. Crumbs on the counter are like germs in an oncology ward: carefully exorcized and kept at bay at all costs, as if the punishment for a breech is death.

In my mom's world, it is.

The rice sock has lavender in it, and as the microwave performs its magic, I lean against the counter and take a deep, cleansing breath. The adrenaline from the night's events drains out of me, the mild rush now turning into the mind-racing of the damned. The entire evening replays itself like a digital film reel being edited on a computer, going in reverse in 2x, 4x, 16x. Then back to the beginning with Ron the Dog Butt Masseuse, to my own massaging of a much more appealing ass.

What have I done?

Ding!

Spritzy comes flying into the kitchen at the sound of the microwave alarm, his little body too fast for his impulses, his nails so long he slides across the kitchen floor and crashes into the wall, jumping up and blinking like the wall attacked him.

He actually growls at it.

Watch out, wall!

I laugh and reach into the microwave, the soothing warmth and waft of lavender giving me some gentle clarity I really need.

Mom's grateful response as I set the rice sock on her shoulders fills me with a kind of sadness I've come to know all too well. It's the sense of a life lived for everyone else. Everything I do involves fixing problems for other people—for my boss, for our clients, for the mystery shoppers I manage, for my friends, for my mom, for the world.

I can't let it go.

Spritzy is on the carpet in the living room as I take a step to go upstairs and put the day behind me. He looks at me, eyes beseeching, and then he plants his little ass on the carpet and uses his front paws to drag himself across the carpet.

Oh, *no*.

My phone buzzes just then as my horrified eyes take in the dog's obvious, uh, clues.

It's a text from a private number. One I haven't seen before.

And all it says is:

Meet me tomorrow in my office at eleven. Your discretion is required. Lipstick is optional. AJM.

AJM?

I frown at the screen while Spritzy violates the carpet. I reach the top of the stairs and it hits me.

Andrew. Andrew James McCormick. AJM.

Andrew is finally texting me. Nearly two years of wondering and waiting, of late nights talking with Amy and Shannon, of dissecting and analyzing and giving up.

I had to slap him to get him to contact me?

Men.

CHAPTER FIVE

The next morning, I park my Turdmobile in the employee parking lot and click my remote to lock it. Then I unlock it. I only lock it out of habit, from when I used to own my own car.

This one? I *hope* someone steals it.

My boss, Greg, got an account where we drive advertisement-covered cars all over town. I inherited Shannon's car when she was offered the ideal job at Anterdec by Mr. Flawless Billionaire and she decided to reach for perfection and we crabs in the pot that is called Consolidated Evalu-Shop couldn't grab her ankles fast enough to pull her back in.

Er, I mean...I'm happy for her.

And I got her car.

It's really an ad for a coffee shop. The brown, roasted coffee bean on top wasn't supposed to look like a giant turd, but it does.

The coffee shop's slogan, *Coffee Gets Everything Moving*, doesn't help.

And yet, it's all a postmodern marketing campaign. None of the companies we advertise is real. We drive around and test whether people will go to the websites advertised on the cars. So far, response has been great. We get the cars for one more year. I sold my junker and have diligently saved a car payment every month so I'll have enough to buy something new if this account goes down the toilet.

To the dogs.

You know—belly up.

Speaking of bellies up, I look over as I walk into the building and see my coworker Josh's car, with Marie's face plastered across the side of it, advertising erectile dysfunction medication. Turns out he's picked up more men with this quirky ad wrap than he ever did driving his nicer car, so he's sticking with what he calls the PickUpMobile.

Get it?

I trudge up the concrete steps. Our office building looks like Leningrad and the Boston Government Service Center building got married and had a baby.

Before I even sling my overloaded purse onto my desktop Josh is standing in my doorway like a sweaty, half-bald vampire living off the blood of the damned.

The DoggieDate Damned.

"How was your date?" he asks, handing me a latte. Ah. There we go. He knows me so well. Almost too well. There are long dry spells in my romantic life where I wish he and I weren't attracted to the same sex. He'd be the perfect boyfriend. He cooks nice meals, he cleans, he gives a good foot rub and he's remarkably tolerant of character disordered people.

Don't discount that last trait. The older I get the more I realize how crucial it is.

"Anal glands," I say, fishing through my purse for my receipts from yesterday's mystery shops.

"You touched his anal glands?" Josh says, his voice going through four octaves. "Isn't that more like a third date phenomenon?"

"No." I'm distracted by a pink plastic box in my purse. Why is my diaphragm in there? Not that I need it these days. At this point, I should just use it as a flexible shot glass. "Wait. Do humans *have* anal glands?"

He just frowns.

I clear my throat and look at him pointedly. "This really is *your* territory. I can't believe you don't know the answer."

"I was a comp sci major. I never took anatomy and physiology."

I just cross my arms over my boobs and stare him down.

He finally flinches and points to the latte. "C'mon. I brought you coffee. Espresso-based coffee."

I take a sip. It tastes like pumpkin-mint. I wince.

"This was a freebie from a mystery shop, wasn't it?"

He goes shifty eyed.

"*Jooooooossssshhhhh!*" I whine.

"What? Carol made me do two of them. The pumpkin-mint taste isn't so bad if you plug your nose while you drink."

He demonstrates for me, pinching his nostrils and tipping his head back.

This is not a ringing endorsement for a new product.

"That coffee tastes like pumpkin mint *gland*."

"What's with the anal gland jokes?" he asks.

"The guy DoggieDate matched me to spent most of the date describing how he saved twenty bucks by learning how to express his dog's anal glands via YouTube videos."

Josh drops his coffee in shock, the top loosening. Half the liquid pours out, covering the brown, industrial carpet. Remarkably, you can't tell. You literally cannot tell that eight ounces of whole milk flavored with espresso, BenGay, and rotten pumpkin just seeped into the carpeting here at Consolidated Evalu-Shop.

SHOPPING FOR A CEO

The room instantly fills with the scent of Lifesavers sacrificed to an angry Pumpkin King.

"Did you kiss him? Sleep with him?" Josh's *non sequitur* throws me for a loop.

"Nothing like changing the subject," I mutter as I fire up my computer. Why did Andrew McCormick's face flash through my mind when he asked me that question? Certainly not Ron's.

"Nothing says romance like spreading your dog's butt cheeks," Josh says cheerfully.

Greg picks that exact moment to walk in. He looks at Josh, frowning.

"Son," he says, placing a hand on Josh's shoulder. "I'm worried about you."

Josh's smile falters.

"Maybe you need a little time off." He gives Josh a sympathetic look. "Unpaid, of course," he quickly adds.

"I wasn't—" Josh sputters. "It's not what—I'm not —we were talking about *dating!*"

Greg's frown deepens.

"Quit talking. You're not helping yourself," Carol hisses, walking in with a coffee tray filled with what I presume are more coffee disasters. "It smells like an air freshener from a T station bathroom had sex with a pumpkin pie in here," she complains.

Greg's phone rings. He answers it, gives Josh a quick squeeze on the neck, and turns away, muttering about compliance and QA into the phone.

Josh turns to me, eyes filled with a strange mix of shame, fury, confusion and impotence.

"This is all your fault!" he cries.

"My fault? How is it my fault you were waxing rhapsodic about dog butts?"

"Hmm, there's a new motto," Carol murmurs. "DoggieDate: For people who *really* love dogs."

"GROSS!" Josh and I snap at her. The apple didn't fall very far from the Marie Tree, did it?

"You were telling us all about your date!"

"And....?"

"And what?"

"Did you sleep with him?"

"No." I shudder.

"Any kisses?"

Any kisses. *Any kisses?* My microscopic pause as I attempt to figure out how to answer that question in the most honest way possible makes Carol and Josh exchange a look so lecherous I feel like I need a pimp to protect me from whatever they're planning for me.

"You kissed him!"

"Who?"

"Anal Gland Hands Man!" Carol exclaims.

Josh's eyebrows go down like The Very Confused Caterpillar. "No, she didn't," he says slowly. "She said so earlier."

They look at me like detectives in an SVU episode. I feel like I'm in an interrogation room with the nondescript character actor whose name you can't recall, but you remember her face from those irritable bowel syndrome commercials.

"Who, exactly, *did* you kiss last night?" Carol asks.

"She kissed Andrew McCormick," announces a voice that is, in timbre, just a few shades off from Carol's.

"Shannon!" Josh squeals, dropping me like he's Ben Affleck and I'm Jennifer Garner. "What are you doing here?"

"Damage control," she gasps as Josh squeezes her like she's a Koosh ball.

Her eyes meet mine.

And narrow.

Uh oh.

She *knows*.

"What were you talking about?" she asks as she looks around the office with an expression that says, *I can't believe I ever worked in this crap hole.*

"Amanda's date! She kissed him." Josh is so breathless he sounds like he's having an asthma attack.

"You never told us you kissed your fake date," Shannon says calmly, eyes a mixture of calculated cool and determined interrogator.

"That's because I didn't."

"You really kissed Andrew? Andrew McCormick?" Carol asks in a low voice. "Again?"

"*Again* again," Shannon says.

Carol frowns. "You mean you've kissed him *three* times?" The woman can't balance a checkbook but she can decode complex inferences to kissing in closets. Sex math has its own logic, apparently.

"Yes."

"Why?" Carol asks.

"Have you *looked* at the man?" Josh says in a disturbingly low voice that sounds exactly like Carol's a moment ago. "He's a delicious *god*."

"He is not," I say weakly. "He's hot, for sure, but *god* might be taking it a bit far."

All three of them snort. Even Greg snorts from the safety of his office. If Spritzy were here, he'd snort, too.

"How about *demigod*?" Josh challenges.

"Fine. He is," I concede. "But that's not why I kissed him."

"Technically, *you* didn't kiss *him*. He kissed *you*. It was like something out of a 1940s Bette Davis film," Shannon explains to Josh and Carol, who pay rapt attention to her words like the good little employees they are. Why do your actual work when you're on the clock if you can gossip about your coworkers instead?

"The Bette Davis movie where she feeds the rat to her invalid sister?" Josh asks, his face screwed tight in confusion.

"Yes," I deadpan. "Exactly like that."

"Did he express the rat's anal glands first?" Carol asks.

"I've heard rat is a delicacy in some parts of southeast Asia," Greg shouts from the other room.

"How did we get from talking about Andrew McCormick to rats?" Josh marvels.

"It's a natural progression." My words hang in the air, hovering like Marie watching Shannon and Declan on their first date.

Minus the wine glass and the dinging and the references to head lice.

My bitterness is leaking out of me like government servers in the hands of Anonymous. I can't stop being hacked by the outside world. Little by little, my sense that I can fix anything is being whittled away by the mystifying reality that everything I've assumed about myself is a lie.

A lie revealed by a kiss.

Or three.

"I thought you liked Andrew," Shannon says, concern creasing her brow. She glows now, like someone ground LED lights and injected them into her bloodstream. Bridal Botox. She is luminescent with love.

I, on the other hand, am bitter with betrayal. Yet how can I be betrayed by a man who has zero attachment or obligation to me?

I inhale slowly, buying time, as I look her over. She's full figured, like me. Her wardrobe has changed along with her income. Everything she wears fits better. The shift is small but noticeable. It's subtle and yet distinct. Somewhere, in the blink of an eye, Shannon has become more herself, a person who is still the old Shannon and yet...more. More present. More aware.

Just...*more*.

Her hands move with the fluid elegance of someone who gestures for emphasis and not out of nervousness. Her eyes gleam with the calculated awareness of someone taking in and observing rather than nervously cataloguing and adjusting. Her smile is more genuine, less anxious. She is a rough diamond, chiseled out of a mine, then cut to near perfection.

Love is the jeweler.

My bitterness fades, replaced by a feeling I can only describe as envy, but that's not right. I don't want to take away what Shannon has with Declan. And I don't even want what she has, because wanting what another person has means settling for less than what is best for you. My own needs differ from Shannon's. My life isn't hers, so why would I want to co-opt the billionaire fiancé and the fabulous marketing job at a Fortune 500 company?

Wait a minute.

Let me pause there.

More money. Better clothes. Financial security. Luxury beyond your wildest dreams. A hot man in her bed—

Forget what I just said.

I want what Shannon has. *Bad*.

"So," Carol says, sipping her coffee, "the bottom line is that Andrew McCormick sniped you from a guy who fondles dog butts for fun and you're not happy?"

I frown. "When you put it that way..."

"Honey, when I put it *any* way, you're not making sense. He has spent most of the past two years sending you mixed signals and you keep picking up what he's putting down, but the two of you are maddening."

"Maddening?" I ask, genuinely confused.

Shannon and Carol move closer to me. It's like having slightly changed, younger versions of Marie and Jason love bombing me.

"He wouldn't kiss you if he didn't like you," Shannon says under her breath.

"I'm still heee—eeerrrre," Josh sings. "I haven't left the room. You don't get to do the chick thing."

"Chick thing?"

"Where you discriminate against me because of my penis."

"When did we start talking about your penis?" I squeak.

"Can we go back to dog butts? I'm less grossed out by that topic," Shannon whispers.

"You are crowding me out of this girl talk because I don't have the right equipment, and I don't appreciate the exclusion." Josh is serious. Oh, boy. He doesn't get like this very often. Normally, the only time he draws this line is when we steal all the massage mystery shops.

"No one's excluding you because of what you have in your pants," Carols says with an eye roll. "We're excluding you because it's really obvious you have a thing for Andrew, too."

That thought never, ever occurred to me.

"I do not!" Josh argues. But his scalp turns red. It's bad enough to be a blusher when all that can turn red are your cheeks and neck, but the poor man is balding. He looks like Hellboy when he's worked up.

A nerdy Hipster Hellboy.

"You came to the mall when Declan was playing Santa last year just so you could sit on his lap!" Shannon's accusation has more bite than I would have expected.

"I did not...okay, I did," Josh admits. "But that doesn't mean I can't gossip about Amanda's sex life!"

"Is *that* what we're doing?" I ask, incredulous.

"Duh," they all say in unison.

"The only one of us with a sex life is Shannon, and she's all settled and happy with her perfect billionaire and her wedding planning, so it's not like there's anything juicy there," Josh explains.

"Other than what they did last night with a stick of butter," I joke.

Oh. Looks like Shannon can blush and look just like Hellboy, too.

"I'm not having sex with anything that doesn't have a battery tech support line," Carol adds. "We have to talk about *someone's* sex life. And Josh is a hopeless cause since his last boyfriend dumped him."

Josh is nodding along to everything Carol says until that last bit.

"Hopeless?" He looks like he's about to cry. "You really think I'm *hopeless*?"

"You use a car that advertises erectile dysfunction meds to find dates."

"Better than dog asses."

"Touché."

Something in the back of my mind won't let go. I feel a thin string unravel, as if a thread were caught from the hem of my skirt, except instead of a skirt, it's my mind. I've forgotten something. It's important.

"What time is it?" Carol finally asks.

"Time for Amanda to come with me to Anterdec for a meeting." Shannon declares. "Eleven-thirty."

Meeting. What is she talking about—

"Oh, my God! Andrew's text. I have a meeting with *him*," I gasp.

"You do?" All three of them raise their eyebrows.

"Yes. Eleven."

Shannon frowns. "He told me to meet him at eleven-thirty. With Declan. Why would he want to meet with *you* earlier?"

This is one of those moments where I have to decide what kind of person I am. Do I lie to my best friend to save face for the man who won't stop turning me into his own little county fair kissing booth, or does loyalty prevail?

"Oh, you know," I say, trying to appear casual. "Maid of honor and best man stuff."

I, apparently, am the kind of person who throws my best friend under a bus.

Shannon smiles, but the grin doesn't meet her eyes. "That's cute. Will you talk about that kiss, too?"

"That's up to him," I huff. "He's never talked to me before about the other kisses."

"Because he's an asshole," Carol says flatly.

"A hot asshole," Josh says.

"You struggling with that, too?" Greg says from the hall as he walks by. "Just lay off the spicy curry. Takes a day or so to go away."

We all wince.

"Is Anterdec hiring?" all three of us ask Shannon at the same time.

She just shakes her head slowly, like she knows something she can't say.

Funny.

Same here.

CHAPTER SIX

"I'll drive," Shannon says as I grab my purse and pointedly ignore Greg. Josh or Carol will tell him I have a meeting at Anterdec. He won't care that it's really about Andrew becoming CEO. He'll think I'm drumming up more business for Consolidated Evalu-Shop.

We get outside and walk down the crumbling concrete steps. There is a limo in front of us.

"Is Declan here?" I ask. He and Andrew travel in the city by limo. The only time I've ever seen Declan drive a car is his SUV, and that almost seems like it's for show. The guy claims he gets more work done when someone else is driving, but then why not let Shannon drive?

As Shannon looks embarrassed but determined, she opens the door and I look in.

No wonder she likes this limo thing. It's the size of her entire old apartment in there.

"Why does it smell like chocolate?" I ask as I bend and settle in.

I look to my left.

"Is that a *cake* bar?"

She pinkens. "Declan just had a new customer come by." She names a celebrity chef you'd gasp to hear mentioned. I do.

"She brought an assortment of desserts from her new line that Anterdec will be using in all their properties in North America. Elite member guests will come in to their hotel rooms with a tray of these, a bottle of sparkling water and chocolate-covered strawberries."

"Any tiramisu?" I joke.

"Only in petit fours form, and no rings attached." She taps on the glass between us and the driver and off we go, headed for the Financial District. As I look back at my office building, it feels like walking out of a Brazilian favela.

"Seriously. Any job openings at Anterdec? Because I would jump ship like the rat that I am," I say, then stuff a little square of cake perfection in my mouth.

She smiles, serene and composed. She's like a Shannonbot.

"Oh, my God, is that pistachio mint?" I groan.

"With a touch of amaretto."

"I think I just orgasmed."

"Wouldn't be the first one in this limo," she sighs.

My mouth goes dry. "Um, thanks? Didn't need that visual."

"Speaking of orgasms," she says, ignoring my comment, "what is going on with you and Andrew?"

My mouth turns into the Sahara.

"Did you have to ruin a perfectly good moment of stress eating by bringing up Andrew?" I whimper.

"Sorry. But yes, I do. What are you hiding about him?"

She's *so* good.

"Nothing."

"Liar."

Rage. An unexpected wave of red fury fills me, wiping away the taste of the divine in my mouth and replacing it with a stark bitterness that fills me with despair.

And anger.

I don't get angry. It's not what I do. Not, at least, with my friends and family. All my life I've been the person who rationalizes and organizes and thinks and plans and plots her way out of emotional messes. I sob quietly in the shower or slink off to let my angry tears come out in vents, but this?

This kind of rage comes after the pressure cooker can't contain it. My inner world is about to become spaghetti stains on the ceiling.

I've never, ever directed it at Shannon. We've known each other since elementary school and I can count on one hand the number of fights we've had. And by "fight" I mean terse words that end with tearful crying and two spoons and a pint of ice cream.

Okay...two pints.

"Isn't your perfect life enough for you?" I hiss, regretting the words instantly even as they come out of me. I sit back and straighten my spine, knowing the inevitability of the moment makes whatever I say all the more odious. I can't stop this. It's an avalanche that has been triggered by her gunshot—the word *liar*—and now here it comes.

Watch out below.

"What—what do you mean?" she stammers. "I was just—"

"You have everything," I whisper through my clenched teeth. "You have it all. And I'm happy for you." My mouth is set in a way that makes the muscles in my face that run along my temple feel like flat pieces of tense wood that can move.

"I really am. This isn't about that. It's about...me." I realize how true that last word is as Shannon looks at me with open, caring eyes and a wary expression. Making eye contact goes against everything in me. I'm a live wire. There is no one in the world I can say this to.

Except my bestie.

"Is it about dumping the Turdmobile off on you? Because I'm so sorry."

I give her a hard look. "Ha ha. No."

"This is really about Andrew and your mom," she says with a sigh.

"Now *that's* a sentence I never expected to have directed at me," I reply, completely stumped. The wind's out of my sails. Only Shannon can do that. "What do Andrew and my mother have to do with each other?"

"You always call yourself a fixer," she says, reaching out to touch my shoulder. Her eyes are so warm, so calm. The Shannon I've known for years has her edges smoothed off. She's coiffed and possessed, and I love her for not yelling at me or rejecting me. Being able to tell her how I really feel means so much more than I think I even understand.

"I am a fixer."

"But who fixes problems for you?"

"Me."

"Exactly."

I frown. "What's your point?"

"That is my point."

"And..."

"You fix your mom's problems. You fix client problems. You came to the rescue and fixed my problem with Declan nearly two years ago. Andrew isn't a problem you can fix."

"I'm not following you."

"He's maddening."

"Okay, *that* I can follow."

"He's unpredictable. He keeps kissing you but never calling. Declan says you confuse his brother."

"*I* confuse *him*? Talk about projecting." A thrill runs up my back, spreading warmth and some salacious throbbing to places that really need more of a pulse. "Wait. Andrew talked to Declan about *me*?"

"Yes."

I feel like a breathless eighth grader. Ah, hell. I *am* a breathless eighth grader.

"And?"

"You're not Andrew's type."

"You mean because I don't charge by the hour?"

She lets go of my shoulder and gives me a glare. "He's my future brother-in-law. Don't talk about him like that."

"You were the one who told me his assistant hires prostitutes for him!"

"No, I didn't!"

"You told me Declan told you that he schedules 'business meetings' with various women and after he's bedded them, they go away. What do you call that?"

"Modern dating?" She smiles.

"Minus the anal glands," I whisper under my breath.

"You're starting to worry me," Shannon says as she squeezes my hand. The limo pulls up to Anterdec's office garage and begins the slow, winding way down to the executive level. Shannon knows how to live now.

"I am the one who is being kissed out of the blue by your future brother-in-law while creating the mystery shopper survey for a dog owners' dating site. I *should* worry you."

Her laughter fills the car. "He has never hired a prostitute. Put that one out of your mind. Plus, Andrew doesn't have a dog."

A pang of guilt hits me. "About that..."

"About doggy dates? You want to dig through the dating database and see if he's in there? Because he's not."

I shudder. "You don't want to know what that database looks like. Trust me."

"Can't be worse than that dating site for married people who want to have affairs."

"There are people in the DoggieDate database who have a sexual fetish for dressing up in dog costumes that match their actual dog's breed and pretending to be a dog."

"Oh. Weird."

"Or the human-dog relationships."

"Oh, gross."

"No, no," I say, hands up in protest. "Not actual human-dog sex. But one person is the human and the other one pretends to be the dog. Wears the costume, eats out of the dog bowl—"

"STOP! I cannot unhear what has been heard."

"The weird part is that there are all these *accessories* for relationships like that. The merchandising opportunities are amazing."

Shannon sticks her fingers in her ears as we climb out of the limo. The driver holds the door open, his face neutral and stoic as I say, "And the human can buy special leashes, and the fetish involves—"

His face is not so stoic now.

"Work. We're talking about a client, Jose," Shannon hastily explains.

"I'm sure you are, ma'am," he says tightly.

"Bet you've heard worse in your line of work," I joke.

He makes eye contact. "No ma'am. That one's in the top three."

Oh, great.

"Let me explain," I say, suddenly deeply humiliated. "I'm a mystery shopping manager and I have to go out on twenty dates with dogs for this new dating service I'm evaluating."

That didn't come out right.

"Not with the dogs," I say, giggling. "With their owners."

"And some of the owners want to pretend to be dogs," Shannon adds, trying to help. "It's a fetish."

Not helpful.

"What you do in your line of....work, ma'am, is your business."

"I'm not a pervert!" I call back as Shannon pulls me away to the elevator, which opens at that exact moment to reveal—you guessed it.

Andrew McCormick.

His eyes light up.

"Shame," is all he says.

"Shame *what*?" I retort.

"Shame you're not a pervert. See you at eleven." And with that, he moves so smoothly it's like he's on wheels, disappearing into the same limo we just got out of, Jose avoiding eye contact with us.

As he pulls away I look at my watch. 10:33 a.m.

"Where is he going?" I ask Shannon, who enters the open elevator and pulls me in. She presses the floor for the main Anterdec offices with a practiced hand. "We have an appointment!"

"Who knows? To grab a cup of coffee?"

Living with a billionaire hasn't rubbed off on her, has it? "He has people who fetch him coffee," I say, as if explaining religion to an alien. "Hell, he has people who test whether it's too hot for him. He probably owns a sugar cane plantation where they hand harvest his personal sweetener. How can you live with the richie riches and not know that?"

"I—"

"And I am not a pervert!" I hiss again.

She starts to laugh. It's a sound of absurdity. There is no mocking in her tone, and I join in, realizing my own over-the-topness.

"You're really not," she gasps. "You're about as vanilla as they come."

"How can I be vanilla when I'm not having sex with anyone?"

The words come out of my mouth just as the elevator slows and the doors open, revealing James McCormick.

Who just heard every word I said.

CHAPTER SEVEN

"That's the difference between men and women," he declares in a voice that's just a notch louder than it needs to be. He's cultivating an audience. James McCormick is a man who is accustomed to instant attention.

Just like Andrew.

"Men pretend to be sleeping with more women than they really are. Women complain endlessly about all the men they're not sleeping with. Both are always lying," James declares with a smug little smile.

"But I'm really not sleeping with anyone!"

I can't believe I just said that in public.

James startles slightly. "You and Andrew aren't...." He makes a series of suggestive sounds from the back of his throat like he's trying out for a sound effects specialist on a porn set.

"What? No! Whatever gave you *that* idea?"

All he does is wink and walk onto the elevator as Shannon drags me off it, the door closing on the grey fox as he whistles to himself.

Panic blooms in my chest like a field of sunflowers all turning toward the light in synchronicity too perfect to be coincidence.

"What did he mean? Is Andrew talking about me? Does he talk about me with his father? Did Declan say something to James about the kiss last night? Is there more going on than I thought?"

"Amanda—"

"Does Andrew like perverts? Because I can be a pervert if that's more his speed. Vanilla is boring. I don't have to be boring. I can be kinky like the best of them."

"AMANDA!"

A firm yank on my wrist and Shannon has me down the hall, inside her office, sitting on a small loveseat, head between my knees, a lavender-filled eye pillow shoved under my nose. She's holding a spritz bottle of water and I'm a little scared.

"What is *wrong* with you?" she demands. "Who stole my level-headed best friend and replaced her with, with...this?" Shannon's wrists flick my way like twin whips.

See? I'm not so vanilla.

"I don't know!" I wail, looking up. "Andrew McCormick has taken every rational brain cell in my head and shaken me like I'm a snow globe."

"With his mouth?" Shannon asks skeptically. "Because so far, all he's done is kiss you and not ask you out."

"Three times! He kissed me in his office the day I tried to fix the mess between you and Declan. He kissed me in the on-call room at the hospital when you swallowed the engagement ring. And then last night, after my anal date, he—"

Tap tap tap.

I look up to find Declan's assistant, Grace, standing in the open doorway.

"Your *what*?" she asks. If my grandmother were alive she'd be Grace's age. Grandma would probably have the same look of untempered disgust and extraordinary curiosity on her face as well.

"Anal *gland* date," Shannon adds. "She forgot a word."

"That really does not clarify," Grace replies. If she frowns any harder she'll be a Shar-Pei.

Why does everything remind me of dogs?

"I went out with a guy last night who likes to express—oh, never mind." I give up. My phone buzzes. I check it.

Reminder: DoggieDate #2 noon

"Oh, shoot!" I snap, standing. "I completely forgot that I have another date today. A lunch date. We're meeting at the Esplanade."

"What's up, Grace?" Shannon asks, trying to change topics.

Grace gives me a look as I check my calendar to see what else I'm forgetting. "Declan wanted me to invite Amanda to your lunch date today at The Fort, but I see she has anal lunch date...er, I mean, *another* lunch date." Grace rushes off like she's retching.

It's hard to rattle that woman.

I'm *that* big a mess, aren't I?

"Look," I say with a long sigh. "This isn't me. This really isn't me. Look at me!"

"You look like Amanda. Brown hair, big eyes, overpainted red lips, and ex-cheerleader body."

"I know, right? I—wait. Overpainted? I'm not overpainted!"

Shannon's mouth tightens like she's been caught making an error. "Er, no. Of course not."

Tap tap tap.

We look toward the door. Declan walks in, his cologne following him by microseconds, a blend of cloves and cotton. He reaches for Shannon and gives her a gentle kiss right under her ear.

What is it like to be known so well by a man? I've had short-term boyfriends. Friends with benefits. A one night stand here or there. I'm no prude, but I'm not the town barfly. Nothing wrong with being somewhere in between, but what Shannon and Declan share feels so out of my league. I can't imagine living in concert with someone where the invisible boundary that makes me *me* and him *him* dissolves at will.

At the power of something greater than simple consent.

Green eyes the color of money look at me. Declan's wearing a suit that costs more than my first year of college. He's holding Shannon against him, arm wrapped across her back, hand cupping one hip like it's a mug handle.

"Amanda," he says pleasantly. "What a surprise to see you here."

"How can it be a surprise when Grace just asked if I'm having lunch with you and Shannon after my meetings?"

Confusion fills his face. "Grace asked that?"

Shannon laughs and turns to me. "Grace runs his entire life. Declan's just a passenger."

"See?" I taunt. "Just like the sugar cane farm for Andrew's sweetener."

Declan's bemusement deepens. "His what?"

Before I can answer, Andrew's executive assistant appears. "Ms. Warrick? Mr. McCormick will see you now."

CHAPTER EIGHT

The last time I was in Andrew's office he was wearing bike shorts. Tight ones. Nice, snug Lycra shorts so fine I really should have shoved a dollar bill in his waistband as a tip for the show. Not that he needed the money.

As his admin guides me to his office, I try to center myself. In an hour I'm meeting Mr. Teacup Chihuahua, a guy matched to me mostly based on my description of Spritzy in the DoggieDate database. We're going to the esplanade so I can meet Muffin, his little teacup sweetie. In our brief email exchanges, my date insisted he needs to make sure Muffin likes me before taking the next step and having her meet Spritzy, lest his dog become too attached to him.

Him.

Not to me.

My mind is racing to think about anything but the image of Andrew McCormick, who is turned away from me, his broad, muscled back on display. His charcoal suit jacket is draped casually over the leather club chair across from his desk. He's looking out the glass wall and over the city. A few floors below I see the Pac-Man-based topiary for the game design company in the building next door.

As I peer closer, I realize they have added a dog run.

And is that a pool...filled with *dogs*?

Huh. Note to self: run a database query on DoggieDate to see how many employees from that company are on DoggieDate, and suggest marketing to them as part of overall strategy for strengthening new accounts.

See? I'm good. As good as Shannon.

Anterdec should hire *me*.

Andrew spins around in his Herman Miller chair and holds one finger up to me. His face is intense, eyes dark in concentration, and he's coiled with the kind of frustration that comes from negotiations that are stalled. The telephone conversation he's having is one that probably requires more privacy, but I instinctively do as told and wait in place.

As I lift his suit jacket from the chair, his cologne fills the air.

It takes every bit of self control I possess not to huff it like a little kid with fruit-scented markers and no adult supervision.

My fingertips can't help it. They've seceded from my rational mind, stroking the fine cloth that has just been resting against those cultured pecs minutes before. The cloth is warm, still, as if he shed the jacket seconds before I walked in. It's almost like being in his arms last night.

Almost.

The pale imitation is worse than nothing. I would rather never, ever see him again than sit here, trying not to lick the wool weave, using every ounce of restraint I possess to maintain a professional exterior that shows my true nature.

I am a fixer.

I can fix this.

I can fix *me*.

Andrew ends the call and gives me his full attention. It's like drinking from a trickle at a water fountain and suddenly having a fire hose aimed at your face.

A sensual, sultry, hot-as-Hades fire hose.

"I assume you've kept your mouth shut?" he starts.

Nothing like cutting to the chase. I see what this meeting is about. We're here to talk business. The business of keeping his secret about becoming the new CEO of Anterdec Industries. Nothing more. I can play this game.

"Except when you're kissing me."

Or I can play my own game. My rules. My board. My pieces.

My *tongue*.

The way he tilts his head just so as his mouth tightens, then spreads into a smile is like watching a rainbow form in the sky.

"I appreciate that." His voice goes low and suggestive. Flirty, even. I'm not imagining this.

"Open-mouthed kisses? I noticed." I match his tone.

He blinks repeatedly, the smile impossible to suppress. Dimples. Dear God, he has the McCormick dimples. Of course he does. His family's DNA has more dimples in it than Tom Brady's.

"I was talking about silence," he says, standing quite suddenly. The movement may be abrupt, but his animal grace is studied. He knows how his body affects mine. Andrew McCormick is a master at knowing how to read other people.

He has a problem, though.

So am I.

Andrew has tells. One eyebrow quirks up right now as he gives away the fact that he's less self-assured than he was when I entered the room. The open discussion about kissing is intriguing him, but it's not distracting him. This meeting has a purpose.

And he's determined to stay focused.

"Silence. You mean the kind of silence that comes after being kissed by you? Or the kind of silence you assume you can kiss your way into?" I ask.

The eyebrow goes down. His face goes slack. Those smoldering eyes narrow.

Now I have his full attention.

"I kissed you because you were about to spill a family secret at a less-than-opportune time."

I look pointedly at the door to the closet in his office. "Really? Which time? After your spin session right there?" I motion toward the door. "Or after Shannon swallowed your mother's engagement ring?"

"You know perfectly well which time." His voice is full of an amused smoothness. Instead of resuming his seat behind the desk, he walks around and sits on the edge, manspreading in front of me, a foot and a half the only space between us.

There goes that cologne again.

"I do?" My words come out breathy, like Marilyn Monroe running after the ice cream truck. "It's getting hard to keep track of all the kisses. I'm nearly ready to draw up a spreadsheet."

"Would you like my assistant to create a database instead?"

"Do you plan to enter me that many times?"

He inhales sharply, then leans forward with the intention of a man who needs to confirm a fact. His hands are folded, forearms resting on his thighs. My mind races to process what I just said.

What I should have said is *Do you plan to enter me into the database that many times?* but I didn't.

What I actually said is not what I meant to say, but that doesn't matter now, does it?

Too late.

The skin around his eyes moves with amusement and a hint of something so dangerous I can't breathe.

"That depends," he says quietly.

"On what?" The less I say, the better.

"On whether you'll slap me every time I," he clears his throat suggestively, "enter you." He smiles, the innuendo giving me permission to smile back. "In the database, I mean."

"Well, now, *that* depends," I reply, matching his voice, trying so hard to keep this light and fun. That's all it is, right? We're just sparring partners taking verbal jabs at each other, with kisses as the topic. I tell myself this because if our conversation means something less, then it won't hurt when he ignores me again, and if it means more, then—

Then I can't even bear to think that way.

I'm inhaling his scent, which changes as we continue, the heat in the air between us altering the space. Like alchemists, we're taking words with specific meanings, fixed characteristics that do not change, and turning them into something wholly forged anew.

His heat is melting me, and I'm not certain what I'll be like when I reform and take on the new element I'm in the process of becoming.

"Depends on what?" he asks. The game is on, and while the rules aren't defined, the outcome most assuredly is. We both know exactly how to score points. The only question that remains is how can we both win?

"On whether you enjoy being slapped. Some men do." I lift one shoulder and bite my upper lip, the look meant to tease, to taunt. I inhale slowly and let him watch me. I'm not a woman you hide from the world in closets, or one you smother with kisses to keep her quiet.

Not anymore.

Bridging the distance between us, he extends a hand to me. I take it and he pulls me up, into the space between those toned thighs. Even though my hips don't touch his legs, I can feel the hardness of those thick muscles, the coiled power in them calling out to be touched.

Without invitation, I reach down, palms on his knees, and watch my own hands ride up to his belt line. Slowly, with a maddening pace that makes seconds feel like lifetimes, I look up.

I never see his eyes, but oh, how I feel his mouth. Unlike all the other kisses we've shared, this one is planned. Seductive. Intentional. Andrew is in no rush, and we're not taken off guard or hiding from anyone— especially ourselves.

His hands circle my waist and mine slide up the hard contours of his back, the soft cotton of his business shirt so smooth it's like silk. My fingertips touch the base of his neck as he bites one of my lips, sucking with just enough intensity to make me wish I were the kind of woman who kept a spare pair of panties in her purse for occasions like this.

Funny how they never covered this topic in Girl Scouts.

He pulls back, then tightens his arms around me, holding on as if he were touching me for the first time, as if we're discovering each other with a serendipitous joy that should be savored and that requires constant contact. The room disappears, the past two years fade, and all my worries and insecurities about this man who kisses me in closets and who is so mysterious and aloof dissolve like the boundary between our bodies as we just let *go*.

"Four," he whispers against my ear as he pulls back, the soft rasp of his cheek against mine just ticklish enough to make me shiver.

"Four what?" I gasp as he nuzzles my neck, those warm arms staying wrapped around me. The longer he holds me, the more I can believe this is real.

"Four kisses. For our database."

"Right. Four," I say weakly. My knees tingle and the feeling travels up. This is real, all right.

"Let's make it five."

"Five is a good number."

A telephone rings in the distance. I twist in his arms and look behind us. To my surprise, his office door is open. He is kissing me in public. That's twice now.

And his arms are still around me.

"Six is even better."

And with that, he adds so many entries to the database that I lose count.

CHAPTER NINE

The sound of a man clearing his throat is the next conscious event that pierces my psyche.

"Excuse me? Eleven-thirty meeting?" It's Declan. I step out of Andrew's arms and close my eyes in embarrassment, like a child who thinks if they can't see the world the world can't see them.

Andrew looks over my shoulder. I feel the movement rather than see it as his palm slides down from the base of my breast to my hip. "Give us a minute. We're wrapping up our meeting."

"You'd better wrap it," Declan mutters. "Shannon and I are having the first grandchild. You don't get to win that one, too—"

"Hey!" Andrew barks, moving swiftly across the room and shutting the door in Declan's smirking face. I watch his body, my mouth buzzing with his taste, the lingering sense of his kisses making me giddy with the sheer nonsense of being in a different layer of life for a few minutes.

How can a kiss (or nine) do that?

Andrew stands at the door, his back to me. He squares his shoulders and begins nodding to himself. I imagine, if he faced me, he would be silently preparing himself for the moment he turns around and tells me this is nothing. We are making a mistake. A kiss (or nine) are enough, and let's just part our separate ways and stay friends.

He turns around, looks at me, and says, "Lunch?"

Not what I expected to hear.

"Excuse me?"

"We'll have lunch. I'll cancel my meeting with Declan and we can continue this database discussion over lunch."

I really, really hope *database discussion* is code for *kissing*.

My stomach flip flops. Lunch. Lunch. I look at the clock.

11:32.

"I...can't."

He looks utterly shocked. "You can't? Why not?"

"Because I have a date."

"A what?"

"A date."

A fake date. I can't say that part, though. First rule of mystery shopping: never, ever reveal your true identity. I can't admit the DoggieDate dates I'm going on are fake. I can't tell him the truth. Some part of me wants to break every professional rule right now, and my body is screaming at me to make an exception.

But I can't.

I just...can't.

He scowls. "A date. You're dating? You have a boyfriend?"

"No boyfriend."

He blinks, alternating between widening his eyes and a furrowed brow. "But you're dating."

"Yes."

"Men?"

"Excuse me?"

"You're dating men?"

"Who else would I date?"

"Shannon."

"*Excuse me?*"

78

"You dated Shannon. For a while there. At least, you pretended to." He looks very confused. "I never really got the whole story from Declan. Something about you and Shannon being married, and then you weren't, and then you stormed into my office and kissed me and demanded that me, Dad and Terry all act in your hotel scheme—"

"Hold on there. *I* kissed *you*?"

"Of all the things I just said, *that's* the detail you're going to focus on? What about my question about men?"

"I did not kiss you! *You* kissed *me*!" As for whether I like men, if he can't tell the answer to that one by now, then we need more kissing.

Er, database discussion.

"You barged into my office and started ranting about what an asshole Declan was, right after my spin session. Then you pulled me into my closet and started kissing me," he recounts.

"You have a memory made of Swiss cheese. There are more holes in that story than in a J. Lo Oscars gown."

"You didn't barge in here?"

"I did," I concede.

"And you didn't pull me into my closet?"

"I did. To hide from Shannon, who magically appeared at the exact worst moment."

"And you didn't kiss me?"

"No, I did NOT. *You* kissed *me*. I remember it perfectly."

"So do I."

"Glad to hear it. Funny how nearly two years went by without a word from you. Good to know you weren't suffering from a rare case of kissing amnesia."

He crosses his arms over his chest and gives me a weird smile. "That's what this is about?"

"What *what's* about?"

"Your attitude."

"I don't have an attitude. You're the one with the attitude. Two minutes ago you were kissing me, then you found out I have a date, and now you're a Neanderthal."

"I'm a Neanderthal? What's that supposed to mean?"

"It means you need to learn to use your words. Silence works for cavemen. Not modern men."

Someone knocks on the door and it opens instantly. Declan is standing there, Shannon right behind him. He taps the threshold.

"Look, little bro, I don't have all day. The resort in Maui needs me for a marketing kickoff meeting about a new merchandising deal we have for branded sunscreen, and—"

"We were just finishing up here. Amanda has to leave for something far more important," Andrew says, his voice closed off and cold.

"More important than Anterdec?" Declan flashes me a dazzling smile, while Shannon's eyes turn suspicious. "What could be more important than a meeting with us?"

Andrew grabs his suit jacket off the chair and shrugs into it, his neck thick with tension. If he tightens his jaw any more he'll crack a tooth. He storms out of the room, calling back over his shoulder:

"A date."

CHAPTER TEN

"The anti-depressants did wonders for little Muffin here." Jordan is forty-two and a short Italian guy who I could never, ever wear heels with if we were dating for real, because I would look like Hagrid next to him. He picked me because I have a teacup chihuahua, too.

He's sweet and friendly, bald, with bushy eyebrows that have erratically long stray grays that extend out like uncoiled springs. Definitely not my type, but the kind of person who deserves to find a low-conflict partner to go to bingo night and chess tournaments and Mass.

Did I mention he goes to Mass seven days a week? His profile on DoggieDate didn't note his Catholicism, but Jordan has managed to bring it up nine times. In fourteen minutes.

As we walk along the esplanade, the Charles River filled with people rowing and sculling, I find myself hunching. I have to. He's so soft spoken and so short that I can't hear him if I don't.

"That's great," I say with as much enthusiasm as I can. Muffin is a tiny little thing that makes my mom's dog, Spritzy, look like the Incredible Hulk by comparison. If Muffin weighs two pounds, I'd be surprised, and she's so nervous she vibrates.

She has also scratched or bitten off most of her hair, so she looks like a rat with a short circuit.

"When my mother died, Muffin just fell apart." Jordan's eyes fill with tears. I'm guessing Muffin wasn't the only one.

"Mama would have loved you," he adds, giving me a shy, sidelong glance that fills me with guilt and a simultaneous sense of relief that this is all pretend.

"Umm..."

"Would you like to meet her?"

I halt. If Mama is dead, what does he mean? Is she sitting in a rocking chair somewhere in his apartment on the North End? Jordan suddenly looks a little too much like Norman Bates for my tastes.

"How would I, uh—"

Muffin sneezes. She scares herself and shakes some more.

"Her grave is a few blocks away. Mama likes it when I bring Muffin to visit her."

I am starting to think that Jordan's favorite toy is a homemade skin suit made from online dating prospects.

"Okay." *It's only pretend. It's only pretend. It's only pretend.*

"Amanda!" We're interrupted by the divine hand of God (or, perhaps, Jordan's disapproving mama) as Marie screeches my name from across the way. She's in the middle of a large patch of grass with about ten people, all on yoga mats, all in Child's Pose.

It would be way too convenient for Marie to just happen to appear in this exact moment at this specific park, right? It's not. We arranged it. You know how some people arrange "rescue calls"? Marie offered some "rescue yoga" for me. She moved her class outdoors for fun, and also to help give me an out when I described Jordan to her.

She's so giving.

"Is that your mother?" Jordan asks a little too eagerly. "She's angelic." His voice goes dreamy and soft, and now...yep.

He's crying.

We walk over to Marie and her outdoor yoga class. Well, *I* do. Jordan follows about three paces behind, sniffing with each step.

"What are you doing here?" Marie asks as she gives me a hug. The question is rhetorical, and she gives me a wink. She's sweaty and radiant, and still manages to smell like lavender even when she's in the middle of teaching a strenuous outdoor class. When *I* sweat, I smell like a teenage boy's locker and tainted cinnamon.

"Hello," Jordan says formally, extending his hand to shake hers. Marie gives me a questioning look but offers her hand, which Jordan rotates slightly so he can kiss the back of it.

How courtly.

And slightly creepy.

Marie gives me a look I can't quite read. It's somewhere between *How sweet* and *Call the police*.

"My name is Jordan Montelcini. This is Muffin." He gestures toward the dog, who is either excited or having a seizure. It's impossible to tell the difference.

Marie's eyebrows go up. Her mouth twitches. Nineteen gears involving my sex life click into place in that scheming mind of hers, and one of them involves Andrew, because she tilts her head, blinks in Morse code, and if I could decipher it I'm sure she'd be saying, *What about Andrew?*

Yeah. I know, I blink back. *What about him?*

"I'm here with Amanda on our first date. Muffin approves so far. It's so nice to meet Amanda's mother."

Muffin puts her jaw on his forearm and closes her eyes. Right. Seal of approval.

Marie looks at the dog. Looks at me. Frowns.

"I'm actually Amanda's best friend's mother," Marie explains, correcting him. Her face explodes into an expression of sheer delight. "Did you say your last name is Montelcini?"

Jordan puffs up. He's almost tall enough now to ride a roller coaster at Six Flags. "Yes."

"Of Montelcini Flowers?"

The man's face spreads with a joyous glow that makes me inhale sharply, for he becomes luminous. It's like watching a caterpillar turn into a butterfly before my very eyes.

"Yes. You've heard of us? I mean," he frowns, swallowing hard. "Me. It's just me now."

Marie looks like she's been slapped. "Just you? But the Montelcini team is renowned for—"

Jordan wails as he drops to the ground with a sob that even his mama must surely hear in heaven. Or, um, wherever she resides.

I'm deeply confused. Who exactly are the Montelcinis, and why is Marie looking at Jordan like he invented salted caramel ice cream?

"Mama!" Jordan sobs. Muffin begins spazzing out and walks three feet away to tinkle on a stray dandelion. A dandelion that is bigger than the dog.

"Is your mother okay?" Marie asks, dropping to the ground and putting her arm around the poor man's shoulders. I'm watching all of this with a strange sort of clinical detachment, as if Jordan isn't my date.

That's because he *isn't* my date.

So far, we're two for two with DoggieDate men. Two weirdos. Two showstoppers.

And I have eighteen more to go.

"My mama is *deaaaadddd*," he cries.

Marie's eyes fill with tears. A few of her yoga students pop their heads up in response to Jordan's cries.

"I'm so sorry, Jordan." She rubs his back. He's genuinely mourning, and I feel for the guy. I do. I'm in my twenties and while my own mother can be an anal retentive, uptight pain in the butt, I love her and don't know what I'd do without her. Jordan seems, to put it mildly, like a mama's boy, and I can only imagine that losing your mom and business partner would be devastating.

"Does this mean Montelcini Flowers isn't doing weddings right now?" Marie asks softly.

Aha.

I roll my tongue inside my mouth and then bite it. If I don't, I'll say something I regret.

Now I understand.

And a lightbulb goes off.

At one of the late night tactical weapons meetings...er, wedding planning sessions, Marie mentioned that the best florist in town was booked three years out.

Montelcini Flowers.

Rescue yoga, indeed. Suddenly her gracious act of bad-date assistance becomes more evident for what it really is.

"How can I do weddings when the bliss of Mama is gone? No one can make her red sauce for me. I had to learn how to do laundry! And make my own bed!" he wails. "Hospital corners are *haaaarrrddd*."

"That is so difficult," Marie says, completely shining him on. Some part of her genuinely cares about the man's pain. Hell, I sure do. But another part of her is clearly emboldened by the idea that she might be able to book *the* premier wedding florist in Boston. The

85

society coup of this one would give her a Momzilla orgasm.

Jordan leans in to Marie's hug, his face pressed against her bosom. He lets out a series of small, hitched sobs. "You smell a little like my mama."

And then he leans in and just cries.

Muffin toddles off, sniffing in a crooked line in the bright sunshine, still within twenty feet of us. It's probably the most freedom that poor little two pounds of flesh has ever had in its coddled little life.

Like Jordan, right now.

As Marie pats him gently on the back, I stand there, my mind occupied by the earlier hour at Anterdec. The kiss. The kisses. Andrew's words cycle through me, his on-off switch so easy to flip, his obvious anger at my "date"—who is now burrowing into Marie's arms in an alarming way—leaving me with more questions than answers.

And then the silence (other than Jordan's sobs) is pierced by a strange cry from the sky.

A red-tailed hawk swoops down and in what feels like slow motion, descends to the grass, plucks little Muffin in its talons, and lifts up, wings pushing down with the effort of getting greater lift with its dinner in its hands.

"Oh, my God!" I scream. Jordan and Marie look up. I'm pointing at the horrific scene as Muffin quakes in the hawk's grasp, twelve feet above us, eyes bulging in terror.

Or is that how she normally looks? It's hard to tell the difference.

"MUFFIN!" Jordan screeches, scrambling to his feet. "No, Muffin! Mama will be so mad if something happens to you!"

"Do something!" Marie cries out, running after the bird, who is lurching up and down as it struggles to hang on to Muffin the Hawk Munchie.

I grab a rock and throw it. I have the pitching arm of a four year old, so all I manage to do is hit a passing dad pushing a stroller as my anemic throw ends in a parabola of shame.

"Hey!" the dad shouts. "Watch it. Babies here."

Great. I hit a dad with twins. The karma on that one is going to be massive.

"Don't hurt Muffin!" Jordan screams at me. "That rock could maim her."

Right. Because throwing a rock to make the hawk drop her is exactly like having her eaten alive by the bird.

Jordan is definitely on my permanent list of people I will never, ever touch.

Marie sprints over to a little boy who has a remote control in his hand. She says something to him and he hands it over. I look up.

A tiny little silver toy helicopter makes a giant U-turn and dive bombs the hawk.

"MUFFIN!" Jordan screams.

In a split second, I race over to the ground under the hawk and Muffin. Someone has to catch the little dog, because at this point, the hawk's a good twenty feet in the air. If he drops her, she'll be a Muffin pancake.

"BOOYAH!" Marie shouts as she manipulates the helicopter. The dad of the twins in the stroller jogs over to the little boy and says soothing things to him. They watch Marie attack the hawk with the toy helicopter.

"Daddy, it's my turn next, right?" the little boy asks. "I wanna hit the hawk. Twenty points!"

Suddenly, the silver copter buzzes loud in my ears, and I hear Muffin whining. The hawk drops her as Marie goes in for one last try, and I aim, barely reaching my arms out in time for falling Muffin to hit my hands, my body stretched as far as it can go in a last-minute lunge that leaves me holding her in my palms, my chest and hips smacking into the solid sidewalk section with a belly-flop that knocks the wind out of me.

My hands shake.

Because Muffin's in them, quaking away.

"MUFFIN!" Jordan snatches her out of my palms as I try to breathe. I fail. My face is smashed into the rough concrete, the blooming pinprick of a bad scrape seeping in to my consciousness. I can't breathe, though. It's like a brick became my lungs. My legs feel like rubber behind me, and my belly is exposed, the lunge to catch the dog pulling my shirt out of my pants.

I'm facedown, palms up, breathless, and about to die.

Then the clapping begins. If I'm going to die because I saved a dog from becoming a Scooby snack, then there damn well *better* be applause.

"That was amazing!" the dad with twins says as Marie gives him back the controller. The little boy looks up into the sky and frowns.

"Where's the bird? I wanna attack the bird! My turn! I'm Player 2!"

I want to say *help*, but I can't. I am lying here and it feels like I have a balloon inside me stopping me from breathing. My ribs spasm and my throat gags and then *bam!*

I'm breathing. The feeling is painful and ragged and god-awfully rippling, like I have layers of skin sticking to each other inside wet lungs, but oxygen gets in.

You don't realize how much you appreciate the simple art of respiration until you can't respire.

"You used that helicopter so well!"

"Mama! Mama was Muffin's guardian angel," Jordan cries out. "And you!" he shouts, pointing at me.

I roll over and sit up. My knees have grass stains on them, my belly and face are scratched, and my hands are covered in what appears to be Muffin's pee.

I wipe them on the grass and unwrap my purse from my neck, fishing around for my wet wipes and antibacterial gel. You mystery shop enough men's bathrooms, you carry those two items everywhere. Who knew I'd be using them to wipe a date's animal pee off my hands?

"What's your name?" Jordan asks Marie.

"Marie Jacoby." She's laughing, a sound of relief and unfettered joy.

"Marie, you are my hero!"

A new round of applause erupts.

Now, wait a minute. It slowly dawns on me that they're clapping for Marie. Not me. I'm the one who threw the rock. Who caught the dog. I look at Jordan, who snuggles Muffin and tightens his grip as he gives me a nasty glare.

"You leave my Muffin alone!"

Wha?

"Excuse me?" I choke out.

"First you threw a rock at her and almost killed her. Then you nearly missed catching her. Mama was holding her in the light the entire time, and sent Marie the angel to me."

I look around. Three or four people are videotaping the entire thing on their phones. A cop on a bicycle appears and stops.

I can barely breathe, and my cheekbone is wet. I can't touch it, though, because *eww*. Dog pee.

I stand and look around. Bathroom. As I walk down the slight slope to it, I hear Marie say in an excited voice:

"Repay me? Oh, Jordan. My dear, sweet boy. You never have to repay me for doing a good deed and helping your mother's precious Muffin. But...if you insist...are you free in July for a wedding at Farmington Country Club?"

CHAPTER ELEVEN

How was your date? the text reads. It's a number I don't know.

Hold on.

Yes I do.

It's AJM.

Uneventful, I type back, lying.

YouTube says otherwise, he replies.

Oh, no.

I tap into my phone's browser and search "hawk dog Boston" on YouTube.

There I am. Nine different video versions.

That was, um... is all I can type back. Words fail me.

You divebomb like that on all your dates? he texts.

Only when there's something interesting to lunge at, I reply. I hit Send before I lose my nerve.

That can be arranged.

I stare at the words and blink. What is he doing?

I let three minutes go by. He made me wait nearly two years. I can make the man wait a hundred and eighty seconds.

He cracks. Hah.

Nothing new to add to your personal database? No entries?

I snort.

Not even a new row, I write back.

Why am I assuring him? Why is he texting me? What game is he playing? The first two times he kissed me I never heard from him again. For nearly two years I had to play a stupid game of Let's Pretend, in which I went to the occasional client meeting where he was present and avoided eye contact.

Now we're maid of honor and best man in Shannon and Declan's wedding and I know his big secret and...what? What's the significance here?

How about we extend one?

I frown. *One what?*

A row.

Which one?

Mine. Dinner tonight. I'll pick you up.

Andrew just changed the game.

I am at home after texting Greg about the incident, which was technically a work related event. You can scare Greg with two simple sentences:

I was hurt at work.

and

I am experiencing my monthly.

Either one is quite effective.

He gave me permission to come home and clean myself up, then just manage mystery shopper updates from home. In addition to the new DoggieDate account, I am still handling all my ongoing mystery shop programs, which currently include Assisted Living evaluations, a chain of coffee houses and their new gluten-free pastries, legal insurance evaluations, hairdresser shops, and my personal favorite: tobacco compliance shops for liquor stores.

Try finding a bunch of twentysomethings who look like fifteen year olds but act like mature adults. Good luck with that.

I stare at Andrew's last text. Our living room has an enormous mirror over the fireplace, and as a kid I used it to study myself. As I've aged, I look less often. Right now, though, I stand in front of it and really take a look at myself. Mom's in her office, on a conference call for her job. I can hear intermittent typing as she takes notes.

Maybe I should be taking notes of a different kind.

My cheekbone is raw red, the nasty abrasion filling in with a few spots that will scab, but it mostly looks like a rug burn. My brown hair is wet and I'm wearing no makeup. I slipped into my comfortable jammies after my shower. Victoria's Secret's got nothing on flannel ducks.

It's like he's in the room with me, staring back from the mirror. Not in some creepy supernatural way, but like I'm looking at myself through the eyes of Andrew McCormick, as imagined by me.

Which doesn't make sense, but falling for someone never does.

I sigh. My wide eyes look back at me with an openness, a pleading, a question. Are you going to leap? Are you prepared to go splat, like Muffin would have if you hadn't been there to catch her? Is Andrew the hawk and I'm the prey?

What will he do with me when he catches me?

Devour me or drop me back to earth?

Only one way to find out.

I pick up my phone and text him back.

* * *

I'm applying makeup for my nine o'clock date with Andrew when my phone rings. I've gotten accustomed to texting after being mercilessly teased by Shannon about my actual telephone calling habits, and the sound of my ringtone is jarring.

It's Queen's "You're My Best Friend," so it must be —

"You're a YouTube sensation," Shannon declares as I put her on speakerphone.

"I'm a what?"

"Hashtags and all!" she crows. "Finally, I'm not the only one!"

"What are you talking about?" I ask, but I feel my voice fade as it dawns on me. All those people recording on their phones. "Oh, no. This is about Muffin, isn't it?"

"Your hashtag is #doghater."

"I have a hashtag? What?"

"Welcome to the club. At least yours doesn't involve the word poop."

"Dog what? Did you say #doghater? How can I be a dog hater? I saved the dog!"

"That's not what I saw. Mom saved the dog. You just threw rocks at it."

"WHAT?" I'm applying foundation so thick it could be memory foam to cover up the abrasion on my cheek from dive-bombing to catch Muffin. "I injured myself rescuing that dog!"

"The videos show otherwise. They show you throwing rocks at the hawk, the creepy little man screaming for someone to help, my mom grabbing the little kid's helicopter remote control, and then Mom saves the day. Videos end with the man cradling the dog."

"I've been cut out of my own rescue video! That's so unfair."

"Why were you even out there? Who was that guy? Mom says you were on a date with him. He's *sooo* not your type. I'm guessing this is part of that dog dating site?"

"Who, him?" I say breezily. "Oh, just some guy I met online."

"You wouldn't date a guy like that with a ten foot pole and a can of troll spray in your hand, Amanda."

"Hey! That's not nice. Jordan's a sweet man."

"I heard. Turns out he's the florist Mom's been whining about for the past six months. I think Mom only saved that dog so she could get him for my wedding."

I finish with the foundation and look at myself.

Tears fill my eyes.

"Hashtag doghater? #Doghater? Who started that?"

"Who do you think?"

"Jessica Coffin?"

"Your Twitter best friend," Shannon says with a grunt.

"She's passé. Like Ann Coulter. So self-absorbed she still thinks she's important."

"She still has lots of followers. People like snark. And poop, apparently."

"But you're not bitter."

She snorts and sounds just enough like Muffin to scare me.

"Can you come over? I need help," I beg.

"Cheetos and marshmallows kind of help?"

"Getting ready for a date kind of help."

"New guy? What's his name? Shrek?"

"Andrew."

"*Andrew* Andrew?"

"Yep."

"He asked you out on a date?" Shannon's obvious incredulity makes me laugh and cry at the same time.

"Yes."

"A real date?"

"He asked me out for dinner."

"Not just business?"

"No."

"And not to talk about my wedding?"

Oh.

Hmm.

Hadn't thought about that.

Spritzy comes into the room and licks my ankle. It stings. I look down. Another abrasion. Great. I bend down and give him loads of attention and even a kiss on the top of his head. Would a dog hater do that?

"I'll be there in ten minutes."

"How can you get here in ten minutes?"

"I was already on my way."

"Why?"

"Because Declan told me Andrew told him he'd asked you out."

"You pretended you didn't know?" I squeak. "Did he include a note with a checkbox that says Do you Like Me: Yes or No?"

She laughs. I laugh. I sniffle. I feel like Jordan suddenly.

"I'm almost there and I do have Cheetos and marshmallows."

"Thank you."

"Thank Declan."

"Why?"

"He made me bring them. Said they're disgusting and doesn't want them cluttering the kitchen."

"Tell him he doesn't know what he's missing out on."

CHAPTER TWELVE

When Shannon arrives, I'm surprised to see her actually driving. At the wheel of a Tesla.

She emerges with a smile, carrying a plastic grocery bag.

I hug her a little tighter than usual.

"Nice wheels."

"Not mine. Declan's new toy."

"They'll be half yours, soon."

She punches me and rolls her eyes as we walk into the house.

"Shannon!" Mom emerges from her home office, a heating pad wrapped around her neck and shoulders. As she hugs Shannon, it starts to slide to the ground. I bend and grab it, my movement effortless and automatic. Mom once watched me do that and explained how jealous she was, knowing I was able to make my limbs move, my joints pivot and bend at will to accomplish a needed task, and to do so without pain.

I've never forgotten that moment.

"What are you doing here?" Mom asks, smiling at my friend. "And please excuse the mess!"

I look around the living room. There is a magazine on the coffee table. Otherwise, the house is spotless. Perfectly, utterly, obsessively spotless. Mom moves like a cleaning ninja to the coffee table and casually slips the magazine into the holder next to the couch.

As she lifts up from her slight crouch, her eyelids flutter, half-closed, her breathing hitched.

Pain.

What seems so easy for some people is an entire universe of complexity for others.

"Hi, Pam. I'm here to deliver Cheetos and marshmallows, and to help rescue Amanda from herself."

"In other words, the usual."

The two laugh. Mom's in good spirits today.

"Which movie are you watching?" Mom asks, then turns to look at me. She pulls back in surprise. "Look at you! You're more beautiful than usual, aside from that nasty cut on your face." She picks up Spritzy and gives him a kiss. "The cut was worth it. You were quite the hero today!" She gives me a big smile, then asks, "Are you two going out?"

I hold my breath. I'm not sure what to say.

Shannon's face splits with a huge grin. "Amanda has a date."

"A *date* date?" Mom asks, stretching her neck. Her face goes tight with tension. It's her muscles, and not me, that she finds troubling.

"I think so."

"You think so?" Her voice goes high and reedy. She's on edge again.

"It's with someone I work with, Mom."

"Not Josh? He's gay, right? Or is he bisexual? Maybe that new sex thing you kids do." Mom turns a furious shade of red. She can't ask for toilet paper, and she just said the word *sex*.

Shannon and I exchange a look. "New sex thing?"

"Identity. I meant to say identity. I was just on a conference call working on insurance rates for people with nonconforming gender identity," she says, her voice shifting from nervousness to authority as she talks about work. "And the consultants were explaining that gender and sexuality isn't black and white like it used to be. It's all shades of grey."

"Fifty of them?" Shannon jokes.

Mom's face goes red again and she won't meet our eyes. "Not quite like that...that book."

"Josh is gay, mom. Hard gay. Confirmed gay. Unyieldingly gay, so no, I'm not going on a date with him."

"Not even a fake date?" Shannon jokes.

"Only if he fake pays."

Mom's brow creases, and not in pain. "Then who? Greg?" She bursts out laughing.

"Actually, it's Andrew McCormick."

"The closet kisser?"

"Yes."

"He asked you out?"

"Yes. For dinner."

"In a closet?" Shannon cracks up.

"At a restaurant."

"And you...accepted?"

"Why wouldn't I?"

"Because he's treated you so shabbily! He kisses you and doesn't call."

She's got me there.

Her eyes narrow. "You've kissed again."

"Yes."

"And this time he asked you out?"

"Yes."

"Why the change of heart?" Her question is directed at Shannon. "You're engaged to his brother. Do you know something we don't?"

I bristle at the word *we*.

"Can we go back to talking about that kinky sex thing you were describing earlier, Pam? I'm still stuck on that," Shannon says.

"Not kinky!" Mom whispers the word. "Gender fluid. No labels. We were trying to determine life insurance rates and roll in gender and sexuality self-identification patterns for determining premium rates and it's quite complicated."

Mom is an actuary for high-risk insurance populations and situations. Take a natural worrywart with a highly analytical mind and find a work-at-home job she can do while suffering from fibromyalgia.

Upshot: it pays well and uses a unique skill set Mom possesses.

Downside: she has some really irrational fears now based on statistics.

"What does gender fluidity have to do with me?"

"You *were* married to Shannon, after all, honey, for those mortgage evaluations."

That joke doesn't get old for everyone but me and Shannon.

I snake my arm around Shannon's waist. "And she's the best wife ever," I say with a laugh as I tip her back and give her a fake kiss, one hand pressed over her mouth, my lips kissing the back of my own hand.

At that exact moment, the silhouette of a man appears at the open screen door.

"Hello?"

It's Andrew.

I nearly drop Shannon, who begins laughing hysterically.

"Am I interrupting something?"

"Just kissing Shannon."

"And not in a closet," Mom mutters. I don't know whether Andrew hears her, as Shannon is opening the screen door and giving him a hug right now. An insane cloud of jealousy strikes me, unfolding like Wolverine's titanium claws sliding out, hidden but deadly.

Where did that come from?

"Hello, Amanda," Andrew says, eyes combing over me. Fortunately, I'm ready. Not having any idea where he's taking me, I went for a smart casual, which means a huge upgrade from my normal fashion sense of shabby chic. I'm wearing an all-black suit made from a shiny silk-linen blend that I got from an upscale boutique mystery shop last year. No stockings. Mary Jane patent leather heels. Bright red dot earrings and red beaded necklace. Dark brown hair and red lips.

And a red shiner.

Concern reflects from those warm, brown eyes the second he sees my cheek. "What happened? Who did that to you?" He's so fierce, his body tensing, that I almost wish I could name someone for him to go avenge me.

Alas...

"A teacup chihuahua named Muffin."

He flinches, stepping closer, examining my eye. "I'd say you lost. The dog has quite a right hook." As his fingertips gently brush against my jaw line as he leans in for a closer look. He smells like limes and cardamom, a fresh, slightly mysterious scent.

"You haven't seen him. I gave him a run for his money."

He smiles, but his eyes remain filled with worry. His hand drops from my face and I want it back.

"Are you sure you're fine for dinner? You could have texted me and postponed." He bends down for a casual hug, his lips brushing against the skin below my cheek, the kiss a formality that makes me quiver.

Like Muffin.

With a politeness blended with unbridled charm, Andrew gives Mom his full attention. "And you must be Amanda's mother. I'm so glad to meet you. Andrew

McCormick." He extends his hand, and I hold my breath. Most people think a strong handshake is a sign of good character, but for someone with fibromyalgia it's a form of torture.

On the other hand, the limp fish handshake that some men extend to women isn't exactly an improvement.

By watching Mom's face, I can see he gets the balance just right. Her eyes comb over him, reading him carefully. Whatever she sees as they make a few sentences of small talk seems to please her while my brain turns into a Vitamix on High that drowns out their words.

He smells so good. An undercurrent of soap and leather fills my senses as he retreats. Mom and Shannon are watching us like television producers on *The Bachelor*. Every second feels both awkward and settled as I walk across the room to get my purse. I have no idea where we're going, no sense of his expectations, I'm trying to rid myself of all of mine, and by the time I reach the front door he's there, holding the screen door open for me, turning back to my mother.

"Nice to meet you, Pam," he says with a radiant smile that makes her flutter her eyelashes and wave goodbye.

And then we're stepping out into the twilight night, leaving behind a curious mother, a bemused bestie, and a plastic grocery bag full of what used to be my favorite thing to do on date night.

CHAPTER THIRTEEN

The limo takes up half my driveway and between it and the Tesla, my Turdmobile looks even more ridiculous. I see it's Lance who is driving tonight, and he's pulled up next to my pile of steel excrement. I know from Shannon that Lance and Gerald are the two drivers who transport Declan and Andrew the most, and that they've been with Anterdec for a long time, largely because of their ability to remain stoic in damn near any situation.

Which is why Lance's expression of unmitigated disgust is all the more alarming as he pokes his head out the limo's driver's window and openly examines my, um—

I realize #poopwatch could have another meaning.

"Nice car," I say to Andrew as he guides me to the back door, his hand hovering over my shoulder. Curiously, he doesn't touch me, keeping his palm an inch or so above my back. How do I know? I can sense it, the heat of attraction like the pull of gravity.

"Wish I could say the same."

Lance snorts. Andrew startles, giving him a curious look. Lance's face goes shockingly blank in a way that makes it clear he's fighting hard to look impassive.

"I make an extra $200 a month to drive that all over Boston," I say as I get in the limo. "Plus expenses."

"I would pay $200 a month *not* to have to drive it," Andrew says.

My laughter fills the night and he joins in, the sound so different from our tight conversations, our tense volleys and verbal jabs that walk a tightrope.

"We can't all be CEOs," I answer as I step into the limo. The cool leather seats feel like I'm sliding into a spa chair.

"No, we can't. Declan just learned that the hard way today," he says as he shuts my door. Within seconds, he's opened his and is climbing in. The limo is so wide we have more than enough room to share the back without touching.

Which is a shame.

"Funny. Shannon didn't say a word about that. You told him?"

"Dad and I did. I'm not sure whether she knows yet. Thank you for not telling him—or her. It was important that he hear it from me and Dad. No one likes to hear bad news secondhand. I worked very hard to keep this information under a tight level of secrecy."

"Of course. How did he take it?"

"Relatively well. I don't have a shiner like yours."

"Muffin didn't like being told I was going to be CEO, either."

Andrew doesn't laugh, but he turns to me and crosses his legs, one ankle to knee, his body open to me. I turn and face him as well, matching his body language, though I cross my legs at the ankles, because if I imitated him perfectly this wouldn't be a date. It would be a peep show.

"Why are you here?" he asks softly.

The limo pulls away and into the night. My mind floats off, as if it were clinging to the back of the vehicle by its fingernails, carried aloft by speed like a stowaway on an airplane.

"What?" There goes my brain's Vitamix again.

"Why did you agree to dinner?"

"Why did you ask?"

"Because it was about time."

"Yes."

"And because I've been stupid."

"Oh, definitely yes."

"And because you're loyal."

Say *what*?

"You mean, like a dog?"

"No. Like a good friend."

"Why did you kiss me the first time? That day when I barged into your office?"

Hey, if we're being blunt, I might as well go for the brass ring.

He nods, eyes looking at everything and nothing, finally settling on my face. "Because you were so passionate about protecting Shannon. You were adorable and irate and you had this energy I wanted to taste."

I'm holding my breath. I thought we would spend this first date doing the awkward getting-to-know you dance. Andrew's gone right to the point. Laser focus.

Just like a CEO.

"Taste?"

"Yes. I know what I want. I don't equivocate. I decide and act. I compartmentalize. I issue orders and execute strategy. You came in that day and started ordering me around and it was cute and exciting and inspiring. Oddly sensual. And when you kissed me—"

"You kissed *me*!"

"And when *we* kissed," he says, eyebrows raised, as if settling this point once and for all, "I got something far more forbidden than I realized I was getting when I went for that simple taste of you."

Forbidden?

SHOPPING FOR A CEO

"What's that?"

He studies me, as if sizing me up, trying to determine whether he should tell me what's next. Or not. Finally, his face changes through a series of three or four emotions, most of them involving some variation of deliberation.

And then:

"You didn't fit in a box."

"I fit in a closet."

He doesn't laugh.

"You intrigued me."

"Not enough to call me after that kiss, though."

He shakes his head. My heart plummets.

"No, Amanda. The opposite. You intrigued me too much."

I get the sense that the word 'intrigued' means something else.

"You mean I scared you."

His eyes flash with emotion I can't read.

"Yes."

Men like Andrew McCormick don't do this. They don't lay their emotions out on the table like this. Why is he doing this?

"Then why did you kiss me again? And again. And *again* again—"

"I don't know."

"C'mon." The driver takes us onto the Mass Pike, lights flying by like spaceships. Little orbs shooting past us, filled with people oblivious to the quantum shift taking place inside this tiny space. "You always know. You're a CEO. You compartmentalize. You execute. You decide. You act. You can't tell me that the great wunderkind Andrew Mc—"

He's on me before I can take a breath to continue speaking, his body so big and bold, so impulsive and

106

unrelenting. The limo becomes its own dimension, his hands seeking to hold all of me as we tumble into some new plane of awareness that doesn't factor into any life we've known until this moment. His mouth finds mine, hands under my suit jacket, palm cupping the lines of my breasts, my waist, my hips, and he's tasting me again, this time with an urgent need that comes from an honesty I don't think he's felt permission to express in a very long time.

If ever.

I break the kiss. His breath is hot against my lips, my chest pushing up as I inhale, trying to synthesize the tactile feel of him in my personal space as the rate of intimacy between us increases at the speed of light.

"What are we doing?" I ask, buying a moment of clarity as I inhale, shaky and shocked. I have never wanted anyone more than I want him right now. This sensation is wholly foreign and delightfully enchanting.

"Whatever it is, let's do more of it."

The reconnection of his mouth against mine, of the sensual weight of him on me in this small space as my legs pull up, closing all gaps between us, feels simultaneously pure and naughty, innocent and illicit, virginal and promiscuous. Once the boundary between our bodies is breached, we navigate every inch with negotiations brokered in sighs and bites, in tongue strokes and caresses, with touch and without words.

My skin rises an inch above my body with a pounding flush that can only be satisfied by no remedy other than his hands, his mouth, his skin, his attentiveness.

More of his skin.

The limo slows, the driver painstaking in his glide to a spot on a city street that is both familiar and daunting.

And then the limo halts entirely.

Andrew sighs, the sound like a churning ocean before a sea storm. His mouth kisses my ear and he murmurs. "We're here. Dinner."

Oh. Right. Dinner.

Date. Public. Food. Single words are all I can muster in my mind. Words like hair. Lipstick. Legs. Skirt.

Throb.

Pulse.

Desire.

Ache.

Andrew.

If he asked me, right now, to skip dinner, I would. One offer. One question is all it would take. I'm past the point of worrying about what he thinks of me. Long gone are the days of sobbing over ice cream and Thai food at Shannon and Amy's apartment back in the suburbs. I'm here to get something out of this *whateveryoucallit* between us, and it's dawning on me that he is, too.

And it's not just kisses in closets.

This is not "just" anything.

CHAPTER FOURTEEN

Andrew sits up and adjusts all sorts of parts of himself, from his shirt tails to his jacket to other pieces that need to be put in place in order to make a public appearance. His hand stays on my knee, like a claiming.

And those eyes watch me.

"Hungry?" he asks, dimples firmly in place as he smiles.

I bite my lips and exhale, a little sound of frustration making the back of my throat vibrate.

"You could say that."

We're in front of a series of brick buildings that look like converted lofts and businesses. As Andrew opens his door, a blast of warm night air fills the limo. April in Boston is a crapshoot. You never know if you'll get a balmy breeze or need your down winter coat.

Salty air, carrying the ocean on it, fills the small space. Aha. I know where we are.

The Seaport district. Congress Street.

I look outside and my eyes adjust. We're just at the curb, not even in a parking spot or an underground garage. The driver simply pulled over and we're blocking traffic.

My door opens. I reach up to touch my hair, then my lips. I must look frightfully disheveled, bright red lipstick smeared across my lips, hair thoroughly mussed.

The second I climb out of this limo it'll be obvious what Andrew and I have been doing. The thought makes me smile.

Andrew reaches one strong hand for me and I take it, lifting up into the dark night, his palm splayed at the small of my back without interruption. He seems incapable of not touching me now.

"Is my lipstick smeared?" I whisper, the intimacy of such a simple question feeling both natural and out of place. I'm living in two different realities right now, second by second, as time flows and I am with him.

There is this dream world, where Andrew McCormick is kissing me. And then there's reality, where I am waiting sorrowfully to wake up.

"Does it matter?"

The limo takes off like a silent jet, disappearing down Congress Street as Andrew guides me up a set of stairs. There is no sign. No obvious door. We might as well be headed into a nondescript, restored historical building that houses tech start-ups rather than a restaurant.

"Where are we?" I ask as I fumble around in my purse, looking for a hand mirror or a compact.

"You'll see."

As he holds open a door, I see a small brass plaque, so subtle I would never have noticed it if I weren't on guard, nerves firing at random intervals as every cell in my body is alert and ripe.

The plaque has the name of the most exclusive new restaurant in town on it, complete with the chef's name.

"We're eating *here*?"

"You've been here before?"

I shake my head, my fingers closing on my compact. I've heard about it. This is the apocryphal restaurant that the celebrity chef created for friends, family, and few of her closest Boston billionaires.

When I look in the mirror, my lipstick's half gone. Where did it go?

Andrew looks down at me and I find my answer.

"You look good in red," I say, pulling on his arm. He gives me a puzzled look and I reach up, using my thumb to wipe some of the lipstick off his mouth and show him.

He laughs, then reaches into his suit jacket for a handkerchief, removing the evidence of our limo encounter. At least, the visible evidence.

I look at my reflection and he gently takes his handkerchief and presses it into my hand. Our eyes lock.

"I must be a mess," I say, suddenly self-conscious, dabbing at my smeared makeup.

"You're gorgeous," he murmurs, bending down, so close his words send shivers down my spine. "And you're even more beautiful when you're a mess, because I know *I* made you that way."

No man has ever talked to me like this. I've never even imagined conversations like this, the kind that cut to the chase. He's so direct, so virile and masculine, filed with the warrior's gaze and the lover's tenderness as he stands there beside me, just...there.

He's finally *here*. It only took him two years.

And I don't know what to do with him now that he's decided to show up.

Andrew takes me to a tiny elevator. It's quite literally just a door, and if I didn't see him wave a small card, like a hotel key, in front of a little circle, I'd think the elevator appeared via magic.

"What's this?" I ask.

"A secret door." We enter it and the elevator lifts us up at a snail's pace.

"How do I know you're not really some kinky billionaire who's taking me to an illicit sex club and I'm about to disappear into an underground world of sexual torture?" I tease.

"I typically save that for the third date," he answers.

The elevator halts and opens onto a rooftop garden. As we step out, I murmur, "Then I have something to look forward to."

The smile he gives me makes my toes curl. A maître d' appears in a suit tailored so well he looks like he just flew in from Milan.

"Mr. McCormick. Ms. Warrick. Welcome."

How does he know my name? Probably the same magic that allows limo drivers to effortlessly glide through the streets of Boston, that gives Andrew cards he can wave in front of sensors to open doors no one else can see, that gives him access not only to luxury, but to the convenience of shaping the entire structure of his life around getting from Point A to Point B with as little friction as possible.

That is the power of money. It's not about buying things. It's about gaining access to shortcuts the 99% can't even fathom. And that buys you an advantage. The McCormick men don't just live in a different economic class—they quite literally function in a completely different world.

One that Andrew has just invited me to visit.

As we're walked to a small table, surrounded by large candles in shimmering glass olive jars the size of toddlers, I realize we are one of only four tables in the entire restaurant. Each has its own pergola, wine grape vines snaking through the wooden slats above us, entwined with strings of pale white lights that give the rooftop an ethereal sense of being a world apart.

Which is pitch perfect for how every second with Andrew feels.

His hand takes mine, fingers slipping into the grooves between my own, palms pressed together like hearts trying to find a common rhythm. Soon we're seated, and as I settle in to my spot I look up, then gasp.

The view of the ocean stretches on into the night, inky and rolling, offering endless possibilities and terrifying enormity.

"It's beautiful," I say, completely smitten with the view.

He looks over his shoulder, as if the panoramic scene behind him were nothing. "Oh. Yeah."

And for him, it probably *is* nothing. Shannon's talked about the everyday luxuries Declan takes for granted, from having groceries delivered and stocked to never touching a cleaning supply or a broom. How he has tailors who come to his office. Dry cleaning picked up dirty and brought back and hung in his closet, neat as a pin.

How the limo driver just delivers him where he needs to go and appears when called. His schedule is managed by people who work for him and he never makes a single logistical arrangement. The McCormick men live a life crafted not so much by whim, she says, but by choice. Other people make their lives run like a well-oiled machine so that they are never, ever inconvenienced by the small tasks in life that trip the rest of us up.

Their lives are fixed by people like *me*.

Wine appears with a first course of grilled octopus and chive aioli that almost tastes as good as Andrew's kisses.

Almost.

We're quiet. He holds one of my hands. We don't really talk for the first few minutes. We don't need to. Either this is super awkward and I'm too clueless to realize it, or we're seamlessly fitting together in a way that is far too easy.

The spectrum is maddeningly long here, and the pendulum has more than enough room to swing in whatever direction fate chooses.

I finish my first glass of wine. Andrew stands and removes his jacket, sliding his arms out of the sleeves and rotating, his form on display. Minutes ago, that body was atop mine, pinning me in place against leather and lust. I enjoy the display, watching the lean stretch of his forearms, the subtle bulge of biceps as they twist and he slips the jacket over the back of his chair, the curve of his legs as he resumes his seat, moving the chair closer to the table, then reaching once more for my hand.

"Nice view," I say.

"You already said that," he replies as he glances over his shoulder.

"I wasn't talking about the ocean."

A gleam in his eyes makes me glad for the boldness of a glass of wine and my own relief at finally having his undivided attention. Maybe I'm being too forward. Perhaps this is far less than I think it is, and I'm making it into more.

I don't care.

Guys like Andrew McCormick don't exist in my world. Not as dating partners. Men like Ron and Jordan are what's out there in my life partner pool, and not only is there no comparison—zero—the fact is that none of that matters.

I spent the last two years waiting for Andrew to make a move I'd given up on ever experiencing. And now here he is, holding my hand and pouring me wine on a private rooftop garden at one of the most exclusive, elite restaurants in the country and I'll be damned if I let this slip out of my hands.

"What are we doing?" he asks, echoing my earlier question.

"You tell me." *Please, tell me, Andrew.*

"We're getting to know each other."

"We've known each other for nearly two years." *Two long years.*

"I know quite a bit about you," he says with an alluring grin.

"Oh yeah? Like what?"

"Shannon spilled all your secrets."

I snort inelegantly. Is there an elegant way to snort, though?

"Right. Not falling for that, bud. Shannon would never, ever spill my secrets. Besides, I don't have any."

"Everyone has secrets."

"Not me. I'm an open book."

He gives me a skeptical look and asks, "What's your greatest fear?"

That this isn't real.

I can't tell him that, so instead I tell him my *second* greatest fear.

"Being naked in public."

His grin widens. "Has this been an issue for you in the past?"

"Only in my nightmares."

"Or *my* dreams."

Did the temperature just rise by ten degrees out here?

A small beet salad with goat cheese and fennel is served, interrupting us and giving me a chance to catch my breath.

"But seriously," I say between bites.

"I was being serious."

"You have dreams about my being naked in public?"

"All the time. Except for the public part."

"You could have said something sooner."

"I'm saying it now."

What else can I do but laugh and pivot?

"What's *your* greatest fear?"

His face goes somber so quickly that I realize my very awful misstep immediately.

"I'm sorry," I rasp. "I know what it is, and I shouldn't have asked that."

He flinches. "You know my greatest fear? How could you know?"

"It's wasps, right?"

Of course it is. Between Shannon's allergy and the story about how Andrew, Declan and Terry's mom died, and Declan's impossible choice, how could I not know? Andrew is deathly allergic to wasp stings. Shannon is deathly allergic to bee stings. It's a weird confluence of events that found Shannon and Declan together, and if I weren't her best friend I would think it was nuts.

But love doesn't care about crazy. It's random that way.

Andrew's head is dipped down, just enough that the strings of lights above us make shadows that cover his face. His hand holding the salad fork is suspended above his plate, arm bent at the elbow, a light breeze blowing the cloth of his shirt to the side. He's blinking furiously and breathing with great care, as if gentling himself.

And then he says, "Yes. That's right."

Except it feels like he's lying by omission.

A million questions pour into my head as I struggle to correct my misstep. I feel so foolish. So sickeningly stupid. Here I go again, ruining what has, so far, been the best night of my life.

I need to fix this.

I need to fix this *now*.

"What's your favorite food?" The words come out of me just as the server clears the plates and a woman in a chef's uniform appears from the shadows. She's tall and lean, elegant in a way that only a European woman can be, with a self-possession that makes me feel like I'm twelve.

"Señor McCormick, so good to see you," she says with a light Spanish accent. Her cheekbones are high and her face long, eyes deeply sunken with a well-painted face and the bone structure of a woman who knows herself all too well. Her hair is streaked with lines of grey that American women in their fifties would dye but she sports proudly.

Andrew stands and kisses her on both cheeks, his movements elegant and possessed. He's so young. Just twenty-nine, and yet here he is, kissing a woman I've seen on television for more than ten years and who chats with him—in Spanish—as if they're old friends.

He switches to English. "May I introduce Amanda Warrick? Amanda, meet—"

"I know who you are," I gush. I've never met a celebrity chef before. Consuela Arroyo is surprisingly pleasant, her face breaking into a warm grin as she reaches for me. Her cool, dry hands reach up to cup my cheeks and plant one kiss on each side. I flail, not quite knowing how to greet her back, and roll my jaw bone against hers, wincing as my shiner scrapes against her cheekbone. This double-cheek-kiss thing makes me feel like an awkward teen at my first school dance.

"Amanda, it is so nice to meet you. I hope you enjoy cilantro," she says in a voice that carries some kind of subtext with Andrew.

I look at him. Andrew makes a face and his lip curls up in disgust.

"I love cilantro!" I chirp.

She gives him a look. "See? It is only *you*."

"Are you one of those people who think it tastes like soap?" I ask him.

"No. I just don't like it."

"How can you not like cilantro?" Consuela and I ask in unison. Her voice contains sheer horror, mine pure curiosity.

He responds by pouring us each a generous glass of wine until the bottle is empty. A server appears as if summoned and replaces it immediately with another.

Good thing neither of us is driving.

"Fine. No cilantro. You will have to suffer through a most exquisite polenta dish without the best herb," Consuela sniffs, her disapproval evident. Those eyes flash with a mock anger that just might hold more anger than teasing.

"I'll survive," Andrew says dryly with a wink.

"You have a savage palate," she retorts, storming off with a wink to me, her hand cradling her glass of wine. Whew. Mockery wins.

"I take it you two are friends," I say as I drink half my wine. It's so smooth. And I'm now more nervous from having met *the* Consuela Arroyo than I am from

118

the fact that this date is going in directions I never fathomed.

"Connie is an old, old friend of Dad's."

"Ah."

"Not *that* kind of friend."

"I never thought that. She's not his type."

"What does that mean?"

"Doesn't James stick to dating women who can't legally purchase alcohol on their own?"

A fine spray of expensive white wine goes flying out of his mouth as he chokes on my words. It's a beautiful sight, really. A kind of performance art I wish I could capture on film.

"Who told you that?"

"Who do you think?"

"Shannon really thinks that about my dad?"

"Well, between Becky and Stacey and Kelly and—"

He holds up one palm, flat. "Got it. Point taken. Don't need to hear my dad's To Do list."

"More like his Done list."

He frowns. "Now that you mention it, when my prom date ditched me to go hang out with my dad, I did think it was a little weird."

I gasp. "That actually happened?"

"No."

I can't find anything to throw at him—other than myself—so I just laugh.

"My dad's not a complete lech, you know."

"I'm sure he's a well-rounded, sophisticated man who's misunderstood."

"Let's not go *too* far. He's a grey fox who likes his women young."

"He dates zygotes."

"He has his reasons."

SHOPPING FOR A CEO

Talking about James McCormick isn't my idea of a fabulous date conversation topic, but there's a reason why we've veered into this territory. "Is everything okay with your father?"

"You mean other than dating women who could star in the Hunger Games movies as tribute?"

"Right."

Andrew closes his eyes, his shoulders rising, then falling, with a deep breath. "Why is it so easy to talk to you?"

I shrug and drink. The wine is loosening me up.

"Because you *are* talking to me?"

"You're not going to let me live that down, are you?"

We both know he's talking about the past. About ignoring me for so long.

"That depends on what happens next."

"What do you want to have happen next, Amanda?" Oh, the way my name spills out of his mouth. It's like being licked up my spine.

Consuela appears at that exact moment and announces, "Polenta with churro in a non-cilantro monstrosity!" and sets down two piping hot cruets on small plates with an overblown flourish that makes us both burst into laughter. His voice is deep and strong, his mirth rumbling and profound. I'm so accustomed to his stoicism that this side of him—which I suspected lingered far beneath the surface—is a joy to experience.

A revelation.

"The salmon is next," Consuela tosses over her shoulder as she disappears into a curtain of greenery.

I roll the stem of my wine glass between my fingers.

"I want more of this," I say with a sigh.

"Polenta?"

"Talking."

"Just talking?"

I smother my smile with a taste of the food. It's divine. So is he.

"What about the wedding?" I ask after finishing my first bite.

He pauses, fork in mid-air. "Isn't that a bit presumptuous? Can we finish our first date before talking about weddings?"

"I meant *Shannon and Declan's* wedding."

He sets down his fork and reaches for his wine, downing the entire glass in a series of gulps that make the thick lines of his neck move like a dancer on stage.

"Of course you did," he declares, pouring more.

I freeze.

There are so many ways I can interpret that. I decide to play dumb.

"Has Marie talked with you about our roles?"

"Best man and maid of honor. We stand at the front of the church and I give a toast and maybe we dance with each other. You throw a bachelorette party and I hire a bunch of hookers for Declan to get in his last chance and—"

I start coughing. "What?"

"Kidding."

"You better be."

"Declan's too head over heels for Shannon. Worst case, we'll go to Vegas for some crazy times and he'll spend half the night blabbering about how great she is."

"Sounds like fun."

"That's true love." He gives me a pointed look. "I guess. I wouldn't know."

"You've never been in love?"

He ponders the question while taking small bites of his food.

"Good question."

"You're stalling."

"No."

"No, you're not stalling, or no, you've never been in love?"

"Never been in love."

"Never? *Ever?*" I can't keep the incredulity from my voice.

"No."

"Wow."

"What about you?"

"Me neither," I admit.

"Then why do you sound so surprised that *I* haven't ever been in love?"

"Because I've never met anyone else who would admit to it, too."

"Then there's a pair of us—don't tell!"

Did he just quote *Emily Dickinson*?

"Are you saying I'm nobody?" I ask with a smirk, my tongue poking out to lick the rim of my wine glass. Let's see if he passes this test.

Please let him pass this test.

"It's quite dreary being somebody." He smiles. "Trust me."

I melt into my chair, and it's not from the wine. My God.

"You are quoting *Dickinson*."

"They shoved it down our throats at Milton Academy."

"I wrote my senior honors thesis on her." I can tell he finds this amusing, and he's sitting across from me with an impish air, but what he doesn't understand is how much I am reeling inside. The unspoken connection between us is now, word by word, being spoken. And it has a language of its own that unfolds like that yearning we all hold, cradled in our hands like a fragile, sleeping bird, in the part of ourselves where we protect our truths.

"Does that make you an expert in being nobody?" he asks.

This is too much.

I stand abruptly, shaken to the core. Every muscle inside me tenses, tightening as if needing to express emotions that cannot come out in any other way. The kinesthetic nature of this is like a keening without mourning, a visceral sense that two different layers of life are colliding and in the resulting chaos nothing makes sense.

"Amanda?"

I wander away from our pergola and over near the edge of the rooftop garden, along the perimeter of the building. The ledge rises to my ribcage, a planter three feet wide surrounding the area. A tiny, hand-written sign says *Chef's Herb Garden*. The scent of lavender and thyme, oregano and basil, fills the air on the ocean's sea salt balm.

The wall of Andrew's body behind me startles me with its warmth, his hands hovering at my shoulders. He's hesitating. All I have to do is lean one inch back. Take one step backwards. He's met me more than half way and now it's my turn, but there is so much inside me whirling like a cyclone that I stand in place, uncertain.

I'm nobody.

Who are you?

"Who are you, Andrew?" I whisper into the night.

He comes to me, hands breaking that final inch of uncertainty.

"I'm somebody who has finally realized he's been a nobody for far too long with you, Amanda," he says, his voice earnest and honest. All banter and jokes are brushed aside like my stray strands of hair that his hand moves, clearing a space on my shoulder for his lips to kiss. He pulls me back against him, arms enveloping me.

We look out into the night.

"That's the same ocean I sat and watched the other night when you were at the marina," I marvel.

"Yes."

"And we're the same people."

"Yes."

"What's changed?"

He turns me around, fingers on my chin, tipping my face up until our eyes meet.

And with one word he answers me before capturing me with a kiss that makes entropy seem like fate.

The word?

"Everything."

CHAPTER FIFTEEN

"Did you sleep with him?" Amy asks as we drink our morning coffee and I relive last night's events.

Well, *most* of them.

We're sitting in her living room, Chuckles ignoring everyone as Marie makes us look at pictures of highlanders in kilt tuxedos.

"I am not going to kiss and tell," I reply.

"I didn't ask if you *kissed* him."

I pretend to zip my lips.

Amy changes topics and tries to convince me that I should move in with her.

"This place is dirt cheap," she urges. "You could see Andrew whenever you want without being texted by your mom. You want independence."

"But I don't want to sleep on the couch like you used to." The apartment only has one bedroom. Shannon let Amy live here rent free but now that she's gone, Amy's paying the entire amount.

"You'd be so much closer to your job. Plus, the landlord says he'll divide the bedroom and turn it into two with a simple wall and a second door."

Tempting.

"Will the guys really go commando?" Marie calls out. "True highlanders don't wear underwear."

"The wedding is in July, Mom," Amy calls back. "In Massachusetts. If you're going to make all those men wear wool kilts and socks, they'll probably gratefully go without underwear just to prevent heat exhaustion."

Marie nods. "Good point."

"But then there's the issue of ball sweat," Amy adds.

Marie frowns and jots down notes on a sticky pad. "Ball sweat? That's a real thing?"

Amy nods. "They make a special product for it."

"There's a product to cure *ball sweat*? Balls have sweat glands? Where do they hide the pores? And how do you know this?"

"Venture capital project at my job. They're coming out with a new product for breast sweat."

"Now *that* I know about first hand," Marie says with a knowing nod. "Breasts do more work than people appreciate. The Girls work up a sweat on a regular basis."

Considering the fact that Marie hasn't been pregnant or breastfed in well over two decades, I don't really want to know what kind of 'work' her chest girls have been up to.

Shannon walks in. Chuckles runs to cuddle with her ankles, then rubs his butthole all over her calf.

"Hi to you too, Chuckles. That's exactly how Declan greets me most nights."

"Ewwwww," Amy says, plugging her ears. "I hear enough about Mom's sex life. Don't need to know more about yours."

"Honey, does Declan have a problem with ball sweat?"

"Huh?" Shannon gives Amy an evil look. "What have you been telling her?"

"Amy says the groom and groomsmen will need testicle powder if I ask them to go commando for the wedding."

"Testicle powder? Is that going to be a wedding favor?"

"Do they make such a thing?" Marie asks, interest piqued.

"Sure," Amy says. "Personalized bottles and everything. Think of the possibilities. *Shannon and Declan, Dry Forever*, with the date stamped on there and a logo of a dove. People will always associate your wedding with smooth sacs."

Shannon throws Chuckles at Amy's head. He lands perfectly in Amy's lap, his butthole sliding down the length of her forearm as he settles into a liquid ball of fur in her lap.

"Don't do that to the flower girl!" Marie barks.

"The *what*? Amy's a bridesmaid, not a flower girl."

"*Chuckles* is the flower girl." Marie says this as if she were saying, *Chicken is the main course*.

Chuckles looks as shocked as Shannon, which is pretty hard to do when you don't have eyebrows, but he pulls it off.

"You're making my cat be my flower girl?"

"The McCormicks don't have any little girls in their family. We only have Jeffrey and Tyler as ring bearers. I saw this adorable idea on Pinterest for how to use family pets as flower girls, and—"

Pinterest is a tool of Satan.

"My cat is going to be my flower girl because of a Pinterest board."

"At least the men will have dry balls," Amy says, um...dryly.

"What about Chuckles?" Marie asks.

"What about him?"

"Will he sweat under his kilt, too?" Marie scribbles on yet another sticky note. "Check to see if they make cat ball sweat powder," she says to herself as she writes.

"Under his *what*? You're making Chuckles wear a kilt tuxedo?" Does Chuckles even have balls? I don't want to look.

I can't help it. I look.

No balls.

"No, silly. Just a kilt. Cat's can't wear tuxedos!" Marie says in a voice filled with scoffing that we would even entertain the thought.

"Cats can't be flower girls, either."

"Of course they can! You're a trendsetter now, Shannon. You're marrying one of the most famous billionaires in the U.S."

"Declan's not a billionaire, Mom."

"Not yet. Soon. Someday James will die and—"

"Mom!"

"What?"

"Don't talk about James dying!"

"Why not? We all die one day."

"But you make it sound so...gauche. Like we're all just waiting around for James to die so Declan can get his money."

Chuckles looks at Marie like he's waiting for her to die so he can get out of being the flower girl at Shannon's wedding. In fact, he looks like he has specific plans to kill Marie in her sleep by smothering her with a—

You guessed it.

Kilt tuxedo.

"Mom, Chuckles doesn't look like he wants to be in the wedding," Amy says out of the blue.

"How do you know what Chuckles wants?" Marie challenges. "Are you the Cat Whisperer?"

"Because I'm the only one who loves him anymore, and because he lives with me. Chuckles is my soul mate. My best friend. He's the only one who *loooooves* me now that Shannon moved out and Amanda won't move in."

Chuckles is frowning at Amy like she's gone off the deep end.

"He's just a cat," Marie says.

"That's right, Mom," Shannon argues. "And cats can't be flower girls."

"We'll talk about it later," Marie says in a voice that really means, *I've made up my mind and will do whatever I want and act like your opinion doesn't matter*.

"Elope," Shannon whispers.

Marie stiffens.

Chuckles smiles.

"Shannon, you and Declan need to have a rehearsal dinner for the bridesmaids and the groomsmen. We all need to be there to begin to talk strategy." Marie's change of topic only serves to confirm the fact that Chuckles the Highlander is a done deal.

"Why would we host it? Isn't that traditionally done by the groom's parents?"

"You know James will just have one of his preschoolers...I mean, assistants, do it for him. A more intimate affair is in order."

Shannon's shoulder's slump with defeat.

"What Mom means is that we need to get everyone together. And by 'everyone,' she means James McCormick. And save a seat for his wallet. It's big enough. In fact, it should be the guest of honor," Amy snarks.

"Huh?" Shannon looks like someone hit her with a rolled-up newspaper.

"Dad doesn't have enough money saved to pay for the kind of wedding Mom's planning, so James will cough up the rest," Amy declares bluntly.

Shannon recoils in resigned horror and turns to me. "Traditionally, it's the bride's family who pays for everything except the rehearsal dinner and the honeymoon. Plus, Daddy's pride is going to take a beating. But James said it's all a business write off under the perfect circumstances, so..." She looks around the apartment. "Do you have an extra spray bottle of water? If Daddy and James get into another fight..."

"That's old-fashioned tradition, honey. When you're marrying into high society like this, it has to be different." Marie sniffs, half-paying attention to the conversation as she rearranges eighty sticky notes. It's like watching someone play Wedding Tetris.

"Right," I say to Shannon. "It's like groom and bride gifts."

Shannon reddens.

"I see." She goes uncharacteristically quiet.

All three of us—make that four, if you include Chuckles—look at her.

"What do you mean, you see?" I ask.

"When you put it that way..."

"*What* way?"

"The bride and groom gifts that they give to each other." She mumbles something I can't quite catch.

"What's that?" Marie asks, cupping an ear.

I'm pretty sure I heard enough, though. Is she kidding? Declan's giving her *that*?

"He's giving you *what* as a wedding present?" I gasp.

"He's paying off all my student loans," Shannon says with a sheepish look, like she's embarrassed to admit it.

"Hmph," Marie grunts. "All Jason gave me was hardcover copy of *The Joy of Sex* and a sweater." She smiles like a Cheshire cat. "Guess which one I got more use out of?"

"What are you giving him?" I ask.

Amy opens her mouth to say something. Shannon cuts her off with a karate chop motion.

"If you say 'anal,' I will turn you into the flower girl, cat tuxedo kilt and all," Shannon says to her.

Amy closes her mouth and bites her lips.

"Speaking of weddings, let's talk about your date with Andrew last night!" Marie chirps.

"What does that have to do with—"

"Did you sleep with him?"

"No."

"Boo." She closes her hand as if she wishes she could take back the high five. "What's wrong with you girls? Enjoy your youth. Spread your wild oats. YOLO!"

Amy and Shannon look at her with twin expressions that say *ugh*. "That's not what you've been saying to us for years!"

Marie pats Amy on the cheek. "Amanda's not my daughter. I can encourage her to be a wanton floozy and it doesn't reflect on me."

"I'm not a wanton floozy!" I protest.

"Of course you're not. You didn't sleep with him on the first date."

"I slept with Declan on the second date," Shannon declares.

"And see where it got you?" Marie's arms spread out over the tiny kitchen table in the apartment, which suddenly looks like a portable version of NORAD. Wherever she goes, folders and sticky notes and brochures and samples follow. How does she do that? It's like Mary Poppins and her magic bag, except instead of pulling out entire lamps Marie extracts caterer plans and photography estimates.

And, oddly enough, cat kilt samples.

"If Shannon slept with Declan on the second date and it got her a wedding, what will I get if I sleep with Andrew on the second date?"

"Hopefully an orgasm," Marie mumbles.

"MOM!" Amy and Shannon shout in unison.

"That was kind of a given in my mind," I say quietly.

"Maybe he'll give you a job," Marie says brightly. "*And* an orgasm."

I glower at her. "I don't need to sleep my way into a job." *And I don't need a man to give me an orgasm*, I want to add, but I've been on too many sex toy shops with Marie to know that this conversation is veering into dangerous territory. Once she starts talking about sex, she'll describe intimate details about her and Jason, and I won't be able to make eye contact with the poor man or look at a dog leash in quite the same way again.

Ever.

Marie studies me, pursing her lips slightly. Her lipstick matches her earrings, a pale peach color that makes her look like a southern belle, coiffed and blessed with a genteel air.

Until she opens her mouth.

"Sleeping your way into a job is nothing to be ashamed of. But sleeping your way *out* of a job is something to be proud of."

"What?" This time, all four of us say the same thing. Even Chuckles has gained the ability to talk, Marie's statement so ridiculous that it instantly catapults his frontal lobe into forming a speech center.

"Shannon's working for Declan right now because he's humoring her," she says with a sigh, as if we're her ignorant little minions and she's extending her wisdom to us. "Once they're married and having babies—"

Shannon pales.

"—she won't be working. She'll become a society wife and manage the children and host lovely weekend dinners with my grandbabies and we'll be all over Boston Magazine and—"

"I'm not quitting my job to become a baby factory!" Shannon argues.

"Not yet," Marie says casually, as if she didn't just spin a tale of wish fulfillment that makes it clear she's already planning Shannon and Declan's kids' birthday parties to look like Royal Family affairs and arranging playdates with Princess Charlotte for 2020.

"Never."

"Everyone says never. I quit my job after we had Carol."

Shannon goes quiet.

"And your father barely made anything. Those were lean years. You'll never have to go through what we went through, honey. I know way too many recipes for Ramen noodles, potatoes and government cheese."

This conversation, like so many with Marie, has taken a U-turn, two corkscrews, a sudden reversal and included a surprise sinkhole, along with nothing but one-way roads.

"I'm, um...right," Shannon whispers, the wind definitely taken out of her outraged sails.

"And that's how it should be. Now, about that rehearsal dinner party. Two weeks before the wedding should do it. We'll invite all the groomsmen and bridesmaids. Parents. Siblings. I think it will be fun. Why don't I just call Grace and get her to arrange everything?" Marie has Grace on speed dial now.

But Grace has Marie's number set to dump directly into voice mail. Marie doesn't know that yet.

"Um, no, Mom. I can make the arrangements."

"You need to learn to let other people do these things for you. It's one of the secrets of the rich."

A chill runs through me. That's exactly what I was thinking about last night with Andrew.

"Plus, I'm sure Grace will do a better job. You aren't exactly polished, dear."

"Huh?"

"When you have your friends over, Thai food and ice cream is fine. But an elegant dinner for twelve people means hiring caterers and taking this to a whole new level."

"Twelve?"

"Me. Daddy. James. Terry. Andrew. Carol. Amanda. You. Declan. Amy."

"That's ten."

"Declan mentioned his delicious Scottish football-playing cousin as a groomsman. He'll be in New York in two weeks for a photo shoot for *Sports Illustrated*'s naked athlete edition."

The drool factor in the room just jumped by three thousand percent.

"That's eleven."

Marie looks at me and says, "And your mother."

"My mother? Mom's not in the wedding."

An uncomfortable silence follows. "Actually, she kind of is, Amanda. I owe her a debt." Marie's uncomfortable. "So I'd like her there."

"A debt?" I'm perplexed. "What did she do?"

"Bagpipes."

"Bagpipes?"

"Your mother went to Carnegie Mellon University and she helped me to round up the twelve final bagpipe players we'll need."

"TWELVE?" Shannon roars. "Are you trying to have my wedding broadcast live to Scotland, without microphones?"

"Twelve out of forty-one," I swear Marie whispers. But that's impossible. Forty-one bagpipes? It'll sound like Godzilla with a vibrator.

"My mom helped with that?" I ask faintly.

"Yes."

Shannon turns away and picks up her phone. Within seconds she's talking to Declan, her face turned down in a kind of dawning confusion, as if she wants to argue with her mother yet it slowly seeps in that maybe Marie has a point. While she speaks with Declan in hushed tones, I watch Marie's hands manipulate all the paperwork she's brought with her, writing check marks on some papers, shaking her head while reading others, and slipping estimates into folders marked Yes, No and Maybe.

Within minutes, Shannon's off the phone, her face filled with shock.

"Declan," she says slowly, "agrees with Mom."

"Did he recently experience head trauma?" Amy asks, her face lined with concern.

Marie gives her a sour look. "I do have good ideas sometimes." She's holding up a sample piece of McCormick tartan fabric against Chuckles' haunches.

Chuckles gives her a look that says, *Not really*.

"He's having Grace arrange everything," Shannon adds as she descends, slowly, into an arm chair, sinking into the upholstery with the air of someone hearing bad news. "He said I just need to give her a few basic ideas and she'll manage the rest."

"Told you." Marie's words are so smug it's like she's channeling Donald Trump. "Let's make a Pinterest board for your rehearsal dinner party!"

See?

Pinterest really is the tool of Satan.

My phone buzzes.

"Is that Andrew?" Marie asks with a leer.

I look.

"Yes."

His text reads, simply: *Tomorrow. Nine p.m. I'll pick you up*.

My reply is one word.

You can guess what it is.

CHAPTER SIXTEEN

The Pinterest board Shannon makes for the big rehearsal dinner party starts to look like every episode of *Kitchen Confidential* shoved in a blender and poured over mashed potatoes. After a while, I give up looking. At one point, someone pins a picture of a can of ball sweat powder in there.

Whoops.

I spend the day alternating between freaking out about tomorrow's date (hint: the word was yes), wondering how Shannon's going to pull off a fancy dinner party (her idea of "elegant" is adding guacamole to her taco order at Chipotle) and thinking about Amy's offer to move in with her.

I mull over all this as I struggle to fall asleep, slumber finally overtaking me, my stupid naked-in-public dream—the one I've had for more than twenty years—making its boring old appearance, yet forcing me awake in darkness, clutching the sheet to my chest, my skin crawling.

I look at the clock.

6:13 a.m.

I slump back on the pillow and will my heart to slow down. Remarkably, it listens.

If only Andrew McCormick were so easy to tame.

By 6:21 a.m. it's hopeless. I pad downstairs in search of caffeinated relief.

"What does your day look like today, honey?" Mom asks. She's up and showered, drinking coffee in front of her tablet, which bodes well. Maybe she's coming out of this pain flare.

"Oh, the usual." I grab my phone and look at my schedule. "I have to go on a date with a man who breeds German shepherds. Then I need to get the oil changed on the Turdmobile, talk with Greg about a new account we have at a hospital, and do a special sex toy shop with Marie."

Her hand twitches at that last comment, sloshing coffee onto the table, which she cleans up before I can even take a single step. Paper towel, wipe, in the trash —*bam!*

Mom's a cleaning ninja. An OCD cleaning ninja.

"What about you?" I ask her.

"Spiders."

"Spiders?"

"My entire day involves assessing spider bite and injury risks for a movie set that involves using more than five thousand live spiders for a scene."

Spiders. I shudder and say, "Did you know that the average person eats eight spiders a year?"

She sighs. "No. That's not true. That's one of those Internet memes someone made up and now everyone accepts it as fact."

"Whew." I push the buttons on the coffee machine and wait for my morning cup.

"However, you do eat ground up cockroaches when you drink most coffees." She picks up her mug and holds it out to me with a gesture of *Cheers*.

My stomach lurches.

"What?" Being the child of an actuary has its downsides. This is the single worst incident, though, by far. You will pry my coffee from my cold, dead, non-twitching hands.

"That is true."

138

"You're making it up!"

She taps her tablet screen a few times and brings up a story from NPR about...cockroaches in ground coffee.

If NPR reports it, it must be true.

I let out a little scream. The scent of my freshly brewed cup wafts across the kitchen like an instrument of torture.

"But we're fine." Mom makes a point of taking a huge gulp from her mug. "As long as you use whole beans and grind them yourself, you aren't eating bugs."

I grab my cup of ambition and take a sip. Ah, what the hell. Life is full of risk.

"You have the best job ever, Mom."

She bursts out laughing. I like the sound. Her face turns ten years younger and she relaxes, her body changing. People have told me my entire life that I look like my dad. Mom is shorter than me and rail thin, with one exception: wide hips that mold into what a friend's father once called an "ass that belongs on Jane Mansfield," whoever that is.

"I think *you* do, Amanda. Massages and free oil changes and a free car and restaurants and hotels." She pauses and squints. "Minus the, um..."

"Dildo shops?"

"Amanda!"

I laugh. She's so easy to embarrass.

"What's your evening like?" she asks. "There's a sing-a-long for *Grease* at that wonderful old film house in Arlington." Mom loves show tunes and for some reason, *Grease* and *The Rocky Horror Picture Show* are her absolute favorites.

I freeze.

"Amanda?"

"I, um, have a date."

"Another doggy date? Or with Andrew? He seemed fine enough."

Do I lie? It would be so easy to lie right now. And *fine*? Andrew is so much more than fine.

"With Andrew."

Her eyebrows go up. "An actual date? Not in a closet? He must like you. Or maybe he's making up for lost time after ignoring you for so long."

Bitterness, meet Mom.

"We've talked that through." Not really, but a defensiveness is rising up in me.

"Good. I hope if I've taught you nothing else, I've imparted the idea that you don't let men walk all over you."

No. You let men walk out *on you.*

I don't say that. It's one of those statements that cracks an emotional planet in half and you can't find enough superglue to put it back together.

Ever.

I cannot think about this right now. I have work to do, mystery shops to manage, dogs to date...er, dog *owners* to meet, and for the next twelve and a half hours I have to try desperately not to think about whether to sleep with Andrew McCormick tonight.

That alone is a job itself. A pretty major one.

The not thinking about it part. Not the actually sleeping with him part. That's not a job. That's a pleasure.

And here I go...thinking about him.

"Gotta run, Mom," I say, stuffing all my emotions into my chest and trapping them there with a big, deep breath. They line up neatly on the shelf inside me, dutifully color-coding themselves and categorizing. Compartmentalizing.

Maybe Andrew and I aren't so different after all.

* * *

"Amanda!" Greg bellows as I walk into the office. He's sitting in the reception area with Josh, who looks like someone made him stick his tongue in an electric socket. "You're pregnant!"

"I'm what?" That's news to me, and I think I'd know long before Greg.

He thumbs toward Josh. "And he's the father."

I laugh. "That's not possible, Greg. Josh is gay."

"Gay men can sleep with women," Greg insists. "My Uncle Angus did for fifty-seven years while he was married to Aunt Joy."

"I'm Gold Star Gay," Josh whispers.

"They give out gold stars for it?" Greg asks, incredulous. "Like, a secret society?"

"Yeah," I say. "It's like the AARP. One day the card just comes in the mail and you wonder how they know you qualify."

Greg frowns. "We don't get gold stars for being straight. I don't understand."

Josh rolls his eyes and rallies, the shade of green in his face replaced by a healthy glow. "Gold star gay men are men who've never slept with a woman."

"Never?" Greg asks. I can tell he's trying to keep his incredulity out of his voice. He accomplishes this by grabbing a donut from the box Carol brought in yesterday and shoving the entire thing in his mouth.

Josh shakes his head.

"Mmmmf evermmmmf?" Greg says. Or tries to say. I'm not sure what he actually says, because I'm dodging the spray of rainbow sprinkles coming out of him.

"Nope. Never." Apparently, Josh can understand the universal language of Donut.

Greg swallows in one giant gulp, like a snake eating a mouse. He sniffs, then looks at me. "Does that make me Gold Star Straight?"

"Huh?" Josh and I ask in unison.

"If I've never slept with a man," Greg says slowly, contemplating the issue while picking crumbs off his tie and licking them from his fingers, "then I'm Gold Star Straight."

"He's got a point," I admit, giving Josh a look that says, *They don't pay us enough for conversations like this*. If any topic can cure me of my obsessive thoughts about sleeping with Andrew McCormick, it's this one.

"That's not how it works," Josh says in a grumpy voice.

"Why not?" Now Greg is indignant. "You get gay marriage now. We should get our own gold stars. I want a gold star."

Josh is speechless. I am struggling to decide whether I would rather go on another date with Mr. Anal Gland Hands or spend one more minute hearing Greg talk about his sex life.

Anal glands for the win.

"You want a gold star for what?" Carol asks, walking in with what looks like a bag full of chocolate foil tractors, scarecrow lollipops, and hard candies shaped like ears of corn. She's wearing denim overalls, a red and white checkered shirt, and her blonde hair is pulled back in a ponytail. If Hee Haw were still on, I'd think she was an extra on the show.

I cock one eyebrow and look at her goodies.

"Farming trade show," she sighs. "You get the wedding trade shows, I get the cranky old farmers who want to talk about bursitis and soybean futures."

"Well," I say magnanimously, stepping behind her and putting one hand on her shoulder, "you can take my place in *this* work conversation."

"Talking about gold stars?" she asks, a bit befuddled. "Is there a special reward system I don't know about?"

"Something like that," Josh mumbles. "Let's stop talking about my sex life."

"Sex life?" Carol snorts, really confused now. She grabs a foil-covered tractor and begins peeling it, taking a bite. The tire snaps off in her mouth. "What do gold stars have to do with sex lives? Now we have sticker charts for sex?"

"That's what I'm wondering!" Greg bellows, reaching for one of the chocolates. "How come Josh gets a gold star for not sleeping with women but I can't get a gold star for not sleeping with men?"

"I'm not sleeping with men or women," Carol says sadly, eating the tractor's engine now. "What do I get for that?"

I reach across my desk and grab a sheaf of papers, sliding them to her. "You get the sex toy shops I took."

She looks at the chocolate in her hand. Glances at the papers. Then the pile of chocolate.

"Why are you giving me those?"

"Because Amanda's pregnant," Greg explains helpfully, his mouth full of a tractor.

"Work pregnant or *pregnant* pregnant?" Carol asks casually. These conversations have become alarmingly normal to me.

"Work pregnant, I assume," I reply. "Because if I'm *pregnant* pregnant, then my vibrator has some explaining to do."

"Or maybe Andrew McCormick?" she adds with a leer.

Josh and Greg give me chocolate-smeared looks. "You're pregnant by Andrew McCormick?" Josh squeals.

"No! We just kissed."

"You're kissing Andrew McCormick?" Greg looks deeply uncomfortable, and it's not his usual acid reflux look.

"We're...something."

"You're somethinging?" We've turned that word into a verb. It's funny when applied to Shannon. To me? Not so much.

"We're dating. I guess?" This is the first time I've had to define whatever Andrew and I are doing.

"Openly?"

"We're not in the closet about it."

"Why would two heterosexuals be in the closet?" Josh asks.

"Ask Andrew."

Greg frowns. "I'm not sure I'm comfortable with this, Amanda. Professionally, I mean."

A chill of shame crawls over my skin, completely unexpected. "What?"

"He's a client."

"Yes, but—"

"He's our biggest client."

"You had no problem when Shannon was dating Declan."

"That's different." Greg's discomfort takes on alarming proportions. "We were in a different phase of the corporate relationship with Anterdec then."

"You mean Shannon helped secure the contract by dating Declan."

"Yes."

"And if I date Andrew you're worried that..."

144

"You could jeopardize some complex business negotiations."

"What does *that* mean?"

Greg's phone rings. He reaches into his pants pocket and walks away abruptly. I hear the words, "Hi, Doctor..." and then his words become indistinct. His wife, Judy, is a breast cancer survivor, and now I wonder if there's even more going on under the surface of every single part of my life—work, home, friends, Andrew—than I ever imagined.

It's like realizing you're perched on an island that turns out to be the tip of an iceberg.

In a boiling pot of water.

"What's he talking about?" I ask Carol, who just shrugs.

"Don't ask me. I'm still the newbie here."

"You've worked here for more than a year."

"I know, but that's my convenient excuse and I'm sticking to it."

"Why can't you be the pregnant one?"

She holds her fingers up in the sign of the cross and shouts to Josh, "Got any garlic? Cast thee out, demon. Don't you dare talk about more spawn in this womb."

"I take it the baby factory is closed."

"The womb has been converted from a factory to an abandoned warehouse. Yours, on the other hand," she says suggestively, "is about to become a playroom."

"Ewww," Josh says from his desk. "I can hear you."

"What? You think we're discriminating against you because you have a penis, but when we talk about vaginas you get grossed out."

"Yes." He shudders.

"Oh, he's going to be a *great* partner in these childbirth classes," I say.

Carol snickers.

145

SHOPPING FOR A CEO

"Why can't *you* do the childbirth class shops with him?" I ask.

She looks at herself, then at Josh. "Look at me. Look at Josh. Not only am I too old for him, but I could crush him like a bug. No one would ever believe we're together."

She's right. They pretty much look like they'd be each other's beard.

"Besides, I'd be the worst candidate for a child birth class, because I've actually been through childbirth. Twice. I know how much bullshit they deal in those classes, and I couldn't keep my mouth shut."

"What do you mean?"

"Oh, honey," she says. "The only part that really helps is the tour of the hospital, so you know exactly where you'll feel all your pain. Contractions in the elevator. Vomiting in the trash can in Waiting Room #4. Actual shredding of your perineum in Delivery Room #3. Stitch popping when you try to poop in Room #535. The tour should be renamed A Map of Your Suffering."

Josh makes a strange gagging sound.

"But they won't tell you that. And they shouldn't. Because what woman in her right mind goes through pregnancy and childbirth knowing the risks and the torture that's coming? So they sugar coat it and tell you that contractions are really just pressure you can use mind techniques to control, or that perineal massage for the entire pregnancy will thin out the tissues so the baby's head doesn't tear two holes into one."

Josh is now retching.

"Or that when you're on the delivery table and they tell you to push, you will end up with hemorrhoids the size of small Pomeranians."

Josh sprints out of his office for the bathroom.

Carol looks over at his empty desk with cat eyes, her expression exactly like the one Chuckles has after coughing up an impressive hairball.

"Why do people reproduce?" I ask, cringing.

"Because it's like making love with your body, but instead of being left with a wet spot, you get an entire human being who you get to love forever."

"Awww."

Josh staggers back, drinking a fresh can of soda from the machine outside the men's room. His eyes are hollow.

"And bonus! If you're really lucky, the flesh donut that forms when your butt hole turns inside out as the head emerges goes back in place. Eventually."

Josh sprints again.

I am really, really glad I'm just *work* pregnant.

CHAPTER SEVENTEEN

As we pull into the parking lot of the sex toy store where Marie and I are mystery shopping today, she turns to me and blurts out, "Amanda, what's a dirty sanchez?"

I set down my foamy hot chocolate. Permanently.

Marie went through the entire mystery shopping certification process so that she could do sex toy shops. So far, she turns out to be a master at them. This one is a little different from the others.

This is a store with its own back room that hosts bachelorette parties. As luck would have it, we need to evaluate the process of being walked through the offer to host a combined bachelorette/sex toy party, complete with catering and strippers.

Timing is everything.

Shannon has begged me to make sure her mother doesn't sign any contracts. Technically, as the maid of honor, it's my job to throw the bachelorette party, and no matter how elegantly awesome this place might be, I have the final say on what Shannon's last night of debauchery looks like.

As far as I'm concerned, it involves alcohol, body oil, and Joe Manganiello.

Not necessarily in that order.

I pointedly ignore Marie's question about a dirty sanchez (Google it—you'll understand why) and we walk up to the smoked glass doors of our day's shop.

You would think we were walking into a spa. A Zen-decorated, grass and glass and polished stones, all muted earth-tones spa. The facility is called O.

Just...O.

A woman dressed in dove grey, with hair pulled back in a bun, greets us with a warm smile, reeking of verbena. She has no idea we're actually mystery shopping. That's the point. We pretend to be regular customers, but quietly document all of the ways the center can improve its customer service.

We're offered cucumber sparkling mineral water. The decor is a mix of raw wood, polished bamboo floors, glass waterfalls and Zen rock stacks, with orange and gold accents throughout.

"O offers a twenty-first century club for sophisticated women," the saleswoman, Chloe, explains. "We want to be a fourth space for women of a discerning taste."

"Fourth space?" Marie asks. She's toned down her entire personality, eyes eager but body controlled.

"Home is the first space. Work is the second space. Third spaces are locations like coffee shops and malls. We're the fourth space. The space where you can arrive. Rest. Relax." Chloe leans forward and whispers in a hushed tone with sultry implications. "Indulge."

Just then, a seven-foot-tall redwood masquerading as a man walks by, covered in oil and ginger hair, all tan and green eyes and...I think he's wearing a shoelace.

And only a shoelace—between his legs.

He bends over and offers an assortment of tiny pieces of sushi on a tray that is so small it can't even cover his, um...chopstick.

"Indulge," Marie says, her voice like a cougar's growl, accepting a piece of something with salmon, her eyes tracking every move the man makes as he leaves the room.

"That is Henry. He's one of our top massage therapists."

"He gives massages?" Marie gives me a look that says, *Please tell me we're required to get a massage as part of this shop. Please. Please!*

I give her a terse head shake.

She pouts.

"Yes," Chloe answers. "We have an array of highly skilled men here, from massage therapists to acupuncturists to Reiki providers and so much more."

"More?" I ask, my lips twitching with amusement.

Chloe takes the bait willingly. She smooths long, elegantly-painted fingers along the tops of her legs, which are covered in a light linen skirt. "Indeed. You wouldn't be here at O if you weren't aware of our full array of services."

"True. My daughter is getting married in a few months and we've heard wonderful stories about your bachelorette parties."

I kick Marie in the ankle, just lightly enough to make a point.

She moves out of target range.

Chloe's face spreads with a grin. "Ah. I see. You want to experience the full package."

Henry walks over with a tray of chocolate mousse in little espresso cups. As he bends over, I see the full package, all right.

I take one of the white chocolate-filled delights and Henry gives me the once over. My face pinkens. A few days ago, this would have been a dream, but now? After my date with Andrew last night and another one scheduled for tonight?

Suddenly Henry is just...work. Nothing more.

Timing really *is* everything.

Chloe pulls out a small remote control and pushes buttons, a large screen sliding down from the ceiling as the lights dim. She begins a slide show, a slick, professional design that takes us through all of the features O has to offer, from private lap dances with the male "talent" to hot tub and massage packages for couples.

"And, of course, we have our Bridal Queen Delight," she says, going in for the kill. None of their services in the brochure have prices next to them.

Five men pour into the room as stripper music starts, the lights changing color. One of them is holding a sex toy that is likely banned in the state of Texas.

We're about to get a full taste of O, all right.

My phone buzzes with a text.

It's Andrew.

Can't wait for tonight. What are you doing now?

Watching a male stripper perform with a sex toy, I text back.

My phone rings instantly.

Marie doesn't even notice. She's watching Henry do a backbend and play with a—

"You're doing *what*?" Andrew's voice barks into my phone. I plug the other ear and try to ignore the show in front of me.

"I'm working."

"Your work involves a male stripper and sex toys?"

"Yes. Today it does."

"Who on earth pays you to do *that*?"

"You do."

Silence.

"WHAT?"

"Anterdec has majority ownership of the parent company that just recently launched the O spas, right?

This is *your* job I'm on, Andrew. Thank you." I practically purr through those last two words.

Silence.

"Shit," he chokes out. "So *I'm* paying you to ogle half-naked men."

I squint and look carefully at the beefcake before me. "Technically, they're about seven-eighths naked."

He groans.

"The only partially naked man I want you to watch is *me*."

My turn to be silent. I am silent because my mouth just filled with drool and I can't stop imagining Andrew in a shoelace offering me chocolate mousse in an espresso cup.

"Amanda?"

"Yes."

"You there?"

"Oh, yes."

"I missed you last night."

"You were *with* me last night."

"I meant after dinner. You didn't take me up on my offer to come back to my place."

"No, I didn't."

"Why not?"

"Too much. Too fast." That's the simple way to explain it. The truth is vastly more complex, but it's hard to concentrate right now when there are five mostly naked men with bodies like something out of Magic Mike shining at me.

Chloe thinks I'm talking about the striptease in front of me and slows everything down. Marie is in some guy's lap, being fed chocolate-covered strawberries and having Champagne poured into a vial between her breasts and sipped by another man.

Maybe that's what she means about 'the girls' doing more work than anyone ever imagines.

"Is it?" he asks softly. "Is tonight too much?"

"No!" I say a little too quickly.

"Yes!" Marie calls out as the music quickens and she's lifted into a—

"Is that a sex swing?" I call out.

"Oh, come on," Andrew mutters. "*My* work day involves discussing currency exchange rates and spreads —"

"This involves some, uh, spreading too," I mutter. And plenty of currency, I imagine.

"Amanda," he growls.

"I think I have to get off the phone before Marie commits a felony or three in front of me, Andrew," I say, trying to stay calm. "Or does something so unforgivable Jason leaves her. I am pretty sure standard wedding vows don't allow for—"

"I want you off this account. Immediately."

"You don't get to decide that," I say, laughing. He has no idea that I would *love* to be taken off all these sex toy shops. I tried to pawn them off on Carol but she wouldn't bite.

Now I'm watching Marie bite.

"If Anterdec's the client, I most certainly do get to decide that. See you tonight."

Click.

Oooooo.

Was that jealousy?

My phone buzzes. It's a text from Andrew:

Is dinner at my place tonight too much, too fast?

I text back:

No.

He replies:

How about asking you to pack an overnight bag?

154

A zing runs through me, and not because of the sudden appearance of Henry in my face, his eight pack inches from my forehead. He's an afterthought. I only have eyes for my blinking blue phone screen.

I type back:

Wait. You cook? You're cooking me dinner?

He replies:

You dodged the question.

I text back:

So did you.

He replies:

Then we're at a standoff.

I answer:

Yes, we are.

And he says:

The only way to break a standoff is to figure out the other person's weak point.

And I reply:

That could take a very long time. I should pack an overnight bag just in case.

He texts back a smiley face.

Hold on.

I think I just lost this standoff before it even began.

CHAPTER EIGHTEEN

Andrew's loft is one story below the penthouse level and right on the water, about a five minute walk from where we had dinner last night. I'm looking out at a wall of glass that shimmers from the reflection of the moon on the water and the city lights bouncing like disco balls. He has a small balcony with two wrought-iron chairs on it and a large, mesh umbrella.

"You live *here*?" I gasp, stunned by the location. "In a waterfront loft? Why were you buying a boat on the marina the other night when you live right on the water?" I can look out his living room window and see the marina in question below. *Way* below.

"Business investment. A way to entertain clients." He's in the kitchen, fussing with food on plates. The apartment smells amazing, but I know that the scent is fake.

"You didn't actually cook for me, did you? You used that old onion trick."

He looks up, face tight with concentration as he arranges food on white, square plates. His hands are big and skilled, moving as if he knows what he's doing. And yet from what I know from Declan, Andrew's got the cooking skills of a preschooler.

After he wipes his hands on a towel, Andrew grabs two wine goblets and pours generous glasses of a lovely white wine. I peek at the label. Domaine Leroy Corton-Charlemagne...something. When rich people put famous historical figures on their wine labels, you know it's going to be expensive.

He hands me one glass.

"What old trick?"

"You fried some onions in olive oil right before I came over. It makes the apartment smell like you slaved away over a hot stove when what really happened was a private chef came by earlier and prepared everything in advance."

Another one of his tells. He blinks slowly, the motion too controlled. His face betrays him.

I take a sip. Great wine. Then I laugh.

"You're good," he says.

"Busted."

"Consuela sends her regards."

"You hired her just for our dinner?"

"Yes. Is that a problem? Would you prefer a different chef?"

"I am fine with a burger and fries."

"Too bad. You're getting filet mignon and cauliflower roasted in avocado oil with a jicama...something."

"You can't even fake cooking well."

He pulls me to him, ending the space gap between us. His mouth tastes like wine and smiles. He's wearing an open-collared business shirt in a shade of blue that makes the grey of his apartment seem crisper. Bolder. There's a black t-shirt underneath, which only serves to mold to the contours of his torso, pecs, and shoulders, outlining his body.

The loft is decorated in shined stainless steel and open support beams, with wallpaper that looks like old black-and-white photos of industrial-age factories. The door to his bedroom is open and I see a nautical theme in there, with the bed covered in a white and blue-striped duvet.

Bed.

His bed.

I shiver and Andrew pulls me ever closer. I feel how much he likes me. Like *this*. His arousal triggers my own, the tête-à-tête fueling a kiss that leaves me on tiptoes, reaching for the soft hair at the back of his head, my hands groping and grasping to bring him as close as two people can be while fully clothed.

Panting hard, he pulls back and stares down at me, eyes alight with more than passion.

"Too much? Too fast?"

"Not yet."

His eyes narrow, those arms cradling my hips in a way that is so comfortable it feels like we've been doing this for years.

"You set the pace," he stresses, letting one arm stray from my waist so he can drink his wine.

"Why?"

"*Why?*"

I just wait. I don't try to explain.

"Because..." His voice fades out with a deliberative sigh. "Because I don't know. It just feels right."

"Do you always do what feels right?"

He jerks his head sharply, breaking eye contact. "No."

"But you try."

"Yes."

"Always?"

"Most of the time."

"Good enough."

"Glad you approve."

I laugh. "Somehow, you don't strike me as the kind of man who worries about having other people's approval in order to do something."

"Other than my dad, that's true. And even with him, it's fading."

I study him. He's not quite nervous, but there's something just slightly off.

"Why's your dad giving over the CEO position to you now? He's barely sixty. That's fairly young. James doesn't strike me as the type to cede control easily."

Andrew's mouth sets in a grim line. His hand is at my elbow and he guides me to the couch. "I'll tell you the answer if you promise to keep it a secret."

"I still haven't said a word to Shannon and Declan about your being CEO."

"I know you haven't. And I appreciate that."

Some layer to Andrew's tone sets an alarm bell off inside me. The wine is loosening me up but this makes me tight with worry.

"Dad has cancer."

And there it is.

"Oh, Andrew," I say, leaning forward to hold his hand. "I am so sorry."

He nods. "It's not that bad. Prostate. Slow growing. He has many years ahead of him. But it's shaken him to the core and he's stepping back. When we make the formal announcement he's not positioning this as a retirement, not at all. In fact, he's becoming a venture capitalist and planning a whole new company around seed money and angel investing."

"Okay." I don't know what else to day.

"But he's freaked out."

"Declan doesn't know yet?"

Andrew shakes his head.

"Your dad confided in you, though?"

"Dad and Declan have a complicated relationship. Dad doesn't like to show any kind of weakness with Dec."

"Why?"

"Goes back to the incident. My mom's death."

"Oh." This is the first time he's ever brought it up with me. He's initiating the conversation, and if I'm careful, he'll open up to me.

"Dad's fumed at Declan for all these years. It's not like Dec could have made a different choice, at least, not the way he tells the story. Mom wanted him to use the EpiPen on me. Dec did as told. Mom died. I lived. The end."

The way he's describing this makes some part of me cry for the teen he was when it all occurred. The man in front of me is telling the story with a clinical detachment that is manufactured. I'm not judging. I'm just observing. His entire demeanor changes as he recounts what happened, and it's giving me insight into Andrew as a man.

What happened that day was horrifying and harrowing for Andrew and Declan and their mother. But the aftermath...oh, how awful. My throat begins to fill with the tangy sense of impeding tears. The bridge of my nose tingles. I blink, hard, trying to drive it away.

Some second date.

I need to reply. He's looking at me like we're playing conversation tennis and it's my turn to return the ball.

"Your father doesn't feel like he has a relationship with Declan where he can tell him these private details?"

"No."

"But he does with you."

Andrew frowns. "Yes. I guess. Apparently so. Dads are so complicated, aren't they?"

I hold my breath.

He picks up on a change in me right away. "What's your dad like?"

"I don't know. He left when I was five."

"Left? Your parents divorced?"

"Um," I say, biting my lower lip. This story never gets easier to tell. "Yes, they divorced."

"Do you see him?"

"No."

"Never?"

"Not since I was five."

"When you say he left, you mean it. He just...*left*?"

"You know the old cliché about the guy who goes to the store one day to get a pack a cigarettes and never comes back?"

He grimaces. "Yes."

"Substitute a twelve pack of beer for cigarettes and you have my dad. Doug Warrick's been gone for more than twenty years."

"And absolutely no contact?"

I wobble. I hesitate. There is a truth here. There really is. But the true truth is deeper below the surface truth than anyone who hasn't lived my life can possibly imagine.

"No."

The lie slips through my teeth so easily, like a wiggly fish on a line that finds a way to escape, the hook deep enough to have caught it but not so embedded as to keep it pinned in place.

"I'm sorry."

"I'm sorry about your mother."

"Is this what they call the Getting to Know You phase?"

We laugh. Laughing is easier than being awkward. So much easier than being raw. Being here with him, in unfamiliar territory, feels remarkably safe. At no point in any of my time I've ever spent with Andrew, from the moment we met in that boardroom at Anterdec for the pitch nearly two years ago (when Hot Guy met Toilet Girl) to these seconds ticking on and onward have I ever felt unsafe.

Unmoored? Yes. Confused? Yes. Uncertain? Sure.

But never unsafe.

He is hard to read and right now, his eyes are on me, as if he's trying to understand me the same way I'm pondering him.

"Where did you go to college?" he asks suddenly.

"UMASS, of course. You?"

He cocks one eyebrow. "Harvard."

"Of course."

"Where were you born?"

"Mendon. But we live in Newton now. You?"

"Weston."

I can't help but laugh. "My guess would have been Wayland, Wellesley or Weston." The expensive western suburbs of Boston.

"Favorite ice cream?"

"Do I have to pick one? That's like asking my favorite Yes song."

Eyes on me, his face changes, evaluating me like he can't quite believe what I just said. His hands reach up to the top button of his shirt, the one right below his open throat. He unbuttons it slowly, then reaches down for the next one.

This is quite a segue. I am getting my second strip tease in the same day, huh? No complaints.

No complaints at all.

Like Superman, he pries open the two sides of his business shirt to reveal—

A Yes concert t-shirt.

"No way!" I crow. "You went last year? At the pavilion?" Right across the bay from Andrew's apartment there is a large outdoor concert center where I saw the band perform just last summer.

"Yes."

We laugh, the sound like threads being woven to make a pattern.

"Too bad about Chris Squire." I don't even have to explain that I'm mourning the loss of the longtime band's bass player recently, for Andrew's face goes sorrowful instantly. He gives me a pensive look, then stands, reaching into his back pocket.

He pulls out his phone, taps a few times on the glass, then inserts the device into a docking stage.

Very familiar music floats through the air.

This is really unreal.

"I don't know anyone under forty who likes Yes," I say.

"And yet here we are. Terry got me into it," he explains. "You?"

"A high school boyfriend with a dad who worked the sound stage for them as a roadie in their earlier years."

"You said you'd never had a boyfriend."

"Not a serious one. High school doesn't count."

He's so appealing right now, sitting there with an openness as he listens to me. Andrew's curiosity feels less like being grilled and more like being known. Something beeps in the distance, and he crosses the room quickly.

The scent of spices tells me it's time for dinner.

"It's much better in the original vinyl, though," I call out as he walks into the kitchen.

"You're a musical Luddite?" he jokes.

"I just like the way it sounds," I explain, the conversation cut short by dinner's readiness.

He's surprisingly fussy, making sure the plates and table are set up correctly, but I understand why when we sit down. He opens a new bottle of wine and by the time we both descend into our seats, nestled in place, everything we could want is within arm's reach.

Including each other.

The food is perfect, a beef dish with flavors that tantalize, and I should appreciate the delicious tastes I'm getting but I can't. Andrew eats with a half-hearted precision that makes me wonder if he feels the same way. As I finish what I know is my final bite of this wonderful meal I sip my water slowly, then replace it with wine, swishing the alcohol in my mouth, savoring the mouth feel.

His tongue would taste even better against my own.

Andrew's face is tipped down, but his eyes flash up at me, framed by those long lashes. "What are you thinking about?" he asks.

I nearly drop my wine glass. My laugh covers up my nervousness. Or so I hope. "Isn't that my line? Aren't women the ones who always ask that?"

"I'm fighting stereotypes."

"I see that. You aren't being texted three hundred times an hour like most CEOs."

"I turned off my phone."

"Oh."

He turned off his phone.

In the range of behaviors C-level executives can exhibit on a date, that's big. Shannon complains incessantly that Declan is constantly being interrupted by his phone. The tech tether that insta-communication creates is more a choke collar than a safety line these days.

He turned off his phone *for me*.

Remembering to breathe is about all I can manage right now, especially when he brings his wine glass to his lips and takes a long, slow drink, his mouth gripping the glass edge like a kiss. His tongue strokes the bottom of the goblet and I work the muscles at the back of my throat so I don't moan.

"No interruptions." His voice is low and deep, punctuated by the heavy breath of someone who is—

Actively remembering to breathe.

"You turned off your phone for me," I say with a long inhale that hitches in my bones. "That's like donating a kidney for a CEO."

One side of that compelling mouth curls up in a smile. "I wouldn't quite go that far."

"You wouldn't donate an organ for me?" I tease, lifting my wine glass to my own lips and taking a sip.

"I have a certain organ you can borrow tonight."

CHAPTER NINETEEN

Wine shoots up the back of my mouth and into my nose. The burning. Dear God, the burning.

"Did you—" *snort* "—seriously just use a frat boy line on me?" I tip my head back and feel white wine dribble down the back of my throat and cough. Hard. If I'm going to lose my voice after spending an evening with Andrew, this is not exactly how I want to lose it.

He dips his head down, biting his lips. "I guess I did." He stands and finds a box of tissues on his fireplace mantel, walking across the room quickly to give them to me.

"Thanks, but what am I going to do with these? Shove them up my nose? I literally just inhaled your Domaine Leroy de whatever."

"I'm out of practice. I haven't done this in a while," he confesses, hands on his hips in a gesture of mild cluelessness.

"Used frat boy lines on women you date?"

"Had a woman over to my apartment for dinner."

"Oh." As my nasal passages recover from being invaded by fermented fruit, I sniff. It hurts. I sniff again, over and over, until the pain in my sinuses and epiglottis dies down enough to swig a bunch of water.

"Are you okay now?"

"I think so. Remind me never to put wine in my Neti pot during allergy season."

He looks relieved.

"When was the last time you had a woman over to your apartment for dinner?"

His arms drop slowly, his breathing controlled as he crosses the room. He's turned the fireplace on, one of those glowing real-wood simulations that casts a gentle light behind his tall frame.

Andrew stops inches in front of me, his hands closing into soft fists.

"Is that important for you to know?"

"Yes."

The kiss he plants on my lips is quick and simple, his mouth wet and warm.

"Never," he says, fingers sliding up from my neck and sinking into my hair. His palms cup my jaw and I look up into eyes that ask me to follow him wherever he leads me.

"Never?"

"You're the first."

"You said you hadn't done this 'in a while'."

"*In a while* is code for *never*."

"You have your own language? I need to become fluent in Andrew."

"It's like speaking in tongues," he murmurs against my neck, his mouth planting open kisses, tongue leaving wet gasps along the way.

"Like in church?" I ask, reaching down to cup parts of him that are speaking to me now. He hisses, the intake of breath the only response I need as I kiss him deeply.

"Oh, God," he groans against my mouth.

"I'll take that as a yes."

I am up in the air, his hands holding me by my ass, my legs temporarily stunned and bending up until my thighs are wrapped around his waist as if they had been programmed by a divine being to do so. My hands are against the hot skin at the back of his neck and I'm blinded by the sheer force of the kiss and our movement. His mouth is a playground, and I'm on the swings. The merry-go-round. The see-saw.

And the slide, down, down, down...

My back hits a smooth, cool softness as I realize he's brought me into his bedroom and set me on his bed. His body folds across mine, covering me with a marbled, muscled fullness that is so exquisite I arch up, seeking more. His hands are everywhere, buried in my hair, cupping each breast, that glorious mouth tonguing and tasting and no longer teasing.

No questions any more. We both know exactly where this is going.

Thank god.

"I have wanted you so much and for so long," he murmurs, rolling off me just enough to prop his jaw in one hand and look at me.

My mind skips. Just...skips. It's like there's a short circuit in the universe and everything halted for two seconds, but resumes.

"You have? Because I've been right here. All along." My words are soft and yielding, just like my body. My skirt is up around my hips and his caress is complete in its savoring of me. The intensity flows through his fingers like a current, a constant flow of emotion and need that surges through him to me.

Being felt like this—not just touched or stroked or catalogued—takes a level of steadiness in me that I'm surprised to find I possess. Maybe I only have it when I'm with him. I don't know. Instead of turning toward him or rolling to hide, I let him use his hands to study my body with a visceral connection that is wholly unknown to me.

His eyes go contemplative, his breath unhurried as I, in turn, touch him. We don't kiss. Not yet. Not now.

"I know you have." His voice crawls along the contours of my skin, as if it's traveling by blood through my veins, seeking to send its message of desire to every pore, each cell. "And thank you."

"Thank you? Thank you for what?" My own hands itch to touch all of him, eagerness more powerful than patience. His waist is tight as I tunnel my fingers between the waistband of his trousers and his shirt and pull the fabric out, seeking the warm expanse of his toned back.

"For—" he says, his voice halting. "For waiting."

"I haven't been waiting," I explain. "I gave up." Being this honest would crush any other interaction with any other man, but not this time. Not this moment.

Not this man.

As I take in the lines of his shoulders, memorizing the angle of his shoulder blades, using my fingertips to chart the curl of muscle against bone, I appreciate the broad stretch of skin that houses the essence of him.

He encircles one nipple with a finger that moves so slowly it feels cruel. Every millimeter makes me gasp. I can only inhale again and again and again until my lungs rise to meet his fingers, begging for release.

He nudges the neckline of my top down, popping one pebbled, rosy breast out and his mouth—oh, sweet heavens.

That mouth.

"Andrew." His name comes out of me in a gasp and a shiver, as if my vocal cords and muscles were unable to discern which biological system to respond with. His mouth plays tricks with my skin as his spare hand slides up between my thighs, where all the blood in my body has pooled and is beating a timpani, a bass drum, and a djun djun all in concert.

I have, singularly, become the pulse point of the universe.

A sudden need to feel him makes me push up against his hand, my fingers at his belt buckle. Unable to see, I use touch as my guide, the hard metal a familiar rectangle, my mind recreating the process for undoing the belt as my hands do my imagination's work.

The belt undone, I release the button, unzip him, and before I can touch him he's kissing me again, the cold night air shocking my wet nipple as the fire of his arousal enflames me, the ice of his brief abandonment making me tug at his shirt tails, pulling up to give me access to more of him.

I need to see him. See everything. Feel everything. Inventory it and ascertain that this is real. This is happening. I am not dreaming or hallucinating. We're in his bedroom, on his bed, and about to make love, naked and deliciously private.

"Amanda," he rasps, his lips against mine, his erection pushing against my thigh, his body moving in short, slow strokes against me in a preview of what is about to unfold. His mouth moves against mine with a steady spiral up, each kiss more intense than the one before, his bare belly against my clothed one, the sensation of him over me nothing short of divine.

He reaches up and under me with swift, nimble fingers, the clasp separating and freeing me. I sit up and he watches with eyes that take in everything as I unbutton my top, peeling off my shirt and leaving me there with the loose bra dangling.

I haven't been naked, in the moonlight, with a man in so long that this feels like the first time.

It's not, but it feels that way.

He takes care of the next step, skimming my arms with his palms, riding up my shoulders and dispatching with the lingerie with a flick of his wrist, leaving me topless.

Without another word, he unbuttons his last bit of his shirt, pulls it off, and grabs the hem of his concert t-shirt, his thick arms reaching up, the cloth covering his face for a moment, giving me a complete view of his upper body on display without his eyes watching me.

And that is the moment when I become utterly, overwhelmingly self-conscious.

He's *gorgeous*. Cut and broad, wild and perfect, with the textured skin of a man who spends hours a day with a personal trainer. I know what his legs look like in bike shorts, and I've caught glimpses of him over the past two years in suits, with and without the jacket, but having Andrew McCormick's half-naked body within inches of mine and on display like this makes me freeze.

This man is about to make love with me. I want him to explore and enjoy all the intimate places in my body and heart that can only be accessed by my *yes*. And my *yes* is throbbing through every nerve cluster, each blush, all the flushed skin on my chest and in the wet, wild parts of me that know we have a huge bed, a magical view of the ocean, and all the time tonight to do delicious, breathtaking, pleasurable things to each other.

"Take off your skirt," he whispers. Andrew is on his knees, his pants undone, hands by his side and inches from me. Towering over me, he's radiating heat and want. His breathing is controlled, and his words make me reach behind me to unzip the skirt, as if there is no other choice, as if I have to do as told because I have already surrendered to him, even if my mind hasn't quite caught up to what my body knows.

I shimmy out of it, wearing only my panties now, and he crawls over me, leaning me back, connecting our bodies only with a kiss that stretches me from toes to ears, turning me into a tingling, breathing soul that knows only sensation and that seeks to understand the world via his touch. His taste. His sound. His gaze.

Him.

"You," he says between kisses and hands, heat and pressure, friction and fire and strokes and *oh*—"are more beautiful in person than I've imagined all this time." With arms like corded steel, he pushes up, impossibly up, and the light from outside catches his face.

I see truth in his eyes.

That truth gives me permission to touch him, to splay my palms against the thick muscles at his waist, to roam and rove and close my eyes and just feel. He's mine to touch and his hitched breath tells me he likes this. I curl up enough to lick the base of his throat, then kiss to his chin, the rasp of a day's beard making me shiver.

Will he? Does he...? My self-consciousness burns off me, like the heat of the morning sunrise evaporating the dawn's dew.

That mouth separates from our kiss and he bends to my breast, sucking in one nipple as one hand reaches between my legs. I'm wetter than wet and while my mind goes on vacation for a few seconds to some ecstasyland I didn't know I possessed, he renders me completely naked.

And then stands, blissfully joining me.

The long, warm stretch of his nude body against mine, thick hair against my own smooth skin, is a study in contrasts.

"I can't believe this is happening," I say, as he crawls into bed and presses against me, but my tone isn't one of disbelief. It's one of confirmation.

"Then I need to up my game, because if you're still not sure this is real, we have quite a bit of work to do." His mouth begins a slow descent between my breasts, over my belly, and to the promised land.

And with that, he keeps his word, all hands and mouth and tongue and taste and sighs and moans and cries of pleasure and release that come from two years of not knowing. We make up for lost time. Again. And again.

And *again* again.

Remember Sex Math? Oh, yeah.

And this game?

We both manage to win.

* * *

I have a confession to make.

I have never spent the night in a man's bed.

I wake up in a total panic, my heart slamming against my chest like a bear whacked a bees' nest and all the bees are trying to escape in one big buzzing wall of fury, synchronized in their brutal attempt to leave. I'm covered in sweat and my legs are sticky.

Why do my hips ache?

And who is this two-hundred pound, six-foot muscled furnace in bed with me?

"Amanda?" he asks, sitting up, bed head smashing his hair against one side of his face, eyes squinty with sleep. In bright daylight, this close to him, his eyes are even browner. How is that possible? "What's wrong?" Warm hands float to my naked back, rising up my shoulders in a gesture that is supposed to comfort me.

Except I'm in a panic because of my stupid naked-in-public dream.

And now I'm naked in public.

For real.

Sort of.

Last night floods my memory, how Mr. Flesh Furnace here used that same mouth that is smiling at me to make me arch up and press against it for more, how that tongue made my thighs shiver, how those hands that gently rub my back elicited sounds from me that involved octaves I'm pretty sure the human throat can only access during orgasm.

Orgasms.

My whole body goes tingly as I reach for the sheet and pull it up over my breasts.

"I'm fine. Just a dream."

His hand rides down over my chest, jarring the sheet loose from one breast. "Your heart is racing. Must have been some dream."

I'm blinking over and over, my face frozen as I try to relax and lower my shoulders. My neck is tight with tension and he's next to me, sitting up, and oh, yes. He most certainly is naked, too.

Daylight is a blessing and a curse.

"It's the same dream I've had almost every night since I was five," I admit. I'm not sure why I tell him this. Maybe actually being naked makes me feel like it's safe to talk about dreaming of being naked.

"Whoa. Same dream almost every night for nearly twenty years?"

"I know."

"That's intense."

I can't stop looking at him, distracted now. He dips his head down to force me to catch his eyes.

"Hi."

"Hi."

Have I mentioned the fact that I have never, *ever* spent the night at a man's house? What am I supposed to do right now? The Walk of Shame never involves the sun. The sun is most certainly out right now, impishly watching as I fumble my way through this morning-after stuff.

Andrew takes care of the *what do I do next?* question by kissing me. This is a slow, deep kiss that I start to pull away from because, hello, morning breath?

And then I don't care, because I melt into the bed as he doesn't care, either. I follow his cues. If he wanted me to leave, this would be awkward and weird, right? He'd be up and showered and drinking coffee, and I would rush to get my clothes on. We would pretend the night before had been just one of those things, and I would depart with that blinking sense of confusion that comes from having a one-night stand and not knowing quite where to compartmentalize the emotions attached to the carnal event.

But that is not happening right now. Not one bit.

This is the kiss of a man who enjoyed last night thoroughly, of a man who is in no rush to separate from me, and as my hand reaches down to stroke his ass and more, I encounter ample evidence of his intentions.

I am following his cues, all right, and he is presenting one very big one right now before me.

"My goodness," I whisper, hand wrapping around his delightfully awake shaft. "Is this breakfast in bed?"

"Oh, God," he sighs as I offer my variation of room service, burrowing under the covers to give him a little of what I got last night. "You are perfect," he adds in a tight voice, which loosens considerably a few minutes later when he finds his own special, lower octave.

He starts to return the favor and it occurs to me that this could all happen again. That last night wasn't an aberration. That he wants more.

And just then, a buzzer sounds in the apartment.

"What is that?" I ask as Andrew's head lifts up from under the sheet with a groan of frustration.

"That is the building concierge, buzzing me."

"A package?"

"No," he groans, rolling off the bed and walking to the bathroom. Ah, the view. The *view*. I didn't know an ass could have that many muscles in it. He comes out of the bathroom wearing a thin silky robe and saunters over to the bed, planting a kiss on my forehead.

"Then what?"

"Someone realized my phone is off and they've resorted to this."

"Oh," I say in a small voice. He reaches for his pants and pulls out his phone, turning it on. It buzzes in fits and starts, like a vibrator with a battery that's dying.

Not that I, uh, know what that looks or sounds like.

"Jesus Christ," he mutters to himself. "Two hundred and forty-seven texts. My phone can't keep up with all the notifications."

Ouch. And I thought it was bad when my mother— oh, no.

My mother.

"Can you hand me my purse?" I ask. He finds it in the living room and brings it back, eyes glued to his phone screen.

The magic is definitely over.

SHOPPING FOR A CEO

By the time I check my messages and text mom back to assure her I haven't been chained to a wall in some lair in Mexico and am not sold into sex slavery by a perverted billionaire, I hear the gurgle of a coffee machine.

It never occurred to me to ask Andrew whether he drinks coffee. Thank God he does, because that would be a show stopper. I can handle a workaholic CEO with a body designed by Crossfit and a tongue that should qualify for the Ironman Triathlon, but if he doesn't drink coffee I'm outta here, because that's just not human.

I also take this chance to snoop.

I hear him talking out in the living room. It sounds like a tense discussion, so I avoid invading his privacy. Last night he welcomed me into his bed and I welcomed him into my body. This morning it's time to go back to reality, where boundaries do, indeed, exist— and respecting those is important.

Even if I really, really need caffeine right now.

Snooping and *respecting boundaries* seem like contradictions. But they're not. Bear with me. I can explain. Everything I know about Andrew is either from him directly, from Shannon, a little from Declan, some from my incessant Google searches, and from my oh-so-careful physical examination of as many nooks and crannies on that hot body as I could reasonably search on Date #2.

This is a chance to learn more.

"Damn it!" he shouts from the other room. The coffee machine sighs.

I am totally not going out there right now. More ammunition for snooping, er...research.

His closet is bigger than my bedroom. He has an affinity for purples and smoky blues, the heathered colors that come from tailors so exclusive they don't have retail stores. His suits line up like good little soldiers, and nothing is out of place. This is one of those closets where the shoes aren't on the floor, or in little cubbies. I reach for a drawer handle and the drawer tips out at a forty-five degree angle, revealing dress shoes in neat lines, three shelves deep.

I tuck the "drawer" back in and leave.

I look out the window and see his little balcony. It really is just two chairs, a table, and an umbrella. Unlike all the other balconies, he has no plants. Nothing. Not a single bit of decoration. It stands out in stark contrast to the rest of the apartment, which is carefully designed and color-coordinated, the look and feel textured and nuanced by someone who knows what they're doing with space.

Weird.

His nightstand is a goldmine. There are a few fitness magazines, a tablet computer, and a bottle of lube. I squeeze my eyes shut and close the drawer. Hey, if he ever snooped in my bedroom, he'd find way more than just a bottle of lube in my nightstand drawers. I single-handedly keep the battery industry going during dry spells.

His dresser drawers are full of rolled socks and underwear, folded t-shirts and jeans. Polo shirts. Workout clothes. Each type of clothing has its own drawer. A hand-carved wooden bowl on one dresser contains an old-fashioned analog watch, some change in various currencies, and a few tie pins. Cuff links.

And a single photo rests on his dresser.

It's him, Declan, Terry, his dad and his mom, all on a boat somewhere on the ocean. I'm guessing it was taken shortly before his mother died, because Andrew's around fifteen or sixteen. He's tall, but not as tall as he is now, and he has the lean look of a teen boy who is just about to fill out as testosterone performs its destiny.

A breeze flows from the left, shoving all their hair to the side, and they're laughing. Andrew is looking at his mom, Declan's staring into the camera, Terry is holding his mom's shoulder, and she's not quite looking at whoever took the picture.

James is just smiling, the grin so bright it's blinding.

Tears hit me like I've been shot from behind, like an arrow pierced me between ribs and struck my heart, the feeling so sudden and unexpected I gasp, an animal sound filling my raw throat.

This is what a real family looks like. A happy family. One filled with joy and love.

And it can all end in seconds.

We have no pictures like this in my house.

I doubt they even exist.

At least Andrew has this. *Had* this. Had a world where people looked at each other like *that*.

"You don't know what you're talking about!" I hear Andrew say, his voice loud but controlled. I sniff and turn away. If I keep looking at that picture a part of me will fall apart, and right now, I can't have anything else inside me vibrate on a different frequency, because too many of those and the dissonance will make me shatter.

I'm dragging the bed sheet everywhere, covering my nakedness, and I decide it's time for coffee. As I reach the threshold between Andrew's bedroom and the living room, I hear:

"Dec, it's not like that. Amanda's not one of those."

I freeze.

Declan? He's been shouting at Declan?

About *me*?

"Look, I know. I know." I hide myself, able to watch him pace across the stainless steel and granite kitchen, his body flickering between low-hanging ceiling lights that drape in regular intervals across a breakfast bar.

"And I won't. I won't hurt her this time." He swipes a frustrated hand through his bedhead hair, leaving locks standing straight up. He's agitated.

"I know she's Shannon's best friend—"

A string of loud, angry sounds comes through his phone. Even I can hear them, and my mouth curls up as I realize Declan is playing the part of the protective older brother.

But for me.

What did Shannon tell him?

"And this is not a one-night stand, Dec. She's still here."

The phone goes silent, and then I hear, quite distinctly:

"What?" The sound of Declan's voice roars out of Andrew's phone. "You've never had a woman stay over."

My whole body goes warm in a flush of radiance.

It's true.

This is a first for both of us.

"I know. That's what I mean. This is something different." Andrew's voice drops. "Don't worry."

Declan says something. Andrew's face tightens.

"Jesus, not this again, Dec. You and I have to agree to disagree. We all have our own risk levels we're comfortable with."

Declan says something I don't understand, and Andrew laughs.

"Right. I won't ruin your wedding. I promise." The sound of Andrew gets closer and I realize I can't be found hiding, so I move, acting as if I were just walking out.

He smiles at me, eyes combing over my body.

I walk past him to find two hot cups of coffee on the counter. I pick one up, then go to the fridge to find milk.

No milk.

The man has three beers, a lime, and a half gallon of orange juice in a fridge the size of an SUV.

I close the door and resign myself to drinking black coffee.

"Gotta go. Okay. Bye." Andrew ends the call and gives me a look I can't read.

"Everything fine?" I ask, blowing on the hot coffee and then taking a sip. I make a face. As much as I need the caffeine, black coffee is bitter.

"Yeah. Business stuff."

Liar.

"You drink your coffee black?" he asks, surprised.

"Actually, no. Your fridge looks like a frat boy lives here."

He laughs. "Yeah, I don't eat in much. How do you normally take your coffee?"

I take another sip of coffee. Then a full swallow. It's not so bad.

"A latte."

"Whole or skim?"

"I'm learning to like breves, actually."

He picks up his phone, types something, and puts it down.

We stand there.

Ah. So *this* is the awkward part.

"Want to go drink coffee on the balcony?" I ask. "It looks gorgeous outside."

A brief moment of panic flashes in his eyes, but he tamps it down so fast I'm not quite sure I ever saw it.

"You look great in a sheet," he says as I choke down more black coffee. He picks up his mug and downs half the liquid in one gulp. He doesn't move toward the balcony, but he doesn't acknowledge my question, either.

"It's my toga look."

"You're prettier without it."

I blush. I also just stand there, because I really don't know what to do next. He doesn't want to go outside, he's acting really strangely...

He decides for me, crossing the room and putting his arms around me. "Last night was amazing."

"Yes."

"And this morning was..." He lets out a puff of air. "Thank you." The kiss he gives me removes half the awkwardness.

But only half.

"I have a business trip," he says as he presses his forehead against mine. Coffee breath fills the space between us.

"Today?"

He nods. "I'll be gone for a week."

My stomach plummets with disappointment, but all say is, "Okay."

"I want to see you when I get back. I wish I could take you with me."

"I have to work." *And go out on dates*, I think. My face must betray my thoughts, because he gives me a questioning look.

I stay silent. No point in telling him I'll be going on six dates while he's gone, right?

"Next Saturday, though, you're mine."

His words give me a jolt no caffeine could ever manage.

"And for the next thirty minutes, too," he says, taking my hand and slowly walking me back to the bed.

Twenty minutes later, Andrew's had breakfast in bed, too. I am a boneless collection of well-satisfied flesh, and the door buzzer buzzes again.

I groan. Andrew gets up.

And returns with a breve latte someone must have just delivered.

"Now that's what I call breakfast in bed," I say as I snuggle against him.

"I liked your version better," he says, giving me a kiss.

By the time we shower and part ways, I realize I never did get a chance to go out on that beautiful balcony and take in the ocean air.

Oh, well.

There's always next time.

CHAPTER TWENTY

"You are sweating more than a woman in her third trimester of pregnancy in Texas in August."

"I can't help it if I'm a stress sweater!" Josh snaps back. "Some of you are stress eaters. I'm a stress perspirer."

"It makes you moist," I say, letting go of his hand. For the sake of this childbirth class mystery shop, we're supposed to pose as a happy couple. Hard to do that when you're holding hands with a gay man whose palm feels like a wet diaper.

"Don't say 'moist.' I hate that word."

It took nearly a month, but the childbirth class evaluation is in full force. Josh and I have to attend two of these four-hour classes here at the hospital with a birthing center attached, which means we get the most "natural birth"-oriented class in the city. Andrew is out of town—again—and I haven't seen him for over a week.

Again.

That night he turned off his phone was the longest stretch of uninterrupted time I've had with him since we started dating. He's supposed to come home today for some board meeting, but so far I haven't heard from him since he boarded the company jet this morning.

Which means I'm cranky.

"Moist," I hiss at my fake baby daddy. I am waddling down the hallway to the media room where our hypnotic childbirth class will be held. Josh looks like he's afraid a giant vagina with teeth is lurking behind every corner, ready to jump out and eat him.

"Is this the right room?" he asks as we stop in front of the clearly-marked Hypnotic Childbirth class sign. His hand is over his eyes as he peeks out between fingers.

"It's not like we're watching *It Follows* or *Friday the Thirteenth*, for goodness sake," I hiss. "It's just the miracle of birth. And no one is going to ambush you with a beaver in the hallway."

He wipes his inner elbow across his brow. "I'm sorry, Amanda," he grouses. "We're not all perfect little mystery shoppers like you. Frankly, this is freaking me out beyond belief and I really wish Greg could have done this with you."

"Greg? As the father of my baby?" I caress the baby bump I'm wearing. It's a weighted pillow underneath a maternity dress, with a layer of loose Spanx between the two. My hips widen as if I'm really pregnant, and I find myself waddling slightly. While I have a few friends from high school who have kids already, for the most part I'm surrounded by twentysomething and early thirtysomething friends and colleagues who remain childless so far.

Other than Jeffrey and Tyler, I don't spend time with kids. And no babies. So walking into the conference room where we will sit for this four hour childbirth class catches me off guard, as a giant watercolor painting the size of the entire wall hits me square in the face.

It's an enormous, layered labia with a red rose coming out of the vagina.

"Oooo, Georgia O'Keeffe!" Josh exclaims, stopping short. His hand is on my elbow now. There's a male possessiveness to the gesture that gives me pause.

"That's not a flower," I whisper. The labia are various shades of beige and mauve, with irregular lines that—

"Oh, my God," Josh gasps, his grasp tightening. "Is that a vag? It's the size of a Transformer."

"It's the newest female Transformer," I whisper. "Vulvatron."

"But what does it transform *into*?" Josh asks, whimpering as he puts his hand over his mouth and grips my arm.

"Do you like the painting?" says a cloud of patchouli oil. "It's one of mine."

We turn and look to our left to find the last hippie in all of Boston. No, really. She looks like someone age-lapsed a picture of one of the flower children at Woodstock and handed her a plastic baby doll with a...pelvis?

"Hi. I'm Sunny." She reaches out to shake Josh's hand. "Congratulations on your blessing."

Her smile is radiant as Josh lets go of my elbow and shakes her hand. "I'm Josh. This is Amanda. My, uh, wife."

That just sounds creepy now.

He puts his arm around my shoulder and looks at the wall labia with enormous eyes. "That's quite a display."

"Pussies usually are," she says, reaching to shake my hand. "So powerful. So divine. So innately in tune with the essence of life and the spirit of oneness."

I've read the Hypnotic Childbirth manual in preparation for this mystery shop, and while I know that the program encourages couples and teachers to use "natural" language, this takes me by surprise.

"P—P—P..." Josh sputters.

"Marie calls it 'Chuckles'," I whisper to him.

187

"That really doesn't help," he hisses back. "Now I won't ever be able to look at that stupid cat without thinking about—" he flails his hands toward the painting "—that."

"It looks like everyone is here," Sunny announces, holding up a clipboard. "My hospital board corporate overlords insist I take attendance." No one laughs except for Sunny, who thinks her own joke is hilarious.

I realize that underneath the patchouli there is a distinct scent of something a little greener.

"We might have some mild interruptions from a big tour going on with the mucky mucks," she adds as she briefly goes through calling out our names. She waves toward the window to the hallway. "Hospital donors. Something about a new cancer wing."

We all turn to see a janitor pushing a mop bucket along.

"If they pop in here, just moan like we're pretending to do controlled breathing for contractions and they'll go away," she says, drawing titters from the crowd.

"Please have a seat," Sunny instructs us. I look around. There are no seats. Only backjacks, like at a meditation retreat, and a giant pile of pillows in the same shades as the labia on the wall.

"Partners, take a seat at the backjack. Mamas, grab as many pillows as you need to get comfy and sit between your partners' legs." I dutifully grab a pillow as I watch four other mamas in various states of pregnancy waddle over and grab four or five pillows.

Josh snickers. "This'll be the first time I've had a woman between my legs."

I whack him with the pillow.

"That's right," Sunny says dreamily. "This is all about fun. You had fun putting the baby in there, and we're gonna make sure you have fun getting the baby out. It's all a dance, people." She shimmies her hips. "We're dancing that baby out."

Josh looks up at me, his back nestled against the backjack, his legs scissored open like he's taking a yoga class and starting to stretch.

I look around the room. There are a total of five couples. One lesbian couple, and four pairs of one man, one woman.

I climb between his legs and as I bend, my pregnancy pillow shoves up between my breasts.

"Breastfeeding comes *after* you've given birth," Josh hisses.

I turn toward him and hide my wardrobe malfunction, reaching up under my skirt to pull the pillow down. As I get it back in place and pull my arm out, I lose my balance and fall face-first into his crotch.

"I know I need to be a convincing hetero here, but you're taking this a little too far, Amanda!"

I scramble up—to the extent that you can scramble with fifteen pounds of pillow attached to your belly— and as I turn around, I see a wall of suits in the window. Must be the mucky muck tour. As I straighten my dress and prepare to sit down, I make eye contact with a man in the crowd.

It's Andrew.

Who looks right at my belly.

And smiles.

"Sometimes the universe works in mysterious ways," Sunny says, opening the class. "We can't know what the divine goddess is thinking when she sends messages our way. All we can do is enjoy the journey."

Andrew looks at me and arches one eyebrow. Then he mouths the word "Work?"

I shrug.

He nods. The suits go by en masse, like a pack of gazelles.

I hold up my hand to my ear and pretend it's a phone.

He nods and turns away, talking to someone who looks like he belongs in a Fidelity Investments commercial.

Josh yanks my hand.

"Get between my legs," he murmurs. "We're supposed to be pretending."

"If a woman's between your legs, you're *definitely* pretending."

"Was that Andrew out there?" he asks, wrapping his moist arms around me. I lean back. Resting against his chest is like leaning back against a line of horizontal marshmallow roasting sticks.

"Do you have an ounce of body fat on you?"

"No!" he crows. "Thank Crossfit. Isn't it great?"

"You're about as comfortable to snuggle with as a croquet set."

"That's not what my boyfriends say!" he retorts, a little too loudly. One of the other dads gives him a funny look.

Josh kisses my temple and says loudly, "I love you, honey." He strokes my hair like he's petting a chinchilla, then reaches down to stroke my belly.

I shiver.

"You're a really bad actor."

"You're a really bad pregnant woman. I wouldn't trust you to raise a Sea Monkey."

"Let's go around the room and introduce ourselves, now that you're snuggled into the arms of your love muffin," Sunny announces.

Muffin. That's what Josh reminds me of. He's starting to shake, and he is about as soft as a hairless chihuahua.

"I'm Sunny. I've given birth three times and have two sons and a daughter. I had water births for all three, and my youngest was born in the ocean, with two dolphins as midwives."

"How do you get medical insurance to cover dolphins?" one of the expectant mothers asks. I snort, loving the sarcasm.

Everyone stares at me.

Oh. She wasn't joking.

Sunny just laughs and smiles beatifically at her. "It's your body. Your baby. You can give birth wherever and whenever you like."

"Can you get an epidural in the parking lot?" another expectant mother asks.

I can't tell if she's joking or not, so I don't laugh.

Everyone else giggles.

Andrew's in the window again. He waves. I swoon.

Josh kisses my temple again.

Andrew glowers.

Introductions are made and Sunny moves on to the always-present birth video. You know the kind. The video of the couple arriving at the hospital, the mother wearing makeup and feeling twinges that will soon erupt into controlled groans of intense concentration, the cries of joy, ending with a baby at the breast and the requisite Mylar balloon bouquets brought by happy grandparents.

At least, that's my understanding of birth from cable television reality shows.

The lights dim, and the movie starts.

"Why are we looking at someone's toupee?" Josh whispers at the opening frame.

"That's not a—"

"*Aieeee!*" Josh squeals as it becomes apparent we're looking at a crotch shot from 1973.

The frame changes and focuses on the silhouette of a very ripe, pregnant body, the woman wearing a diaphanous gown, her hair long and ribboned with white flowers.

If she weren't pregnant, she'd look like an ad for a douche product.

"Childbirth is as natural as time itself," the narrator declares.

"That makes no sense," Josh complains in a whisper. "Who writes the scripts for this shit?"

"You're going to blow our cover," I hiss. "You need to look like all the other partners."

Josh pretends he's a deer caught in headlights.

"Perfect."

"I love you, sweetie," he says in a stage whisper, kissing my temple again.

"You touch my belly with that moist hand and I will make you massage my feet," I declare.

Josh flinches. He hates feet. It's an anti-fetish for him.

A guy behind us taps Josh on the shoulder and says, with sympathy, "Pregnancy hormones are a bitch, dude."

Josh nods and returns his eyes to the movie just in time for the frame to change to an anatomy drawing of a woman's genitals.

Then a live-action picture of the same parts.

"Is it always so pink? And wet?" Josh asks under his breath. "Where does the wetness come from? Is it pee?"

"The *moist*ness, you mean?"

Now I'm just being mean. I blame all the fake pregnancy hormones.

"Stop saying moist!" He looks like he ate a bad peanut. "Why is it so wet?"

"The vulva?"

"The vagina."

"You're looking at the labia, the vulva, and the clitoris. The vagina is the tunnel where the baby comes out." I feel like a tour director on the Vagina Express. Greg does not pay me enough to provide sex education to co-workers. I should put out a tip can.

"Where, exactly, is the clitoris?" Josh questions.

"That's what *every* man asks."

"How in the hell am I supposed to know? I've never seen one of these," he bites back. "By choice." He wrinkles his nose. "And now I know why."

I snort. "As if penises are aesthetically pleasing."

He looks offended. "What's wrong with penises? Penises are awesome."

"They have two looks. Deflated fire hose or Washington Monument wearing a firefighter's hat. While they're certainly useful and sensual and exciting under the right circumstances, they're not exactly works of art."

Josh ponders that for a minute, chewing on the inside of his cheek. He tilts his head back and forth as if weighing out my words, then finally whispers in my ear. "I'll give you that."

"Shhhh," someone rasps from the back of the room.

We go silent.

Silence is pretty much the only rational response to what we watch for the next ten minutes as the video describes the process of the development of a baby from conception to birth.

"You can grow your own organs?" Josh whispers in my ear, his hot breath frantic and punctuated by weird little hitches. Is he on the verge of hyperventilating?

"Women can. Not men. Hah! Isn't that cool? The placenta gets built from my body. Breast milk, too."

"You realize you're not really pregnant, right? *You* didn't build a placenta from spare body parts and cells inside you. And it's an organ that just goes to waste after the baby's born."

"Unless you eat it," I say, distracted by the sight of a baby's foot pressing up against the thinly stretched wall of the mother's huge belly on screen.

"Eat *what*?"

"The placenta."

"People eat it?" he shrieks. "Isn't that a form of cannibalism?" His eyes search the perimeter of the room for available exits. "I had no idea how violent childbirth is!"

"Shhhh," Sunny says, her eyes glazed. "We'll talk about how to desiccate and eat the placenta later, after I teach perineal massage."

"What's a perineal?" Josh asks, suspicious.

"It's part of the woman's neck," I lie.

"Whew," he says, his shoulders relaxing. But he's still shaking, and now his arms are covered with a thin sheen of cold sweat.

He is the very definition of all the reasons the word *moist* is so disgusting.

"Would it kill these women to try a little with their appearance?" he whispers as we watch more of the video presentation.

"What?"

"I mean, look at them. No makeup. No toenail polish on those feet." He makes a sour face. "Hairy legs. Bushes that look like they spread chia seeds on their—" he waves his hands vaguely around the crotch area "—you know."

"Mons."

He shivers. "That word is worse than moist!"

"You expect women who are experiencing the most painful and athletic event of their life to put on *makeup*?"

He half shrugs. "Just saying. A pedicure or some eye shadow would at least show they tried. The poor baby's going to be born and mama will be in all the pictures looking like a Jersey Devil with an overdue mani pedi."

The slide changes to an image of a woman's legs spread wide, with a baby's head crowning.

"Oh, my lordy lord it's got hair teeth!" Josh screams. His eyes roll up the back of his head and *bam* —he's in a dead faint, falling on the floor and rolling on his side on the industrial carpet.

"He acts like he's never seen a vagina before in his life," one of the dad's murmurs. His words carry throughout the room, and all eyes are on me. "How could she be pregnant and he's never—"

"We're strict Mormons," I lie, grasping at straws.

All the expressions soften into understanding, as if *that* explains everything.

"He's bleeding!" someone gasps. I look at Josh's head and yes—he is.

The next few minutes are a blur of activity as the class teacher administers First Aid, someone is pulled in from the emergency room, and a nurse assures me that lots of husbands faint during class from nervousness, though "never quite this early in the lesson."

As Josh comes to, he looks around the room, wild and unfocused.

"Labia is a lovely name if it's a girl," he whispers, then faints again.

I like him better unconscious.

The wall of suits appear, because it's not enough to have my gay, unconscious co-worker who is my fake husband bleeding all over the floor of a conference room where a baby's head emerges from a woman's vagina and—ouch!—we see the evidence for why stitches have to happen after birth.

Let's throw in a few grey-haired CEOs and their bean counters. And one delightfully delicious CEO who has most definitely seen a vag before.

Mine.

"You have quite the track record with fake spouses," Andrew says quietly in my ear as people in the crowd either fret over Josh's prone body or murmur about liability issues.

Sunny lights a sage smudge stick and starts muttering something while waving the burning leaves over my "husband".

Andrew looks at my belly with a mixture of amusement and protectiveness. I want to touch him but I can't. He has, obviously, figured out the ruse. While I technically can't tell him that Josh and I are working, he clearly knows.

"Are you stalking me, Mr. McCormick?" I murmur, rubbing my pretend bump. "You appear in the most unusual moments in my life."

"I'm on the board of directors of the hospital, Ms. Warrick," he replies with a smile. "We're doing an annual walk through."

"I'm preparing for the most precious moment I never expected," I answer, giving him a wink.

He smothers a grin.

Sunny glides over. She smells like roasted chicken, which makes my tummy growl. I am eating for two after all.

Me and *Josh*. He's so green there's no way he'll be able to go out with me for dinner after this.

"Your husband is down for the count, I'm afraid," Sunny says sadly.

A warrior's cry erupts in the tiny room. We all turn toward the source of the sound.

A bloody baby's head emerges on screen. Sunny pauses the video right there, the frame frozen in graphic detail.

"The miracle of life," Sunny calls out. She claps her hands. "Let's resume class now that Amanda's husband is feeling better." I shiver at the words *Amanda's husband*.

"I'm not feeling better," Josh argues as two nurses help him stand.

"We're going to take him into the ER for a quick eval," one of them tells me.

"But Amanda needs a partner for the next lesson!" Sunny says with a loud, slow sigh. "Who will help her to make the clay molds of cervixes that we'll stretch open to welcome the baby?"

Josh retches violently as they lead him out the door.

"I guess I'll handle my cervix by myself," I say pleasantly to Sunny, who gives me a funny look.

"I can help you with your cervix," Andrew replies. He catches the eye of one of the receding suits and gestures that he's staying in the class.

"Don't you have evil corporate overlords to entertain?" I ask, trying desperately not to lunge at him and kiss him silly. After more than a week apart, I can feel the pulsing parts of me trying to attach to him like suckers on the ends of tentacles.

"Who are you?" Sunny asks Andrew.

Oh, boy.

"This is my, um...brother," I mumble.

Andrew's shoulders begin to shake with repressed laughter.

She gives him a once over, then looks at me. "I see the family resemblance."

What resemblance?

"Let's try to resume some semblance of normalcy," Sunny says, dimming the lights again and pressing Play on the video.

"I think that shark got jumped a while ago," I mutter. Andrew looks around the room, tugs up lightly on his trouser legs, and bends to sit on the floor.

He looks up at me with an expression of expectation.

"What are you doing?" I ask.

"Waiting for you to get between my legs." His hand is extended toward me. I take it and bend down.

My fake pregnant belly goes right up between my breasts again.

"Now there's a look," Andrew says, staring at my boobs.

"Pregnancy does strange things to a woman's body."

"I heard that breasts get bigger, but this is something *else*."

I reach under my skirt—again—to pull the belly back in place.

A warm, helping palm slides up my leg.

"Excuse me?"

"I'm assisting you. Remember? I'm your birthing partner."

"I'm not birthing anything right now."

"Just practicing." He gives me a hotter-than-hot smile.

"Practicing what? The childbirth part or the conception part?"

"I get a choice? Because I pick conception without the conception."

"Then that's not conception. It's just sex."

"You're on to something there, Amanda. What a good student you are. Quick study."

As I nestle in his arms, belly back where it belongs, his hand rests on my outer thigh. When I lean back against his chest, it's a thick, warm wall of *ahhhhhh*.

"You have body fat," I murmur as we watch a gooey baby being placed on a mother's flaccid belly and crawl up, in search of a nipple. The scene reminds me of that one time I had sex with this really weird guy I met on Craigslist....

"I do." An appreciative palm gives my thigh a squeeze. "So do you, in all the luscious places."

"I thought she said he was her brother," one of the women behind me hisses. "Why's his hand up her skirt?"

"Ewww," her husband grunts.

Andrew reluctantly removes his hand and sighs. Warm breath that smells like coffee and spices tickles my ear.

The video shows a woman latching the baby to her breast, a look of blissful contentment on her face. As the camera pans out, we see a doctor merrily stitching away at her torn bits, using a needle the size of an aluminum baseball bat with a meat hook at the end.

At least, that's how my panicked brain views it.

All of the women in the room collectively gasp and bring our knees together.

"Don't worry!" Sunny says cheerfully. "That won't happen to you! Daily perineal massage for months before birth will make you stretch to fit anything in there."

"What if she already had to stretch to fit anything in there to make the conception possible?" one of the dads jokes.

"Like a turkey baster," the lone lesbian partner cracks.

"Perineal massage?" Andrew whispers. "Is that what they call it? I just call it foreplay."

And I'm moist.

He stays right there, cocooning me from behind, his hands roaming over my pretend belly.

"You ever think about having kids?" he asks.

A joke sticks in my throat. I have to swallow twice before I can speak.

"Yes," I say.

"Yes, you've thought about it, or yes, you want them?"

"Both. I want them."

I can feel his smile against my cheek and earlobe.

"How about you?" I ask in a hushed tone.

"Me, too. Not for a little while, but yeah. Some day." He cups my pregnancy pillow and lovingly pats it.

And just like that, I fall even more in love with my fake brother.

* * *

I'm walking down the sidewalk through Faneuil Hall in downtown Boston. Street performers juggle on stilts, crowds surrounding them, errant children clapping and running up to throw dollar bills in open music cases. The sky glows as if it's daylight and yet it's not. A dark chill in the air, a smoky mist that billows and blanks out the rest of the city, makes it clear that nighttime prevails.

The scent of freshly-made caramel corn and sour beer fills my nose, and I'm walking, step by step, looking up at the faces of moms and dads, of street people and college students, of people I don't know.

They all ignore me. I smile harder.

A shriek. A sigh. A raucous laugh. A baby crying. All the sounds pop in and out of the glow and the smoke, as if playing a symphony with the human voice as instruments, following a music score I can't read.

I stumble slightly on cobblestone, grabbing the corner of a produce cart for support. It is laden with melons and apples, cucumbers and oranges, fresh fruits from the Haymarket stands nearby.

As I look down to catch my footing, I see I'm naked.

Completely nude.

The chill of the night runs up my spine like a mouse escaping a predator, tiny claws making their way from the small of my back to the top of my head. I can't shout. Can't move. Can't bear to do anything that might draw attention to me.

And so I freeze in the center of everything that glows and obscures, my heart receding as if it, too, wants to fade away to nothing so it can't be seen.

A police siren begins, abrupt and alarming, as if a cruiser hid in the shadows behind the crowd and suddenly flipped a switch.

Instead of turning toward the source of the sound, every single person in the crowd looks at me.

I look down at my chest.

My heart is a red, screaming glow, calling out for a kind of help I don't have words to ask for.

Andrew's apartment door buzzes and I sit up, whacking my half-asleep head against a cantaloupe.

"Shit!" shouts the melon.

Oh. That's not a piece of produce.

The dream lingers, my hand on my chest where the bright red glow of my shrieking heart just was moments ago. I feel my breasts with frantic palms, fingers sliding into the grooves between my ribs, solid and warm but not on fire. The crowd's eyes are not on me. There are no street performers.

It was, as always, just a dream.

I'm in Andrew's bed and he's rubbing his eye socket, squinting at me like a pirate through a white tunnel made of cotton.

I'm under the covers and disoriented. How in the hell do baby kangaroos instinctively find their way out of the birth canal into the mama's pouch when I can't disentangle myself from a simple bed sheet?

Andrew's naked ass walks away, his hand rubbing his head, by the time I extricate myself.

He comes back into the room wearing nothing, but carrying two lattes.

I enjoy the view.

"You answered the door like that?" I accept my morning treat with gratitude.

He leers at my naked chest. "They know to leave it outside the door now."

"You've done this *that* often?"

"Only with you." He winks.

"I'm honored."

"You should be." He gives me a puzzled look and brushes his fingers against the eyebrow I whacked. "You okay? Bad dream?"

I laugh through my nose, suddenly tongue-tied. "Just my usual. Naked in public nightmare."

"Ouch." He gives me a searching look, but one of companionship and acceptance. *It's okay*, that look says. *Take your time. I'll be here.*

The residue of the discomfort from that other world persists, like an oily sheen on my skin. I want to talk about anything but the dream, especially when I am, indeed, naked right now.

I look outside at the gorgeous spring day. "How about we have coffee outside on the balcony?"

His face goes blank. A pinprick sensation, a tingly sense that there is a misalignment in the room, washes over me.

"Let's just stay here in bed," he says in a clipped voice, avoiding my eyes.

I shove my hair out of my face and feel a thick thatch at the back of my head. This is no normal case of bedhead. This is, most firmly, sexhead, which is a physical manifestation of being well-thumped in ways where by *thumped*, I mean *fu*—

"I love how you look when I wake up next to you," he says, his eyes tipping down to look at the top of his coffee. Shyness is endearing on most men, but on Andrew, it damn near makes my heart implode.

I'm going to need more caffeine for this level of emotional engagement and nakedness combined at 7:07 a.m. Whatever weirdness I just felt fades instantly.

"I love waking up next to you, my fake brother."

His laughter carries across the room and out the open window, toward that family picture on his dresser.

"That felt a little porny if I'm your brother."

"As if creating a clay mold of my cervix last night in class wasn't inappropriate enough?"

"It certainly was interesting when that instructor took your cervix and shoved the plastic doll through it." He shudders as he drinks his coffee, his shoulders round and contoured, corded tendons popping out as he moves. I don't need Netflix.

I just need Andrewflix. Twenty-four seven. I could watch him all day.

I shudder, too. "She seemed way too enthusiastic about perineal massage."

His hand goes for my naked hip. "I don't know. I'm not sure you can ever be too excited about that part of a woman's anatomy."

"You have an endless supply of frat boy lines." I can't stop giggling. He joins me, his deep chuckles rippling on the air, weaving with my laughter to form a cloud of contentment that fills the room.

"What were you really doing at the hospital last night?" I ask. We didn't exactly, um, talk much last night after the childbirth class was over. In fact, I think my panties are still in the limo. Now that I have coffee and we've thoroughly reacquainted ourselves with every inch of each other's skin, it's time to turn to conversation.

"Board meeting."

"Sunny said something about a cancer wing."

He blinks fast, suddenly, and his neck tenses. "Right. Dad's donating to the hospital. Wants to help bring new technology to the cancer center."

"To help him?"

"To help everyone. He's always had his hand in smaller philanthropic causes, but for this one he wants to pour a ton of his personal fortune into the new wing."

"How do you feel about that?"

Andrew shrugs. "His money. His choice."

"I'm sorry. I shouldn't ask questions like this," I say, suddenly feeling like I've gone in the wrong direction.

"What?" He holds my hand. "No. Nothing wrong with talking."

"You seem closed off."

"I do?" He purses his lips, eyebrows tilting down in an expression that's not quite a frown. "I guess...I just don't talk to people like this. It's new."

"Like what?"

"Like a human being."

"You are one, you know."

His eyes light up with mischief, little flecks of amber shining in the sunlight. "I'll have to drive that out of me. Such a weakness."

The heavy moment is over. I take a big gulp of my coffee and stay quiet.

He squeezes my hand. "You can ask me anything, Amanda. No subject is off limits."

"Really?"

"Really. For instance, you could ask me about that family resemblance the instructor noticed last night—"

"Can we change the subject? You are *so* not my brother. Not even my fake brother. I'm an only child."

"Lucky." He drinks a big sip and looks at me. "You never had to compete for attention."

"Nope. Just me and my mom."

A shadow passes over his face. If I weren't staring at him, I'd have missed it.

"Right. For us, it was just the three sons and our dad and our tutors and his assistant, Grace."

"You mean Declan's assistant."

"She is now. But back then, she worked for Dad." Andrew's face goes wistful, the light stubble on his face the only manifestation of adulthood holding him back from looking like a teen as he remembers. "Grace was the one who helped keep us functioning after Mom died."

I look at the family picture. He looks at me.

"Have you seen that?"

I nod as I drink more coffee. A salty gust of wind lifts up and into the room, carrying my heart with it, lifting so high in my chest it seems to cry out as it bangs against its limits.

Crawling to the end of his bed, he stretches and grabs the frame, then settles next to me, holding it.

"She—" His voice cracks like a preteen's. Having him sit here, post night-time lovemaking, drinking coffee in bed while going into the very vulnerable center of his being is a gift. I want to spend the rest of my life just sitting next to him. Holding his hand. Drinking coffee.

Just *being*.

That feeling rolls through me with a resounding certainty that clears my mind.

"She what?" I ask, urging him on. This is like having a windowless room turn out to have an enormous skylight buried under three feet of snow that has just thawed.

"Nothing. Not important."

"It's important to me."

The fluttering of his eyelashes as emotions fight against each other within him makes me ache for what his life must be like on the inside. Andrew McCormick, CEO of Anterdec. He's a wheeler and dealer, the young CEO everyone is watching for his first big mis-step, eyes of the business world on him not in admiration but with a smirk, just waiting for him to screw up.

And here I am, in his bed, listening to him talk about missing his mom.

"She would have liked you." His hand crawls under the sheet, seeking mine again. The threaded pull of our ten fingers intertwined like roots makes me smile.

The stinging pain of unexpected tears and a protective tenderness towards him makes me inhale slowly, like discovering a new flower so beautiful you have to smell it.

"I'm sorry I never got to meet her."

He leans over and kisses my cheek, all while squeezing my hand. "Me, too."

The picture frame set aside, he reaches for my coffee and puts it on the end table, then slowly, sweetly, makes love to me as if I'm his entire world, as if eternity were an unending loop of all that is good and right in the world and each time our bodies connect, we create a new universe.

CHAPTER TWENTY-ONE

I think there is a checklist of Things You Do in a Relationship When You Live in Boston, and going to a Red Sox game at Fenway Park is one of them.

Except when you're dating a CEO and a near-billionaire, the experience is a wee bit different from the masses. I'm standing in a premium suite behind home plate, after spending an hour drinking beer and munching on little lobster and sushi bites. Andrew's company is hosting an event here for some investors in a new office building in the Financial District, and I'm arm candy.

I'm enjoying being arm candy. It's a new role for me.

We're here for a mid-afternoon day game. Being Andrew McCormick, we've come by limo, doorstep to doorstep, from the underground garage in his apartment building to a back door he walked through so quickly you would think he was on fire.

He is certainly in his element, dressed in a polo shirt and khaki casual trousers, wearing the requisite Red Sox cap. I am dressed in a too-tight V-neck Red Sox jersey that he gave me last night, especially for this event, and I'm learning something about myself as I make small talk with eight men who each are worth more than the Gross National Product of half the countries in the world.

I am pretty hot.

That sounds so braggy. I know. But coming from someone who has never based her self-worth on her looks, but rather on her ability to fix problems, this is new. Being with Andrew makes me feel attractive. Desirable. Worth the male gaze.

And this jersey he gave me is eating up gazes, all right. My boobs have never had so many conversations.

Most of them with Andrew himself.

He extracts himself from some scintillating talk about reinforced steel and snakes an arm around my waist.

"Nice shirt."

"Someone gave it to me."

"He has great taste."

"He doesn't know my size." I tug at the hem to cover my quarter inch of exposed belly. All that does is expose another half-inch of breast.

"Oh," he sighs, so hard I feel his hot breath on my cleavage. "He most certainly does."

"Game starts in ten minutes!" someone shouts.

"Ready to get to our seats?" he asks my breasts.

I touch his chin and make his eyes meet mine.

"They don't talk, you know."

"If they could, though, they'd say really nice things about me," he says with a smile. "That Andrew is so attentive." He pretends to be my breasts, his voice shifting into a falsetto. "He's so sweet. We wish Amanda would let him touch us more."

I hit him gently, right above his belt buckle.

"Oof."

"My breasts don't talk like that. They have a genteel southern accent."

He starts to put his ear on my cleavage. "This I have to hear."

I sprint for the door, knowing that only propriety stops him from hungry-handing my ass.

We wind our way up stairs to the pavilion suites, where a wall of glass faces the ball field. One of the men in the group lets out a low whistle. I join him.

Andrew whistles, too, but I don't think he's looking at the ball park.

"That is a view," I say.

"Sure is," he agrees, staring at my rack.

"Can that glass wall open up?" one of the men asks.

Andrew tenses and answers, "No. We're keeping it closed. It's too humid out there." While he's right that it's a nasty, swampy June day in Massachusetts, he's not telling the whole truth.

"The glass wall does open," I correct him. "This can become an open-air suite if we want."

Andrew's glare makes me feel like I've done something wrong, so I shut up instantly. My teeth snap together from the force of how fast I close my mouth. He doesn't even have to ask.

Suddenly, this shirt is all wrong. Being in this suite is intolerable. I can't be here. I give him a shaky smile and go back downstairs to grab my sweater, practically running. The suite is over air-conditioned anyhow, so I have my excuse if anyone wonders.

In the downstairs lounge, I give myself a few minutes to catch my breath.

What the hell just changed upstairs?

"Honey?" one of the female bartenders asks as she dries a fresh rack of washed glasses. "You okay? Those guys harassing you?" She gives me one of those looks that only two single women can give each other in a sports setting where alcohol is everywhere.

"I'm fine," I assure her. "Just, you know. My date is here with his clients and I needed a break."

Her eyebrow shoots up. "Andrew McCormick's your boyfriend?" She makes a *whew* sound. "Nice."

I smile. "Thanks." It definitely feels weird to hear someone call him my boyfriend. Andrew and I haven't had that conversation yet. I let it slide, because I can. He's nowhere nearby to overhear.

"Have fun. Not that you won't," she says with a wink. "You're living on a whole different plane of existence from the rest of us."

As I walk to the staircase, slipping my arms into my sweater, it hits me how true that is. I zip up the cardigan and square my shoulders, pasting on a smile.

The game opens just as I reach the suite, and all the men are lined up in their tall stools at a long counter, facing the glass wall. The room smells like freshly-popped popcorn and a burnt sugar scent. A quick glance at the counter reveals the source of that.

Caramel corn.

Andrew pats an empty chair next to him, on the end, with no one else next to me. "Saved you a seat." There's no trace of his earlier anger, which is a huge relief. As I settle in, he hands me a small cone of popcorn and we face the field.

Play ball.

As I look over the crowd at Fenway Park, an uneasy familiarity creeps over my skin. Andrew's hand is on my knee and he's avidly watching as the players get ready for the pitcher, the first inning about to open. Loud organ music pounds through the air, muted in here.

I've been here.

Not in this suite, but I've been here. At Fenway Park.

When Andrew asked me to this game, he questioned whether I'd attended a baseball game before. Other than once, in high school, I told him I had a vague memory of my mom bringing me to a game when I was really little. Or maybe my grandpa? I couldn't remember.

Suddenly, an image of myself as a tiny girl and the faint olfactory memory of peanuts transports me back two decades. My hand is in the warm clasp of a man's calloused palm, the back of his hand covered with black hair. He puts a baseball cap on my head and it's too big.

His laughter rumbles and he's hugging me, the vibration of his chest against my ear so loud. His breath is sour against my cheek. I look up to find his face surrounded by a halo of bright sunshine. I have to squint hard to see his face.

Crack!

One of the pitches hits the bat and the shortstop makes a long throw to first base, barely beating the runner. Everyone's on their feet, cheering.

The roar of the crowd.

A flash of sunlight and I'm blinded, except there is no sun outside right now. It's a partly cloudy day, with no chance of rain, and no bright orb in the sky.

What am I remembering?

"You okay?" Andrew asks, concern in his eyes as I drop my cone of popcorn, the pieces spilling over my leg. Except my leg is tiny, and I'm wearing a gingham dress. It's my favorite. It's the one I wore for my kindergarten school picture, with tiny pink flowers against a chocolate backdrop, and brown piping along the hem.

I look at Andrew and see my father's face.

"Mandy?" he says.

Except Andrew actually says, "Amanda."

No one has called me Mandy since I was five. Since my dad disappeared. That was my father's nickname

213

for me. My dad, though, never brought me to a baseball game.

I stand abruptly, shaking my head fast. "Uh, excuse me."

"Amanda," Andrew repeats. "What's going on? Are you sick?" He follows me to the doorway, his hand on my elbow. The gesture is protective and genuine. I'm worrying him.

I'm worrying *me*.

"I, um...can we just go for a walk?" I beg. The room closes in on me, even with the expansive view. The billboard flashes with numbers and videos. I can't blink hard enough to get clarity.

"Now?" If I were in a better frame of mind I would see the fear in his eyes. Not anger. Not disappointment.

Fear.

"Yeah. I'm having this weird memory about Fenway Park."

"From high school?"

I start to breathe through my nose in short little spurts. "No. Earlier."

He cocks his head and bends down. I can smell the popcorn he's been eating. "I thought you said you were maybe here with your mom or grandpa once."

"I thought so, too. But now I'm remembering coming here with my *dad*."

Shock registers in the way he moves. "Your father? But he abandoned you."

"Right. This memory...I don't know. I just need to go for a walk. I need fresh air. Please, Andrew? Please?"

Adrenaline pours through me like an overflowing bucket under a full-throttle faucet. I am nothing but one big, nauseated cell.

He looks over my head and outside, where the game is underway. His eyes scan the entire perimeter of the glass that faces the park.

Then he looks down at me.

Back up at the wall.

Down at me.

His face hardens. "I can't. This is an important client meeting. And besides," he adds, "you, um...photographers might be out there."

"Photographers?" What is he talking about? Who cares about my picture being taken?

My breathing quickens. If I don't get out of here, I'm going to pass out. Or vomit. Or just plain old die as my dad's face takes over, the backs of his hands covering his face, his sobs cutting through me like a razor blade as I pat him on the back and ask Daddy for more ice cream.

"Right," Andrew says quickly, his rapid-fire speech an anomaly, his eyes nervously bouncing across sights outside. "You know. *Boston Magazine*, media outlets. You don't really want—"

Wrenching my elbow away from him, I walk as fast as I can down the stairs, pounding down them until I find a door I can burst through, the scent of the outdoor air sickening as I find myself next to a short man with a beard, making balloon hats for a crowd of children.

Rushing past them, I round a corner and find myself on the sidewalk behind the park, where street vendors offer me Cuban sandwiches and Italian sausage.

Deep breath. Deep breath. Deep breath.

How can I have a memory of something that never actually happened?

Only one way to find out.

I call my mom.

As her phone rings, I look toward the building, praying Andrew will follow. Yes, I ran away. Yes, I broke contact. But I need someone right now, because I am about as out of my own head and body as a person can get, and this feels suspiciously like I'm going a little—or a lot—insane.

"Hello?"

"Mom?"

"What's wrong, Amanda?" she asks with alarm.

It's that obvious, huh?

"Did my dad ever bring me to a baseball game at Fenway Park when I was little?" My words come out in gasps and half-chokes, cracked in two like an egg just before the whites spit on the griddle in bubbling oil.

"What?" she gasps. "*What?*"

I find a tiny patch of grass next to the curb and sink to the ground, my forehead pressing into my knee.

"Mom? I'm here at a game with Andrew and I keep seeing my dad. In my mind. Like we were in the stands watching a game. He put a baseball cap on my head."

"Oh, sweetie," she says through a voice so thick it feels like it's coming across twenty years of pain. "Oh, Amanda. I thought you'd forgotten."

"Forgotten? I really *was* here once with him?" A blast of relief counteracts all my fear. I'm not crazy. I'm not unraveling. I'm not insane.

I look down the street toward the back of the building.

Still no Andrew.

"Mom?" She's gone silent.

"Yes, sweetie," she says reluctantly. "You were."

"Oh," I say, the sound coming out in waves, like it's seven syllables, the same on repeat. "Oh, thank God. I'm not crazy. This is a real memory."

"It is." She's breathing slowly. Too slowly. Mom defaults to deep breaths when she has to control her pain. I hope I haven't triggered any.

"Why don't I remember it all?" I ask. "Just bits and pieces."

"Do you remember anything more than the game?"

I close my eyes and try. All I see is a void.

"No."

"Okay." She lets out a long sigh.

"Why? What else happened?"

My phone buzzes. I'm sure it's a text from Andrew, who is probably trying to figure out where the hell I am.

"Can you hop the Green Line? Come home now? Or grab a cab?"

"I can do any of those, but I'm here with Andrew and he's going to wonder."

"Is he still entertaining clients?"

"Yes."

"Then text him. Tell him you need a couple hours. Then go back to him. We need to talk."

I just blink as I stare across the street at the graffiti.

"Talk?"

"Honey, you're remembering the very last day you ever saw your dad. Let's just say it was the worst day of my life, and probably one of the worst of yours, even if you don't remember everything."

I look around wildly. Where is Andrew? Why didn't he follow?

"Okay."

"I'd feel better if we talked in person. I can come get you."

"No, I can get a ride. I'll be home soon, Mom."

I end the call and pull up a ride share app. Estimated time for pick up: two minutes.

Then I check my texts, expecting one from Andrew. Instead, it's a text from Marie:

Chuckles doesn't have balls, so no worries about lotion for him.

I click out of the text function and stand, then turn the text feature back on as the driver appears. I climb in. He has my address from the app and we speed off. I look back one last time.

No Andrew.

As a courtesy I type out a short text to him.

Got sick. Went home. Talk later.

I press Send and then turn off my phone completely.

When I arrive at home, Mom's in the door, hovering behind the screen. The shadow of her body shows her shoulders tight, her eyebrows high, face a mask of pain and despair.

I hate knowing that I've triggered her pain.

"You want coffee?" We walk into the kitchen, her arm around my waist. I'm taller than her, and ever since her car accident this is how it is. She can't reach up very high without pinching a nerve in her neck. I'm grateful for the affection and take what I can get, leaning into the half hug.

On the counter there is a tray of Cheeto marshmallow treats. I look at her fingernails.

They're stained orange.

My eyes fill to the point of near blindness. "Mom? What's going on?"

"Where's Andrew?"

Half an answer suffices for most people. It's startling how much you can get away with when you learn this. "He's back at Fenway, entertaining his investors still."

"Oh." Her eyes bounce from the tray of treats to the coffee she just poured to me. "Okay."

I grab milk from the fridge, my eyes blurred by hands acting from physical memory, and prepare my coffee. She takes a splash of milk as well.

"Tell me," I ask. It's not an order.

"I don't want to make it bigger than it is, Man—Amanda."

"You haven't called me Mandy in years, Mom. That's what Dad called me."

"I know." Her voice is contrite. Why?

"Make *what* bigger?"

"The day your father abandoned you."

"Why would you make it bigger?"

She sighs and uses a spatula to dig out two pieces of Cheeto treat, munching on one as she hands me mine. I take a relieved bite, the familiar salty-sweet taste so comforting.

"Do you remember the police station?" she whispers, the question stripped down to such a basic handful of words that it dawns on me: Mom knows the trick of giving half the information needed, too.

"Police station?" I lower my brow, trying to understand what she means. Stuffing my face with another bite, I mumble around the mouthful. "What police station?"

"The one you found that day. In South Boston." She's handing out pieces of information like I'm—

And then *wham!* The entire memory floods me at once, like torn pieces of a watercolor all whirling together in a wind tunnel, my fingers grasping and reaching to gather them all until the wind dies down and I can assemble the whole.

I inhale so sharply that a piece of the treat lodges in the back of my throat, making me choke. I cough it up immediately, but the ragged edge leaves a stinging scrape along my tonsil. Mom hands me my coffee, which is just cool enough to gulp, helping to quell the pain.

My mind, meanwhile, is like a memory factory, taking pieces along an assembly line and playing Tetris.

"I do remember being in a police station," I say. "The police officer gave me a Dr. Pepper. I remember because you never let me have soda and he asked me if I wanted something from the machine. I thought I was being very naughty, but you also taught me that police officers were good people, so I decided it was okay."

She makes a barking sound like laughter and tears competing to emerge from her throat.

"You remember that," she gasps. "You were drinking it when you arrived."

"Did this have something to do with Dad? Did that all happen on the same..." My voice trails off as I remember long walks on the sidewalk. Feeling buried in the shadows of tall buildings. Being thirsty. Needing to pee. Tripping and skinning my knee.

Being alone.

"Same day." She reaches for my hand. "Yes."

"The same day." I haven't forgotten any of it. The word *forget* doesn't describe it. It's more like all the details have been stored in different shelves in my brain, disparate places that don't feel connected to each other.

"I went to the baseball game with my dad?"

"Yes."

"Was that the day he left for good?"

"Oh, yes."

"What *happened*, Mom?"

Her face crumples, hand covering her mouth. The long, thin veins on the back of her hand stand out in stark relief, making her seem so much older. Like grandma.

"He took you to the ball game. He had just been laid off. Drinking on the job. But he had tickets from some raffle he won at a bar, and he was determined to take you. Against my better judgment, I let him. We didn't have money to buy a third ticket, and you were so excited."

An eerie calm descends over the kitchen. I stop chewing. It sounds cavernous in the silence.

"We didn't have cell phones back then. I mean, some people did, but we sure didn't." She makes a scoffing sound. "Your father drank away all the extra we had."

"He was a good man, Mandy." My skin crawls with her use of the old nickname. "He tried. But he had his own demons, and after seven years together I think they just ate him up alive."

She's rambling, and I let her, because this is the most I've ever heard about my father from her in years. My grandma has pieced together some of it for me, but when every third word out of her mouth is *bastard* it's kind of hard to get a sense of anything beyond the worst.

"He got drunk at the game. Leo probably got drunk before he even left with you," she says in a bitter tone I don't hear often. "But at the game I'll bet he was a big spender. Bought you anything you wanted."

I remember popcorn. The baseball hat. An ice cream.

"I guess?"

"Here's what we reconstructed from you, the police, and the short time Leo was here," Mom starts.

Reconstructed?

"Your dad got drunk. You left the game. Some time between the game ending and the time we found you —"

Found me?

"—your father got in the car without you, drove home drunk, and got into a crash."

I can't breathe.

"I got a call from a state trooper. That call. The one no one ever wants. Leo came out of the crash with a few scratches. The car was totaled. And when I asked about you—" Her voice just halts, the sob turning into a high-pitched sound that makes my mouth fill with the acrid taste of her buried fear.

"Mom?"

"Oh, that poor state trooper. When I asked about my little girl he screamed. *Screamed.* He was at the scene with Leo and all those men, all those firefighters and paramedics ran back to the scene and started combing the long grasses by the side of the road and roamed into the woods, searching."

"For me?"

Her eyes meet mine, red and wet, filled with the haunting of memory. "For your little body."

"My *body*?"

"Leo was too drunk to be coherent and I just cried and prayed into the phone. I thought you were with him. We didn't know that you weren't. Those poor men. They spent hours looking for you. Hours, expecting to find a little girl thrown from the car from the crash's impact."

The full horror of what she's saying hits me like I've been kicked in the chest.

"Oh, Mom." Her words sink in. "But I wasn't with dad?"

She shakes her head, her eyes glassy. "No. Sweet Jesus, no. Thank God, Mandy. We don't know how, but we think Leo just left you at Fenway Park. Maybe you went to tinkle, maybe you wandered off to get an ice cream. Maybe he walked away to get a beer for the road...we don't know. We just know that after hours of trying, those responders never found you. And then...."

"You—" She's clinging to the kitchen island with those hands, her fingertips white with pressure. "You had walked all the way from Fenway Park to some police station in South Boston. Hell of a distance. Back then, it wasn't safe. Southie was no place for a little kid alone. You had to cross that enormous bridge. The cop told us you walked in to the station and sweetly asked for help calling your mom. That you had lost your dad. You knew our phone number and he called and called, but it was busy."

"Busy?"

She sniffs and snorts and makes a funny laugh. "Yeah. Busy. Back then we didn't have call waiting for two lines and Leo and I sold the answering machine at a yard sale, so...yeah. Busy. The cop spent the next hour calling."

I'm remembering the nice police officer with the ginger hair and the wide brown eyes. His eyelashes were the color of my peach crayons in my box at school. His name tag flashes through my mind.

"Murphy. Officer Murphy."

She jumps like I shocked her.

"Holy shit. You *do* remember. I still send that man a Christmas card every year."

Mom doesn't curse. Ever.

"I remember how he gave me a second Dr. Pepper and told me my mom wouldn't yell at me for it. How he talked to the other officers and they kept looking at me. Then one of them grabbed his hat and took off, then came back. And how Officer Murphy said we were going for a ride in a police car. That was really cool."

Mom slowly drops to the floor, her back against the kitchen cabinet under the sink. Twilight's descending and the change from the sun's disappearance gives the room a kind of faerie light that makes me feel like a child.

I hold her hand. She clings to it like a lifeline.

"That man—that beautiful man—put two and two together and brought you home." Her throat is jumping in spasms and she's sniffing. I pull the hem of my shirt out and wipe her eyes. She doesn't move, just sits there, shoulders shaking. "He kept it quiet. Pulled the police cruiser over a half block from home and just walked you up. Kept it calm."

She takes in a hitched series of breaths, then lets it all out. "That moment is etched in my mind forever, Amanda. I had just started to force myself to assume you were dead."

I reach out and hold her. She holds me right back. I'm not sure how long we both just sob, but it feels like hours.

Finally, I break the silence.

"But I wasn't."

"No. You weren't. You later told us that when you couldn't find your dad, you decided to start walking until you found a police officer. You ended up taking an alley away from all the traffic. One different turn and you'd have found a cop right away. You headed for the Financial District and...just kept going. I guess. That's how we reconstructed it all."

I just nod. That's how I remember it.

Minus the whole car accident part.

"What about dad?"

"Your father? Your fuckin' fathah." Mom's Revere accent comes roaring out of her. She's smoothed it out over the years, but I've heard it leak through in times of extreme anger. "When he sobered up, we still hadn't found you. I said...some things."

"I'd have said them, too."

"Told him he'd killed you."

"Jesus."

"And the cops took him away. He was booked with a DUI and when you came home, child services got involved. They interviewed you at school and me here at home but Leo...Leo disappeared."

"He just left?"

She nods.

Reconstructed, indeed.

"I don't...Mom, I had no idea all this happened. I remember parts of the baseball game and walking around Boston. It was an adventure. I felt like the little kids in that book. The one where they live in New York at the museums for fun. *From The Mixed Up Files of Mrs. Basil E. Frankenweiler*. I was just fine and all I needed was a police officer and I'd find my way home. I remember being pretty proud of myself for figuring it all out. The Dr. Peppers were a bonus."

We share a laugh. It feels good.

"That's how I wanted it. You were always such a smart little girl. Unflappable. The counselor at your school and the lady from children's services said you didn't need to know. About the car accident. And I just told you Leo went out to get some beer and didn't come back. Which was probably true." She buries her head in her arms, which are resting on her knees.

"You hid me from all that."

"I thought it was best. I didn't know. You're my one and only, kiddo. I'm not an expert in this parenting stuff. We all start out completely clueless and..." She laughs, the sound buried by sadness. "And we stay clueless."

I understand so much now. Why Mom worries when I don't check in. How she was such a hovermother for so long. What it must have done to her emotionally and psychologically to go through an alcoholic husband and the horror of thinking I was dead.

Why she's always been so obsessive-compulsive about controlling so much of our life.

"Did my dad ever find out I was alive?"

She looks at me. Her eyes narrow, brown triangles of deliberation.

"You tell me, Amanda," she whispers.

My turn to share something she only knows bits and pieces of.

"He came to my school. Once. When I was in second grade."

Her shoulders slump. "I thought so."

"He stood on the other side of the chainlink fence. He cried, Mom. Said I was beautiful and he was sorry and that he'd make it up to me some day. My teacher came over to see why I was talking to a strange man and he ran away."

"She told me." Mom uses the hem of her own shirt to wipe her face now. There's more I could say, but I can feel her limit. Pain radiates from her limbs like love in twisted form. I'm not adding to that right now.

I stand. My knees pop. I reach down to offer her a hand and as she lifts up, she groans with pain.

"I'll regret sitting like that in the morning."

The front screen door opens. A man's voice calls out. "Hello?"

Andrew.

He did follow, after all.

I wonder what he thinks when he walks into the kitchen to find two orange-stained-finger women crying their eyes out in the darkness. Whatever his internal reaction, on the outside he's polite. Concerned. Downright courtly.

"I've been calling and texting for the past few hours. Are you okay?" He crosses the room and stops a few feet in front of me. His eyes take in my mom. Then me.

Then the tray of Cheeto treats.

Mom smooths her hands on her slacks and gives me a hopeful smile. "I'll leave you two alone," she says, grabbing me for a very tight hug.

"No, Mom. I—"

She looks at Andrew, then at me, then back at Andrew. "Glad you're here," she says to him. "Amanda needs someone right now."

"Mom, but—"

"It's all old territory for me, honey. But it's new for you." And with that she steps out of the kitchen, leaving me with a very perplexed Andrew.

"What's going on?" he asks in a voice filled with grave alarm. His tone drops down to a low, sedate level.

I tell him. The whole story, from the moment in the pavilion suite until just now, right before he came in the house.

I spill it all in one long, crazy ramble. It's the kind of story I'll have to tell many times going forward, so the telling from start to finish feels good in its own odd way.

By the time I'm done, we're standing in complete darkness, the only light peeping in from other rooms in the house and digital clock displays on appliances in the kitchen. We're bathed in a strange greenish glow.

"That's one hell of a story." He exhales as if he's been holding his breath. "I'm so sorry I didn't understand earlier."

"It's fine." It isn't. Not really. But I don't know what else I can say.

"I'm here now." He opens his arms wide and I walk into them, my drained eyes resting against the soft fabric of his fleece top.

"You know what's funny?"

"What?"

"Those naked-in-public dreams I have?"

"Yeah?"

"They started when I was five. Now I know why."

He squeezes me tighter. "Oh, Amanda." He gives me a soft kiss on the temple and moves me, slowly, to an oversized chair in the living room. It's the one mom used to sit in with me when I was little and we'd read picture books from the library, one after the other from a big basket she always kept next to the fireplace.

Andrew sits down and pulls me into his lap. I curl up, my cheek pressed against his heart. His breath is my anchor.

I cry for everything I didn't know I'd lost and gained until I fall asleep in his arms.

And do not dream.

CHAPTER TWENTY-TWO

The man sitting across from me at this lovely bistro is remarkably normal. Better than normal, in fact. He's downright *hot*.

"What is someone like you doing using an online dating service like this?" Chris asks, bringing his beer to his lips. We're in a brew pub, with little wooden boards containing six little glasses of beer samplers. So far, we've determined we have the same taste in brew choices.

Dark and hoppy.

On this, my ninth DoggieDate date, I have found the Holy Grail of men: a decent one. A better-than-decent one.

A guy I, Amanda Warrick, for real, would actually date.

Lord have mercy.

Chris Stieg is taller than me, with the slim, toned look of a tech guy, which he is. He's the lead architect for some new publishing technology that analyzes books to track narrative arcs and reader engagement.

The man has read Italo Calvino.

And Jennifer Weiner.

Avant-garde lit fic *and* commercial fiction? He's someone's wet book dream.

Maybe even mine.

Don't get me wrong—I'm technically still dating Andrew. But after that weird blip at the baseball game, and after he finally found me at home that night, things have been bumpy. He's been in Tokyo for a week and our texts have been erratic. Falling asleep in his arms in my comfy chair in the living room was wonderful.

But I had awoken alone in the daylight, in my own bed, with a text that simply read: *See you soon*.

Mr. Hot and Cold is blowing more chilly arctic air these days, and it's killing me.

Besides, this is a DoggieDate date. It's for work. I'm just doing my job.

Is it my fault that some days I love my job more than others?

"I, well, you know. It's not like Tinder or Ashley Madison are my speed," I reply.

Chris laughs, throwing his head back just enough for me to take in the golden blonde hair. He wears glasses and has these sweet eyes the color of honey lager.

"Let me guess. Loads of disgusting come-ons from guys who think that crap works."

"I have quite the collection of unwanted dick pics."

He chokes through his laughter.

"And all I did was send you a picture of my dog," he says with a smile that reaches those warm eyes.

The beer is loosening me up. I lean back and stretch, pushing my breasts out inadvertently. Chris is too much of a gentleman to look. We're seated right by the big, plate-glass window along the sidewalk. Outside, the streets are filled with people straggling back from an art-in-the-city festival.

Chris reaches across the table as I go to taste another sample, and our hands bump.

"I'm grateful for that. Snoozer is a real cutie, by the way. I love affenpinschers," I say.

Chris smiles, looking down at our hands, which are an inch away.

And then a rush of memory hits me, of Andrew and I naked in bed.

Heat runs from my belly to my mouth like a brushfire. I hastily grab the final glass of beer from the taster board and chug it.

Chris's eyebrows shoot up. "That good?"

I realize my mistake. We're sharing this, to decide which pints to buy. "Oh. Um, I'm so sorry." I look at the empty glass and make a face. "It actually wasn't."

"You saved me from bad beer. Friends don't let friends drink bad beer."

"Then I had some really bad friends back in college."

He laughs, and I see him watching my hand. Oh, boy. He's sending all the good signals now.

When Greg informed me I was perfect for the DoggieDate account, I figured I would slog through twenty insufferable dates with weirdos who use a site like DoggieDate for a reason. Because they're weirdos.

I never—not once—thought I'd meet an actual hot guy who I'd *want* to date.

And here I am.

Andrew.

His name slides through my mind with an echo of need. My eyes take in Chris as the waiter comes over and he orders pints for us, picking our two professed favorites. I could date him. Kiss him. Maybe even sleep with him.

There really are plenty of fish in the sea after all.

Too bad the fish I want is in Tokyo right now.

I have a choice here. If I'd met Chris on the very first DoggieDate, life might be very different.

Then it hits me.

I don't want different.

I want *Andrew.*

At that precise moment, warm fingers take my hand. That zing? The one you're supposed to feel the first time you experience affection from someone you're getting to know romantically?

It's not there. Holding hands with Chris is nice. It's comfortable and sweet, and as I look up and meet his eyes and smile, I remember that I am playing a role here. We're supposed to be talking about our dogs and bonding over my teacup chihuahua and his little affen puppy.

"What's Snoozer like?" I ask, bringing this back to my actual job requirements. The mystery shopping evaluation form has been taking shape slowly as I go through enough of these dates to start to form an idea of what we need to evaluate in terms of customer service and client experience.

Chris gets an uncomfortable look on his face. His eyes drop to my boobs. I'm wearing a shirt that could pass muster in a convent, so I'm not sure what he thinks he's actually looking at.

"I have a confession to make," he says in a sheepish voice, squeezing my hand. I have to lean forward slightly to hear him.

Outside, cabs stop and go, dropping off and picking up customers right outside the window. The brew pub takes up nearly half a block in this trendy neighborhood, and it's a bustling area that's gentrifying. Enormous old factories are being renovated into new lofts, hotels, and business spaces. I'm guessing the brew pub has two to three years, tops, at this location, before the rent increases drive them away.

"I, um..." Chris stumbles, then sits back with a long sigh, letting go of my hand. The waiter brings our pints and we clink glasses, then each chug about half our respective beers. I fight back a belch.

Chris leans forward again and puts his palm on my shoulder. Our faces are half a foot apart.

"Are you okay? Is something wrong with Snoozer?" I've learned to direct all the attention to talk about the dogs whenever anything gets strange on these dates. Works like a charm.

"No, no. Nothing's wrong with him. Actually, though," he says, leaning in another inch. "This is about Snoozer. He, um, he's not my dog."

I press my lips together and frown. "Huh?"

"I don't actually have a dog."

"You don't?" My voice contains a little more glee than it should, because I predicted this exact scenario when I spoke with the client. I said there would be fakers, and my God, here we are. The thrill of being right mixes with the beer, which I grab and finish off with a flourish.

"No. I just invented him so I could join this dating service," he says as he gets closer. Any closer and my eyes will cross to a blur.

But just then, he freezes.

"Don't look," he whispers, "but there's a creepy guy outside staring right at you."

I turn and look in defiance of his order and—

Andrew McCormick is standing three feet away, his limo behind him.

And if looks really could kill, Chris would be dead right now.

Chris pulls back and gives me a menacing stare. "You know him? Because—"

I'm on my feet, throwing the napkin down before he can finish. "Hang on," is all I say as I fly through the warehouse-style restaurant, the enormous painted duct work above me, metal ceiling fans dropped along thick wires that lend the place the feel of a hipster brew pub.

I run out the door and find Andrew exactly where he was seconds ago, his hands in his suit trouser pockets, his face a grim scowl.

Directed entirely at Chris.

"What are you doing here?" I cry out, fighting twin urges to smack him and hug him.

"Interrupting something, apparently," he answers, eyes staying on Chris, who has pulled out his phone and has a bad case of self-invoked text neck as he pretends to ignore Andrew's ire.

"No, I mean, aren't you in Tokyo?"

"I came back early."

"What are you doing *here*? In this part of town? Did you come to find me? Are you stalking me?"

His nose pugs up, jaw tight, like he's trying hard not to let his temper fly. He still won't look at me. "Gerald had to take the limo on a detour. We were stuck at the light. I looked out the window to see you on your...." He clears his throat like he's eaten a bug. "Date."

I'm stuck.

I can't tell him the truth. I just can't. And technically, we're not exclusive. He's sending me mixed signals and if this were a real date, that would be fine. He has no claim on me. We're not—

"Is he your boyfriend?" Andrew asks, eyes narrowing as he stares at Chris.

"What? Him? No. First date."

"Why?"

"Why what?"

"Why are you dating?"

"Because I can?"

"No, you can't."

"Excuse me? I most certainly can."

"Do you want to?"

"Want to what?"

"Date other men."

I open my mouth to answer and stop mid-movement, eyes blinking. The cool night air dries out my mouth quickly, and with my hammering heart and beer-soaked blood, I realize that everything in me is screaming:

"No."

"Then why?"

"Because you haven't given me a reason not to."

Okay, technically, that's not true, either. But knowing how competitive Andrew is, and being stuck in this absolutely, utterly impossible horror of a situation with three brain cells left for making decisions, it's the best I can come up with on the fly.

Suddenly, his mouth is on me, slanted against mine, tongue ravaging and claiming. This is no welcome kiss, no soft *hi there* after a week apart. The rough push of his lips, scruffy with a day's growth of beard, will leave my mouth raw with the demand of this man who is making it quite clear that this is the only reason I need to stop dating anyone else.

This kiss.

This man.

His hands fill with my ass, fingers digging in to the flesh, his hardness against my belly, my arms hanging loose by my sides as my mouth knows what it's doing but the rest of me needs a few seconds to catch up. The *zing!* that fills every square inch of my skin screams out his name in ecstasy, as if all the vibrations in the world came into one single frequency that pumps through my veins like thunder.

And then my body remembers what to do, hands clutching his waist, sliding up over those rolling shoulders that are attached to fingers that won't stop giving me reason after reason after reason not to date anyone else.

And promise to give me multiple, mind-shattering *reasons* right now, if I just go with him.

"Ahem."

Someone is clearing their throat, but *my* throat is currently occupied by Andrew's delicious tongue, so I—

"This is not how my dates typically end," declares Chris.

I reach between me and Andrew, brushing against his erection as my palms slide up his hard wall of abs and chest, then make a space between us. Our mouths separate with near violence, and I turn to look through blurred vision at—

Oh. Yeah.

My date.

"Normally *I'm* the one kissing my date," Chris adds.

"Go away," Andrew growls.

And Chris does.

I'm not torn. I should be, but I'm not. As I watch Chris the Fake Dog Dater roam off into the night, my staring is interrupted by a strong hand on my cheek, fingers raking through my hair, my head tipped up for another kiss that leaves me breathless and knowing even less than I knew a moment ago.

Until:

"You won't date anyone else."

"I won't?"

The savagery in his tone and the bluntness of the words makes my feminist heart rise up and shake its outraged fist.

"No."

"Says who?"

"Says your boyfriend."

"He sounds like a troglodyte."

"He prefers the term Neanderthal. Someone applied it to him once."

"Boyfriend? That makes me your girlfriend?"

I'm thrilled and horrified at the same time, because I have eleven dates to go for DoggieDate. And I can't say a word about this, because the owner of DoggieDate is a rival of Anterdec's. I would not only be violating the basic tenets of mystery shopping, but also a slew of non-disclosure agreements. I'd lose my job in a heartbeat.

"Yes." His voice softens.

"Is that what you want?"

"I just said so." He kisses me again.

"You know what I want?" I stand on tiptoes, my lips against his ear.

"Mmmm?"

"A breve latte for breakfast."

He leers at me. "How about that latte for second breakfast. First breakfast in bed can be...you know..."

I leer back.

He grabs my hand and pulls me to the limo, whispering, "Okay, girlfriend. Done."

I fall into his lap in a tumble of giggles and gasps—then groans.

His groans. I've missed the sound of his sigh in my ear, how his breath lifts the hair from my neck, how his throaty laugh rumbles along my skin.

Andrew reaches behind me and grasps the door handle, shutting the limo closed with a thump. We begin to move, but I don't really notice much, as Andrew's kissing me like we haven't touched in years.

How can a week of distance feel so much longer?

"I missed you," he whispers, dragging the tip of his nose along my neck, from earlobe to collarbone, his lips hard and soft at the same time, arms circling me like I'm meant only to be here.

"I missed you, too." A thin wisp of guilt floats through the air as I inhale. I must tense, because he stops moving his hands, his arms tightening.

"Is this okay?"

"Of course," I reply, my laughter muted. "I just feel bad about ditching my, uh..." The word *date* feels dangerous right now. Inappropriate.

Incendiary.

"Your date?"

"Yeah." When he names it, I'm off the hook.

"Why?"

"Because he was a nice person."

"Just because he was nice doesn't mean he gets to be shielded from consequences."

"Consequences?"

"Right."

"Explain."

Andrew's head dips down, and as he moves his chin glides along the top of my breasts. A fireball of want replaces whatever silly little bit of guilt was there a second ago.

"People don't live with a rope tied between you and them emotionally. Not people you aren't attached to, I mean."

I frown, tilting my head as if the physical shift will give me a different perspective on his words. "Explain again."

"I see you doing this. Shannon, too."

My ears perk up at the mention of Shannon. Although she's about to become his sister-in-law, I've rarely heard him mention her. This is definitely new territory.

"You both," he continues, "act like you owe some debt to people you aren't attached to. As if you have to take care of everyone else's feelings, even when you're not asked."

My cheeks begin to blaze. It's not from arousal.

"I don't understand," I admit.

He swallows, and I feel the tension in his neck. "Ah, maybe I'm getting too serious here."

"No," I whisper. "You're not. This is interesting. I'm really trying to understand. I think you're on to something. Please," I urge him.

What I don't say is that there's a deep intimacy to his words, to this discussion, that I don't get from him elsewhere. Not in restaurants, not in the boardroom—not even in the bedroom.

I feel his shrug. "Maybe it's a male/female difference. Maybe it's personality. I don't know. That guy back there—"

"Chris. His name is Chris."

"Who cares. Anyhow, *that guy* is walking home right now, probably a little pissed that I sniped his date, but he certainly doesn't feel an attachment to you. There's no connection. No mutuality. You don't owe him a thing and he doesn't owe you a thing. He's a separate person who has autonomy over his behaviors and emotions."

"Still not getting you." And yet, something deep inside me is stirring. I can feel it. A dawning recognition that Andrew has zeroed in on an essential part of who I am, a piece of me that I know subconsciously is there, but that lurks within the subterranean mess of my chaotic soul. The fact that he intuitively sees this part of me is both thrilling and terrifying, because it involves being more real than I've ever been with anyone.

"Amanda, you have a loyalty and a need to fix problems for other people. You do this not because you want the accolades, but because you deeply enjoy being the person who solves problems." He tightens his grasp of me, touching my elbow with a stroke. "You connect ideas with solutions and implement them. You're the perfect operations person."

Coming from the former VP of Operations at Anterdec and now CEO, that's high praise.

"If you're just saying that to get into my pants," I tease, "I'm a sure thing tonight."

His laugh makes my body lift and bounce slightly as I burrow into the embrace. "I don't say anything I don't mean. Take the compliment."

"Then...thank you. I'm still not sure I understand everything you said, but I find it fascinating."

"My middle name is Freud."

"I thought your middle name was James."

"Don't ruin a witty comeback," he says, crushing my mouth with his so that, indeed, I cannot say another word.

Five minutes later we come up for air. Oxygen deprivation is the only explanation for why I reach for his face, caress his cheek, look him square in the eyes and murmur, "I've never felt this way about any man before."

He smiles, then reaches up to brush my unruly hair from my forehead, the movement profound and fleeting.

"What do you feel? For me?" he asks, head tipped slightly down, eyes lifting up.

"Attachment."

Love, I want to say, but the word is like a fire starter, inert until it gets close to a flame.

And then it ignites.

I don't say it. Can't. Not yet.

His face breaks into a wide smile at the word I *do* use.

"Good."

"I thought you just told me I attach to people too easily!" My heart is pounding. My skin feels exquisitely sensitive. What I'm saying and what I'm thinking are wildly divergent, and yet totally integrated.

"You attach emotional outcomes to the *wrong* people too readily." As he nuzzles my neck, a whiff of his cologne takes over the tiny space.

"Semantics," I scoff, trying to pretend that this is banter. It's not. This is a kind of truth I'm trying so hard to be ready for.

I get a long, hot kiss as an answer.

Before I can turn the tables and ask him what he feels for me, the limo slows and motors into the garage at his building.

And then we're out, walking to the elevator, hand in hand, Andrew pushing the button and like magic, the doors float open.

"Nice trick," I say as we walk on, my heart bouncing like popcorn on a stove.

"I have lots of them."

The stakes tonight feel higher. The question of whether to sleep with Andrew isn't part of this experience. And the aroused speculation of what it's like to be naked with him in bed is gone. I know what that is like.

And it is *damn* fine.

What I feel, as the doors close and his fingers unlace from mine, his body closing the distance, mouth finding my own as his hands skim up my spine, is the wholly unfamiliar sense of familiarity. I *do* know what this is like. The fact that I get more is what is so startling.

I'm sleeping with him again.

I'm spending the night again.

His tongue is lush and ripe and doing *that* again.

And again.

Oh, God, please.

Again.

He pushes me forward, using his thighs and hips, his hardness making me lose my breath.

And my sense of control.

Yet I have to know.

"What about you?" My words come out in a rush, as if I can cram them in between passion, as if they have to be hurried and said before this all goes away.

But he takes his time as he thinks about his answer. He is in no rush.

And then:

"I spend long stretches away," he murmurs against my mouth, "sitting in stupid business meetings with people from around the world who think a merger is more important than anything else, or that a change in online branding will change the world. I fly in planes at crazy hours of the night and do whirlwind tours in countries that changed names during my lifetime. And lately, Amanda, I spend every waking hour away from you wondering what the hell I'm doing."

Something in me breaks and blossoms at the same time, illogical and breathtaking, like cracking open an egg and finding a beautiful rainbow inside that takes over the sky.

"I'm good at what I do. Top of my game," he continues as I splay my palm flat against his abs. He's talking, and he needs to, and the words wash over me like the warm sea, welcoming and eternal, ancient and true.

"But not one bit of it matters. I have everything. Everything I could possibly want. Or, at least, I did. Until I realized I didn't have you."

"Is that why you really kissed me that night after the marina?" I ask.

"I already told you why I kissed you that night."

"Tell me again."

"How about I show you?"

My back is against the wall, my body craving all of this, every second of his attention, every commanding movement as he pulls me closer, pinning me between him and the moving elevator, and all I can think about is this.

Him.

Us.

What if I just stopped trying to fix problems in life and, instead, starting living?

One kiss, one lick, one groan, one cry at a time.

The elevator doors open and we lurch, Andrew's steady hold keeping me upright. But his hands are under my shirt as he walks me backwards into his hallway. He punches the door code and it opens. I lose my footing and tumble backwards, a mass of heat and giggles as I look up at him, standing in the doorway, smiling down on me.

"That's the view I love. Except you're wearing too many clothes."

He shuts the door.

"How many is too many?" I ask.

"Any."

We're playful and in pleasure mode now, the relief of just being together making us move fast suddenly, as if we have to capture the moment and pin it down, enjoy it first and savor it later.

There will be a next time, our bodies tell each other. *There will. But let's make sure there is a* now.

Our clothes in a puddle of discarded propriety at the edge of his front door, we kiss our way to the bedroom. His bed is unmade, a surprising display of messiness that makes me smile. I'm currently kissing him as the grin trips over my lips, so he stops and bites my earlobe. The hard warmth of his ticklish skin, scattered with hair that makes my hands rake across his skin with delight as he rubs against me, makes me heady.

"What's so funny?" he asks just as my hand reaches for his hardness, fingers wrapping around his thickness.

I can't answer because I'm laughing. I halt in the doorway to his bedroom and, because he's attached to the part of him I'm holding, he has to stop, too.

"I know you're not laughing at *that*!" he adds, clearing his throat meaningfully.

I descend into giggles that take minutes to recover from, my whoops of uncontrolled devolution breaking down slowly, like a music box whose key is finally unwinding down to the last few notes.

"No," I finally gasp. I'm still holding him. "I'm laughing because your bed is unmade."

"So? We're just going to mess it even more." His abs slide against mine and a shiver runs through me.

"Also, you're tickling me. On your skin. The hair on your legs." I reach down to touch the tops of his thighs. "Your belly." I reach up. "Your happy trail."

I slide my palm down.

"My habitrail? I know I have some body hair, but did you just refer to that patch as a *habitrail*? Like a hamster?"

With great flourish, he takes a step back and points both sets of fingers, palms facing in, at his navel and below, and declares, "*This* does not involve furry monsters."

Cue more giggling for the next seven minutes.

"I said Happy Trail. Two different words. No hamsters." I can't stop gasping.

A look of confusion, relief, and amusement fills his face. "Well, that's an improvement, but what the hell is a 'happy trail?'"

I point with my index finger at the thickening hair below his navel, tracing it down for him on his torso until he inhales sharply.

And then I drop to my knees.

"*That*, Mr. McCormick, is a happy trail. And while I see no furry monsters, I am discovering definite signs of a male animal here."

His growl of satisfaction confirms it, in fact.

A few minutes later, he stops me.

"I don't want to...this isn't how I want....well., I just.." Andrew isn't a stammerer, so this is charming. *I* do this to him. My mouth, my hands, my attentions take away his poise and leave him more real.

I stand on tiptoes and kiss him.

"You want me."

"I want to be in you. I want you in my arms. Not on your knees." He's breathing hard, his eyes dark and intense. "I want to make love with you, Amanda. In my bed, under me, on top of me—but together."

Rather than answer, I lead him to the bed and he takes control, crawling over my body as he warms my heart, my toes, my eyes and arms and legs and everything.

"I wanted to ask you a question in the car," I whisper as he kisses my collarbone, his breath coming in sighs and sounds like restraint becoming frayed by too much use.

"Yes?"

"What do *you* feel? For me?" I murmur. His face hovers above my breast, brow relaxed and smooth. One second passes. Two. Three. I lose count because time becomes a blur of chaos as I wait to hear my anchor in the endless river of hope.

He lifts his head up and moves so our faces are inches apart. The moon pokes out from clouds here and there, making the light erratic, carrying a dewy glow like gossamer flattened with an iron and spread thin. I cannot see his eyes in full, but I feel the soft energy of his breath against my chest.

"I," he says sweetly, "feel...." He sighs, then gives me a look of earnest connection that makes all my doubts disappear.

"Everything, Amanda. I feel *everything*."

The kiss that seals my fate comes with a sense that time itself ripples right now, like a stone thrown into a pond. The water will go back to being placid and smooth, but the stone remains forever moved, the water displaced *just so* forever. And ever.

And everything.

Discreet and quiet, he reaches into his nightstand and finds what he needs for protection, the same way he has each time we've made love before. I'm grateful for the smooth integration, for his responsibility, for the thoughtful resoluteness in making sure that making love is safe.

His words make all the blood in my body rush to places where his touch thrills and sates, where we get as close as two individuals can possibly be. I want him in me, too, and as I stretch back and pull him to me, I wrap my legs around him, inviting him the only way I know how without words.

He finds me wet and wanting, his hips moving against me with a measured distraction that I find alluring. His fingers trace a circle around one nipple as he thrusts gently, all the way, making me tip my hips to take him in.

The fresh heat of him over me captivates every part of my being. Andrew is in me, over me, arms around me and I am enraptured. The strands of web that make up Amanda are woven by time, experience, emotion and senses, and right now he is threaded in me, weaving new patterns into the tapestry of my essence.

We move against each other with slow strokes that carry the groundswell of urge and need, of fire and ice, of everything.

Everything.

"I feel you, Amanda," he murmurs, his voice harder to control. "And you're *all* I want to feel. I want you." My own control is fading, too, as impulse driven by logic dissolves under the moans that build in my throat. Too many years of no one, too many memories of loneliness, and far too many missed chances flood me as my blood skyrockets and crests, fevered and pulsing, searching for ways to find more of him.

From the way his hands grasp and explore, seeking to find new ways to touch and ignite, I think he feels it, too.

"You have me now," I say, my words caught in my throat as my pulse quickens and the glow inside spreads, so powerful it pulls him in, too. As we come together we integrate, those threads of passion and respect, of shared time and futures to come, all mixing with flesh and bone. He's carrying me away to some place we create between our hearts, where the only risk is in never taking a chance at all.

I tuck my head up against his shoulder and lick his neck, then give him a soulful kiss. He tastes like some exotic flavor, alluring and new. As we move against each other in the night, he fills me with a joyous bliss and hearing him call out my name in the throes of intimacy is, well....

Everything.

CHAPTER TWENTY-THREE

"He's in Tokyo again." Shannon whines. "Why do they *both* have to be there?" Declan went with Andrew for this round of negotiations. We're both feeling their absence. They come home tomorrow after nine days away. I'm squeezing in as many DoggieDates as I can while Andrew's out of town and can't magically appear at any of them.

I know. I'm lying to him. Great way to start a relationship, right? But it's for a higher cause. The Paycheck Cause. Can't pay my bills with kisses and breve lattes in bed. Oh, if only I could...

"They come home tomorrow," Marie says with an eye roll. She and Carol are getting ready to go out for work, purses in hand, faces excited. But first, Marie fiddles with some folders on the dining table. Jason has let Marie turn their dining room into a wedding Command Central that puts the White House emergency bunker to shame. The Jacoby family dining room looks like the War Room at the White House. No —not quite.

It is more organized.

And speaking of the White House...

"We still haven't received an RSVP from the president or vice president," Marie says with a disappointed sigh as she goes through the mail and sorts response cards.

"You expected the President of the United States to attend Declan and Shannon's wedding?" Carol snorts.

"I expected a gentle decline, if nothing else. Or he could send the First Lady. But would it kill the man to stop by for twenty minutes?"

I'm not sure which is more remarkable: that these sorts of conversations don't shock me, or that Marie actually holds out hope that the president might just pop in for the wedding.

"Where are you going?" Jason asks pleasantly, stepping into the house via the sliding patio door. His hair is half on end and half flat. There's a giant smear of grease on his right cheek, and he looks like he hasn't shaved in a couple of days. His face is sprinkled with streaks of cotton.

Oh. Wait. That's not cotton. I guess his beard is mostly white, which is weird, because his hair is such a rich shade of auburn.

Marie turns an uncharacteristic shade of pink. She's embarrassed. I didn't think Marie was capable of embarrassment, much like the Queen isn't capable of smiling without looking like she's constipated.

"Um, we're going to a mystery shop," she says in a breathy voice.

Carol gives her the side-eye. "This mystery shop is one of Mom's favorites."

"A sex toy shop?" Jason asks, as if he were asking about a garden supply store or an insurance agent evaluation. The level of casual discourse we have these days about anal beads and dildos is disturbing, especially since I can't talk about tampons with my own mother without needing smelling salts.

"No. Even better," Carol says in a voice filled with amusement. "A *department store* shop."

Jason frowns. He's picking up on the subtext. "What's so special about that?" he asks Marie, who is avoiding eye contact.

"Nothing! It's just a shop," she murmurs, pretending to paw through her purse.

Carol seems to enjoy tormenting her mom. "This is a men's clothing experience." She looks at me. "From top to bottom."

My quizzical look must match Jason's, because Carol bursts into laughter.

"It's porn for women," she says, as if that explains everything.

It doesn't.

"Shopping for men's clothing is porn for women?" Jason asks in an incredulous tone.

"Have you seen the men's underwear display lately?" Marie bursts out. "All these models. David Gandy. David Beckham. All wearing underwear and nothing more and their pictures are on the posters and on every single package. It's like they went and got Minions except instead of a crowd of little yellow beings staring at you, it's thirty or forty pictures of hot men in underwear all asking you to touch them."

"Pick up their package," Carol murmurs. Marie elbows her in the ribs as Carol giggles silently.

Jason just blinks, over and over.

"Hey, don't judge. You have your Victoria's Secret catalog obsession," Marie says in a threatening tone.

He throws his hands in the air, one of which is clutching a wrench. "I don't judge, honey!"

"Then why the stare?"

"I was just thinking that you should stop teaching yoga classes and do this mystery shopping thing full time. It suits you better." And with that, he walks over, drops the wrench, and bends her backwards, giving her the kind of kiss you see in old movie posters, the kind that curls a woman's toes and makes her body melt.

I turn away.

Now *I'm* embarrassed.

"Get a room," Carol mutters, clearly used to this. But I'm not. I've never seen my father kiss my mother. I don't even have a memory of it. Not one, single mental image of my mom and dad touching. Ever.

Now that I know the full story about what happened with my dad, I find myself even more interested in watching men who are about his age. I've always struggled with the concept of a father. So many of the men in my life who represent dads are wildly different. James McCormick terrifies me. Jason is a cuddly teddy bear, but I keep my distance with him because, well, I'm not one of his daughters. He reserves a kind of overflowing love for all of them that stands out in stark contrast to what I don't have.

I keep him at arm's length because it's too painful to think about sometimes.

I've told everyone the story my mom poured out after the baseball game, and Marie's been more pleasant to her. Not just because Mom pulled strings to get the bagpipers from Carnegie Mellon, but because, as Marie put it, "Oh, lord, those hours of pure despair. That would shred anyone to the bone. I understand why she's a hovermother now."

Yeah. I guess I do, too.

"We're going to stare at pictures of mostly naked men on underwear packages," Carol says pleasantly, all dimples and blue eyes and blonde hair. "What's your work day look like?"

"I am dating a man named Eagle," I declare.

"Eagle?" Jason has pried his lips off Marie and is now looking through receipts on the table with the air of a man who needs a barf bag. "You're dating a man named—sweet Jesus, Marie, you bought $3,100 worth of tartan ribbons?"

Marie bustles over to the table and physically blocks Jason's access to the folders by shoving her ample boobage right in his line of vision.

"Don't worry, Jason. It's all covered."

"We have a seventeen-thousand dollar budget and you've spent a fifth of it on *ribbons*?"

Shannon closes her eyes in resignation. The moment of truth has arrived. Turns out I'm not the only one hiding the truth from someone.

"Uh, Dad? Our budget is bigger than that."

Jason frowns. "What do you mean? I took Carol's wedding fund and split it between you and Amy and—"

"Anterdec is footing the bill, Dad."

"Anterdec is *what*?"

Shannon and Marie share a look. "Right after Declan proposed, we had a meeting with James, who asked that this be a thousand-guest wedding."

"A thousand?" Jason's been involved in some of the details, but for the most part has been happy to let all the women in his life do their thing.

"Yes. And most of those are business associates. He said this will be great, free publicity for Anterdec and if we invite enough business colleagues it becomes a corporate write off."

"The bastard coopted my own daughter's wedding," Jason fumes.

This, I know, is exactly why Marie and Shannon have kept things quiet, though at some point didn't Jason question some of the arrangements, like the forty-one piece bagpipe band and the ice sculptor from Finland?

"We didn't want to hurt your feelings, Daddy," Shannon says, reaching for his hand. I turn away. It's moments like that that make it hard to be around Jason. What's it like to reach out and just touch your dad like that, with a father-daughter bond that has been forged by decades of love?

"Why would you hurt my feelings? It's obvious James McCormick has a bigger...wallet...than I do." He sighs and swallows, hard.

"That's not what this is about," Shannon pleads.

"I know it's not, sweetie. I do. I just worry that the love between you and Declan is getting lost in all the tartans and cake frosting flavors and elephant discussions."

Shannon turns sharply to Marie. "Elephants?"

Marie shrugs one shoulder. "We thought about it. Bring you and Declan to the ceremony on an elephant, but mahouts are notoriously difficult and the dung is big and messy, and it turns out elephants don't like to wear diapers."

"No elephants!" Shannon shrieks.

"Plus, they don't make tartan-pattern elephant diapers, so—"

"What's a mahout?" Jason asks.

Bzzzz.

Marie and Carol look at their phones. "Gotta go! Our mystery shop reports are due by six p.m. and our boss is a real bitch."

"Hey!" I protest. "*I'm* in charge of that account!"

Carol just laughs as they sprint out the door, leaving a puzzled, slightly hurt Jason.

"Cowards," Shannon mutters. She looks around Command Central and shuffles through some papers. Frowns.

"What?" I ask, afraid to do so, but...

"Mom has a deposit for that place. The one you went to," Shannon tells me.

"O? The stripper spa?" I'm surprised. Not shocked, though.

"Yeah."

"Oh, boy."

"No. Just O."

Shannon makes a sound like Declan makes when he's displeased with Marie.

"She's sniping the bachelorette party." I am stunned. I can't say I'm truly surprised, because this is Marie, after all. The woman who is turning a cat into a flower girl and making the cat wear a kilt.

"Oh, no, she isn't." Shannon's expression is smugger than smug. "We're outwitting her."

"We are?"

"Let's find a way around her. Swear Amy and Carol and everyone to secrecy."

"Yeah," I say. "About that. The, um, party list."

"What about it?"

"Josh asked if he could go."

"Why would we include Josh?"

"Because he likes male strippers, too? Plus he's technically part of the wedding."

"He is?"

"Marie made him web developer for your live streaming video channel."

"My *what*? My wedding is being broadcast live over the Internet?"

"Yes. You even have corporate sponsors."

"WHAT? Why would we need corporate sponsors when Anterdec is paying for everything?"

"Marie's trying to get them to sponsor her live yoga channel after the wedding is over."

"And no one told me any of this? I feel like Dad!"

"Ouch." We share twin looks of horror because being left out of the loop is one of the most insulting actions you can take against a Jacoby woman.

A soon-to-be McCormick woman.

"You're telling me," she says slowly, a sound of cunning permeating her voice as the gears turn, "that Mom already booked O for my bachelorette party." She repeats what she knows as if chewing her way through the harsh reality.

"Yes."

"And Josh thinks he's coming, too?"

"Mmmm hmmm."

She blinks a few times, chewing on her lower lip. Then her mouth curls in victory.

"I know exactly what we need to do next."

And when she tells me, I execute the plan to perfection.

Why?

Because this problem I can fix.

* * *

My final DoggieDate before Andrew gets home is an eight p.m. dinner date. My date was supposed to be an outdoor lunch on a marina in the Seaport district, but the guy canceled at the last minute. "Eagle" said he forgot a parole officer appointment and sent his apologies, and that Killer would meet Spritzy some other day.

Um, yeah.

Like never.

The new DoggieDate dude wants a dinner appointment, so here I am, waiting at a table in a rather elegant waterfront restaurant behind a glass wall. The night lights from the city and various boats along the wharf cast more bobbing orbs my way. I've been asked to bring Spritzy, who is resting comfortably in his little purse. Mom acquiesced when I explained it was a work issue.

She wasn't planning to leave the house anyhow, and while Spritzy isn't technically a service dog, Mom won't leave home without him. I once joked she should rename the dog American Express, but Mom didn't laugh.

I slip Spritzy a tiny piece of bread and he munches down, happy.

I wish I could be made happy with a simple bite of bread.

I'm sickly aware of Andrew's pending arrival in town and hoping to get through this dinner in two hours, tops, so I can go home to—

Andrew?

"Amanda?" he asks, standing a safe distance away from me. In his arms is a tiny little terrier wearing a pale green ribbon. The dog is freshly groomed and the incongruity of:

a) Andrew standing there
b) a dog in his arms
c) Spritzy jumping up to hump Andrew's ankle

makes the room spin for a moment.

"What are you doing here?" I hiss, searching the room for witnesses, as if Andrew might appear again like he did on my date with Chris and crash it.

"I'm your date."

"You're my date?" I fish around my purse for my DoggieDate paperwork and ignore Spritzy's sexytime with Andrew's wingtips. My mom's dog is having more sex with Andrew than me.

If Mr. Spritzy keeps this up, I'm going to have to offer him a cigarette. Whoa.

"Could you call your dog off?" he asks, gently nudging Spritzy off him. The movement just makes the little chihuahua redouble his efforts. "Spritzy has good taste, but I'm not a foot fetish guy."

I reach down and grab the little dog, tucking him back in Mom's purse and shoving a thin breadstick at him.

"Who's this?" I ask, seething but pretending to be someone capable of behaving in public without becoming a screaming banshee. My cover is clearly blown. Someone's told Andrew the truth. I hope to God I don't lose the account for the client and that Greg doesn't fire me. Then again, I didn't break any of my NDAs.

"This is my dog. Mr. Wiffles." He is holding the calmest little Yorkie I have ever seen. Its eyes are sharp and alert behind long, beribboned hair that frames the most adorable face. Mr. Wiffles looks like something out of the Westminster Dog Show, like a well-pampered beast of luxury, and he's sweet, to boot.

"You have a dog?"

His eyes go shifty. "I do." Andrew looks about as comfortable holding the dog as I do being naked in public.

"I've been to your apartment numerous times and never saw him."

"He's quiet. Well trained." Andrew pats his head like he's blotting a spot of ketchup off a shirt.

I snort. Spritzy imitates me. Mr. Wiffles joins in.

"Andrew. I have stayed at your apartment for more than twelve hours at a time and never heard a dog."

As I talk, Andrew takes a seat across the way from me. He sets Mr. Wiffles down on the chair next to him and pulls the linen napkin out, spreading it on his lap. Andrew's basically acting like nothing's wrong. Nothing to see here.

We're just two nobodies.

With dogs.

He looks up, eyes hard yet amused. "How many dates?"

"How many what?"

"How many of these dates have you been on?"

"That is privileged information. And how did you find out about all this?"

His mouth tightens.

"I'm a smart guy."

"What did you promise Marie in exchange for the info?"

He has the decency to pretend to be offended, then gives up the ruse. "I told her I'd make sure the guys go commando for the wedding."

"How'd you get Declan to agree to *that*?"

"Don't ask. But I'll be spending a lot of time in Indonesia with tech support people next month."

"You went through all that to stalk me?"

"I'd hardly call this stalking."

I'm about to reply that this is, pretty much, the very *definition* of stalking when an enormous man who looks like an angry bear comes barreling through the restaurant like his ass is on fire. He's dressed in well-loved Birkenstocks, a torn concert t-shirt, and jeans that look like they were being worn when Bruce Springsteen made "Born in the USA" a hit.

"Where is my Mr. Wiffles?" says a deep bass voice that sounds like it's percolating up from the ground.

Oh. It's Terry. Andrew's brother.

Andrew pretends he isn't there, which is pretty hard to do when the human equivalent of a subwoofer is standing three inches from your head and about to blow.

"*Your* Mr. Wiffles?" I ask. Ah. This is starting to make more sense.

The Yorkie perks up and begins wagging its tail. Terry bends down and picks it up, kissing its little head between the ears. This is like watching big, shirtless, cut firefighters collect kittens from trees or a police officer nursing a baby bird with a broken wing.

It makes my ovaries not only leap out of my body and do jumping jacks, I'm pretty sure they're desperately searching for a baby registry right now.

"I can't believe you stole my dog, Andrew!" Terry bellows. The salt shaker on the table quivers.

"I did not steal your dog."

"Don't lie."

"I'm not lying. I did not steal your dog."

Terry's nostrils flare. "Fine. Your *chauffeur* stole my dog."

Andrew says nothing, but his eye roll is epic.

"You had your chauffeur slip Mr. Wiffles' trainer a fifty and you stole her! She's a very nervous type and can't handle this."

Mr. Wiffles wags her tail and licks Terry. She looks about as nervous as Marie is discreet.

"Wait. Mr. Wiffles is a *she*?" I ask.

Andrew makes a noise of disgust. "Don't ask."

I look at Terry. He shrugs.

"Terry has a transgendered dog," Andrew intones, nodding slowly, like that explains *everything*.

"That is not funny!" Terry booms. The sound is like a shockwave that ripples through the restaurant. I think he messed up some hairdos and may have given three women orgasms.

"Then why does she have a male name?" I ask, assuming it's a perfectly reasonable question to ask.

Terry glares at Andrew like it's his fault Mr. Wiffles' name doesn't match the, er, parts.

"Mr. Wiffles was bred in Amish country," he says with a sigh, as if the sentence were self-explanatory. A familiar sense of confusion rolls over me.

Talking to Terry is just a little too similar to talking to Marie sometimes.

"And...?" I ask, my voice rising as I draw out the word.

"And, apparently, the man who bred her had his young daughter name her. The daughter was too shy to look at the parts and just decided Mr. Wiffles was a he."

"That doesn't make sense," I say.

Andrew gives Terry a look that only an impish little brother can shoot the oldest in a family. "Yeah. I know. We have all said that. Even Mr. Wiffles' trainer."

"I am not traumatizing my poor dog by changing her name now," Terry hisses. Is he actually covering the dog's ears so she can't hear this? "It's bad enough you stole her, but now you're making her feel bad, and if her self-esteem is harmed, you're in trouble."

I've been on enough DoggieDate dates to realize that Terry's behavior, though loony as hell in the general population, is actually well within the bounds of normal for the ultra dog-loving dating pool I'm in.

That said, Terry's lips twitch on that final statement. I think some legs are being pulled.

Andrew's jaw clenches. "You can have her now."

"Why did you steal her?" Terry looks at me as if he's noticing me for the first time. Which he is. "Oh. Hi, Amanda. Did you change your hair?"

I reach up and realize I've gone auburn. Yet another hair coloring shop, this one with temporary dye. "Yes."

"You two having a business meeting?" I can tell from his tone that he has no idea Andrew and I have been...*whatevering* we've been doing for a while now. Hmm. Tuck that away for later.

"No. Date," I say, trying to seem casual.

"You needed Mr. Wiffles for a date?" He gives Andrew a scandalized look, then holds up a palm the size of a catcher's mitt. "Never mind. I don't want to know. I just—"

Andrew frowns and interrupts Terry. "How in the hell did you know where to find me?"

Terry smirks. "You gave the trainer a fifty. I gave her a hundred. As you like to say all the time, money makes people talk."

I watch them like I've been drop-shipped into Burma and don't understand a thing.

"You bribed the person *I* bribed?" Andrew says with outrage.

"And I did it better, bro." Terry tries to high-five Mr. Wiffles, but the dog just wags her tail and licks his hand.

"I'm firing that trainer," Andrew mutters.

Terry bends down, his hand constantly petting Mr. Wiffles. "You can't fire her. *I'm* the one who hired her."

Andrew's eyes narrow. Hah.

Out-alpha'd by a guy who is now kissing a female dog named Mr. Wiffles.

"I am taking Mr. Wiffles now," Terry declares. He gives Andrew a look only a much-older brother can give. "You steal her again and I'll tell Dad about your limo elimination plan."

"You wouldn't."

Terry adjusts Mr. Wiffles' bow. "Try me." And with that, he's off, happy dog in arms.

I take a long drink of my iced tea and say, "My last date pretended he had a dog he never had, but he didn't resort to actual *theft* of a dog to go out with me."

"I didn't steal her. She's part of the family."

"I am honored that you'd go to such extremes just to spend time with me. But you don't have to resort to canine crime."

"Except when you're dating other men."

"Which you now know I'm not."

"Right."

The air between us is so thick with tension. We're on shaky ground, and every move, each sigh, all the breaths and sips and looks add up to uncertainty. The stable, steady sense of togetherness that we had just begun to develop feels like an illusion, as if we created it for a specific need in the past and it floated off on the wind, gone to seed.

The waiter arrives. Andrew orders for us both and I let him. Not because of a power struggle or from a place of submission, but because what he orders sounds damn good. Water glasses filled, iced tea in hand, and a pitcher of sangria delivered and poured, we're ready to talk *sans* Mr. Wiffles.

And, maybe, *sans* pretense.

"Why didn't you tell me about the dates? How many did you go on?"

"I can't talk about this."

"Why not?"

"NDA. I sign NDAs for my work with Anterdec, and I sign them with other clients."

His brow lowers. "You take your work very seriously."

"I do."

"It's one of the many qualities I admire in you."

"Thank you."

"Though your mouth is your best feature."

I nearly spray him with a mouthful of iced tea.

"You always know the right things to say," he elaborates, though he suppresses a smile.

I feel like I can't string a sentence together. Like I can't take syllables from my mind and connect them to form words any more. What once was easy with Andrew—though hard won—is now back to that topsy-turvy state where he's joking, and I'm bantering, and we're in that will-he-won't-he-will-she-won't-she place that I am, frankly, tired of being in.

We were supposed to be past this quite some time ago. The spiral backwards feels as if we're losing ground.

And yet I can't walk away. I can't even hope to do anything other than smile at this man who is willing to steal a dog to come and see me.

"I've missed you," he says softly. "And I forgive you."

I sit up sharply. "You *what*?"

"I forgive you. You obviously take your promises very seriously, and any woman who keeps her word like this is someone I value."

Damn. I was all worked up over that forgiveness comment, because I have nothing to ask forgiveness *for*, and then he neutralizes it with a compliment.

Well played, Andrew. Well played.

"I also know you're still processing everything you learned that day after Fenway Park."

The waiter delivers salads, giving me a chance to take a shaky breath and try to calm the unending loop of questions that runs through me.

Andrew ignores his food.

"And I want to help."

He reaches in his suit jacket pocket and slides a half-size manila envelope across the table.

"What's this?"

His face wears a sad smile. "Open it."

Spritzy whines. I dig through my purse and find the zippered baggie with doggie treats in it. Satisfied with two, he resumes his pretend sleep.

My fingers fumble on the back of the envelope, but I get it open.

To find a fairly familiar packet of paperwork. At the top there is a name:

Leo Rossi Warrick.

"Jesus, Andrew," I gasp. "You had my father tracked down."

This is the part where I'm supposed to look up at him from across the table with adoration and gratitude. In Andrew's mind, I'm sure, he's performed a wonderful act of compassion. A gesture of caring. Finding my father is supposed to help me to heal. To absorb and integrate and process and find a place for the maelstrom of emotions that don't know where to rest.

All I feel is *fury*.

"It was remarkably easy," he says in a voice that doesn't boast. He isn't proud. He's just here, looking at me with eyes that say he's giving me what he thinks I need, and that ask me to accept what he's offering as a bridge to some new place we can be together.

Except I'm about to set fire to that bridge.

I can't help it. I spontaneously combust so quickly there isn't time to contain it.

"I don't want this," I snap, shoving it back at him. The papers fall in erratic patterns, one landing in his salad, one scraping across Spritzy's head. The dog begins to whine.

"What? I don't understand." He's sitting back, the papers scattered across the table. He leans forward, his suit jacket open, his waist pressing into the table's edge.

"I said *I don't want it*," I repeat through clenched teeth, my voice vibrating with anger. I can only imagine what my face looks like based on the way he frowns.

"I thought you'd want to know."

"You think I didn't already know where he is? I research these issues for a living! I've known where Leo is for years." I swallow, my saliva bitter with the tangy taste of disappointment. I'm not sure who I'm more disappointed in, though. "Vehicular homicide. He has three more years to go." Mom's story was a gut punch in more ways than one. While he didn't, obviously, kill me twenty-two years ago, he went on to kill someone else. Two someones, while driving drunk in Iowa.

"You..." He flinches, as if my words were blows.

"I tried to visit him. Once. The prison authorities told me he refused."

I'm looking down on Andrew from a standing position I don't recall moving into. His face is tipped up, dark brows covering eyes that seem to fight inside, his pupils dilating then constricting, his face a flickering field of light and shadow.

"Amanda, I thought I was being helpful." His voice wavers between bewilderment and a cold control that turns up the fury flame inside me. "And I am so sorry," he says, his voice softening slightly. "Sorry that he would refuse you."

"You could have asked, first. Before you went snooping." Shame pours over my skin like lighter fluid, the tiny hairs on my arms standing as gooseflesh ripples across the space between us. Why would he find out the truth about my father? What possible purpose would that serve?

"You're right. I see I made a mistake." The balance between his bewilderment and control is shifting, his voice going tight.

Our eyes lock, and as second pass we don't look away. The intensity that flows between us feels like a shockwave that shatters everything fragile for miles.

And then it hits me.

"Is that what this is about?" I continue. "Is this why you don't want to be seen in public with me?"

"What?" Incredulity clears up any ambiguity in his expression. "Where the hell did that come from?"

Gloves are off.

"The evidence is pretty clear, Andrew. We've only ever had dates in private places. You only see me at night. You wouldn't go for a walk with me when I really needed you at the Fenway. You told me you were worried about photographers. You still haven't introduced me as your girlfriend to your dad or, obviously, to Terry. He was just here and had no clue! And now you dug up the truth about my father—a truth I knew a long time ago—and what else am I supposed to think?"

I am dying inside. A familiar shower of shame rolls over my skin, like I'm bathed in the flow of every naked-in-public dream I've experienced for twenty years, all rolled into one.

Right here. Right now.

With the one man who is supposed to be safe.

For the briefest of moments I swear I catch a glimpse of untempered vulnerability in his eyes as he looks at me, then at the papers strewn across the table. He frowns, his breathing quickening.

Andrew stands.

His hands stay at his sides.

"You think that? You think that of me? That I am *ashamed* of you?" His back is straight, his eyes fixed on me, blinking with a slow, hypnotic constancy that triggers something primal in me. My breath comes in short spurts and I realize I have to flee.

"What other conclusion am I supposed to draw? Hell, Andrew, you won't even sit on your balcony for morning coffee outside with me where someone might see!"

I am completely illogical now. I know I am. The fear that he's avoiding being seen in public with me is one that's been brewing beneath the surface for a while, but I haven't articulated it before. Not even to Shannon. It is flimsy. I might be wrong. I hope I'm wrong. But the alternative is to be truly open and raw and to stop trying to fix everything and let the world spin without my efforts—and *that*?

That's worse than being naked in public.

Spritzy begins to whine, so I take the convenient way out and reach for him, clasping him in my arms like a football I have to protect as I make my way through a crowd and avoid being tackled.

Andrew's on my heels as I reach the door of the restaurant. He blocks my way, his arm going up above me, braced against a support post.

"Don't," I beg. Fire burns behind my tongue. I will turn him into a crisp if he doesn't move.

"Amanda." The way he says my name makes me cringe, because this feels unfixable. I feel unfixable. In the space of a handful of minutes I've ruined everything and all I can do is escape. Run away.

Leave.

"I am not, and never have been, ashamed of you." He reaches out to touch me, then stops himself. A coiled anger seeps out of his eyes as he looks at me in a way that makes it clear I do not have permission to look away.

"I—"

"I'm a busy man. I'm taking over for my father, who is embroiled in medical appointments and business transitions and this damned wedding and if I am not as available as you would like, when you want access to me at the exact moments you prefer, then I apologize."

The ice in his voice physically *hurts*.

And yet I don't quite buy what he's saying.

"Your father's prison record has no bearing on how I feel about you." He moves his arm. "I had my security team seek him out so you would have some answers."

"That's a remarkable spin on violating my privacy."

"His whereabouts is public record." The more Andrew speaks, the colder I become.

"Just because you *can* learn something about a person doesn't mean you *should*."

"And just because someone isn't where you want them to be doesn't mean they've abandoned you."

I race out the doors, a shaking Spritzy in Mom's purse bag, my vision blurred. I drove into the city so I have to find the garage I used and walk down two flights of stairs to the underground level where I parked.

Coming face to face with my piece of...car doesn't help either. Two college students walk past me. One of them holds his nose and the other guffaws, grabbing his phone to take a picture of the Turdmobile. I can't really see their faces, because my eyes are reflective lenses filled with pooled tears that beg for release.

I open the back door, put Spritzy in her secured little dog crate, click her seat belt, then climb in the front.

And cry through smoke and ashes until all that's left is nobody.

* * *

A long time ago, just as Shannon was moving in with Declan, she told me that in a true emergency I could drive right up to their building and a valet would take care of my car.

If anything qualifies as an emergency, it's this.

I take Spritzy out of his crate and hand my Turdmobile over to the smirking valet parking dude, who is already on his phone, probably live-tweeting his experience.

The elevator feels like a coffin.

I walk into their apartment and Shannon runs to me with a big hug.

"You." I point at Declan. "Plug your ears."

He ignores me and starts tapping on his phone. He stops, then walks into the bedroom. Half a minute later, he interrupts me and Shannon as I furiously whisper all the details to her. Declan's carrying a gym bag.

"I'll be back in a few hours," he says, leaning in to give her a kiss.

"Where are you going?" she asks, clearly surprised.

"Workout with Andrew."

I give him my death glare. It doesn't quite work, because he stays alive.

"Why?"

"So I can learn the truth." He gives me an unsmiling look that only a suave, sophisticated billionaire can give a woman, and he's out the door, off to the little nook to wait for the elevator.

270

"The truth!" I sputter. "What is that supposed to mean?"

"Don't try to dissect it," Shannon says reassuringly. "It's like trying to understand why the Kardashians get any news coverage. You'll just drive yourself nuts."

"I'll tell you the truth," I fume. "The truth is that Andrew stole Terry's dog and appeared on my DoggieDate and he researched and found out my father's in prison and now everything is ruined."

"That's a lot of truth."

"I know!" I wail, picking through their fridge. Now that Shannon lives with Declan she eats paleo, and that means there are hardly any carbs here. How in the hell do you have an asshole boyfriend talk without carbs?

"He really found your dad?"

"Yeah."

"But you already know where he is."

"I know. Andrew didn't know that."

"He thought he was helping?"

I sigh, deflating like an emotional balloon. "I know. But he has this way of just barging in and taking over, then backing off. He's really strange. I think—" No. I can't say it. Once my suspicions are spoken, I can't unspeak them. I just dumped them all out on Andrew and they feel even more illogical now.

"What do you think?"

"I think he doesn't want to be seen in public with me."

There. Said. Done.

A man's deep sigh shatters Shannon's stunned silence. We turn and find Declan standing there, gym bag in hand, a grim look on his face.

"That's not what's going on," he says.

Let me halt here for a moment and attempt to explain how utterly incomprehensible his appearance at this moment really is. Declan does not—I repeat, does *not*—ever insert himself into any conversation Shannon and I have about relationships. He has been a silent sentry through the past two years and while I know he knows Andrew's feelings on the subject, he has never uttered a word to me about it.

Until now.

"Huh?" Shannon grunts. She's as shocked as I am. Spritzy tries to make love to Declan's ankle. Shannon cocks an eyebrow and Declan nudges Spritzy away.

"I swore to myself I would never intervene," Declan mumbles under his breath. "This kind of thing never ends well."

"What's he talking about?" I hiss to Shannon.

"I don't know." She throws her hands in the air. "He mutters nonsense like this all the time whenever Mom and I try to troubleshoot other people's problems."

"And we all know how well that turns out," Declan says in a tight voice. "But I can tell you that the problem here is not that Andrew doesn't want to be seen in public with you or that your father being in prison has anything to do with Andrew's actions."

"Then what?" I croak out.

"The problem is that my brother is a vampire."

That really doesn't help clear up *anything*.

"You mean, like Edward Cullen?"

"What does my vibrator have to do with this?" Shannon gasps.

Declan glares at her and mutters, "I still can't believe you named that thing." His frown deepens. "Or that you still own it."

"Can we stick to the whole *your brother is a bloodsucking creature* part?"

"What does being a CEO have to do with this?" Shannon jokes.

We both give her a look.

Declan turns to me after a spectacular eye roll that even his helicopter pilot must have felt. "I mean that Andrew will never go outside in daylight."

I whip to face Shannon. "I thought you were *joking* when you said that!" I think back to the time in the ER when Shannon swallowed her engagement ring and Andrew made a comment about not going outside. How everyone told stories.

How I didn't believe it.

"He's too afraid of being stung," Declan adds, giving Shannon a nervous glance. We all know why Declan subconsciously does that, but it doesn't stop my stomach from hurting.

"Never? He *never* goes out in daylight? What about winter?"

Declan nods. "He does then. He's an avid skier. But from March to November, no way."

"He's crafted his entire life around this giant fear?" My mind races to piece this together. "Is this why he has a balcony but no plants? Why he always wants to meet for dinner but never lunch? Why he has drivers who take him from underground garage to—oh, my God." I slump against the couch. "You two aren't kidding."

"I wouldn't joke about this," Declan says, his voice sincere and full of compassion. "He's not rejecting you. He's not embarrassed to be seen in public with you, Amanda. He's terrified to be in any situation where there's the smallest risk he might get stung."

"That's crazy!" I cry out, looking at Shannon, who now has fat tears filling her eyes. "He's *crazy*! Shannon

273

doesn't live like that! You can't live a life where there's no risk."

"Not no risk. Just no risk in this one, particular part of his life. He's surprisingly bold when it comes to taking huge leaps in business. It's one reason why Dad plucked him for the CEO spot. Whatever risks he doesn't take in real life with his physical body he has no problem making on paper or in the boardroom." Declan's mouth twists with a smile that is equal parts admiration and contempt.

"How does he—I don't understand—what does he..." But my voice fades out as I run through the possibility—the *probability*, that Declan is right.

Andrew lives a life driven entirely by fear.

"Why didn't he just say that?" I beg, pleading with Declan to explain this to me so I can fix it. Make it better. Clear it all up and get everything back in order.

"He'll never say it."

Bzzzzz.

The intercom by the elevator crackles. "Mr. McCormick?" That's Gerald's voice.

Declan jogs over to the elevator. The doors are shutting. He sticks his foot in the opening and lodges the doors open again. "One second, Gerald."

"No problem." The crackling ends.

With a pained expression, Declan looks at me. "I don't know how else to explain it, but facts are facts. I didn't want you thinking that he's rejecting you for the wrong reasons."

"There are *right* reasons?" I choke out.

With a shrug, he gets on the elevator, the doors closing over troubled eyes.

"But why won't he say it?" I call out.

And...he's gone.

I look at Shannon. Her eyes are a mix of pity and confusion.

"Oh, God, Shannon. What have I done?"

CHAPTER TWENTY-FOUR

It's showtime. Shannon and Declan's rehearsal dinner party night. It's T-minus two weeks for the wedding and now everything shifts into high gear. My calendar is filled with bridesmaid dress fittings and re-fittings, photographer walk-throughs, final confirmations for the bachelorette party, florist checks, and a million texts from Marie asking about details and a million more from Shannon hot on her heels, complaining about her mom.

But no Andrew.

We actually did the rehearsal part earlier in the day at the minister's office because of a slew of calls from New Zealand and Indonesia that Andrew and Declan had to take. Andrew's head was bent over his phone the entire time, his distraction so bad he had to be physically moved by Grace throughout most of the practice ceremony. At least he was present. Sort of.

We've confirmed that everyone knows where to walk, even though rain made us just do this at the church where Declan's parents married. Quite some time ago, Shannon, Declan and Marie decided to just hold the wedding outdoors at Farmington Country Club, so the rehearsal is a formality.

Marie has been studying the layout of Farmington Country Club weddings for so long she should get an honorary Army Corps of Engineers membership card.

Tonight, Shannon and Declan's apartment looks like something out of one of those HGTV television shows combined with a Gordon Ramsey kitchen. My mom and I arrive before all the guests to provide Shannon with some much-needed support, only to find her crying over a small frying pan full of onions.

"I can't do this! Mom is insane! I can't host a dinner for twelve people! I can barely assemble a Lunchable correctly," she sobs.

Declan is nowhere to be seen.

A tall, slim woman with blonde hair and the tight smile of an overly officious school teacher interrupts us.

"You're burning the onions," she says kindly.

Shannon looks down and cries out.

"And there's no need for that old trick. The odors from our meal will more than fill the apartment."

Shannon tosses the spitting frying pan into one half of the divided sink and throws her hands in the air.

"I give up!"

"Thank goodness," the woman mutters. I look at her apron. The logo for a very well known restaurant is on it.

"Where is Declan?" When in doubt, stick the man in the hot seat.

"I don't know! He said he'd be here by now and everyone is coming and Mom put me up to this and I can't *even*."

Remember how I said Shannon has become so poised, so confident, so mature and composed?

Yeah. That's long gone now. Momzillas can unravel anything.

"You can go take a shower and get ready." I will fix this. She just has to get out of the way. Shannon can be her own worst enemy.

"I can't! I—"

"Come here, dear," my mother says, guiding Shannon in that way only a mother can, her voice firm and no-nonsense, Spritzy in her purse on her arm, his tail thumping against leather. DNA and training make Shannon obey *her*.

The door buzzes.

I march across the room and see James's face at the video screen. I let him in.

And we're off.

Over the course of the next hour, the following people arrive: Marie, Jason, Carol, Terry, Amy, Jamie from Outlander. Add in me, my mom, Andrew, Declan and Shannon and we are twelve total.

That's right.

Jamie.

All right, not technically, but the man in the video screen—and the second-to-last to arrive—was a cool 6'2", with bright green McCormick eyes and the threaded gold of a ginger-haired god.

A cousin *god*.

Turns out the Boston McCormicks still had some contact with the Edinburgh McCormicks and Declan asked Hamish to be a groomsman. In his native Scotland, Hamish is a rock star. Not because he's a musician.

Because he plays football.

Or, as we call it here, soccer.

Which means Hamish is a nobody in Boston. He may have his face splashed all over all the major newspapers in Europe and South America, but he's a complete unknown in the U.S.

And he doesn't seem to realize it.

He's headed to New York City for a *Sports Illustrated* nude athlete photo spread after this dinner, then back for the bachelor party and wedding day. Marie's eyes comb over him and it's very clear she's doing her best camera imitation right now.

Andrew still hasn't arrived as the wine's poured, the hors d'oeurves are distributed, and Shannon tries hard to pretend she cares about McCormick tartan ribbons tied around the birdseed packets that people will throw as she and Declan leave the church.

Marie won't shut up about them.

I'm too preoccupied by Andrew's absence to care.

"It's all a bit much, aye?" Hamish says to Amy, who is giving him the critical once over of a woman who knows she's supposed to be impressed but most decidedly isn't. His accent makes my panties melt. Maybe that's why people in Scotland go commando when they wear kilts and skirts.

It's the hot accent.

"What's a bit much?" Carol asks. *She* looks like she needs a McCormick tartan handkerchief to mop up her drool as she looks at Hamish.

"The tartan." The word *tartan* rolls off his tongue like it's a cocker spaniel being sprung from a cage. "By the time the wedding comes, we'll look like Nessie ingested a bunch of highlanders and vomited everywhere."

Carol laughs like that's the funniest joke she's ever heard.

"Hamish!" Marie exclaims, walking over and offering herself up to him for a hug like he's a rock climbing wall and there's a prize for reaching the top. "So good to meet you!" Her eyes are bright and excited as he pulls away from the embrace and she asks, "You're a sports star in Europe, I hear. What position do you play? Shortstop?"

Hamish's golden eyebrows turn down. "I play football, Marie." Jason stifles a laugh.

"Oh. Tight end, then?" She cranes her neck around behind him to check out *his* tight end.

"No—not American football. I play soccer." His voice is filled with a frustrated resignation, as if he's had this same conversation far too often for his liking.

"Point guard?" she tries.

Jason hands the poor Scot another shot and claps him on the back. "Just give up, man."

"Americans," Hamish mutters before downing the drink.

Where in the hell is Andrew?

I shouldn't care. I know I shouldn't care. I blew it. But he could have told me. We're grown-ups. We each have the ability to exchange emotional truths in an honest way.

Barring that, would it kill the man to send a basic text?

While Amy sulks and Marie and Carol moon over Hamish, I try to find Shannon. She's disappeared. I grab two glasses of wine from an increasingly-attractive male waiter who walks by with a tray of poured Pinot Grigio. I work on drinking part of my second? third? glass of wine.

After searching everywhere, I finally find her in the bedroom, in a walk-in closet, trying not to cry.

"What's wrong?" I ask. She's holding a tartan garter in her hands and just standing there, staring at Declan's shoehorn, which hangs from a hook behind his suits.

"I'm not sure I can do this."

There is a point in every maid of honor's stretch of time in this role where we expect the bride to get cold feet. If you're a woman in modern America, you've been steeped in the wedding articles since you were about nine or so, and could read the *Cosmopolitan* and *Glamour* magazines your mom left all over the house. You know Ten Ways To Make Her Wedding Rock and

Five Mistakes Bridesmaids Make and Why Good Friends Throw Naughty Bachelorette Parties.

Cold feet are just a part of the wedding process.

"You love Declan. Being Mrs. McCormick is going to be awesome," I assure her. I offer her the untouched wine goblet.

She looks at me like I just ate a Madagascar hissing cockroach in front of her. "I know that! I'm not talking about the wedding. I'm talking about this stupid dinner party!" She ignores the wine I'm offering.

That's how I really know she's upset.

"Oh."

"And where's Andrew?" she snaps.

I finish my third glass (definitely third) and start in on her reject.

"No clue," I say.

Bzzz.

I pull my phone out of my pocket and gently guide Shannon back into the living room. She pivots at the doorway and tosses the garter onto her bed.

I haven't seen Andrew since the night he stole Mr. Wiffles and we fought nearly a month ago. He texted a half-hearted apology and I texted back a lame half-acceptance. After that, his assistant has asked me a few wedding-related questions regarding schedules. No other contact.

And Declan won't reveal what Andrew told him that night they worked out. He's been in New York on business, then in Paris, and finally he's back—for this party. Andrew and Declan made it clear that he has to leave early and board the helicopter to go back to New York again.

I look at my phone and bark out a weird laugh.

"Is that him?" Shannon asks.

"Oh, my God!" I hold up my phone so she can read this.

She gives me a knowing look. "I know he's traveling so much these days, and he's only in town for a few hours, but you guys have to talk this out—"

Chug. Hmm. That fourth glass went down well.

"Does that text say what I think it says?" Shannon looks gut-punched. "Did he seriously just text you with, *Only here for the party. Not even time for a quickie*."

"Yep."

Andrew walks in the living room at that precise moment. The force of our glares should have propelled him right through the wall, but instead he lurches slightly to the right, one hand in his pocket, the other on the wood counter near the kitchen.

He gives me a wave.

"A wave?" she hisses. "You get a wave? That's it?"

"Yep. A fight, a month of mostly silence, a bizarre text and a wave."

We contemplate that one by stewing in the silence of the outraged. It has a very bitter taste.

"What man doesn't make time for a quickie?" she huffs.

"A gay man?"

Her eyes go wide. "He's *gay*?"

That question makes me remember the last time we made love. "No. Definitely not gay. Just sayin'. There are two kinds of men who aren't interested in quickies: gay men and dead men."

Her eyes narrow.

"Gay men like quickies."

"Not with Vulvatron." I gesture vaguely at my crotch and realize my wine glass is empty. Hmm. Have to remedy that.

"Vulva-*what*?"

"Never mind."

"Declan would rappel down from a helicopter with his pants off in a hurricane if we went weeks without sex and he was in town for a few hours and it were the only way to fit in a quickie."

I throw my hands up in the air and brush lightly against that fine, fine waiter who is carrying my sweet love juice. Ah, Pinot Grigio. How have I never cozied up to a bottle of you between my breasts? I grab another glass of wine.

"That is because you're marrying Superbillionaire."

Shannon eyes my wine. "Time to slow down?"

I take a gulp. "I'm just getting started."

Andrew's walking toward me with a determined look in his eye and oh, sweet mercy, I go loose and wet and fuzzy inside as he reaches for me, planting a kiss on either cheek. He just flew back from Paris, so maybe that's the drill.

As I go in for a kiss on the lips, though, he grazes my cheek again.

My blood stops pumping.

What
Fresh
Hell
Is
This?

Mixed signals is one thing. Andrew's confusing set of clues is more like a computer system short circuiting.

I look around, my hands out in a gesture of *WTF?* and I scan the crowd as if I'll catch someone's eye and we can share in our disbelief that my boyfriend just dodged a kiss from me after a month of nothing. Nada. I actually resorted to my nightstand collection for the first time in months and let me tell you, they need to put little speakers on vibrators with audio recordings of

284

men sighing and groaning at appropriate intervals, because *bzzz bzzz bzzz* is not sexy.

It just isn't.

The first sex toy company who designs a vibrator that says, "I love when you just let go like that," or "Your O face is so hot," or groans, "Have you lost weight? Because I need more to grab" will dominate the industry and blow up the stock market.

Especially if the voices are programmable, like GPS systems. Male, female, British, Irish, Spanish, French, Shrek—imagine the possibilities. Mr. Darcy could be your vibrator's voice. You could have tie-ins with major video game characters.

Thor.

Thor could utter phrases from down below, like, "This mortal form requires orgasms."

You could even have your significant other record special messages to be played at intervals of their choosing (or yours). If your partner dies, you'd cherish the memory of them forever.

I may be on to something here. I come up with some amazing ideas sometimes. Man, this Pinot Grigio is some good stuff.

While I contemplate these philosophical questions about the meaning of life and finish my fifth (I'm not counting) glass of wine, Marie calls everyone to attention.

"Dinner is served!" she announces.

Declan hands Andrew and Hamish a shot of something amber. The two clink glasses and down the alcohol. Then Hamish pours another. By the time we're all assembled at the table, I count three rounds.

Fine, then. I pluck a sixth glass of wine from the hot waiter and take my seat.

Next to Andrew.

SHOPPING FOR A CEO

Before my ass is even in the chair Marie is banging on her wine glass with a salad fork like it's a dinner bell at a dude ranch and we're all cows out to pasture who need to come home.

Get along little dogie.

"Kiss! Kiss!" she calls out, smiling at Declan and Shannon.

In response, Jason bends over Marie and gives her one hell of a hot, probing scorcher that she starts to fight off, then melts into. After a while, we all start to shift in our seats as it goes on and on...

"I don't think that's quite what Marie was going for," James says dryly.

"You don't know my mom and dad," Amy replies.

"A typical kiss contains more than two hundred strains of bacteria," my mom announces.

Jason pulls away.

"Research," my mom says awkwardly.

"What do you do for a living? Work on a porn set?" Marie jokes.

"Actuary."

"Oh." Marie frowns. "That's like the opposite of porn."

"I compute premium rates for various high-risk pools. Just did a kissing evaluation last year for some Hollywood projects." Mom shudders. "You wouldn't believe how much herpes there is in that population."

And with a single sentence, my mother silences even Marie.

"You are just a wealth of interesting facts," James says. I do a double-take as I realize James is holding Spritzy in his lap, rubbing his little head with affection. He's smiling at my mother with a look that makes me understand why people call him The Grey Wolf, though lately they're calling him The Silver Wolf. Not sure what the difference is.

Andrew's hand lands on my knee.

Oh.

It's The Asshole Wolf.

I turn to face him. He is, basically, James. Only three and a half decades younger and a little lighter.

"Would you help me get Hamish's attention?" Andrew asks, the hand withdrawing quickly.

I pick up a bread roll and pull my arm back to throw it across the table, but Andrew's faster.

"What the hell are you doing?"

"Getting Hamish's attention."

"Are you drunk?"

"No," I lie. I take the opportunity to really look at him. He has five o'clock shadow, a genetic trait that runs through the McCormick men even at noon, and his tie is loose. His eyes are floating in his head and he's staring at my boobs like they talk.

"Are *you*?"

He ignores my question.

I put down the dinner roll and reach down, pressing my breasts together to form the Grand Canyon.

"Why Andrew, well fiddle-dee-dee," I say in my best Scarlett O'Hara imitation. "How nice of you to drop by."

Hamish is watching us from across the table and nudges Amy, pointing. "Is this a party trick in the U.S.? Do women actually make their breasts talk?"

She gives him a hard look. "No. Most of us just double knot a cherry stem with our tongues."

Hamish sprays a fine mist of what I now realize is Glenfiddich scotch whisky all over his arm.

"I need to spend more time with my American cousins," he mutters, eyeing Amy with renewed interest as she reaches for the Maraschino cherry in her amaretto sour.

And promptly bites down, hard, on the fruit's flesh, tearing it in half with her teeth.

Hamish flinches.

"Or not," he declares.

"Why are you making your boobs sound like one of the women in Duck Dynasty?" Andrew says with a sad little look. "I've lost respect for them."

"You apologize to my boobs," I demand. Maybe a little too loudly, because suddenly everyone is looking at me.

Shannon's face ripples with horror. Her eyes skip to my wine. She makes a throat-cutting gesture with her finger.

"She wants you to stop drinking," Andrew hisses in my ear.

"Or cut off your balls," I say pleasantly. "It's hard to tell which one would make the world a better place." I reach for my butter knife and Andrew shifts away from me, turning to try to speak with no one, because he's at the end of the table.

I overhear Terry saying something about Farmington Country Club to Carol.

"Last time I was there was for my mother's funeral."

She flinches and puts her hand on his wrist. "I'm so sorry. Is the location going to be hard for your brothers and your dad? Because I can talk to my mother and—"

Terry's deep laugh makes his eyebrows go up, and he sits back in his chair, stretching out, like he and Carol are old friends.

"We're all fine. Farmington isn't ruined for us. And you're about as likely to change your mother's mind as you are to find my dad dating someone who was born before Reagan was president."

Declan stands abruptly, Carol interrupting her own laughter as his movement catches her eye.

"Well," says Declan, in a voice I can't read. Either he's overcome with emotion, barely holding himself back from strangling Marie, or pissed as hell.

Sometimes you just can't tell the difference with him.

Most of the time you can't tell the difference with him.

"I found the perfect woman for me," he chokes out as the toast ends and we all smile.

Overcome. I see. I'll learn to read him eventually.

He and Shannon share a sweet kiss. Marie looks like she's a split second away from chiming her wine glass with a spoon again. I catch her attention and give her a wide-eyed stare that I hope looks earnest like Thumper the rabbit in Bambi, but also deathly, like one of those scary prison women from *Orange is the New Black*.

It works.

My hairstylist shops are back, and I've returned to my onyx hair color. I need to rock this black hair look more. When you look like a dominatrix and walk like an Ice Queen Warrior, people defer to you.

Especially Jason, which is kind of disturbing.

"And Shannon looks great naked," Andrew adds with a smile and a voice that carries.

All movement, all breathing, all linear thought halts. Splat. Like dropping a watermelon from James McCormick's office window.

SHOPPING FOR A CEO

All the air leaves the room like a (c'mon, you knew this was coming) New England Patriots football.

Shannon's face contorts like something out of a circus show. Declan looks like he's about to leap across the table and give Andrew a vasectomy with a shrimp skewer.

This is my best friend. My bestie. The woman I can call at 5:47 a.m. on my way to a 7 a.m. appointment and beg to bring me tampons after my period makes an inelegant appearance mid-night. The woman who knows my secret passion for marshmallow treats made with Cheetos instead of Rice Krispies. The friend who I could, seriously, call to help me move a body and who would dance on the grave if the person was bad enough.

She may help me move Andrew McCormick's body at this rate. And not in some male fantasy FMF kind of way.

No one makes a sound. All eyes are on Andrew, who is obliviously chowing through his salad. He stabs a pecan and eats it, then reaches for his glass of white wine. *My* white wine, in fact.

I imagine Andrew's ankle is his crotch.

And then I jab it, hard, with my high heel.

He yelps, wine spilling down his wrist.

You know that one note in The Star Spangled Banner? The one no one can ever quite nail when they sing it before a Red Sox or Patriots game?

Yeah. He should change careers, because that sound is pitch perfect.

"You've seen Shannon naked?" James asks Andrew, who is reaching under the table to rub his ankle and muttering curses in three different languages. Ah, the rich. They even curse better.

"Who hasn't?" Marie says in a too-chipper voice.

Terry's eyebrows hit a CNN satellite orbiting in space. He's been quiet so far, the only McCormick brother at the table who seems to avoid power or attention. I like him the most. He is my new best friend.

Marie continues, very obviously counting heads at the table. Me. Andrew. Declan. Marie. Jason. Amy. Terry. Carol. Hamish. James. Shannon. Declan. "By my count," she adds, "about seventy-five percent of the room has."

"Who else here *hasn't* seen Shannon naked?" James replies. It dawns on me that he's not shocked by this conversation.

He's pissed to be an outsider.

Hamish starts to raise his hand and wiggles his fingers. Amy smacks his hand down.

"You've seen her naked?" Andrew growls at me from a position half under the table. Is he snarling?

"Yes," I whisper back.

"Hmph," he grunts, sounding remarkably like his Scottish cousin. "That's kind of hot."

I stab the back of his neck with my dessert fork.

A strong hand reaches up, grabs my wrist, and I find myself yanked, hard, under the table. My face is inches from Andrew's, and he's hissing at me in that voice only men can do. The low, deep vibrating baritone that makes hissing sound like pure sex in vocal form.

"What the hell do you think you're doing?" he growls at me.

His eyes are red and floating. "Did you show up here drunk?" I ask, my voice full of accusation. "Is that what your quickie text is all about? You're drunk texting?"

He's very, very angry. Which makes him even hotter, which makes me tingle in places that feel like they're vibrating from pure animal magnetism. He's the magnet and I have iron shavings running through my bloodstream.

"Raise your hand if you *haven't* seen Shannon naked," I hear James say above us. "Apparently, there's a club and some of us are excluded."

"DAD!" Declan shouts, his voice filled with warning.

I don't know what happens next, because Andrew's mouth takes mine, hard and furious, the kiss more like retaliation for my neck stab.

Retaliate away, bud. And do it a little more to the left like that. Oh, and that.

And...oh.

A month's worth of lust comes pouring out between us. If my panties hadn't already melted off from listening to Hamish recite the MBTA Red Line station list, they would melt off again.

"Are you two making out down there?" Shannon cries out. Her beautiful Tom Ford high heel turns into a weapon, jabbing at us like a toothpick going after a jumbo piece of shrimp at a cocktail party.

Fortunately, she gets Andrew, an inch to the left of his crotch.

"Jesus Christ!" he screams, sitting up so fast his head whacks against the underside of the table, making people murmur and gasp above.

"Direct hit!" I shout. "You sunk my battleship!"

Shannon pulls me out from under the table and directs me to my seat. "Don't do this to me," she whispers furiously.

Andrew crawls out as well, clutching his phone. "Found it!" he says, pretending that's why we were under there. He does not realize three inches to the left of his lips, he's covered in my red lipstick. He looks like the subject of a South American anthropology documentary.

"Found what? Mandy's mouth?" my mom quips. James' lips twitch. I don't appreciate the childhood name, but I let it slide.

Until...

"Mandy!" Marie squeals, her eyes jumping from me to Andrew like she's on a scavenger hunt and we're on the list. "And Andy!" She claps like a child, jumping up and down in her seat.

"No one has ever called me Andy," Andrew declares in a cold voice as he takes his seat and angrily wipes his face with his napkin.

Hamish waggles his eyebrows and holds up the bottle of scotch, offering to pour Andrew a shot. Andrew takes the entire bottle from him and fills his wine glass instead.

"Hardcore," Hamish murmurs admiringly.

"And I haven't been Mandy since I was five," I say. Andrew and I exchange a look. I give my mom an arched eyebrow. She reaches into her bag and pretends Spritzy needs attention, except Spritzy is in James' lap, now licking the herbed butter bowl.

Andrew and I have something in common, after all. At least there's this: a hatred for diminution.

Marie pretends not to hear, or maybe she does and simply decides our protests do not fit her delusion and therefore are dispensable.

She zeroes in on Hamish, then Amy.

"Weel," Hamish says in that low Scottish accent of his. "Ye dinna have a nickname you can use for me, Marie. Hamish is—"

"Hamy and Amy!" Marie interjects, pronouncing Hamish's new moniker as if it rhymes with Amy.

The man's face turns green. It's astonishing, and too bad he's not Irish, because that would be one hell of a party trick if he were, especially in Boston every March for the famous St. Patrick's Day parade.

"Oh, God," Amy mutters, reaching for her wine. She drinks the whole glass down, grabs the bottle of white wine, and starts chugging from the mouth.

Declan grabs the red and it looks like he's about to imitate her. Or use the bottle as a weapon against Marie.

When he starts drinking, I exhale sharply. Whew. Marie's safe.

Terry is watching all of this with a look of inappropriate glee, most of his attention focused on his brothers and James. Of all the McCormick men, he seems to be the only one who genuinely likes Marie.

"Carol and Terry," Marie announces, squinching up her face. "Hmmm. You two don't match."

"And I'm not changing my name to Terrel," Terry says, winking at Carol, who manages to roll her eyes and blush at the same time.

"That's fine. Carol can just go by Carrie! Carrie and Terry works!" Marie looks like she just discovered Fermat's Last Theorem.

"What rhymes with Chuckles?" Declan mutters.

James clears his throat. "I know a word. It starts with F—"

"Too bad 'Shannon' and 'Declan' don't rhyme," Marie says sadly. Is she pouting? Her lower lip pokes out like a cash register drawer.

"Where's that sword that goes with the kilt tuxedo? I need it sooner than later," Declan whispers to Shannon.

"Quit joking," she says, poking him in the ribs.

"Who's joking?" he, Andrew and James say in unison. Andrew pops back all the whisky in his wine glass and slams it on the table.

And then the caterer begins the next course.

We manage to eat in relative peace for an entire four minutes or so before someone—okay, me—opens her big, fat mouth and says, "Jason and Marie don't rhyme."

"Your names don't need to rhyme to have a fabulous marriage," Declan says, giving Shannon a lovely kiss on the cheek.

My eyes tear up.

"That was fucking beautiful, Declan," Andrew says, giving him a slow golf clap.

Declan gives him a look that silences Andrew.

"I would like to make an announcement," James says, handing Spritzy off to my mother and standing slowly, with the grace of a man who is accustomed to being watched.

"Is this about your cancer?" Andrew asks, the words coming out of his mouth with little tethers on them, and as they roll out you can see in Andrew's eyes a series of tiny little men desperately yanking on the ropes as they try to put them back behind his teeth.

"What?" Declan gasps. The table erupts into chaos.

Andrew has the wherewithal to just close his eyes and wince.

"I'm sorry, Dad." He bows his head like a toy being powered off. My heart softens for him and I reach under the table to take his hand, but stop myself. I don't really know what role I play in his life right now and the boundary between us is there. Undefined, but there.

James is blinking, his face a neutral mask as he stands above the seated group, clearly trying to figure out the best approach to salvage the situation.

"I was about to propose a toast to Shannon, but it looks like I will make a quiet personal announcement instead," James says in a jovial voice. Either he's really this grounded and centered about the cancer, or he's a damn fine actor.

"Yes, it's true. I have very slow-growing prostate cancer." He looks at Declan with the closest thing to love I've ever seen him express toward his son. "And I wanted to tell you privately, Declan, but this is how you're learning."

Both Terry and Andrew shift uncomfortably in their seats.

Ah. Terry knows, too. Sympathy for Declan makes me pour myself another glass of wine, because...well.

Because I'm pretty sloshed here.

Declan stands and looks across the table at his father, who is already on his feet for the aborted toast. "Are you sick now? Do you need chemotherapy? What do the doctors—"

James' eyes go soft and concerned. Fatherly. "I'm fine, son. My prognosis is fantastic. I'm one of those old coots," he says with a laugh, exchanging a look with Jason that makes my throat ache, "who will be around to watch my grandchildren graduate high school. As long as you two get cracking," he adds, giving Shannon a wink.

The table erupts into polite chuckling.

My mother and Shannon have one thing in common: when they get nervous, they babble. This is important, because Mom, who is sitting right next to James, turns to him and says,

"I recently did an analysis on prostate cancer issues for health insurance purposes. New research shows that men who orgasm more than twenty times a month have reduced prostate cancer rates."

He smiles, giving her a look like he's seeing her in a new light. "Is that an offer to help?"

Mom turns the color of my lipstick and mumbles into her wine. She's blushing. James reaches down and touching her shoulder with a gesture that strikes me as friendly.

James doesn't *do* friendly.

Then again, people change. Especially when they have no choice.

I look at Andrew.

"I'm so sorry," numerous folks at the table murmur. It's hard to tell who says what because I can't drink wine and listen at the same time. Sure, I was a cheerleader in high school and was able to be the base of three-person-tall formations, but get six (seven?) glasses of wine in me and it's a freaking miracle if I can remember to—.

Andrew's hand goes on my knee.

Apparently, my body remembers how to respond to his touch.

"May I have a word with you?"

"Now?"

"Yes. In private," he says through the corner of his mouth.

I start to crawl under the table. He pulls me back.

"Not there."

"Oh."

We stand. The ground got *way* lower since I sat down at the dinner table.

"I know you're not taking me outside," I say with far more cynicism than I should. He winces. I bite my lips to shut up.

He directs me to Shannon and Declan's bedroom.

"Oh, no, bud. You're not having sex with me here. Mr. I Don't Have Time for a Quickie isn't getting any." I use a mocking tone that feels right when the angel inside me whispers sweet nothings in my ear, but that feels wrong when the devil tells me I should just shut up and unwind.

"What are you talking about?" He sounds genuinely perplexed.

I reach between my boobs. He stares. I pull out my phone. He smiles.

"What else do you keep in there?"

"Not quickies."

His face falls. I shove my phone in front of him and show him his earlier text.

He frowns. "I wrote *that*?"

"The text is from your phone number."

"I'm an idiot."

I don't argue.

His warm hand presses between my shoulder blades as he looks behind us and guides me into Declan's walk in closet. He closes the door and turns around, giving me a smile that not only melts my non-existent panties, but I think my clitoris just became a Roman candle.

"No way," I declare before my body can override my circuits. "I am not regressing."

"Regressing?"

"This whole relationship started out in closets. We moved up to limos and beds and restaurants. I will not let you take us back to the dreaded closets. Nope, nope, nope."

He looks down at the soft carpeting.

"Closets can be good."

"For storing clothes."

"For making up."

"Is that what this is?"

"I'm trying, Amanda." He steps into my space and our heat mingles. His eyelids flutter and he sighs, a sound of hope. "I'm really trying."

"I am, too," I confess.

"I'm sorry," he says, his hands on my hips, reaching out like twin olive branches. "I don't care about your father being in prison and I like your mother and I followed you that night at the marina because I had just learned about my dad's cancer the week before and it made me think. Really think. It made me realize that life is short." He makes a small, earnest sound. "Not that I didn't learn that a long time ago."

I start to open my mouth to say something about his mother, but he continues.

"When I saw you there, I didn't chase you down to keep you quiet. I followed you because it seemed like more than coincidence to meet you there. Like fate was trying to tell me something."

Oh.

"For the past two years I've been stupid. I thought you weren't my type. I have watched Declan fall in love with Shannon and listened to our father tell my brother what a fool he is to take such a huge risk with her. I live a life where all my risk is poured into my work. Not my personal life."

"No girlfriend," I say.

He shakes his head. "Never. Easier that way."

My heart tightens like someone's pulling a drawstring.

"But not better."

I stretch up to meet his mouth, the movement like smoke seeking the sky as I burn for him. He tastes like fine whisky and apologies, his mouth tender and loose, the kiss lush with that gentle moment when everything you thought had dark, thick borders around it turns out to be an optical illusion you invented by accident.

I'm blurring in his arms, my lips becoming his, his hard shoulder muscles now mine, the soft curve of my waist a part of Andrew, his hardness against my thigh a part of me.

Or it would be, soon.

In me, at any rate.

For weeks I have ached for him. Dreamed of him. Given over my mind to the endless recriminations of *what ifs* and rifled through my self-doubt like a woman who has lost her wedding ring in the trash. Did I throw away my one best hope for love because I can't handle the hint of abandonment? Was Andrew right? Has his absence been a misunderstanding fueled by the ghosts of my past?

Shannon is the overthinker. Always has been. I'm the one who pretends to listen and then acts to fix whatever's wrong. My mind loosened by too many fermented grapes and adrenaline, my blood thickened by want and proximity, I pull back.

It's time to act.

"If I sleep with you right now, it'll be hate sex," I say, then frown. Where in the hell did that come from? I thought I was about to reach for his belt buckle, but clearly my hands and my head have two different agendas.

"Nothing wrong with hate sex."

"*Boozy* hate sex we'll both regret in the morning."

"I might regret the booze in the morning, Amanda," he says with a voice filled with longing and urgency, "but I would never, ever regret having sex with you."

"How long have you been practicing that line?"

"Since you stabbed me in the neck with the fork."

"You're a planner."

"I am very good at risk assessment."

"And you've determined..."

"That there is no downside to sex with you. Ever."

"No wonder you're so good at negotiations in the boardroom."

"I'm even better in the bedroom."

"How about closets?"

His hands reach up to cup my breasts and I lean into the touch, his thumbs tracing circles around nipples that strain against the cloth of my bra to be closer to him. We could, you know? Make love right here, right now, against the row of ties that hang like ribbons on a vine. On the carpeted floor amidst the sterile, organized cabinetry.

I could tell him I'm sorry. That I got all the wrong ideas from all the right actions. He's scared and vulnerable, so he creates a life that reduces risk. I understand that. I can honor it, even if it means never going outside in the sun with him eight months a year, extreme as that may be. Yielding to his obsessiveness to eliminate risk is nothing new to me.

I've done that most of my life with my mom.

Now, at least, I know why.

Exponentially.

All these thoughts mix in my mind like word salad, each making sense alone until they're all blended together. He just needs to be open with me, to tell me how he feels.

And how he feels about *me*.

301

It would be so easy to say yes to sex right now. I could use a few minutes of bursting passion where I lose myself in him. The word is on the tip of my tongue, which is currently sliding against his teeth, rising up to the top of his mouth as his welcome touch makes me wonder why I'd ever say no. That *yes* bounces from my mouth to his, then back, and I am about to release it and claim him for myself when we hear:

Tap tap tap.

Andrew groans.

"Are you two having sex in my *closet?*" Declan says in a voice that makes it clear that we do not, under any circumstances, have permission to have sex in his closet.

"Yes."

"No."

We answer simultaneously, then giggle.

The doorknob jiggles.

"Don't come in!" Andrew shouts, reaching between us to adjust himself.

"Why not? Afraid I'll see Amanda naked? We'd just be even, then."

"I am not a bag of flesh you get to parade to settle some score!" I shout.

Andrew's eyebrows go up.

The doorknob stops shaking.

"Get out here. Now. You two are the maid of honor and the best man at this wedding and you're acting like horny teenagers. You have responsibilities. And not just announcing Dad's cancer to a group of people and violating his privacy."

"Shit," Andrew hisses through his teeth. His gaze drops and he sighs.

I fling open the door and look up into the eyes of a very angry Declan McCormick.

"See here," I say, shoving my finger in his face. "You don't get to blame Andrew for the fact that your father doesn't want to share his private information with you."

"Amanda—" Andrew grabs my other arm and tries to stop me.

"Are you blaming *me* for what Andrew just did?" Declan's voice goes low and dangerous, like a coiled snake preparing for a full strike.

"No."

"Sounds like it."

"That's your interpretation."

I can feel Andrew's eyes on me, though I can't see his face. I'm not fighting his battle for him; he can do that just fine.

I don't really know why I'm taking on Declan. Six (seven?) glasses of wine, maybe? Does everything I do have to make sense? Everyone around me has tacit permission from the universe to act in irrational ways.

Maybe it's my turn.

Finally.

Declan's face is a study in how to exude power without actually doing anything. No words. No expression. No movement. Just the steady breath of a man who is accustomed to having time stop for him while he deliberates.

And then:

"Not now. I am not having this conversation now. Dad," he says, looking around me and catching Andrew's eye, "is out there trying to salvage everything after that bomb you dropped. You owe him, at the very least, the courtesy of your attendance."

And with that, Declan slams the door shut in my face.

Andrew looks at me.

I look back.

He runs a shaking hand through his hair and asks, "I'm guessing sex is out of the question now?"

CHAPTER TWENTY-FIVE

The wedding is in one week, and it's time for final fittings, not-so-final fits, and a lot of frustration.

Plenty of words that start with the letter F.

Which means grumpy men, lots of wine, and a mother of the bride who is like a hummingbird on crack.

We are at Shannon and Declan's apartment yet again, though there's no fancy dinner for us to ruin. Just an assemblage of snacks, some beer and wine, and a tailor flown in from Edinburgh to make sure the men in their kilt tuxedos fit the part. Marie has gone for the modern Scottish look, with the men in tight, tailored, short jackets and bow ties, and kilts that look more complicated than a corset to assemble and wear properly. The look is more Royal Family than Eighteenth Century Highlander, thank goodness.

I see swords and sporrans, special socks and strange shoes, and for once I'm relieved to deal with the familiar drudgery of a strapless bridesmaid dress. We women have our wedding seamstress, and she's doing all the last-minute tucks and loosenings and fussy little tweaks that make everything perfect.

"No, Marie, I will not dye my hair auburn for the wedding," Declan insists as the tailor adjusts his skirt...er, kilt. Sorry. I called it a skirt in front of the Scottish tailor and he hissed at me like that time I stepped on Chuckles' tail.

"But you'll wear the tuxedo kilt," Marie replies.

"Of course." Declan gestures down at his body. He's clad in a white t-shirt that fits quite well, the kilt in question, a sporran and the woolen socks. All the pieces are being carefully checked to make sure that the suits can be delivered as planned to the Farmington Country Club groom's quarters on D-Day.

"And the sword?"

"Mooooooooom," Shannon says in a low voice of warning.

"The sword is a wee bit much," the tailor mutters under his breath.

"Sure," Declan answers. "I need to have something to fall on when you finally tip me over the edge."

"Ye might do better with a Sgian Dubh." He pronounces it like *skee-an-doo*.

"A what?" Declan asks, twitching suddenly as the kilt pin gets a wee too close to his, um...wee wee.

"A small knife you can hide in your hand and use quietly." The smile he shares with Declan creeps me out. "Ye do more damage faster that way and put yourself out o' your misery."

Marie splays her palm over her heart. The tips of her fingernails are a lovely lilac that matches her eye shadow. Her own hair is a rich auburn now, permed to be curly. She's gone from platinum blonde to auburn so fast it's disconcerting.

Then again, who am I to talk when it comes to changing hair color?

"I am just trying to make sure I...er, you and Shannon have the best wedding ever!" She sniffs, clearly hurt. Or pretending to be hurt. Now that she's become a Momzilla, it's hard to tell the difference.

She gives the tailor a withering glance. He doesn't notice. I have the distinct impression he couldn't care if he did notice, anyhow.

Declan's eyes narrow. Shannon puts her hand on his biceps and whispers something in his ear that makes him tense, then arch an eyebrow.

"And I'll do the authentic kilt thing," he says in a tight voice.

My turn to arch some eyebrows as I look at Shannon, whose cheeks are flushed.

"You'll go commando?" Marie chirps, clapping her hands with glee.

"It turns out it might have some benefits I hadn't considered," Declan mutters. What I thought was a tone of frustration sounds more and more like arousal.

Get a room, you two.

Andrew lets out a snort and looks at Shannon.

Then right at me. All the blood in my body stops, pulsing in place, as if trying to decide what to do next. It's as if my red blood cells have become sentient and aware, attuned to Andrew's presence at all times.

Every day that this wedding planning goes on and we both have to be in the same room is a kind of exquisite torture. My breath feels charged. He won't stop looking at me.

So what can I do?

I look back.

And imagine him commando.

My heart tugs a little every time I see him. I want to go back to that night we spent in bed, after he found me at the brew pub. It's not the sex that I miss. I miss the intimacy. Our talks. The loose and easy way I can strip myself down to my essence and be real with him. Andrew looks like he could use a loving dose of *real* right now, too.

Why does all the rest of life have to get in the way?

I know he's hurting after blurting out his father's secret. Declan was livid. Shannon told me later that he nearly withdrew his offer for Andrew to be his best man, but she'd talked him down. James and Declan have had a contentious relationship for years, and for Declan, it felt like one more way of being unmoored in the world, untethered from the man who should be an anchor.

I know from that night when Andrew opened up to me that Declan's not that far off base. The strain between his father and brother is one with roots so deep and searching.

Roots that wrap right around Andrew's heart, nourished by blood and denial.

Here I am, fighting back the real and working on my mask.

Once you taste real, though, the fakery is hard to swallow.

"Why in the hell would ye wear pants?" the tailor asks, his face a blistering pink. He has dark hair like Declan's, though it's gone to salt and pepper. His beard is thick like a squirrel's tail, and he has bright blue eyes. "Yer bollocks need airing out."

"My balls need lots of things," Andrew mumbles.

This is the first time I've seen him since the dinner party. We're taking it slow. And by *slow*, I mean we're taking it *nowhere*, if by "it" you mean this relationship thing.

I'm nobody. Who are you?

I'm nobody who really does regret not indulging in boozy sex with Andrew in that closet.

He was right.

He's texted me a few times. Between his traveling to New York and Europe and my last-minute wedding stuff, plus a spectacularly dull series of a few extra DoggieDates and my second childbirth class with Josh, the past few weeks have been a blur.

Not a wine-induced blur. Worse.

An ambiguous blur.

"Yer turn," the tailor, Mr. MacNevin, tells Andrew.

Hamish saunters in at that moment, beer bottle in hand, and he reaches into a bowl of snacks someone's put out on the kitchen counter. I see him munch on day-glo cheese balls and something chocolate.

Intrigued, I go and look.

And my joyful little heart sings.

"Cheetos and chocolate-covered pretzels!" I say, clapping, then shoving a handful in my mouth. "Hoo eatz deeze?"

"You, clearly," Hamish says, then swigs his beer. He makes a face and looks at the label. "Jay-zuz. Piss water. All these Americans drink is piss water. Ye canna get a good lager here."

"You're eating Andrew's favorite snack food," Shannon says, ignoring Hamish. The seamstress is cupping her boobs, on her knees in front of Shannon, and Declan is watching with a leering fascination.

Andrew is staring down at his own version of seamstress, on his knees with the kilt and sporran, and a very long kilt pin that could, with a shove of two inches, turn Andrew's unprotected balls into a pin cushion.

I swallow my mouthful and reach for my own bottle of watered-down piss.

Or, as we Americans call it, light beer.

"Oh, hi!" Marie says to Hamish, squinting. "Are you the stripper we called about? That woman who owns the company said she'd send over a nice, tall redhead, but..."

"Remember Hamish? My cousin?" Declan says pointedly.

Marie puts on her glasses. "Oh, yes. Hamish! You look so much like one of the male strippers I tried out for Shannon's bachelorette party that I didn't recognize you."

Let's unpack that sentence, shall we? Because it contains so many whoppers in such a brief stretch of words.

"Stripper you *tried out*?" howls Jason from across the room, where one of Mr. MacNevin's assistants flails in an attempt not to poke himself in the eyeball with Jason's kilt pin.

"You're planning my bachelorette party?" Shannon yells, turning in such a way that her dress falls in a puddle beneath her, revealing a strange combination of a red UMASS t-shirt and a tartan garter.

"Garters," Declan says, drooling.

"I didn't *literally* try him out," Marie titters.

"If it's the same guy from O," I counter, "then drinking that shot of white Russian out of his navel while he massaged lavender oil into your—

"MARIE!"

"MOM!"

"I was *working*!" Marie argues back. She pointedly walks to the kitchen table and shuffles more papers, mumbling something to herself about the tents and the weather forecast.

"Garters," Declan says, still drooling.

Shannon walks over to him and presses up on his chin, rolling her eyes.

Mr. MacNevin looks to Hamish with a conspirator's stare. "Are they all like this?"

"Like what?"

"So...American."

"Aye."

The two sigh and make a weird grumpy sound in the back of their throats.

A warm flush starts at the hollow of my throat, and not because the seamstress has moved on to me. She hands me my dress and I go into the changing room with her at my heels. We're trying everything on, so I have to add the many layers of underclothes, the corset, and finally the dress and sash.

"Amanda," the seamstress, Holly, says, huffing and puffing as she tightens the corset. "You have more cleavage than Dolly Parton."

I look down. I don't have to look far, because my chin brushes against the top of my boobs.

"Can you loosen it?"

"The corset, yes." Holly is not much older than me, with slim, surgeon's hands that move fast. "Are you fine with that? Most American women hate not wearing a bra, even a strapless one."

"No problem."

"But your dress buttons won't budge. They're as far out as can go."

I take a deep breath and nearly smother myself with these airbags that double as breasts.

"I will pass out before the ceremony starts."

She tugs on her long, brown braid, looking at me from various angles. "We could try Velcro."

"Velcro?"

Holly's eyes dart about the room like were talking about meth. Marie won't be happy with Velcro. "Yeah. Velcro. Just don't say a word to the crazy wench, and —"

"Is that your name for Marie?"

She snorts. "MacNevin's name for her is far, far worse." She gets back to the matter at hand, touching this and tugging that. "I can buy you another inch or

311

two with some well-placed buttons and a few changes. Can hide it so no one else notices. What do you say?"

"It's Velcro or death by asphyxiation."

She stares at me like that's not an answer.

"Um, Velcro, of course. There's no other choice."

"No. There is. You'd be surprised how many mothers of the bride insist on possible asphyxiation as a perfectly acceptable plan."

And with that, she helps me out of the entire contraption, giving me privacy to change back into my street clothes, then wander back into the main room. Holly guides me back to our spot, where she makes some small adjustments with a sash over my shoulder.

Marie is the queen at court.

"Amanda, did you order extra chairs and those shade sails for the sides of the seating areas? With a thousand guests outdoors, it's going to be—"

Andrew interrupts Marie with a sharp word. "Outdoors?"

Either she ignores him, or doesn't hear him. You can never tell the difference with Marie. "—a logistical nightmare making sure everything is—"

Without caring that he's upended the poor tailor's assistant by moving swiftly across the room to get in Marie's face, Andrew bends down in a curled stature, towering over Marie, who slowly tips her head up like she's realizing she's in danger from a beast she hasn't noticed before.

"Yes?" she squeaks.

"Did you say the wedding is *outdoors*?"

"Yes?" Her voice goes up like a question.

"I thought the actual wedding was at the same church where Mom and Dad married. Where practiced." His nostrils flare and his face goes blank in a manner that makes my skin start to crawl. "And then an outdoor, evening reception."

Marie's eyes dart to Shannon, who is watching the exchange while chewing on her thumbnail. Declan is in a small room, off to the side, being fitted for some part of the garment that requires privacy.

"Um, we moved it?" Marie's entire face lifts up, like she's asking permission. "There is some parade and festival in that part of the city, and when we looked at the calendar and—"

"No one told me." Andrew's words silence the room. I'm not about to open my mouth right now and mention that if he'd paid a smidge of attention at the rehearsal, he'd have known.

Just then, Declan walks in. An uncharacteristic expression of panic flitters across his face like a ghost.

"What's going on?"

"Outdoor wedding?" Andrew snaps.

Declan's eyebrows drop and those green eyes turn dark as he looks at Marie. "You didn't tell him?"

"*You* didn't tell him?" she cries back. She turns to Andrew. "But you were at the rehearsal! We were talking about the outdoor logistics, and—"

"No one told me!" Andrew roars. He reaches down and tries to unbuckle the complex series of straps and fabric that is cinched about his waist. I see a pin fall and he flinches, a streak of blood on his arm. He then finally rips the entire thing off in a spectacular display of physical self-abuse, revealing bicycle shorts underneath. Gasping with anger, he stands there wearing a white, molded t-shirt, black shorts, and a look of outrage so clear it feels like he's a different person.

He looks at Terry, who is watching the display with the kind of dispassionate observation only an older sibling can have, and says coldly, "You can be best man. I'm done."

Thick woolen stockings and dress shoes still on, he storms out of the apartment and, instead of using the elevator, appears to take the steps.

We look at each other in stunned silence.

"Andrew got Mom's temper," Terry murmurs.

I want to ask what that means, but Marie is falling to pieces before my eyes.

"Oh, my God, Shannon, is he serious? Why would he refuse to be in the wedding? What on earth is going on?"

I race out of the room, managing to make it about ten feet before I hear a gut-wrenching sound of torn fabric, then feel something yank me backwards just enough to make me gag.

The seamstress's cry is one of surprise, not pain. "Amanda!" she says. "I'm so sorry! I was standing on your sash!"

I untangle my neck and run to the elevator, pushing the button over and over, as if that will make the machine move faster.

The chatter in the living room is a mix of sobs and anger, of surprise and accusations. All the voices in different timbres and tones form a sort of solid pain in my ears, and when the elevator doors open with a soft *ding!*, I am relieved to hear it fade in the background, like the receding shock of an unexpected blow.

The ride down is glacial. At the rate Andrew was running, he may damn well beat me to the street, and if he does, he'll climb in a limo and be gone.

Or will he?

It's daylight outside. He won't venture into the fresh air. That limits where I need to search. Declan and Shannon's building has a fitness center, one that's in the basement, and there's a public pool attached to it. Spin bikes, treadmills, free weights.

I never exercise in there, but there's a twelve-person hot tub we use frequently.

I quickly press the button for that floor and hope.

Finding him will be so much easier than knowing what to actually say to him. He can't do this. He simply cannot pull out of the wedding. Andrew is Declan's best friend in the world. You want your best friend there when you change from just a person to someone *else's* person. You need someone who has seen you through all the different phases of yourself and watched you grow into who you are now stand before the world and claim that self.

Claim it via true love.

Of all the days for Andrew to set aside his fear, this wedding should be it. Twelve years is too long for him to hang on to this notion that he's too fragile to be outside. There is something so irrational going on, so fueled by all the impulsive emotions we develop when trauma happens, that I feel a cool detachment forming even as my increasing love—yes, *love*—for Andrew clouds my judgment.

As the elevator doors open, I walk into the small hallway in front of the fitness center. I am in a lounge, with lean chairs covered in colorful leather, shaggy carpets in patterns like butterfly wings, and a series of coolers offering various electrolyte-infused waters.

You cannot access the fitness center without a special residents-only key, so I find a seat facing the stairs and wait.

And wait.

I wait just long enough to experience the dread of determining that I should go back upstairs when I see Andrew walk out of the door to the staircase. He is coated in sweat, his hair dripping with it, shirt like something from a spring break wet t-shirt contest.

His eyes are wild and he avoids looking at me until he can't help himself.

"Did you know?"

"Does it matter?"

As his fist bangs into the doorway, I see twelve years of something he can't even name leaking out of him.

"Fuck yes, it matters, Amanda!"

"If it helps, I thought you knew. You were right there during the rehearsal. I know you were busy with business issues and on your phone a lot, but I thought you had decided you were fine with it and willing to take the risk and..." I cut off my chatter with a sudden shrug, the look on his face like an emergency brake.

"I would be an incompetent fool at best, and a reckless jerk at worst, to spend an hour or more outside on a hot July day in a flower-filled wedding at Farmington Country Club's enormous garden, with cakes and sweets and alcohol and pretty much every substance you can imagine drawing bees and wasps like a damn death magnet," he says coldly.

At least he's admitting why he's upset about the wedding being outdoors. This is progress.

"You can bring EpiPens. The chance is so, so slim. And Marie has even arranged to have an ambulance and paramedic on hand for any medical emergency—"

"Listen to yourself!" he shouts. "Shannon is a fool! She's going to break Declan's heart!"

"What? No. She loves him so much, Andrew. So, so much. She would never—"

"My mother," he says through gritted teeth, "never thought she would snap my father in two, either. But she did. And she broke Declan. Just...broke him."

316

"What about *you*?"

"I wish she had broken me!" he rasps, his voice cracking at the end. I see his throat ripple, emotion in kinetic form. "I wish she'd just..."

"No," I say fiercely. "*No.*"

"It would have been better than what happened that day! What happened after. Do you have any idea," he says, his voice going low and taut, like a tightrope between twelve years ago and now, "what it is like to wake up in a hospital with a hollow brother with shell-shocked eyes, an enraged father, and a nurse kindly holding your hand as you're informed your mother died because of—"

"No, no, Andrew, it wasn't—"

"Because of *me.*"

He said it. The ragged savagery of his voice feels like my heart has been clawed out of its chest by a bear and rests on the ground between us, beating.

Right alongside his.

I have stayed in my seat, looking up at him, respecting his space, but instinct makes me leap up and go to him. Touch him. He is impossibly hot and icily cold all at once, heat pouring off clammy skin.

"Your mother did not die because of you!"

He makes a keening sound and begins to pace. At least he's not leaving. At least there's that.

"Your mother died because of a freak, one-in-a-million accident that was so unfair."

"One that was *preventable*," he spits out.

"How? *How* was it preventable? Your parents did everything they could. They tested you. No one knew you had the same allergy. Your mom and dad and you and Declan did everything right—"

"Even when you do everything right people still leave you. You of all people should understand that."

317

I am *struck dumb*.

"When people pick me, their lives fall apart. They lose everyone they love," Andrew continues, his voice soft and quiet, the unsophisticated tone of a teen. He drops into a chair and holds his head in his hands, elbows on his knees. The back of his neck is vulnerable. A tiny hint of sweat darkens the hairline, making the edge of his hair curl. It's boyish. Childlike.

Remarkably innocent. I can see the teen he once was. The emergent man. If only I could unwind time. Time is the one thing I cannot fix.

He lets out a long sigh, like the past is being pushed out, like memory being born and crossing from one life to the next. Andrew stands, the movement so abrupt my eyes flit from his neck to his waist to shoe laces, like a series of still images scattered across a cinema screen in rapid-fire sequence.

As I scramble to meet him, he turns away. His shoulders are squared, the fabric tight across the wide upper back. My eyes take in the white cotton cloth, how it hugs his ribs and waist, tucked in and rumpled, the flat lines of wrinkles at odd angles, as if the cloth forgot how to listen and behave.

And then he looks at me with eyes so wounded and ragged its as if they've been torn.

"Don't pick me, Amanda. Don't pick me."

"What?" Suddenly, this conversation has nothing to do with the wedding. Not one bit.

"You heard me. Don't pick me."

"I—" With numb legs, I move toward him. So many words fill my mind. I want to reach up and wipe the crease of worry from his brow. I want to heal those eyes, to reach back in time and cradle his soul to my heart and let it find my rhythm. I want to breathe for him, just long enough so he can rest.

318

I want to make him know that my world will fall apart if I pick him, but not for the reasons he thinks.

And I'm ready to fall right along with it.

"Andrew, oh, Andrew, I'm falling for you and I don't care about the wasps or the risks or—"

He steps back and shakes his head, eyes clear in the way that can only come from a deep abyss of despair.

His voice is full of regret and longing. "I won't *let* you pick me."

And with that he turns, long, determined strides taking him down the hallway, out of my sight, and out of my heart.

Leaving me out of my mind.

CHAPTER TWENTY-SIX

"The problem with having so many women all working together on this wedding is that we are spending a ton of time together. Too much time. So much time that our cycles suddenly, painfully, align themselves," I lie to Marie, who has just arrived at Amy's apartment to get ready to caravan over to the party Marie scheduled.

Remember how Marie tried to take over the bachelorette soirée and I found a fix?

Well. Here we go.

"Poor Shannon! My baby!" Marie descends on morose, aching Shannon with a level of motherly sympathy that triggers a massive guilt complex in me. I don't like to lie. But if it fixes a problem...

"I am an entire week early!" Shannon screams as we ply her with ice cream and salt-n-vinegar potato chips and ibuprofen and heating wraps filled with lavender and aerosolized Xanax.

(Kidding about that last one, but wouldn't that be *awesome* if it existed?)

"Amy, Shannon, Carol and I all have our periods. Everyone started today. We're like lemmings, only instead of jumping off cliffs, we're using tampons," I say to Marie, whose face is scrunched in sympathy, eyes impossibly framed by lashes that could only be created by a penis enlargement device maker.

They're *that* long.

"How could this happen?" Marie moans. "It seems so bizarre." My mom is behind her, at the front door, and shoots me a look so skeptical she might as well rename herself Sherlock Holmes. Even Spritzy, dangling from her forearm, rolls his eyes.

Chuckles makes a hiss of warning at Spritzy, who starts to quiver in his bag and hunkers down.

"Yeah," my mom says. "Statistically impossible, in fact."

Uh oh.

Never try to pull one over an on actuary. I hadn't counted on my mother being part of a drinking sexfest.

She comes over to me, gives me a longer-than-usual hug, and whispers, "What are you all up to?" in my ear.

As I pull back I play the innocent, wide eyes and all. "I don't know what you're talking about."

I get a cocked eyebrow in return.

Huh. She looks just like me right now.

"See?" Marie crows as we sit around Amy's apartment looking like a bunch of post-roller-derby players, curled into fetal positions with various cold and hot packs on our body parts, groaning in pain. "Finally, that stupid menopause comes in handy!" She glances at my mother and they share a look that makes me want to rip out my uterus and beat them with it.

"I can't eat any of this!" Shannon cries out, then shoves another mouthful of caramel chunk ice cream between her teeth. "I'll never fit into my wedding dress."

"That's okay, dear," Marie says with sympathy, patting her arm. "We never thought you could manage anyway, so I had the seamstress add some gussets for the inevitable."

"WHAT?"

"I have not spent twenty-six years as your mother to not realize that you have the self control of Agnes at a yoga class for male underwear models."

My mom clears her throat and asks, blushing, "You offer yoga classes for male underwear models?"

"No, but isn't that a *great* idea?"

My mom nods. "I'd exercise more if that were an option."

Marie just beams.

"I am going to stand in front of a thousand people in two days and look like a big, white whale next to a god in a kilt!" Shannon sobs. I'm impressed. She's taking this acting thing way too far, but it seems to be fooling Marie.

"A *billionaire* god," Amy adds.

"That's not helpful!" Shannon snaps. She scrapes the bottom of her ice cream pint and pokes furiously with a spoon, as if viciously stabbing Ben and Jerry.

"Don't be silly," Marie soothes. "The photographer is an expert in Photoshop. You won't look like a whale. I promise."

"I don't want to have my wedding photographs doctored!"

"Not doctored. More like....finessed."

"That's fakery!"

"That's reality, Shannon," Marie argues. "Fake is the new black."

"What is that supposed to mean? That makes no sense!"

"Just eat your ice cream and wait for the pills to kick in, dear." Marie and my mother sling their purses over their shoulders and start to walk out the door.

"Where are you going?" Carol asks.

"To Shannon's bachelorette party."

"There is no party."

Marie and my mom share an uneasy look. Marie taps one fingernail against her front teeth as she screws up some courage.

"Spit it out, Mom," Carol says with a resigned sigh. "Whatever this is, it's gonna be good."

"Well, just because you all have uncooperative uterii doesn't mean Pam and I need to miss out on all the fun!"

"Uncooperative Uterii sounds like the name of a garage band at Smith College," Amy groans.

"You're going to," Shannon says slowly, her eyes still closed, head slung up against the back of the couch, "have my bachelorette party without *me*?"

"If you insist, sweetie!" Marie chirps. She and my mom high tail it for the door. "We'll do a blow job in your honor!"

"A what?"

"It's a drink. A shot. Don't worry. She's not really...they're not really, you know...." My mother sputters more than a lawn mower warming up.

"Although, Pam isn't married. She can whore it up all she wants."

The words *whore* and *my mother* should never, ever be in the same sentence.

My mom just winks at me. Winks!

And with that, they're off, Spritzy as their mascot. Mom has a letter from her doctor that sort of certifies Spritzy as a service dog. Not really, but the letterhead shuts people up fairly quickly. Mom's anxiety over her pain from the fibromyalgia means having Spritzy helps.

Not sure how having Spritzy at a bachelorette party is going to work, but...

Carol's phone buzzes with a text. She reads it and makes a sound of disbelief.

"Everything okay with Jeffrey and Tyler?" Shannon asks, her brow creased with concern.

"What? That? Oh, yeah. Dad's keeping them overnight. Taking them out to their favorite restaurant and spoiling them rotten."

"You gave poor Jason earplugs for Chuck E. Cheese, right?" I ask.

Carol smiles and looks just like Marie. "We gave him a twelve pack for Christmas this year."

"Then what's wrong?"

"*Josh* just sent me a text asking where the party is."

"Josh? Why would Josh think he's been invited to my bachelorette party?" Shannon asks.

"Let me find out." Carol taps her screen a few times and we wait.

And wait.

Bzzzzz.

She reads the text aloud:

"Your mother invited me."

Jaws drop in disbelief.

"He has a penis! He can't come to my party!"

"He likes the same eye candy."

"Besides, I'm pretty sure Andrew invited him to Declan's bachelor party."

"And there will be plenty of penises at your bachelorette party," Carol groans.

"Not Josh's penis! Stripper penii!"

"Tell him where Mom and Pam are," Shannon says with a gleam in her eye. She looks at Carol and adds a mopey sigh.

Carol taps on her screen. "Done. Josh says he'll save some stripper belly lint for us to keep as a memento."

"Ewww," I say, recoiling.

Amy has been standing by the front door, looking outside. She turns around, slowly pulling her long, auburn curls out of the crooked ponytail she made.

"They're gone. It's safe."

"Whew!" Shannon exclaims. "I thought I was going to have to eat the entire pint and get sick before they left."

"That whole 'I'm going to look like a whale in my dress' act was great! You really sold it, Shannon," I tell her.

"I wasn't joking," Shannon says weakly.

Carol looks at us in confusion as Amy starts finger-combing her hair and Shannon grabs a small gym bag and heads for the bathroom.

"What are you doing?"

The three of us stop our bustling around. Amy gets an uneasy look, her eyes floating to me. Clearly, I'm the one who is going to have to explain what just happened.

"We, um...there actually *is* a bachelorette party."

"I know! Mom booked it behind your and Shannon's back and now...oh...." She's looking at us critically, as if she's processing nanosecond by nanosecond what we're up to.

We're silent as I struggle to figure out how to say this.

"We faked Mom out," Amy says bluntly. "We all pretended to get our periods and cancel the bachelorette party because we knew Mom would crash it."

The brownie in Carol's hand breaks in half. Chuckles is in her lap and it falls on his head. He sniffs it like it's a live hand grenade, then scurries off.

"You *what*?"

326

"It was easy for Amanda to pretend she was in pain," Amy says, coming over to me and rubbing my back compassionately. "She's in break-up mode. That's worse than period mode."

I nod.

Shannon comes back into the room wearing a glittery outfit clearly designed for pub crawling fun. It's a pale purple, with a shiny silver sheen, and a cowl neckline. Retro '70s.

"That just means Amanda can drink alcohol out of a man's navel and not worry about remembering his name when she wakes up next to him in the morning," she says with a wink.

"But he won't know to get me a breve latte," I joke, mortified to find that real tears are threatening my eyelids as I say the words.

"Wait. Hold on. Back up," Carol insists. "This is all...you were just *pretending* you all got your periods to get Mom to go off on a snipe hunt? Isn't that really cruel?"

"A half-naked man stripper snipe hunt," Amy adds.

Carol wavers. "That's not so bad, I guess."

"Amy probably has something you can borrow to wear," Shannon says to her older sister. "I'm sorry we didn't tell you so you could prepare," Shannon adds nervously, her words coming out like air from a tire pump. "But you're the worst liar, Carol, and—"

"Hey! I am not! I'm a very good liar. You try eloping with Todd and being married to that jackass and not learn how to lie."

"But you can't lie to Daddy. And he can't lie to Mom. We had to limit the circle of knowledge." Shannon fluffs her hair with Amy's hair pick, but because Shannon has hair with the consistency of Easter

327

basket grass and the waviness of a straight edge, she just looks like she's picking through brown corn silk.

"The circle of knowledge? And hold on. You mean you all *don't* have your periods right now?"

We three shake our heads.

"Damn it! I *do*!" she cries out, clasping the heating pad hard to her belly.

"Oh, man," Amy mumbles in sympathy.

"And I'm the only one in here who can't get pregnant!" Carol grouses. "But I still get my stupid periods. I'm between you three and Mom and Pam. I'm stuck in the middle." I'm assuming that's an allusion to having her tubes tied after she had her youngest son.

No one is listening to her as we change clothes and fluff and primp and get ready for a night on the town.

Carol jumps up, sighs, and pops some ibuprofen.

"All right. What can I squeeze into from Amy's closet? Dad's got Jeffrey and Tyler for the night." She sets down a half-eaten pint of ice cream, licking the spoon clean and shoving it in the treat. "Might as well have some fun that doesn't involve using my mouth."

We all practically crack our necks looking at her.

She grins back.

And looks just like her mom.

* * *

A long time ago, Shannon informed me she wanted a private room at a huge piano bar for singalongs and strippers. Hiring male strippers who can sing surprisingly easy.

As we walk in to the private room, a familiar Billy Joel tunes carries through the air from twin baby grand pianos that face each other. A row of tables sits in front of them, with layers radiating out from the center formed by the two pianos.

There is no bar tonight. It's all an open bar with table service, and all bankrolled by Anterdec. The only stipulation James McCormick placed on me when I made the bachelorette party arrangements was that I invite enough Anterdec employees, contractors, and subsidiary company workers to make it a legitimate business deduction.

That was easy.

Half of the male performers from O are here. I invited Declan's assistant, Grace, and Andrew's assistant. Shannon invited a gaggle of women she works with in Marketing at Anterdec, so we're pretty much covered there.

As we settle in at the table of honor, one of the cocktail servers plunks a bottle of chilled Champagne and a bucket of chilled wine coolers on the table.

Actually, that's not a bucket.

That's a *trough*. It takes two servers to lift the ice-and-bottle-filled bucket onto the table in front of us.

"Now that's what I call table service!" shouts a familiar voice.

Shannon gives me a look, as if Satan himself were whispering our names from the depths of Hell.

Right behind us.

We turn around slowly to find a *very* pleased with herself Marie, holding an open bottle of Champagne, standing next to my mother, who appears to be as drunk as I have ever seen her.

And Josh is behind them, giving us a sour look.

Mom and Marie do a surprisingly good imitation of Edina and Patsy from Absolutely Fabulous.

"Uh...." Shannon and I say in twin voices that sound like a boat propeller revving down.

"Thought you could outsmart us, huh?" Marie crows, nudging my mother, who falls against Josh, who knocks into a six-foot-tall stripper wearing less around his waist than Josh has on his balding head.

They're a game of human drunk dominoes.

The stripper holds Josh up with big, thick hands and winks. "Most people slip a five dollar bill in there after touching me like that."

"I—uh—um," Josh flounders, reaching in his back pocket for his wallet.

"It's okay. I give one free grab per cutie," the stripper says, walking off with a gait that shows off every butt muscle.

Josh grabs the Champagne from Marie and guzzles half the bottle.

"We, uh...." I look wildly around the room for Amy and Carol, who appear to be hiding. "We weren't ditching you."

Busted.

Shannon rolls her eyes and stands, giving Marie a grudging hug. "You win, Mom. You figured it out."

"See?" Marie says, then hiccups, slinging her arm around my mom. "Told you they tried to exclude us old birds."

"Actually, I figured it out," my mom protests.

Seventysomething Grace picks that moment to appear, a Corona in hand. "Marie! Good to see you. Shannon's got one hell of a party here, huh? I could use a different kind of eye candy myself, but a woman can admire the fine lines of a man without wanting to sleep with him, right?" She turns to Josh and clicks her beer bottle against his Champagne.

Josh and Marie share a horrified look.

"I don't understand what she just said," Josh whispers.

"Me either," Marie says.

Josh takes the bottle and drains it.

I leave Marie to do the introductions. I pull Shannon aside, but before we can escape, Marie is huffing with indignity, hissing in our faces. She's abandoned Josh and Mom. I hope someone, somewhere, introduces them all to each other.

"You invited Grace and tried to ditch me and Pam?"

"Grace isn't my *mother*," Shannon says with a *grrrr*. Literally. Like a dog. She makes noises like I imagine Mr. Wiffles sounds when upset.

"She could be your grandmother!" Marie snaps back.

"She works for Anterdec! She's Declan's longtime assistant and like a mother to him."

"*I* am like a mother to him! If you're going to include Grace, you should have included me!"

"MOM!" Shannon bellows. Her eyes are rimmed with red rage and she looks like she is about to pop. "You have taken my entire wedding and turned it into a giant clusterfuck!"

Marie gasps in horror, because Shannon rarely curses.

"I never wanted the Scottish-themed wedding. Didn't care about Farmington," Shannon screeches. The piano players vacillate between playing louder to cover up the argument, and softer to listen in. A small crowd of Shannon's coworkers and friends is forming around the two women.

"I have put up with the tartan thongs. With having a cat as a flower girl. With the spun sugar, life-size likeness of me and Declan next to the wedding cake. And the ice sculpture. And the ninety-minute video that takes our lives and turns it all into a time capsule. The live streaming video thing was way over the top, but did I complain? NO!"

The crowd tightens.

"All I wanted was one night. One tradition. One ritual that was mine. Just mine, exactly the way I wanted it, with a bunch of women I could let loose with and party. But no. You had to crash it. You had to ruin this for me. I'm not going to worry about your feelings of hurt because I didn't invite you, when you show no concern for my feelings!"

Marie blinks, then sniffs, then blinks again.

Shannon is panting, her top glimmering in the dark lights of the club, her breasts turning into shiny waves.

"Are you done?" Marie asks in a patient voice.

"Yes."

Marie reaches out and pats Shannon on the cheek. "It's okay, dear," she whispers. "I can tell you're *really* having your period and this is just the hormones talking."

And with that, Marie walks over to a stripper who is on his back on a long table, his body covered with little green vodka jigglers, and slurps one up with more tongue than Chuckles licking a bowl of cream.

I resist the urge to shove Shannon's eyeballs back in her head.

"HOW DOES SHE DO THAT?" Shannon screeches.

My own mother comes over and gives Shannon a sympathetic pat on the back, then stumbles slightly.

"'sokay Shannon, honey," Mom says. "Did you know that nine percent of all brides don't even have a bachelorette party?"

We look at her.

"Wedding insurance project," she adds, giving us a big smile. It lifts twenty years off her face, and I see

332

myself in her. I look more like my dad, so this is a revelation.

"And," she says, pulling Shannon closer, whispering in her ear, "between twenty-five and fifty percent of brides and grooms don't even have sex on their wedding night."

Oh, now I *know* my mother is drunk.

She's talking about sex.

"Don' be one of those, Shannon. Have sex with Declan. It's okay to lose your virginity on your wedding night."

"I already lost my—"

I grab Shannon and leave my mom to stagger over to Marie, where I don't want to know what happens next. I hear her say to Marie, "You know, I haven't had sex in seven years..." and that is when my circuits overload.

Hold on.

Mom doesn't date.

Ever. And dad left twenty-two years ago.

So, who did she—?

Not my business. Not my business. Not my business.

Tonight, I am determined not to drink. At all. I've had too much over the past few months. I'm normally a two-to-three drink a month person. Shannon and Marie have overindulged, too, and while a bachelorette party is the place to let loose and go wild, for some reason I'm living life backwards, anyway, so I might as well stay sober tonight.

Someone has to keep an eye on everyone anyhow.

And I'm the fixer.

Over the course of the next few hours we sing Garth Brooks, Billy Joel, Snow Lion, a hair-raising version of "Macarena", and we learn that both Marie and my mother know all the words to "Paradise by the Dashboard Light".

Even the baseball announcer's part.

After that last song ends, there's a short break. The room is so quiet my ears ring. Shannon is laughing it up with Grace and some other women from Anterdec. My mom and Marie are giggling in a booth over something they're watching on Marie's phone. Carol is flirting with a stripper who has more tattoos than he has skin. Amy is dancing to nothing. Just by herself, glass held high above her auburn hair, dancing to silence.

"HEY!" booms a loud, man's voice. It is, to my surprise, Josh.

Josh, who is shirtless and stretched across a long bar table on his back, with his navel filled with liquor.

And Spritzy is on his abs, happily licking from the little pool.

Henry the stripper walks by, taps me on the head, and says, "I've seen some kinky shit before, but..."

"Get your dog off me!" Josh screeches as my mom grabs Spritzy off his belly and stuffs her in her purse.

"DoggieDate indeed," mumbles Carol as Henry tosses Josh a bar towel and he cleans himself, muttering about wasted tequila.

I briefly wonder if tequila is okay for Spritzy but figure if it's a problem, Mom would panic, and given her current state of chill, I'm guessing the crisis has been averted.

The bar sound system starts up with—yep.

The song "The Dog Days Are Over" by Florence + The Machine. Henry looks at me from the stereo and winks.

Amy's dancing takes on a distinct beat and soon, the crowd is lost in the relentless pounding of the tune, clapping and stomping in time.

Staying dry while everyone around you drinks is its own little world. I am an island.

And then I am on my knees doing a blow job.

Hold on—it's a *drink*.

Fine, fine. *One* won't hurt anybody.

Every woman is being asked by the strippers to do a blow job as a way of honoring the bride, and who am *I* to dishonor my bestie?

You might even say I'm *required* to do this blow job. Might.

The splash of liquor and mocha against the back of my throat reminds me of "breakfast in bed" with Andrew, of antics under the sheets and the morning breve that followed. Funny how viscerally we embed memories via physical events. A scent. A sound. A texture. An image. Our senses store memories in our physical bodies as much as our minds are computer banks filled with the recall.

And as I swallow, on my knees and bent down to the floor to bite the shot glass between my teeth and tip its contents back, mind and body work together to make me recall what I've lost.

Who I've lost.

When Henry offers me a second blow job, I don't say no.

And this time, his navel is the shot glass.

"A-MAN-DA! A-MAN-DA!" the crowd chants. They start banging shot glasses against the scarred wood tables, the sound like that popular Queen song, the one people sang at football games back when I was a cheerleader.

That's what this reminds me of. The spotlight. The fun. Being the center of attention for highly-structured entertainment that delivers exactly according to audience expectations.

I deliver.

Six blow jobs later and boy, does my jaw ache. Marie and my mom are sitting next to one of the piano players, stuffing bills into a pint glass and begging them to play "Freebird".

Other women are stuffing even more money in the tip jar to stop the "Freebird" madness.

"C'mon," my mom pleads. "If you won't do 'Freebird', then how about 'Dog and Butterfly'?"

"Pammy! I love that song!" Marie squeals, stuffing what looks like a free coupon for a Starbucks latte into the tip jar.

"I hate being called Pammy," my mom mutters.

"You're my new best friend, Pammy!"

Meanwhile, the piano player just watches with a languid amusement.

I get the distinct impression he's been through this more than once.

"I am the bride, so I pick the last song!" Shannon slurs. I look at the big clock behind the bar, shocked it's nearly one a.m. already. I lost track of time slurping off the navel of a man.

Sue me.

"'Imagine'!" Shannon cries out.

The entire room groans in unison.

"We'll all start crying if you play that!" I argue. "How about something happier?"

"'The Wreck of the Edmund Fitzgerald'!" my mom suggests.

"Not happier, Mom."

Mom gives me a petulant look.

"I know!" I whisper it in Shannon's ear and she nods vigorously. She goes to the pianos players, and within seconds the opening lines of Van Morrison's "Brown Eyed Girl" start playing.

And we dance, Shannon's brown eyes wild and full of unfettered joy as she spends her second-to-last night as a single woman surrounded by women who love her.

Plus Josh, who is happily pouring shots into some guy's belly button. Except I'm not sure he's a stripper....

We dance until they kick us out.

And then we puke.

Okay, so technically, my *mom* is the only one who pukes. There's always one in every crowd when you go clubbing, and tonight it's the woman who gave birth to me.

"I'll hold your hair, Pammy! 'Cause tha's what bess frienns do." Marie proceeds to grab my mom's purse from her.

"That's *not* her hair."

"What?" Marie looks at mom's purse cross-eyed.

I sigh and reach for mom's hair.

The retching definitely puts a damper on the night. Luckily, I am not a sympathy gagger. Poor Mom has a system clearly not cut out for alcohol, and I'm actually surprised she drank at all tonight. We don't keep alcohol in the house. I've never seen her even tipsy.

"I'm sorry, honey," she says, trying to compose herself. "I think I drank more tonight than in the past twenty years combined. I also touched more man skin tonight than in the past two decades."

"Go Pammy!" Marie says, high-fiving my mom. She misses and goes flat on the ground, purse clutched in her other hand.

Growing up means realizing your parents are flawed human beings who are just twenty-five-year-older versions of your friends. Does that mean there's no such thing as actual adults? We're all just pretending?

"Pammy, you need to learn to hold your liquor." Marie pulls herself up and brushes grass off her knees.

"Something old, something new, something borrowed, something spew," Mom says in a sing-songy voice that immediately turns into a snore as I drag her to the open limo and tuck her into a spot.

"That's not how it goes," Marie protests. She follows Mom and doesn't seem to realize she's passed out.

And then she climbs inside and crashes on the seat, right in Mom's lap.

Shannon walks up from behind. Carol's already in the limo, and Amy is—oh, God, is she crouched around a corner, peeing in public? I'm going to pretend I didn't see that.

"Is that going to be us in a few decades?" Shannon ponders, her arm on my shoulder.

Marie's hand cups my mom's boob just as Amy walks over, adjusting her skirt.

"Oh, that needs to be captured on camera," she says, reaching into her cleavage and pulling out a camera.

Click.

"Nothing on social media!" Shannon cautions.

Amy gets an uneasy look on her face. I instinctively reach for her hair and pull it back.

"What are you doing?" she says, recoiling.

"You looked queasy."

"I was trying to decide whether to say something or not."

"About what?"

"About social media."

Shannon's eyes narrow like a hawk's. "Spill."

Amy sighs. "Jessica Coffin was here."

"WHAT?"

"Yeah. We had the bouncers kick her out, but we don't know how much she saw."

"I didn't notice her," I say.

Josh's voice pops up behind me. "That's because every single one of your senses was engaged in a piece of man beast named Zeke."

"Who?"

"Your blow job man."

We all nod as if this is a normal conversation.

"You guys see Jessica earlier?" Josh asks. When he drinks he gets chipper. "She heard a rumor Andrew and Amanda were dating."

Ouch.

Were.

"If she took pictures, I'll kill her," Shannon warns.

"You want me to hack her again?" Josh asks, then slaps his hand over his mouth. "Er, I mean...*someone* should hack her Twitter account again."

A light snore floats out from the limo. Then it's in harmony and melody as both Mom and Marie make beautiful music together. I peer in to see Amy and Carol on either side of them. Josh is sitting across the way now, staring at the inside of the limo like it's the deck of the U.S.S. Enterprise.

To my surprise, Shannon walks over to the driver's side, says something to a chauffeur I've never met, and closes the back doors, thumping the hood like a pro.

The limo takes off.

"What are you doing?" I ask, watching the tail lights narrow to red, glowing pupils as the car disappears into the night down the city street.

"Gerald will arrive in ten minutes with another car." Her sigh tells me everything and nothing. "I just needed to, you know...breathe."

"Need me to hold your hair?"

"Hah. No. Poor Pam."

"I think my mom got twenty years of teetotaling karma in one night."

"No one can keep up with my mom when it comes to alcohol, I guess." Shannon's voice is wistful. A cool breeze cuts the night and I shiver, all gooseflesh and gobsmacked. The alcohol is wearing off and I feel myself spiraling down, gently, like an autumn leaf. The maudlin mood feels fine, given the night we've had.

"I think my mom was last in a club in 1991 or something," I marvel. "I mean, asking the piano player for some song called 'Walk the Dinosaur'? What the hell?"

We snort and snicker until another gust of wind makes us wrap our arms around ourselves as we wait.

"You okay?" she asks, giving me a look that says I need to tell the truth or she'll just pull it out of me anyhow.

"No."

"You miss Andrew."

"Yes."

"I'm so sorry."

"He's an asshole."

"Yeah. I wish I could storm into his office and line all the McCormick men up as my puppets and make him see reason like a certain *someone* I know did for me two years ago."

"You didn't, um, do that by any chance, did you?" I ask in panic. "Because this isn't the same as you and Declan."

"No, no office storming. That's your deal. But I did talk to him."

Lightbulb.

That's why she sent everyone off in the limo.

"And?" My gooseflesh now has nothing to do with the weather.

Trouble seeps into her expression. "Andrew's terrified. He would never admit it, but he is the son who does whatever James wants. Dec says before their mom died, Terry was the rebel and Andrew was the cocky, carefree player. He did well in sports and that was it. Mouthed off to James because James let him. He was headed for pro sports and the wasp sting ended that."

"What does this have to do with me?"

"Have you ever talked to Andrew about what happened when he woke up?"

Our conversation from the last time we made love hits me.

"Yes."

"How James couldn't stop being so angry with Declan for the choice he made?"

"Yes." My own anger rises so fast.

"And how it makes Andrew feel like he's here only because Declan made a choice James might not have chosen himself, in the moment."

My heart stops. No, really. We can't survive without the push of blood through the sixty thousand miles of blood vessels within us, delivering oxygen and nutrients, but Shannon's words deprive me of one beat.

Just one.

"Andrew doesn't *really* think his father would prefer he'd died?"

"It's so complicated," Shannon groans, starting to pace. "No. Of course not. He loves Andrew. But Dec has described how he just shut down because of his own trauma from the event, and how James put Andrew into boarding school and he had to change sports, and how Andrew told him once—and he told me this, too—that he feels like when their mom chose him to survive, she didn't realize that the family would be destroyed."

"Oh, God. It's like what he said to me."

She stops in front of me. We must look like mangy raccoons by now, makeup long worn off and hair like magpie nests. I have a hair clip and probably a stray shot glass in there. Shannon's disco top looks like crumpled aluminum foil, and her eyes are tired.

So tired.

"He won't let you pick him, right?"

I nod.

"He woke up to a world where his mother made this huge sacrifice, but he felt unworthy. Andrew has spent the last twelve years trying to make up for the fact that his mother loved him so much she chose to leave James and her boys behind for his sake."

"And James never got the choice," I say, the reality hitting me.

Headlights glimmer, then triangulate, the rectangles stretching and skewing with the turn into the parking lot.

"Ms. Warrick. Ms. Jacoby." It's Gerald. "Soon to be Mrs. McCormick," he adds with a wink.

Shannon shivers as we climb in.

"Let's go to Amanda's place first," she tells him on the intercom.

My head is in my hands with the blinding grief of what I'm hearing. "Andrew knows what the aftermath of losing someone so fragile is like."

"Hey, I may have a life-threatening allergy, but fragile is a bit much, isn't it?" Shannon chides.

"Honestly? No. No. It's not. You and Andrew are at opposite ends of the risk spectrum on this, Shannon."

342

She frowns and says nothing.

"He isn't afraid of what I thought he was afraid of."

"Commitment?" she asks.

I shake my head. "He's afraid of the mess his death would leave behind. That one-in-a-gazillion chance that he'd be stung and not have an EpiPen and not get medical attention and...the Hobson's Choice that Declan was stuck with is so rooted in Andrew and...I give up. I can't puzzle through it any more. I feel like I'm just going around and around in a never-ending loop."

"Like Andrew." She sighs. "Like Declan."

I jolt. "What do you mean?"

"They can't, you know..." We're exhausted, and the strain of months of wedding planning shows in her shoulders, the dark circles under her eyes, and I can hear it in her emotional voice. Shannon's like a guitar string pulled too tight. "Declan is still haunted by the fact that he couldn't save them both. James is angry he had his life ripped out from under him and couldn't control the outcome."

"And Andrew?"

"I don't know." Her voice goes quiet. "I think Andrew feels like he owes it to the world to make sure he never puts himself in any true risk."

"Why do you?"

"Why do I what?"

"Live like a normal person. Go out into nature. Let yourself be around bees."

"Because I'd go crazy spending my life mitigating all the what ifs. That's not really living."

"Why can't Andrew see that?"

Newton is just close enough to the piano bar that the drive is almost over, especially at this hour of the night. As Gerald guides the limo into my driveway, I'm assured by the sight of lights on in the house. Mom made it home safe.

"I'm guessing it's like Declan and James. I don't know Terry well enough to know if it's true for him, but I know that Dec and James can't let go of the fact that this happened without their being able to fix it."

Fix. There's that word.

"And Andrew? I don't think it's the same thing, Amanda. I think he feels like he's a sacrificial lamb. Like he got saved without his input. Like he has to live with the consequences of his mother's decision and if anything bad ever happens again, everyone around him will fall to pieces. That's one hell of a burden to carry."

I won't let you pick me.

The air becomes thick, my lungs like wet balloons as I open the door and wheeze, inhaling fresh air so quickly I feel faint. Three breaths later and I'm around the car, normal. Shannon walks me into my house and, without a word, zips into the downstairs bathroom.

Mom is snoring lightly on the couch. I walk over and reposition her bent arm so she doesn't wake up with a cramped neck. A thick fleece throw blanket over her will help keep her from getting chilled. I can't prevent the nasty hangover that is coming in the morning, though. For that, she's on her own.

The sound of running water comes from the bathroom as I notice a large, flat package. It's in a delivery envelope with a familiar logo. My name is on the label.

"I didn't order anything," I mumble to myself, rotating the large, thin package in my hands. With a perplexed sigh, I rip open the pull tab and remove the contents.

And gasp.

It's from Andrew.

Fragile.

One of Yes's best albums, and from the looks of it, this was from the original release in the 1970s, long before I was born.

Shannon walks in to find me holding the vinyl album in one shaking hand, the other fishing around in the envelope. My fingers brush against a piece of paper. I remove it, handing her the album. Eyebrows crashing together as she puzzles over it all, she nonetheless stays silent, and as if reading my mind, goes over to Mom's record player and loads the album, setting the needle to the first song.

"Roundabout" begins, the first notes low and jaunty, strumming through my blood like tidal waves caused by dropping many moons into the ocean in rapid-fire succession.

Dear Amanda,

Enjoy.

AJM

She's reading over my shoulder and inhales sharply. "That's it? That's it? Oh, Andrew..." Shannon's voice gives me permission to let the tears flow, her exasperation and polite outrage confirming that all the mixed feelings I'm experiencing are the only rational reaction to this chaos.

"Why did he send me this? Why now?" I look at the outer package. The date is from weeks ago. It was mailed from the UK. Ah. A remnant of the past.

Just like everything involving Andrew.

One look at the album cover and Shannon smiles. "'Fragile', huh?"

All I can do is weep.

"You want me to stay?"

I shake my head. "I'm okay. I need to be alone." *Sniff.*

Except I'm not alone. The music is a talisman of something I've lost, yet it's also a comfort, reminding me of a world where it was once safe to imagine I could just be with someone and not feel an obligation to prove my worth. That I could risk my heart and not be left behind.

That I could choose love.

But love didn't let me pick him.

Shannon hugs me, a good, tight embrace that speaks of change on the horizon. Then she leaves.

Good change is still change.

It destabilizes the world you thought you knew for just long enough to make you question everything.

Everything.

CHAPTER TWENTY-SEVEN

"I'm reconsidering this whole wedding," Shannon announces to no one in the room as I crash in, carrying a coffee tray filled with love and caffeine. Mostly caffeine, because on this morning of her wedding Shannon has finally morphed into Bridezilla, and I have to really dig deep to find the love.

"Dude, the room is empty. You're talking to yourself." I hand her a white cardboard cup of inspiration.

"No, it's not." Shannon points down.

To a very angry pile of tartan and flowers.

"That is a table setting," I say, giving her the hairy eyeball. "You are talking to inanimate objects. Did you get enough sleep last night?"

"Look closer."

The centerpiece *moves*.

"Oh, no," I say, jumping back in self-defense, palms out in a gesture of supplication.

That pile of tartan and flowers is *Chuckles*.

"Meow."

That is the first time Chuckles has ever said a word to me.

He's *that* desperate.

I reach down to pick him up and he snuggles in my arms. Either that, or he's using me for friction to wriggle out of the atrocity that is his outfit.

"What is he wearing?"

"Mom put him in a tartan kilt. See the pin? She made Mr. MacNevin secure an infant's kilt pin for the —"

"Hold up. Infant kilt pin?"

She shrugs, two of her long, perfect curls sliding on her bare shoulder. "I guess it's a thing. Anyhow, then they took the flower girl basket and Mom had it custom made for Chuckles."

He looks like he's wearing a saddle with two open baskets on either side, filled with rose petals.

"Mom says that as he walks, the petals will spill on the white silk runner behind him, and he's the flower girl."

Chuckles drops out of my hands and wanders over to the corner, curling into a ball and spilling all the rose petals on the floor.

Then he stands up and pees all over them.

"I hate to think about what he's going to do when you throw the bouquet."

Shannon bursts into tears.

"My mother is ruining my wedding!" she wails.

I can't say all the normal niceties you say to your best friend in this kind of situation, because she's right.

"Well, there's always elopement," I joke.

"Is Declan using you now to get to me?" she snaps.

"Whoa, whoa there!" I hold up my hands. "That was just a joke!"

"Sorry," she sniffs, the word wispy and fragile in her mouth. "He's spent the last month or so begging me to just run away with him and bag this whole stupid big wedding thing."

"He has?"

"Plus he's angry I made him abstain."

"For a month?" I'd be angry, too. It's only been a few weeks for me and I'm pretty grouchy.

"No. Three days."

"Oh. Poor baby." My sarcasm is as thick as the mocha syrup in her latte.

"You're not being very sympathetic! The maid of honor is supposed to be supportive."

I point to the lattes I brought her, mochas in the largest size Starbucks carries. There's more caffeine in there than in a UMASS student's bloodstream on the last day of finals.

"I am supportive!"

"Not when you suggest eloping," she whimpers. "I'm so tempted."

Tap tap tap.

Before I can answer the door, two little boys spill into the room, a bundle of nervous energy and out-of-control limbs.

"Auntie Shannon!" Jeffrey shouts, his lisp finally gone. He's almost ten now, and growing like a weed. He races to her, clearly not caring or conscious of the fact that she's in a slip, her corset loose around her torso, and she's showing more skin than a Hannibal Lechter victim.

Jeffrey's hug is full-force, all-love, and no holding back.

And it makes Shannon cry even harder.

"Why are you crying? Mom says this is the happiest day of your life, Auntie Shannon!" Jeffrey's words are muffled because his face is buried in nineteen layers of muslin and taffeta and wool.

Shannon cries more. If she sobs with much more force her brain will slide out her nostril.

Tyler's little face appears from around the open door. He's painfully shy, but when he walks in the room he lights up at the sight of Shannon.

"Pretty!"

349

They are the ring bearers and dressed—you guessed it—in kilt tuxedos. Traditional kilt shoes, called Ghillie brogues, are like dress shoes without tongues and feature extra-long laces that wrap around the boys' ankles. In fact, all the men in the wedding party are wearing the same shoes.

Chuckles rubs his side up against Tyler's left foot, his leg lifting, and—

"No kitty! No! Turn the kitty off!" Tyler screams as he half-kicks poor Chuckles a few feet, sending a cascade of rose petals all over the corner.

Chuckles finds his footing quickly, but his attached basket inverts, making it impossible for him to walk, an extra inch of wicker rubbing along the ground.

He stops and lays on his side, like a female cat nursing her brood.

"You don't kick animals, Tyler!" Jeffrey shouts.

"I sorry! I sorry!" Tyler's speech disorder comes back when he's nervous. "Turn the kitty off!" That's his way of saying, *Go away*.

Carol rushes in, taking everything in with the practiced eye of a parent of two young boys.

"Did you kick Chuckles?"

Tyler buries his face in Shannon's skirts and says nothing.

Carol turns to Jeffrey for an answer.

He looks at Tyler, then me and Shannon, assessing where his loyalties rest.

Just then, Jason arrives, whistling and happy as can be, wearing half his tuxedo kilt, a tool company t-shirt covering the top of him.

"Why does Chuckles look like a dying Tauntaun?"

"Tyler kicked him," Jeffrey starts to explain.

"Did NOT!" Tyler wails from under Shannon's skirt now, where he's taken up residence.

"Why?"

"Because Chuckles was going to pee on him, I think. Look, Grandpa. All our shoes have laces."

Jason's face goes blank, then beet red. "Oh, shit. You're right."

"Dad! Language!"

"Sorry, Carol."

"Shit," mutters Shannon's skirt.

Carol shoots Jason an exasperated look. "Great! It took two weeks to get him to stop saying that word last time."

"Hey, Tyler," Jason says to the skirt.

"What?"

"If I give you M&Ms, will you stop saying 'shit'?"

"Okay," he mutters as he comes out.

"Shit!" Jeffrey shouts.

Carol and Jason glare at him.

"What? If he gets M&Ms for *not* saying 'shit,' I thought I'd say 'shit' and then you can give me M&Ms for stopping saying it, too."

Jeffrey is going to grow up to be a political campaign manager.

Or a pawn shop owner.

I point to the coffee tray and Jason and Carol give me looks of thanks as they guzzle their lattes. I take in the room. The groom, his new best man, and his groomsmen are supposed to be in a wing on the other side of the pool and reception courtyard outside. Each wing is a wall of glass, covered with thick curtains. From what Shannon's told me, Andrew is here. He just refuses to be best man, or to go outside until the temperature cools down enough to reduce the risk of wasps and bees.

He insisted on confirming that the ambulance is here as well.

351

And planted EpiPens everywhere.

I hope one is shoved way up his butt, because if you're going to have a stick up there, it might as well serve a functional purpose, too. My sympathy for his complex fear withers away in the face of not overcoming it for the sake of his own brother on his big day.

"What are you thinking about?' Carol asks, interrupting my evil thoughts. "You look just like Chuckles."

"Oh. Um...nothing." I shake my head and drink the rest of my mocha latte. I'm not a fan of sweet coffee, but I just ordered on autopilot and here I am, letting sugar cut in on my caffeine dance.

"You okay?" She's worried. "I'm sorry about Andrew."

"I'm fine. Really."

"Can you handle being around him?"

"No problem. Could you handle being around Todd after you two split up?"

She laughs through her nose. "He never gave me a chance to find out."

Before I can apologize for my unthinking question, Jason bellows, "CHUCKLES!" and shakes out his foot.

The cat looks about as apologetic as Marie crashing Shannon's bachelorette party.

"Damn it!" Jason adds.

"Dammit," says Tyler the Human Mina Bird.

"Ten bucks and I'll get him to stop," pipes up Jeffrey, holding out an open palm.

I hand him the money and shoo him and Tyler out of the room. Easiest problem I'll fix all day.

"What are you doing here, Daddy?" Shannon asks as Jason gives her a barely-there hug, clearly a bit less enthusiastic as she's half-clothed. "You should be on the men's side, getting ready."

"They're fine. Hamish is passing around another bottle of whisky, and Declan isn't even here yet. Just me, James, and Terry." He laughs. "And Jeffrey and Tyler. Have to count them with men, right?"

No Andrew.

"Hamish is passing out shots right now? Before the wedding?" Shannon isn't wearing her makeup yet, so she grabs the hem of Jason's shirt and uses it to wipe her eyes. That closeness, that comfortable assumption that Jason will let her, sets my teeth on edge.

"The guys need a bit of the hair of the dog. Last night was brutal."

"Last night?" Shannon has been living with Amy during the three days before the wedding, so she has no idea that the bachelor party went on for two nights in a row. I only know because Hamish called Amy last night, insisting that "Hamy and Amy" have a meeting to talk about proper hand positioning for the walk down the aisle.

And on other parts of her body.

A Scottish booty call at three a.m. is better left unmentioned the next day.

Amy rushes in, red-faced and fuming. She's carrying her dress and wearing sweats, but her hair is clean and slightly damp. She has creamy skin, long, ringlet red curls, and bright blue eyes. Amy is the complete package: smart, emotionally secure, and gorgeous.

"How's Hamy?" I tease.

Marie's head whips around.

"He's an ass! A complete ass! The arrogance of that man!" But her red-face is not from anger.

"Did he acknowledge the booty call?" I ask. Marie already knows about it, and Jason just left the room to check on the little boys. He scoops up Chuckles on his way out, holding the cat gingerly a foot away from his midsection.

"He says *I* made the booty call!" Amy wails.

"What?"

"He told me he was flattered, but he remembers receiving the call and that I'm cute, but not his type."

"WHAT?" Marie, Shannon, Carol and I all roar with indignation on her part.

"So I put him firmly in his place, and then you know what he did?"

"What?" we ask in unison.

"He tried to get me to introduce him to Jessica Coffin."

"Why would he try to do that?" Shannon asks.

"He says she's the best person for going viral."

"She's a disease, all right," Shannon mutters.

"I mean for publicity. He can't stand the fact that he's a celebrity in Europe, and here in the U.S. no one knows who he is."

Shannon snorts as Marie fusses with a ringlet. Fighting physics, Shannon's hairdresser somehow managed to make her straight, thin, brown hair curl into magical strands that make her look like a princess. I think there's a sewage treatment plant somewhere in the city that is currently befuddling its engineers who have encountered a seven-hundred-pound block of excess mousse, hair gel and hairspray, though.

Carol looks outside and sees Tyler bending down, dipping his hand in the small reflecting pool. It's covered with tastefully-placed lily pads, and is both decorative and functional, as Marie informed us when she booked this facility. For the wedding, they'll close it off, but the gate is open.

"I'm worried about Tyler and that damn pool," Carol says in a tight voice.

"We'll have someone close the gate," Marie promises.

"So," Amy says absent-mindedly as she peers out a crack in the curtains further down the line, "are you ready for your wedding night?"

And Shannon's tears come back.

"Is Declan hung over this morning? I want to see him."

"It's bad luck," Marie chides. She motions for Shannon to close her eyes and pulls out a makeup brush the size of a street sweeper.

"I don't care. I haven't gone this long without seeing him other than business trips, and I'm falling apart on the inside, and what if he's changed his mind and wants to call off the wedding and run away with Jessica Coffin and make beautiful Barbies with her forever and ever and marry a woman who knows you don't drink white wine with beef!"

"I had wedding day jitters the day I married Jason, honey," Marie says with a sigh, putting down all her beauty supplies and just reaching out to hold Shannon's hands. "Every bride gets them."

"I know he loves me," Shannon says as Marie looks at her with so much love peeking out from raw, makeup-less eyes that it's like watching a mother look at her newborn for the first time. "It's just..." She flings herself at Marie and the two sob, each hitched breath like a tug that pulls Shannon further away into her new life.

Just then, a little man who looks like a troll carrying a hair-covered electric drill walks into the room and claps his hands three times.

"Flowers for the bridal party!"

Ah. It's Jordan. And he's carrying Muffin, who now has fuzz all over her.

Marie drops Shannon and practically wins the Olympic 100-meter sprint trying to hug Jordan, whose face lights up as he scans the room over her shoulder.

Until he sees me.

Is he actually baring his fangs at me? The man has unusually large incisors.

"Marie," he croons. "Let's make this wedding even more beautiful with my creations." He takes over, offering the bridal bouquet and the reception bouquet, our pinned corsages and explaining in tremendous detail how the groom and his men will be attired in various flowers native to Scotland, like primrose and bluebell, combined with white roses and a touch of red, all color-coordinated to match the tartan.

While on paper (and Pinterest) it seemed an awful, gaudy mess to me, in person it works. Adding real, live people to the plan makes a huge difference.

Like pretty much everything.

"One hour to showtime!" Marie squeals, sending seamstresses and photographers into frantic activity as we finish dressing, primping, painting and all the accompanying rituals that come with getting wedding-perfect.

As promised, the seamstress fixed the back of my dress so that as long as I keep the corset fairly loose, and the strings tied in a simple slip knot, the Velcro holds the back of the strapless dress in place. We're all showing shoulders, with a McCormick tartan sash draped over one, and the dresses touch the ground in spite of our high heels.

Between tartan underwear (don't ask), tartan sashes, tartan ribbons in our hair and flowers, and tartan fingernails, we do, indeed, look like the Loch Ness Monster ate a bunch of highlanders and vomited. Hamish is right.

Shannon is also exquisite, and she and Declan will be smashing together.

Speaking of the groom, I can't stop looking across the courtyard at the closed curtains on the men's side.

No Andrew.

Is he really going to stand in the shadows, letting fear keep him from being at the front lines?

"How's the crowd?" Amy asks, peering over my shoulder.

"Looks like about half of them are here already, getting seats."

"It's supposed to be a mild day for July in Boston."

"Which means only one of the four of us will faint in these dresses," I groan. I'm wearing about thirty pounds of clothing, from slips to petticoats to thick tartan wool, with sashes and red silk and various cotton blends all swirling around me. I am so weighted down I have to take great care walking in my high heeled shoes, waiting for the swish of my skirts, laden with so much cloth, to catch up to my center of gravity before proceeding.

This forces me to walk like I am in a wedding processional.

Perfect.

"Amanda! Oh, Amanda! You're so beautiful!" Mom's voice makes me turn around, the drag of my delayed motion nearly tipping me over as she gives me a big hug. Her hugs comes with an extra side of groping, as Spritzy licks the underside of my boob. I elbow him out of the way, his purse swaying slightly. He's tightly zippered into a big bag that has thick beige leather handles.

"So do you!" Mom clearly made an effort this morning, in spite of significant pain. All that drinking triggered a fibromyalgia flare, and I can see in her face how fatigued she is. But the beige dress she's wearing cuts nicely against the lines of her body, and she's done her hair in a French knot. She shifts and puts Spritzy on her other arm, wincing slightly. If you didn't know my mother, you wouldn't realize she's having a tough morning.

"Are those grandma's pearls?" I ask.

She beams. "Yes. Remember?"

"I haven't seen you wear those since Aunt Jody's wedding when I was in middle school."

She fiddles with the back of the earring clasp. "That's probably the last time I wore them!"

Jason and James come around a corner, both outfitted to the nines in their fine Scottish dress, swords dangling from their hips.

Mom lets out a low whistle.

Jason blushes.

James doesn't.

"Pam! Nice to see you! Don't you look stunning," James says as he walks over to my mother and gives her a kiss on both cheeks.

The entire scene moves like someone has pushed a slow-motion button in the hallway.

James is kissing my mother.

And is he touching her hip? With his palm? Is he...

"James," Mom says, her voice like warm butter. "So good to see you again."

"Have any good statistics for me to use to improve my life?" he asks with a wink. "How about some good wedding stats?"

Mom blushes, and looks up, as if retrieving them from her mind. "Married men live longer than single men. That's all I've got."

"Is that true for women, too?"

Mom smiles and nods.

"Then I'm glad to hear my son and new daughter-in-law are giving themselves more time together by spending nearly seven figures of my money on this beast of a day!"

Jason, who is drinking a cup of coffee from the catering service, sprays it all over the trash can he's standing next to.

As he turns to James with a look of empty shock on his face, a blood-curdling scream from the women's prep room shatters the moment.

"YOU
INVITED
JESSICA
COFFIN
TO
MY
WEDDING,
MOM?"

CHAPTER TWENTY-EIGHT

Jason, having no choice in the matter, recovers quickly from James' wedding cost comment and rushes to the source of the sound. I look out the window and yes, indeed, there's Jessica Coffin, a wall of long, straight blonde hair attached to the heart of a demon.

I abandon my mom and James and take off after Jason, if by *take off* you mean run like a sloth being transported by a snail.

This dress is so heavy I am sure that when I remove it at the end of the day I'll just float up and be carried off into the clouds.

Marie and Shannon are face to face now, the bride screaming so loudly and inches from her mother's face that it's like watching wounded rage in pure form come out via fingertips and travel into Marie's body. I swear a tri-colored arc of electricity leaps from Shannon's eyes to her mother's heart. The cycle is so complete, their screaming in synchronicity, that there's a certain magic to it, a mellifluous quality that makes me stop and take in the sound.

Meanwhile, Shannon's ex-boyfriend, Steve, is out there, looking at Jessica's ass and pretending to talk to her, all while grabbing canapes from wandering wait staff.

Brave man that he is, Jason inserts himself between Shannon and Marie, who each try to bring him over to their respective dark sides. Declan comes rushing in to the doorway just as Shannon's voice gives out and she picks up the bridal bouquet, arm pulled back like a baseball pitcher, aimed straight for her mother.

"You wouldn't!" Marie screams.

"TRY ME!"

Declan is across the room and holding Shannon's elbow with a mobile grace that makes it seem staged.

"You can't see the bride before the wedding!" Marie scolds. Her hair is wild and flat on one side, and mascara flakes from the nine layers she uses to get eyelashes longer than Donald Trump's actual hair freckle her face.

"Watch me," he shouts.

"You *can't*!" The pitch of her voice drops two octaves, as if the hounds of hell have been dispatched from her vocal cords. Muffin and Spritzy start barking back. It's *101 Dalmatians* all over again, and Marie is looking like Cruella herself, only instead of collecting puppies, she's collecting tartan.

Jason shuttles her out of the room quickly, giving Declan a look that says, *I think this is the first of many such situations.* Soon they'll have a protocol. But for now, we're all first-timers here.

Shannon is bent in half, her corset loosened, her carefully coiffed curls spilling around her face like sentries in crooked formation as she sits in a chair now and cries like the world has ended.

Marie tries to enter the room, but I block her with the door, using it as a half-closed shield.

"What are you doing?"

"Protecting my bestie." I close the door all the way and stand there, knowing I need to act as a bouncer at my best friend's wedding to protect her from...

Her mother.

It's finally come to that.

Forty-five minutes before the ceremony.

"What are you doing here?" Shannon asks, her voice a mixture of half-horror and half-relief as Declan drops to one knee and looks at her, eyes filled with the kind of love most people spend three lifetimes trying to find.

"I heard you screaming. What did Marie do now?"

"She invited Jessica Coffin to the wedding."

An uncharacteristic set of emotions marches across Declan's face. "Why doesn't she just drop a ring in your coffee for you to swallow while she's at it?"

"I know! She invited the woman who almost ruined our getting together, and who is my biggest online bully, to the most important day of my life!"

"Honey, *this* isn't the most important day of your life. It's the first day of the long series of days that will, if I have anything to say about it, be one day after the other of the most important day of your life. Right up until the day we die together, well into our nineties, after I give you the best orgasm *ever*." The way he looks at her as he speaks is like watching love come to life.

She sniffs and laughs, all giggles and twitches. "That's one hell of a bucket list you have, Declan."

"I never back down from a challenge." He pulls her up and kisses her temple. She lets out a shaky breath, then cries softly.

"I don't want this," Shannon whispers.

"Don't want to marry me?"

"God, yes I want to marry you! But this? The pompous pageantry of it? No! Mom's completely taken over and no matter how hard I try to stand up against it, I can't win."

He holds her while she cries, then says in a deep, determined voice, "Sometimes the only way to win is not to play."

"What?"

"Bow out. Fold."

"Our wedding isn't a game of poker!"

"It sort of is, Shannon," he insists. "Is this—" He gestures around the room and outside "—how you imagined our wedding would be?"

"Hell, no."

"Do you want this?"

"Do *you*?"

"No. But I'll go along with it because I love you."

"*I* don't want any of this! I would have been happy getting married on one of the Harbor Islands with just family and close friends! Or eloping in Vegas!"

"I can arrange both. You pick which one." Declan reaches into his tuxedo jacket pocket and pulls out his phone. "We can be gone in twenty minutes."

"What? You're joking."

"You know me. I don't joke when it comes to making something you want happen."

In retrospect, I'm pretty sure Shannon would have said *no* to eloping if what happened next had not unfurled.

Marie begins banging on the door, insisting to be let in and hissing about Jessica Coffin's importance in high society and how Shannon needs to learn to put petty differences aside for the sake of a higher purpose —

At the exact moment Jessica herself moves just enough to be seen through the windows to the courtyard, chatting with Shannon's ex-boyfriend, Steve.

And his mother, Monica.

"Is that *Steve*?" Declan roars as he spots the ex, the sound so forceful it makes an empty coffee cup on a table shake. "Your mother invited STEVE?"

"My God," Shannon whimpers. "I give up. I just give up." She turns to me as I lean hard against the door, my fingers sweaty, thumb joint aching from holding on to the doorknob to stop Marie from coming in.

I look beyond the trio outside and see another face across the way, peering through the glass in the men's dressing wing.

Andrew.

He's *here*. My body blooms with a kind of anticipatory pain, the knowledge that we can't be together juxtaposed against the happiness I can't control when I see him. The twinning of those two emotions leaves me in a perceptive state, the edges of everything I see a little too bright.

"What do I do, Amanda?" Shannon pleads, her face dotted with the splotchiness of sadness and fear.

I need to fix this.

I want to fix this.

I should fix this.

But I *can't* fix this.

Andrew was right. This isn't mine to fix.

"Hon, you're on your own." I exchange a look with Declan that makes it clear I chose the right words. "I love you, and I'll lie for you. I'll block a door for you. I'll hold Jessica down while you rip out her hair extensions, but I can't decide for you."

She looks outside at the triad of destructive distortion.

Looks back at the door, which is rippling with the force of Marie's blows.

Then, eyes only for Declan, she says, "Do it. I don't care how you do it, but let's escape. Now. I am not going to be ridiculed by Jessica Coffin on the one day where I am supposed to be the *positive* center of attention. Mom has gone too far."

"I'll give you all the positive attention you need," Declan declares, kissing her. He's on the phone in seconds, delivering orders.

"Are you really going to run away from your own wedding? Like in The Graduate?" I marvel.

She looks around the room, then outside, then down at her body. "It's not really my wedding, though, is it? Mom ran roughshod over everyone. Declan has a point. Sometimes the best way to fight is to leave."

"Give up?"

"No. Just...not engage. She's turned this spectacle into something that doesn't actually need me or Declan to even happen. We could make cardboard cutouts of ourselves on wheels and it would take her an hour to notice the difference."

I can't help but laugh sadly.

"Do you think that would really work?" Shannon asks with such innocent hope that I laugh harder.

"If it did, you and Amy and Carol would have tried it by now."

Declan gives me a tight look. "Will you lie for us?"

"Lie?"

"I think I have a good cover story for escaping."

"Escaping your own thousand-guest wedding? The story better be damned good."

He whispers his plan in my ear.

I suddenly sound like a hyena in labor. "You *what*?"

"Marie will buy it. Let's just play on her biggest weakness. Give her what she's dreamed of," Declan explains.

I'm floored by what he whispered. There is no way this plan is going to work. None.

I look outside to see that Jessica has separated herself from Steve and Monica and is now taking pictures of everything, then tapping on her phone. Uploading? Probably to various social media sites with hashtags that will follow Shannon for months.

#doghater leaves a bad taste in my mouth, too.

"I'll do it. I'll lie. But you're crazy if you think Marie'll believe this."

"Don't say a word. Go along with it. Pretend just long enough for us to escape. Just...trust me," Declan says in a voice filled with so much authority that I can't help it.

I do.

"There will be a point after we leave when she will try to squeeze the truth out of you. Don't cave in," he demands.

This is unreal.

"You're serious! You're ditching your own wedding?"

Shannon is beaming. Beaming! She looks happier than I've seen her in nearly a year.

And Declan is a man with a mission.

She walks over to me, where the door is thumping and Marie is muttering compromises in the background, something about stopping all the sex toy shops if we'll just come out there.

I kiss Shannon on the cheek and whisper, "Go for it. I'm here. I'll fix whatever mess is left."

And with that, I let go of the doorknob.

Marie comes flying into the room, disheveled, followed by a very addled Jason.

"Marie! There you are!" Declan reaches for her and sweeps her into a huge hug, followed by a kiss on each cheek that makes him seem like James. "We were wondering what happened to you. Come on, now! We need to get this wedding going. You need to get moving!"

"I—what?"

Jason shoots Declan a sly look.

"We're behind schedule! The ceremony starts in forty minutes. You need to get with the program," Declan adds, giving Shannon a secret wink.

"What is he—he's the one who—I wasn't delaying anything!" Marie sputters.

"Then get moving!" He spanks Marie on the ass, the slap making a *snap!* sound that echoes all the way to Pinterest.

And with that, he saunters out of the room.

Like a boss.

* * *

The ceremony starts like any other wedding ceremony happening on that same Saturday in July across the United States. The classical pianist begins the pre-ceremony music, giving guests the chance to settle into their spots. From the glass doorway I see familiar clusters along the fifty rows of twenty white chairs, each row decorated with festive flowers that Jordan has lovingly created, the Scottish feel evident.

Each row of twenty white chairs is bisected by the aisle, and as the ushers lead people to seats, with the bride and groom guests all mixed together, the wedding takes on a beauty and order of its own.

There are Shannon's distant relatives from the midwest. Marie's yoga students are all together, Agnes in beautiful, bright-red glory with a hat attached to her pin curls that might well have been original when Jackie Kennedy wore the same kind. Corrine is next to her in a Coco Chanel inspired get-up, too. A ton of

Anterdec employees dot the crowd. Some high school friends. Greg, his wife, Josh and...is that one of the strippers from the piano bar with him, in a suit?

And hundreds and hundreds of people Shannon and Declan don't know.

Declan's at the altar with the minister, Terry next to him. James is in the front row, and I see my mom right behind him, obliviously sitting next to Jessica Coffin, who is admiring Spritzy and talking animatedly to my innocent mother, who appears to be inviting Jessica to take pictures.

Great. That's like asking Dorothy Parker to write a poem about you.

Someone sets Chuckles on the ground at the back of the large garden display, right in the center of the aisle he needs to walk down. Like a game lion, he takes large, slow steps, scanning the crowd to the left, then to the right, as if to say, *That's right. You people are my subjects.*

And then he hisses.

And then a dog barks.

And after *that*? Five minutes of my life just disappear.

Muffin, who is in Jordan's arms, shoots across the laps of all the guests in his row and tackles Chuckles, who takes the direct hit of a two-pound vibrating teacup chihuahua with what appears to be a bad case of psoriasis as an attack on his sovereignty.

The cat and dog begin a tumbling log roll that takes them back towards us, and various members of the crowd stand to see the source of the ruckus. The pianists, bless their hearts, keep going.

"Chuckles!" Jason grunts, trying to pin down the exact location of the Muffin-Chuckles fleshfest. Out of the corner of my eye I see my mother come running over with James.

The barking and hissing make it impossible to understand the human commands people are delivering, and then an animated purse make its way into the melee.

"Don't hurt my Muffin, you vile cat!" Jordan screams as Muffin sinks her teeth into Chuckles' back leg, Muffin's leash tangling with the flower basket attached to Chuckles, tying the two together in a kind of cross-species bondage that is just so *wrong*.

"Don't ruin the kilt!" Marie shouts.

Spritzy, who is so tightly zipped into the purse that only his head pokes out, yaps and barks until Chuckles attacks him, Muffin's leash tangling all three into one big mess.

They make their way right past me, and I drop my flowers and bend down, running in almost a bear walk to catch them, oblivious to the large metal hook embedded in an enormous cement planter.

The cheery display of peonies and geraniums—a flash of red, white and purple—blurs as a significant portion of my dress catches on the hook at the same time as I watch the clump of two dogs and one furious cat roll through the open pool gate and into the deep reflecting pool.

I try to run faster but in my panic, I just pull and pull, fighting against whatever hand is holding me back, determined to get to the animals, who are now sinking. One of the heels of my shoes snaps off and my ankle leans to one side, making me lose my bearings as all my weight pulls and I fall.

RRRRRRRIIIIIIIIIIPPPPPPPPPP

I stand and run to the edge of the pool, looking at the thrashing water, then stop as I feel a cool breeze in places where one normally does not.

A thousand gasps and a hundred giggles fill the air like bubbles in a swimming pool.

I am naked to the waist.

Completely naked.

In public.

"Amanda!" my mom shouts. Her voice sounds like it is coming from under water. Two thousand eyes are on me, eyeballs reaching across the courtyard to slime their way along my skin, blinking like headlights, chanting like gnomes. Someone has flayed me, scraped all my skin clean off, leaving blood vessels and tendons, fat and muscle, flesh and bone exposed for the world to critique and catalog, to condescend and shame.

Worse.

To look at, then walk away, a silent judge without comment. Without explanation.

Being frozen in place means prolonging the humiliation, the horror cloud of the crowd lingering over me like the storm no town wants, but every town eventually gets.

Jessica Coffin just holds up her phone and taps.

And taps and taps and taps.

There is only one thing I can do right now.

I jump into the water to save the little beastly mammals who cannot save themselves.

Sinking down to their level is no problem. Holding my breath is. I've forgotten to take in a huge gulp of air and now I feel the weight of that mistake as thirty pounds of dress sink me down, down, down to a scratching furball of pain.

The leash on Muffin is the problem. If I can untangle that, I can get the animals to the surface.

My chest hitches with the automatic need to inhale. I fight instinct.

Closing my eyes, I will away the pain that the animals' claws cause on my forearms, going by feel to separate them. The water is warm and salty, not chlorinated. One collar—no leash. A second head and collar—no leash. Teeth sink into my hand and I shake them off.

My lungs spasm.

Finally, I find Muffin's collar and free the leash, shoving him up with a push. Mere seconds have gone by, maybe twenty, but more than I can bear for much longer.

Chuckles' basket is twisted in the leash with Muffin, their bodies impossible to disentangle, and someone bites me again.

Black spots begin to fill in my vision, yet my eyes are closed.

The serene simplicity of this underwater world stands in stark contrast to the calamity above, and as my hands slow down and find the leash, unweaving it until, alas, Spritzy floats up and away, allowing me to shove Chuckles up, too, I feel a stillness.

They're free.

I kick my legs hard, willing my body up. Time for me to be free, too.

The animals are rising in the buoyant waters, but I am not. I reach back to my waistband, to find the hooks and buttons to undo my skirts. The fasteners are a network of laces and metal, of buttons and fabric, old combined with new to make beauty.

I kick.

I try to breathe in.

I fight the impulse.

Panic sets in, my hands more frantic as I hold on to the pattern in my mind for how to organize my own ascent, the orderly steps of actions to take to get sweet oxygen, to rise back to the surface and just breathe.

Just breathe and *be*.

And then I inhale water, my muscles too powerful to battle.

There is a point where instinct overrides self-preservation.

A loud splash at the surface makes me hope someone got the animals, and I bite my lips to stop from breathing in again, my chest going concave, the struggle to hold my breath one I am losing.

My fingers fumble and then strong arms grab me, wrenching my shoulder with a tearing sensation that makes my neck scream. One of the stranger's arms slides under my bare armpits, pressing my breasts flat as the stranger's second arm pulls the water down, down, down to drag me up, up up—

Ah.

Air.

He freed me.

"Hold onto the side. Hold onto the side," a man's voice urges. He's kicking the water, treading next to me, one hand on mine as he guides my fingers to the curled cement edge, my hands shaking but capable.

"Get the paramedics!" he booms to the crowd, who I can't see or hear, but know surround us.

Hacking and coughing, spitting out water, I try to breathe. My windpipe feels like it has shredded pieces of melted tires hanging from it, and I can't cough hard enough to get the water out. A giant lily pad covers my shoulder, and as I finally find some semblance of a pattern for getting a thin, striated hole of air through my throat, I realize I'm still bare breasted.

In public.

"Jesus, Amanda, please say something," says Andrew, who is the man, drenched and next to me, holding my hand, his dark hair soaked and wrapped like feathers around his forehead, his white shirt clinging to his shoulders, the only part of him I can see. "Please. Oh, God, please say something."

My vision begins to focus, the blackness fading, lingering only at the edges of what I can see, like a shadow that doesn't know what to do with itself.

"Chuckles," is all my hoarse throat can choke out.

"We got 'em!" James bellows back. "All three of these little stinkers are just fine thanks to you!"

I'm shaking, still trying to breathe, as a uniformed paramedic bends down and offers me a hand.

"Ah, no." I look down. "Naked." I move one hand and start to sink again.

Andrew winds one arm around my waist and holds me up, his fist filling with the thick cloth of my wet skirts. He looks at the paramedic.

"Got a knife?"

"A knife?"

"A blade. Anything. I need to cut her dress off."

In seconds, the guy hands Andrew a knife and he cuts loose the wool tartan overlay, which slides down around my legs like a mermaid shedding her tail.

I take in a deep breath and cough. The next breaths feel more regular. Andrew's hands are on my face, my shoulders, my back and waist, an endless sequence of touches that seem less about checking my status and more about verifying that I am above water and safe and really here.

Really here.

Wait.

He's really here.

374

"You're outside!" I gasp.

"And you're insane!" he says with a finality that I can't argue with. "What in the hell did you jump in the pool for?" His voice shakes with a kind of post-trauma agony that makes me wince. With a caring hand, he holds my waist, his strong legs kicking for me. Salty water drips into my eyes, the stinging bringing on more tears.

"To save the cat and doggies," I croak out.

"You nearly *died*. Don't you ever, *ever* do that again! What in the hell were you thinking?" A crack in his voice, then a deep, sharp inhale and he starts to breathe hard, his eyes boring into me like he can only keep me alive if he looks at me.

He can't stop touching me, his steady kicking keeping him afloat, my own legs too weak to move. I'm clinging to the edge of the pool, one hand too sore to grasp anything. I look at it and see puncture wounds swelling at an alarmingly fast rate, the salt water lapping at them and hurting. My torso is smashed as far up against the cool mosaic of tiles as possible. I'll probably have an imprint of that pattern permanently etched into my boobs and belly.

"But I didn't die. I didn't die because of you," I say, resting my forehead against the edge. If I had the energy, I would look at him. Say more. Adrenaline that kept me going underwater drains out of me as if osmosis were at work, the water sucking all my focus from me. I am wet and my hand throbs and I am naked in front of other people and oh, God, Andrew is here with me.

"He shot out of that glass door over there like a human rocket when you jumped in, Amanda." Mom is holding a wet Spritzy while James feeds the dog a piece of cheese. "Only stopped to rip off his suit jacket and shoes, leaped into the air, launched off the black iron fence and—" Emotion overtakes her. "James plucked the animals out with the net and scooped them up just as Andrew dove in."

"You're outside," I repeat. "In the sunlight. In July." Andrew's face is inches from mine and he's clearly unnerved, body vibrating so fast he's making the water radiate away from him in rippling waves. It's warm, like bath water, and it's not even four p.m., so I know he's not cold.

"I knew that dress would keep you on the bottom of the pool. *Drown* you." He can barely say those last two words.

"Huh?"

"I was a competitive swimmer. We trained in weighted clothes. I knew the second you jumped in you were doomed. And my heart just about died on the spot, Amanda." He presses his forehead against mine. "I ran out and dove in on pure instinct."

"Just like me jumping in to save the animals."

So many thoughts race through my mind as I float, his body protecting me, keeping me anchored to the pool wall so I can find my breath. Except I can't feel the difference between my own air and Andrew's, between the water and my body, for I'm bathed in the warmth of his proximity. What he just did tells me I do get to pick him, after all.

He didn't just save me.

He saved *himself*.

A slow golf clap starts in the distance, then gets louder as Jessica Coffin begins it, other people joining in, not realizing the smirk on her face means the applause is born of sarcasm, not an invitation to celebrate. She holds up her cell phone and snaps photos the entire time.

Chuckles rubs against her leg, now free of all his human clothing and the basket.

And he pees on her lace-up high heels.

She screams.

I don't care.

My chin starts to chatter against the backs of my hands.

"Thank you for the Yes album," I say under my breath, as if talking to the water. "And, you know, for saving my life."

"You're welcome for both," he says with a disbelieving sound of amusement. "But I don't need your thanks. Just promise me you'll never do that again." He pulls me into the closest embrace you can manage while treading water. He smells like salt and pain, his scent a beacon for me to follow.

"I can't promise I'll never listen to 'Roundabout'." I shake my head.

He bites his lower lip as he holds me, my words muffled against his wet shoulder, his cheek scratching against my face.

"I see you're recovering," he says drolly. "Let's get you out of here," Andrew says softly, strong hand urging my own away from the pool's edge, nudging me towards the set of stairs to ascend.

"I'm naked," I whisper. "In public." Most people among the wedding guests have the decency not to stare, but I can feel plenty of eyes on me, and the murmurs and titters of the crowd sound like bees buzzing in the distance.

"I know," he says, low and sweet. His voice aches with a kind of modesty on my behalf that is winsome. "I felt so bad for you when I saw your dress rip. Your worst nightmare."

377

I reach up and run my fingers through his wet hair, our eyes locked. In his smile I see the remnants of his fast action. Those worried eyes are hollow, carrying echoes of the receding panic that drove him to override his own instinct, too.

For *me*.

"Your worst nightmare, too," I say, looking pointedly at the cake, the flowers, the whole garden.

"No."

"No *what*?"

"Being outside like this and at risk for a wasp sting isn't my worst nightmare anymore, Amanda."

"Then what is?"

"Losing you."

My breathing quickens at his words, the heat from his touch and the gentle relief that comes from being with him now, in such a dark moment, buoying me. I'm floating on his sacrifice, on my freedom, the sense that I've faced my entrenched fear and lived in spite of it.

I'm being loved because of it.

He cradles my cheek with one hand, still kicking, the water brushing against my stockinged legs. "Amanda, I—"

"If you two are done with your—" Marie waves her hand "—whatever you call this, we'd like to resume the, you know, giant wedding that is taking place right here with the thousand people who are all staring at you two, the heroine and the hero!"

People tap camera phones. The professional photographers use flashes here and there.

Great.

I'm naked in public *and* on camera.

And I don't care.

I turn back to Andrew.

"Remember that first date at Consuela's rooftop garden?"

"Yes."

"You asked me what my biggest fear was."

"Yes."

"I lied," I confess.

Unless I'm mistaken, Mr. Andrew James McCormick, CEO of Anterdec Industries and competitive swimmer, has tears in his eyes. The sunlight makes them shine, his brown irises shimmering beneath.

"And?"

"My biggest fear was that being with you wasn't real."

"Oh," he says, the word like a pained sigh, as if I've punctured his heart. "I want to be real with you, Amanda. More than anything in the world. I thought bowing out of the wedding would save everyone from risk. I never wanted to put Declan in the position of having my life in his hands. Never wanted to put you in a place where you'd experience the—" His words break off, segmented by a harsh sound of being overcome by intensity. "Where you'd know what it's like to watch your world turn out to be more fragile than you expected, and to see it all fall apart without being able to stop it."

Fragile.

"I know." I'm crying now, my words unfiltered, my thoughts racing as everything I feel for him rushes out of me. "I know why you walked away. I just didn't know how to fix it."

"Watching you risk everything just now and seeing you—oh, God—it made me understand that the biggest risk isn't dying. It isn't even being left behind to pick up the pieces." He smooths my hair away from my face, his thumb on my cheekbone, his hand steadying me. "It's the mistake of never trying."

I start to shiver uncontrollably.

Andrew peels off his shirt, bobbing in the water and dipping beneath the surface. As he comes up, he urges me back from the side of the pool by an inch, and then guides one of my hands into the wet armhole.

"Ow!" I cry out.

I look at my hand. It's swollen, covered in nasty welts from the scratches, and the spot he touched has two clear puncture marks.

Horror fills his face, his hair wet and plastered against his forehead. "You fought to free the animals underwater while they did this to you?" he asks in a voice filled with disbelief.

I shrug. But because I'm shivering, I just look like I'm twitching. All his words run through my mind in a blur, and I want to talk and touch and feel and spend every waking minute with him, but all my energy is leaking out of me so fast. Too fast.

He takes the shirt and drapes it over my front. Gently, he moves me off the side of the pool and clasps me in an embrace, my breasts mashed up against his wet shirt. Warmth pours out of him like melted love, heated to just the right temperature. I stop shivering and let out a long, grateful sigh of relief.

Andrew laughs, his throat working hard, his eyes so full of—dare I say it?—love. "Is this," he says, looking pointedly at my wet, cotton-covered top, "real enough for you?"

And then he kisses me so hard he makes me really, *truly* real.

"I love you," he rasps against my neck. "I never thought I could feel this way about anyone in my life, and I've been such an ass thinking that I was somehow saving you from the pain of risk with me. What I didn't realize was that the pain of not being together was worse than the pain of losing you. I wasn't saving you anything by walking away. I was just making life agony for us both."

He looks at me, his face filled with a dawning earnestness.

"I love you too, Andrew. I truly do," I whisper, amazed at how real the words feel.

When he kisses me, there is a stillness like I felt minutes ago underwater, but instead of struggling not to breathe, I feel like I have inhaled all the air in the world and absorbed every bit of love.

"There goes the maid of honor," Marie howls. "She's useless now! Carol, you're her understudy. Get over there!"

Carol looks completely confused and Andrew moves us to the edge of the lily pond pool where a set of stairs leads up. Shannon's standing next to Declan, and both them wave, Shannon's face split into a grin of pure joy that reflects into the courtyard like a lighthouse beam. She splits from him, walking toward me.

"Follow me," he says, keeping my front pressed against him, walking with a smooth, steady series of steps until we're out of the water, where the paramedic runs over, throwing a thick fleece and wool blanket over my shoulders, finally giving me some modesty.

"I can't lose you again, Amanda. I'm so sorry," Andrew says as the paramedic asks me questions and tends to the bites and scratches all over my arms. The antiseptic he spreads liberally stings, but compared to the salt water pool, it's heaven.

"You won't lose me. Ever." We share a smile I've been waiting to give my whole life.

"Amanda!" Mom crushes me with a side hug. "I can't believe how brave you were!" She turns to Andrew, her eyes red from crying. "And you!" She forces Andrew to let her hug him. He waggles his eyebrows at me over her shoulder, but he takes the embrace, giving it right back.

Spritzy is at my feet, licking my stocking-covered toes.

"Mr. McCormick! Mr. McCormick!" shouts Jordan, who is running over, cradling a wet wool sock.

Wait.

That's Muffin.

Andrew, James, Declan and Terry all turn toward the little man, who approaches James.

"Thank you so, so much, Mr. McCormick, for saving my precious Muffin! You were so brave to use that pool skimmer and to pluck her out of her watery grave. I am forever in your debt."

And then he bows and actually takes James' hand, kissing his ring.

"What?!" I am about to blow a gasket. Jordan must hear me going nuclear, because he slowly cranes his neck toward me, eyes bulging out with the hard look of sanctimony.

Andrew tries not to laugh, but I can feel his body bouncing with mirth. "Hashtag doghater," he whispers in my ear, giving me an affectionate squeeze.

I growl back.

"You!" Jordan's fingers are long, like a surgeon's, and when he points at me I feel like an accused witch in a seventeenth century Salem trial. "You tried to kill my Muffin again."

"Oh, brother," I mutter. "OW!" I squeal as the paramedic puts something that stings all over a bite.

The physical pain doesn't distract me from the indignity of being unfairly accused yet again.

He turns to James, red-faced and righteous. "When we went on our date, she threw rocks at my mama's little dog! And now she she tried to drown Muffin!"

"She *saved* your dog!" Andrew says, starting to stand up and confront Jordan, who is shaking as hard as his mama's teacup chihuahua now.

I reach up with my good hand and pull Andrew back to the chair next to mine. "Not worth it. Don't even try to reason with him."

"Hold on," Andrew says, halting. "Date? Did he say *date*? You dated *him*?"

"Yes. For work."

Whatever laughter Andrew has been holding back comes rushing out, his body bent in half, his gloriously unclothed chest and back on display as he lets it *all* out.

"And—" Andrew gasps "—I was worried about..." He's so amused by all of it that I can't help but join in, our laughter more than just relief. We're joyfully celebrating the unspoken brilliance of living each minute and taking what life throws our way. No more guessing. No more fear.

Not when we're together.

And then he sweeps in for an exuberant kiss that is so nakedly passionate and marvelously delicious that whatever pain I'm in fades away in the presence of his whole self.

In the sunlight.

In July.

As Jordan shakes James' hand and bows again, I overhear him say, "I'm happy to do your next son's wedding as a thank you to you for your courage, but you'll have to keep *her* away from my Muffin."

I'm about to give Jordan a piece of my mind when a great *shhh-shhh-shhh* begins in the distance in the sky. We all stare up, following the source of the sound.

The black helicopter has no markings of any kind as it descends onto the lawn, the whoop-whoop-whoop of the blades making the air feel like it's sliced into pieces, as if sound itself were being chopped. The helicopter pilot's face is obscured as he comes into focus. This is not an Anterdec helicopter, and yet in all the images I've seen of the President of the United States of America's helicopter, there's always been a circular seal. A sign.

A marker.

Declan excuses himself from a talk with his dad and my mom and marches with determination toward us, Marie wending her way through the crowd to intervene.

"What is going on?" she shouts. You have to raise your voice, because the chopper is so close, engines still on.

Declan cups his hand and bends to her, saying something in her ear.

Her eyes go wide with exhilaration and her hands clap over her mouth.

"No!"

"Yes!" he calls back.

"You—he—*he* is here?" Marie screams, giddy. "This will save the wedding! No one will remember naked Amanda now!"

"I will," Andrew shouts.

My mom blushes.

"But they'll remember that the President of the United States came to my—er, your—wedding! Everyone! Everyone!" Marie shouts, trying to get the crowd's attention. "The President of the United States is in that helicopter! He's a guest at the wedding!"

"We need to go talk to him first!" Declan shouts to Marie, his voice loud enough for me to hear over the blades. He pulls Shannon out from the cluster of people hovering around the pool.

They do not stop. Shannon's dress is swept up in the rush of air, her train heavy and twisting, her tartan plaid accents ruined by the blast of air flow. Shannon and Declan share a look of anticipation, an *Are you sure?* interlude that they both confirm with twin nods of determination.

Marie shoos them, her wrists flicking like shotguns. "Go! Go! Of course you need to greet him. My goodness!" She turns to me with a look of exaltation. "Please tell me Jessica Coffin is seeing this!" she begs. "And Monica Raleigh!"

"Monica who?'

"Steve's mother!"

"Oh."

"Bet she'll never have the President of the United States at Steve's wedding! She brags about knowing a state senator. Hah!"

Shannon and Declan have put me in the worst position possible right now. As they both make their way to the helicopter, I know what they're about to do.

Andrew has his arm around me, helping to keep the blanket about my shoulders, and he leans in and says, "They're headed to Vegas for a quickie wedding. This is delicious to watch. Marie is about to get five lifetimes of karma."

All I can do is lean against his shoulder and rest.

And cringe.

Declan boards first, the wind picking up his kilt and oh, sweet creator, he most certainly is commando. I thought Shannon was exaggerating when she talked about the size of Declan's, ah...ego, but she was telling the truth.

The whole truth.

The whole long, thick truth.

I reach over for Andrew's thigh and slide my hand up, meeting the soft flesh of, um, confirmation that he, too, went authentic. Truthiness never felt so...

"Is that an offer?" he shouts, his hand slipping to my ribs as I scramble to grab the sliding blanket. Immediately, he rights it, wrapping me protectively in the only item that keeps me from reliving my public nakedness. I give his thigh a squeeze and he kisses my temple, his cheek resting against me, his body relaxing into mine.

"Mr. President!" Marie screams, waving her tartan fan.

Behind us, I see Jason ambling on the grass toward Marie, walking with the steady, strong steps of a warrior, Chuckles in his arms.

Shannon climbs into the helicopter and what happens next is so fast it will take me a solid month to reconstruct it properly.

The helicopter begins to lift, Shannon's train hanging down just a few feet from the open door to the passenger area. Declan bends down to grab it and Marie takes off at a little jog, her high heels making that difficult.

The helicopter lifts five feet. Then ten feet, and stops, hovering for seconds.

"Where are you going, Mr. President?" she screams, her jog turning into a canter I haven't seen since I learned horsemanship at Girl Scout camp in fourth grade.

I bury my face in Andrew's chest.

"This is painful to watch!" I shout.

"She deserves it," Andrew shouts back.

I turn back. It's like rubbernecking. I know I shouldn't look, but curiosity gets the better of me. Besides, I'm going to hear about this for the rest of my life. Might as well actually witness it so I can know the truth before it gets wildly distorted.

The helicopter lurches up, about two more feet, as Marie reaches the spot where it just was, her shoes in the deep grooves in the green grass where the landing gear just rested.

"WHAT ARE YOU DOING?" she screams. "WHERE IS THE PRESIDENT?"

Declan gives Marie a handsome, victorious grin and waves like he's the Prince of Wales. Shannon's head peeks out behind him and she shouts, "I love you!"

"What?" Marie shouts. "Where is the president? I have a seat for him down here, right next to me!"

And then Shannon answers with one word.

One simple, earth-shattering word.

"ELOPE!" she screams as the helicopter lifts, up, up, up, with Marie staring into the sky, her face a mask of dawning horror.

My heart ripples with Marie's pain.

Until I look back and see Jessica Coffin, her head bent down with text neck, typing away furiously on her phone, grinning like the Joker.

"WHERE ARE YOU GOING!" Marie shouts, jumping up in the sky as if she could grab the bottom edge of the helicopter. "GET BACK HERE!"

As the chopper gains height and starts to move forward, away to the west, Jason reaches Marie. He watches the helicopter, his hand shielding his eyes, then looks at Marie, who is shaking her fist in the air.

The blades no longer producing overwhelming noise, it's possible to hear her.

"ELOPE? THEY CAN'T ELOPE! GET THEM BACK HERE, JASON! THEY ARE RUINING MY WEDDING!"

Jason is very clearly trying to reconcile what he just saw with the reality of his wife's Momzilla tantrum.

"This is better than cheesy reality television," Andrew whispers.

"Did you know," my mother says, her voice carrying on the wind as if she were addressing someone near her. I turn around to see her talking to Carol, Terry and James. "Did you know that people who elope are more than twelve times as likely to divorce versus those who marry with a wedding of two hundred or more guests?"

"I eloped," Carol snaps.

"Elena and I had more than two hundred guests at our wedding and were happily married for more than twenty years," James says with a wistful sigh.

"I eloped," my mom admits, giving me a nervous look. "And we know how that turned out."

I watch the receding helicopter in the sky. Somehow, I don't think this elopement meets any statistical category, though. Shannon and Declan are their own standard deviation. Or two.

"ANDREW!" Marie's voice splits the air like a cannonball. I've never seen her this angry. Not even that time in high school when we got sent home from high school for rearranging the letters on the school sign. Instead of "Congratulations Warriors Hockey" it said, "Congratulations Hairy Coworkers."

Andrew's eyes fly open like he's a human experimentation victim with lid retractors attached. "What? Why me?"

"YOU NEED TO GET ANTERDEC'S HELICOPTER NOW. NOW. NOW NOW NOW."

"I'm sorry, Marie. The helicopter is being used right now in central America to help deliver medical supplies for a corporate humanitarian mission."

"THAT IS NO EXCUSE. WE HAVE MORE IMPORTANT PROBLEMS HERE. CALL IT BACK."

Marie has one volume right now.

"Honey," Jason says, trying to soothe her. "We can't do anything about this. Shannon and Declan decided they want to get away and—"

"DON'T YOU DARE TELL ME THAT! I AM NOT MISSING WATCHING MY DAUGHTER GET MARRIED. I DID NOT SPEND THE LAST YEAR OF MY LIFE RESEARCHING TARTAN THONGS FOR THIS!"

Jason gives Marie's ass an appraising look. "Tartan *thongs*?"

Andrew slides his hand on my butt. "Tartan thongs?" he whispers.

"We were forced to match."

"Why not go commando like we kilt wearers?"

"We tried! Marie wouldn't let us. Said if we didn't have balls, we couldn't go commando."

"*You* have balls," Andrew says. "Bigger than most men's."

Can't say I disagree.

"But not mine," he adds.

"JASON! CALL THE POLICE AND REPORT A KIDNAPPING!"

"Shannon hasn't been kidnapped, Marie," he says with a weary sigh.

"MY WEDDING HAS BEEN KIDNAPPED!"

"Oh, God." Jason burrows his fingers into his sporran and pulls out a half-used roll of antacids. He carefully peels off the entire remainder of the wrapping and pops all of the pieces into his mouth at once.

See? Aerosolized Xanax would come in handy now, wouldn't it?

"WHERE ARE THEY GOING?" Marie is screaming, enraged beyond the point of all reason, and I really do wish she'd hired that elephant and trainer after all, because an animal tranquilizer gun would come in handy right about now.

James, my mom, and Jason all put up their hands in a gesture of ignorance.

Carol and Terry are drinking Champagne near the fountain. The caterers look like they've pretty much picked up on the fact that there won't be an actual marriage ceremony given the sudden escape of the bride and groom, so they're putting out food.

Hamish is standing next to Amy, his hot soccer player legs half-bare, kilt ending at the knees and Agnes is on the ground, bent down in—huh? Is she doing yoga? Why would a ninetysomething woman be doing yoga at a wedding, in a suit?

Her red hat slides under Hamish's legs and she shoves her arm in the air, brushing against his kilt. Hamish looks down, one eyebrow flying high in consternation.

"He's authentic, Corrine!" Agnes gives her old friend a thumbs' up. Corrine hobbles over and smiles down at Agnes.

"I owe you ten bucks," Agnes adds with a disagreeable sigh.

"Here. We'll call it even," Corrine says, fishing in her purse for a powder compact, her knees popping as she bends downs. "Take this, open the mirror, and angle it just so—"

"Americans are so weird," Hamish grumbles. But he doesn't move.

Andrew reaches around me, careful to preserve my modesty, as he leans in for a kiss, the touch and taste of him a reunion that fills my heart with—

"STOP THAT! YOU SHOULD BE ON THE PHONE ARRANGING THE CORPORATE JET FOR US!" Marie shouts at Andrew. Her hair flies around her face in a swirl of hairsprayed plates, like someone has molded her hairdo in a factory and clicked it together like Pergo flooring. Click. Click. Click.

And someone just unfastened it all.

"To go where?"

Marie zeroes in on me and Andrew, eyes like snake slits. "YOU TWO KNOW!"

My heart pounds hard and suddenly, like someone is practicing handball in my chest.

Remember how I said Andrew has tells? Well, I do too, apparently. My eyes flicker over to Carol, who is loudly explaining to Jeffrey that just because I got to "swim" doesn't mean he and Tyler can, too.

Marie follows my gaze and while she might not be the crispiest taco shell in the package, she gets my subconscious glance's meaning instantly.

"Ohhhhhhh, nooooooooo. Not Las Vegas! Not like Carol and Todd. Please tell me they didn't just run off to Vegas," she whimpers, her voice going soft, the volume change disconcerting.

"They didn't just run off to Vegas," Andrew says in a robot voice, then takes my face in his hands and kisses me again, the touch of his mouth and the texture of his breath so delightful.

"ORDER THE CORPORATE JET TO TAKE US THERE."

And she's back.

SHOPPING FOR A CEO

"Where?" Andrew asks, his mouth still on mine. "And Marie? We're kind of busy."

Hysterical laughter ripples out of her like clowns pouring out of a car at a circus. "BUSY? BUSY? YOU ARE BUSY GROPING AMANDA AND I AM BUSY PICKING UP THE SHATTERED PIECES OF THIS—"

"We're trying to make up!" Andrew grinds out, clearly upset at her interruption.

"MAKE UP IN VEGAS!" she screams back, reaching out to pluck a very wet, very angry Chuckles from Jason as she storms off, her tartan sash snagging on chair legs.

Andrew looks at me, eyebrows raised.

"Vegas? Why would I want to go to Vegas?"

"Make up sex in Vegas?" I ask.

He grabs his phone. "You have a way with words."

THE END...until Vegas...

And speaking of Vegas, wonder what's happening in that helicopter as Declan and Shannon escape their own wedding?

Who needs a SWAT team to escape from their own wedding? Me.

My Momzilla turned us into hostages at our own ceremony, so Declan and I are getting married the good old-fashioned way, just like everybody else.

By calling in his private security team, stealing away before the ceremony by helicopter, connecting to his corporate jet and heading for Las Vegas.

The Boston wedding of the year is about to become a trashy Elvis drive-thru ceremony.

Until the best man spills the beans and Mom, Dad, my sisters, his brothers, my maid of honor, my friend Josh, and even my cat, Chuckles, all come along for the ride.

I can't win, can I?

Oh. Yeah. I already did.

Love conquers all.

Even my crazy family.

* * *

Shopping for a Billionaire's Wife is the 8th book in the New York Times and USA Today bestselling Shopping for a Billionaire series. After Declan convinces Shannon to escape from their own wedding minutes before the ceremony begins, the madcap adventures are just getting started. When the mother of the bride pries their location out of the tortured best man, the whole crazy crew follows the bride and groom to Las Vegas in this romantic comedy from Julia Kent.

Pre-order *Shopping for a Billionaire's Wife*, book 8 in the Shopping series, now!

Watch my Facebook and newsletters for details on pre-order links.

* * *

Shopping for a Billionaire's Wife is coming in March 2016. Join my newsletter mailing list at jkentauthor.com or like my Facebook page (facebook.com/jkentauthor) to stay tuned for release dates.

SHOPPING FOR A CEO

If you haven't read Declan and Shannon's story in the *Shopping for a Billionaire Boxed Set,* go read it right now! This series began in May 2014 as a serial, and the boxed set has 670+ pages of their hilarious, hot, and crazy story.

Read more now!

Shopping for a Billionaire Boxed Set

OTHER BOOKS BY JULIA KENT

Suggested Reading Order

Shopping for a Billionaire: The Collection (Parts 1-5 in one bundle, 670 pages!)
- Shopping for a Billionaire 1
- Shopping for a Billionaire 2
- Shopping for a Billionaire 3
- Shopping for a Billionaire 4
- Christmas Shopping for a Billionaire

Shopping for a Billionaire's Fiancée
Shopping for a CEO

Before Her Billionaires
Her Billionaires: Boxed Set
- Her First Billionaire—FREE ebook
- Her Second Billionaire
- Her Two Billionaires
- Her Two Billionaires and a Baby

It's Complicated
Complete Abandon (A Her Billionaires novella)
Complete Harmony (A Her Billionaires novella #2)
Complete Bliss (A Her Billionaires novella #3)
Complete We (A Her Billionaires novella #4)

Random Acts of Crazy
Random Acts of Trust

SHOPPING FOR A CEO

Random Acts of Fantasy
Random Acts of Hope
Randomly Ever After: Sam and Amy
Random Acts of Love
Random on Tour: Los Angeles

Maliciously Obedient
Suspiciously Obedient
Deliciously Obedient

ABOUT THE AUTHOR

Text JKentBooks to 77948 and get a text message on release dates!

New York Times and *USA Today* bestselling author Julia Kent turned to writing contemporary romance after deciding that life is too short not to have fun. She writes romantic comedy with an edge, and new adult books that push contemporary boundaries. From billionaires to BBWs to rock stars, Julia finds a sensual, goofy joy in every book she writes, but unlike Trevor from *Random Acts of Crazy*, she has never kissed a chicken.

She loves to hear from her readers by email at jkentauthor@gmail.com, on Twitter @jkentauthor, and on Facebook at facebook.com/jkentauthor

Visit her website at http://jkentauthor.com

Made in the USA
Middletown, DE
27 September 2015